Dreaming Mill Valley

Christie Nelson

San Rafael, CA

ISBN 978-0-9848261-1-7
Library Of Congress Card Number: 2012903612

The Hobbit
by J.R.R. Tolkien
September 21, 1937
George Allen & Unwin, UK

Book Design & Composition by Julie Valin
Cover Woodcut Art by Tom Killion
Author Photo by Dedalus Hyde

Author website:
www.christienelson.com

Printed in the United States of America

For Andrew and Dedalus
and all the children of Mill Valley
who survived the 70's

Acknowledgements

IF IT'S TRUE THAT A SUBJECT CHOOSES THE WRITER—not the other way round—this novel is a prime example. I set out to write a story about friendship between women. Then the muse stepped in and had her way with me.

I did, on the other hand, choose the places where the story happens. How could I not? My love affair with the glorious and gritty town of San Francisco and beauty and majesty of Marin County has no end in sight.

When I wrote my first novel, one of the pleasures was hearing from readers who said, "I know exactly where that creek/waterhole/bar is. I've been there, too." May this book hold some of the same discovery of familiar haunts for new as well as faithful readers.

To native sons and daughters who may know the landmarks in this territory better than I, an explanation seems appropriate. Sometimes I've altered geography and architecture in the service of the story, which I trust has not caused your hair to burst into flame.

To historians, the accuracy and chronology of events, like Governor Moonbeam's first inauguration, has also been bent to fit the story. I did this on purpose. In short, all errors are mine.

Along the way, I've had many supporters and champions. Here are a few of them.

Bust Out Writers led by the inestimable Guy Biederman who organized soirees in the Garden Shack and then kept it going at The Downtown Art Center and Atelier: Chuck Culver, Sam Friedlander, Damon Yeargain, Toni Piccinni, Rosie Sorenson, Akasha Halsey, Mark Krahling, Carolyn Ingram, Ellen Swain Veen, and Taylor Teegarden.

West Marin Writers Gang: Brenda Kinsel, Molly Fisk, Elisabeth Ptak, Jules Evans, and David Clarkson.

The 4th Street Writers: Colleen Rae, Barbara Toohey, Kathy Revue, and Lum Franco.

Pit Crew and Confidants: Betsy Graziani Fasbinder, Amy Peele, and Linda Joy Myers.

Jessica Barksdale Inclan who told me to go back and finish "that novel."

The Librarians of Marin County, Elaine Petrocelli and Booksellers of Book Passage, and Michael Whyte of Booksmith.

Brooke Warner, Editor, Coach, and Exceptionally Lovely Person.

Julie Valin, Book Designer, Poet, and Fellow Race Car Driver.

Penny Dufficy, Proof Reader, Fact Checker and Sheep Ranch Provocateur.

Dear Friends and Family, where would I be without you?

Kudos to Undercover Agent and BFF Liz Mamorsky, Trail Guide Suellen LaMorte, Catherine Flaxman, Dreamweaver and Soul Sister, and Linda Verdone, Brave Sister and Laugh Maker.

And to my Numero Uno, Heart Throb, Chief Financial Officer, Bottle Washer, Legal Beagle, Trip Planner, Inventor, Suduko Player, Steam Locomotive/Streetcar Heir, Spare Parts Guy, Fancy Dancer, Ditch Digger, Officer and Gentleman, and Orchardist, Ron Moore.

Christie Nelson
San Rafael, CA
June 2012

Our truest nature
is when we are
in dreams awake.

- Henry David Thoreau

No facet of nature
is as unlikely as we,
the tiny bipeds,
with giant dreams.

- Diane Ackerman

Prologue

She is called Tamalpais, Coast Miwok for the Sleeping Lady. Long ago she rose from the sea to rest upon her back as if in repose. Approaching from the inland roads across the great tidal basin toward the shining coast, her reclining body, from the crown of her forehead to the tips of her toes, is etched in silhouette high against the sky.

Face to heaven, the Sleeping Lady dreams of love. Above her in the clouds, unseen and unheard, her beloved weeps. As he cries, his tears mix with the bosky sea-scented air, turn to fog, and cover her like a blanket. Whenever you look at the mountain, you'll know when his heart is breaking.

During the day, she is smoky emerald against an azure sky. At night, lights twinkle on her shoulder, which is the town of Mill Valley, and twinkle on her thigh, which is another town named after the purple wildflower, Larkspur. And so it goes all the way to the coast, towns and hamlets nestled into the rises and hollows of the Sleeping Lady. From the air she is one sublime landform laid out like a green finger bordered against the slate blue Pacific.

If you hike her trails on a brilliant spring day there will be so many trees, shrubs, rocks, boulders, grasses and wildflowers that it will be impossible to take it all in. Maybe you'll notice one oak tree or granite outcropping; the next time it will appear familiar yet entirely new. You'll run along the trails, the knee-high grasses brushing your legs. The sun will be in your eyes, and the voices of the children will mingle with the wind and the call of the hawks. You'll search for just the right meadow with a clear view to the sea where you'll spread a blanket on tender grass and lie down upon your back. There the Sleeping Lady will hold you in her embrace while deer graze in her meadows, and woodland creatures roam in her forests.

When you return home dazed and peaceful from the sunshine, and the air, and the endless blue expanse of sky, darkness will fall over her and upon the towns and hamlets. Before you sleep, if you glance from your window, you may see that fog has returned to shroud the Sleeping Lady. On those nights, your dreams will be filled with strange haunting visions. You'll dream of winding staircases leading nowhere or waves carrying you across a warm sea toward a shore you cannot see or the embrace of a stranger whose caresses intoxicate your soul. In those dreams you'll hear voices softly calling your name or the strains of a melody you've heard before but cannot place or bells faintly chiming from a distant hilltop. If you awake, you'll wonder what spell you've fallen under, and then you'll hear the whisper of love longing for what is lost and must be found again.

Chapter 1

April 1, 1974

IN THE ALCOVE of a second-story corner apartment tucked under the eaves of the former Congregational Church in Mill Valley, Jess McCarty awakened beneath a layer of wool blankets and a patchwork quilt. She had a tendency to sleep cool. As dawn turned the sky opalescent like the inside of oyster shells, she pulled the covers to her chin and squinted at the unfamiliar planes and angles of the room taking shape in the pale light. The thought of the parishioners singing "Just A Closer Walk With Thee" up into the rafters caused her to smile. The ogee-arched windows and onion spires were like something she'd seen in a Turkish mosque; they lent an exotic flavor to the building like belly dancers at a potluck social.

Jess listened for her daughter, Sarah, in the adjoining room. Quiet answered and she burrowed deeper under the warm covers. The air smelled like Christmas. A tenant was burning pinecones in a potbelly stove in the apartment below, and a thin, smoky haze seeped through the floorboards.

From her wide bed, she imagined she was poised at the brink of a new world. Here the rallying cry was freedom. Everyone wanted space—open space, green space, space to be themselves. Canyons and hilltops were being saved; women, farm workers and prisoners were organizing; Indians were claiming Alcatraz; men were joining encounter groups and beating drums, and across the bay in San Francisco, the gay revolution was in full swing. Pan, god of woods and fields, ran through the streets playing a zither. The Avatar was coming; anything was possible.

As the light began to brighten, she rolled onto her side and imagined the township of Woodacre, just miles away, the place where she and Sarah had spent three years, first in a mossy cottage by a creek that threatened each winter to overflow. Although it was only a short distance to the northwest, it was a world away. On first sighting Woodacre had been all she had wanted—a landscape without memories or association—but within reach of San Francisco, her hometown, and the alleys of Chinatown, their smell of rotting cabbages, the wide boulevards downtown, the lanes and streets of the ethnic neighborhoods that clung to the seven hills, and the deep briny cold of Ocean Beach.

She recalled in the beginning how the beauty of Woodacre dazzled her, but soon she saw the woods darkening houses built under trees or hanging off hillsides, vegetable gardens reaching for the sun, lamps glowing in windows at midday, and she admitted to herself how impetuous it had been to settle there. Gradually, it became the most isolated and wild and lonesome-making place she'd ever known. She'd retreated from Parker, her husband, and collided with Mickey, the man she loved when they were eighteen.

The night before, while shaking out her daughter's clothing, she'd discovered a pouch in Sarah's jacket pocket. A breathless fear ran through her when her hand touched the leathery material. Instantly she knew it contained objects found on the trails around Woodacre—arrowheads and small rocks given to her daughter by Mickey. She spilled the arrowheads, inky and black, into her palm. To hold the objects was like having him standing beside her. Her fingers turned cold, and she pushed back tears. We turned ourselves inside out for each other, she reasoned. But as she stared down at the objects in her hand, she knew that as much as she'd gambled with her heart, she'd risked emotional injury to her daughter. What else had he given Sarah that she was hiding? Jess resolved to do whatever it took to mend any attachment her daughter had to him. She'd root out the hurt and try to explain. Her love would nurture Sarah and, she reassured herself, children were resilient. After all, Sarah's relationship with Parker was primary and inviolate, and if there were any sadness or confusion now, her daughter would bounce back.

She fumbled for the clock on the plastic top of the portable radio and peered into its round face. Water hummed in the pipes behind the walls. Gradually she dozed as if on a becalmed sea clinging to a dream of love's sensations. She reconstructed her world not as it was, but as she wanted it to be. If unable to conjure a lover's face, she would smell his scent on her fingertips. If unable to know his name, his kisses would touch her lips and his voice would sound in her ears. The promise of love was a bulwark against night fears and the future's interminable length.

Had she actually known love could not be summoned, she might have prepared herself. She might have stepped away from men with their hair curling past their collars, a faraway look in their eyes, car keys jingling in their pockets. She might have considered the consequences of acting like real love was merely a breath away. But like many women who could no more wait for the world to come to their doorstep than to stop breathing, she flung herself into the fray. She believed she was living in paradise.

"Wake up, Mom," her daughter said into her ear.

"I'm awake," she answered.

"How come your eyes are closed?" Sarah climbed onto the bed and nestled into the crook of her mother's arm.

"Let's lie here for a minute." Outside the windows fog swirled around the redwood trees, their boughs drenched with moisture, pattering onto the windowsill.

"Is it today yet?" Sarah asked.

Jess's eyes snapped open. "Yes, it is. Your first day of school at Old Mill." She smoothed a fan of sun-bleached hair pleated across her daughter's forehead. Timbers creaked overhead.

"Do you think Daddy remembers?"

"I'm sure he does." Jess exercised caution when compensating for Parker's neglect. If she built glass castles around Sarah, she reasoned it was for her protection.

"How come he didn't call last night?"

"I don't know. Maybe he's out of town or involved in important meetings." She held Sarah closer and stroked her slender shoulders through her flannel pajama top. Jess's anger at Parker ignited, and she tamped it down, trying to modulate her voice. "Shall we try and call him later?"

"What time is it in Hartford if it's afternoon here?"

"East coast time is three hours ahead so if it's three o'clock here that would make it…"

"Six o'clock," Sarah replied. "He probably won't be home anyway."

"Don't worry, sweetheart, he's thinking of you. Daddy loves you."

"What if no one likes me at my new school?"

Eyes stretched open, she held her daughter at arm's length. "Are you kidding? *Everyone* liked you at San Geronimo. And you're already friends with Noah and Matthew. Wait a minute. Did you change overnight? Maybe I should check?"

Sarah squirmed away, bounced off the bed, and ran across the floor. "No checking. I'm getting dressed."

"I'll fix breakfast."

"I'm not hungry."

"You're still going to eat," Jess replied and rolled out of bed, dug into a canvas bag at her feet, and pulled out dance leotards and tights. Peeling on the rumpled clothes, she clicked on the radio tuned to KPFA, Radio Free Berkeley.

The noose was tightening around Nixon's neck; all programming had been suspended to broadcast the Watergate hearings. Senator Sam Ervin, all Southern drawl and deadly serious, bellowed over the airwaves and pounded the gavel, "There will be order in the chambers! Everyone take your seat and simmer down. I said there will be *order*!"

"This is unprecedented," the announcer exclaimed. "Nixon has defied the court's subpoenas to turn over the tapes. Instead he's released 1,254 pages of edited transcripts. These documents reveal his frequent use of obscene language and conversations with Haldeman and Ehrlichman to get money to silence the Watergate burglars. The reporters are going wild!"

Oh, this is good, Jess thought, pulling a velour top over her head. On the radio, she heard papers rustling, shouting in the background and Senator Ervin's exhalations reverberating through the microphone. She notched up the volume. Maneuvering around books and boxes stacked on the floor, she walked to the kitchen area built along one wall of the open room—a carpenter's dream of unpainted cabinets and plywood countertops glazed with a coat of shellac. From the wood shelving, she removed a Mason jar, unscrewed the lid and sprinkled granola into two bowls. Triscuit, the calico cat, wandered in from the hall and wound her body back and forth around her ankles.

"I'm all dressed," Sarah declared, pulling a red shirt over her stomach and tucking the ends into red and green plaid pants.

"Don't forget to tie your laces. Here, have a seat."

"I told you I'm not hungry."

"Sit down," she ordered. The battle over food infuriated her. Sarah would boycott breakfast, or stubbornly reject dinner because the peas on the plate touched the mashed potatoes tainted by the juices from the meatloaf, or scornfully disdain any vegetable even slightly soft like cooked carrots, while raw carrots were acceptable.

She leveled her I've-had-it stare at Sarah. "It's important to eat. I won't have you going to school without something in your stomach." She poured soymilk into the bowls and set one down in front of Sarah. "There will be no discussion, no negotiation, and no funny business. Now eat."

At the countertop, she plucked a thick-skinned avocado out of a basket with one hand, spooned cereal into her mouth with the other, and with one ear cocked to the radio, listened to the august Democrat from North Carolina thunder over the airwaves.

Sarah kneeled on the chair and nibbled from the spoon. "How come we have to listen to this stupid radio program every morning with the same old boring men talking?"

"Keep eating," Jess said, preparing one of her standard school lunches—avocado, jack cheese, and sprouts on wheat with mayonnaise—and slipped it inside a wax paper bag. She laid the sandwich, a bunch of grapes, two Fig Newtons, and a napkin inside a lunch box.

At noon on the playground, in a display of new-kid bravado, Sarah would trade the entire meal to an undernourished stick of a girl for two chocolate Hostess Twinkies, each decorated with a thin ribbon of white sugary frosting, nestled in cellophane.

Jess eyed Sarah's bowl. "Keep it up. You're getting there," she said, clicked off the radio, walked down the hall into a room she had designated as her studio.

Jess heard Sarah say, "Keep it up," and the wet sound of spitting. A spurt of water rattled the plumbing in the walls. Jess smiled and shook her head. Half a battle won was victory enough for this morning. She turned on a tape recorder on the floor. The cascading notes of Debussy piano suites filled the room and Jess, inhaling the music like fresh air, began deep *plies* at the ballet bar. The cat mewed, Sarah dashed down the hall into her room, and outside the windows the fog began to lift.

* * *

When Jess and Sarah stepped from the apartment building, a flock of Cedar Waxwings chatted in the high branches of a pine tree. Sarah ran down the brick stairs and skipped across the gravel drive. Jess caught up with her, grabbed her by the hand, and hummed a few bars of "Mill Valley!" Together they rounded the driveway onto the road.

Before them, Mt. Tamalpais loomed in the sky. Everywhere Jess looked she saw the upward, green cant of the mountain and its curved ridgeline against the sky. The mountain would become her mother, her Greenwich meantime, latitude and longitude, and she its servant. The molded swell of the mountain's face and redwoods standing along its knolls would hold her days like calendar months around a year.

Here, the climate was welcoming and the town wholesome. The air was moist, tempered by ocean breezes and tinged with the scent of redwoods, pine, and bay. The streets were laid out against the lower reaches of the mountain and meandered to the tide flats. Houses shared hillsides with trees and deer; commerce intermingled with open space and bird sanctuaries; Wing Tips played footsie with Birkenstocks; Edward Curtis sepia prints of the

American Indian hung on living room walls alongside woolly textile art studded with feathers and shells; *The Pacific Sun* and *Bay Guardian* were read as faithfully as *The Chronicle* and *The Examiner*, and down at the Depot Bookstore and Café, the local literati gathered to sip coffee while financial wizards boarded the bus for San Francisco's Montgomery Street.

"Can't you walk faster?" Sarah pleaded.

"I'm walking as fast as I can," Jess said.

"There's the playground!" Sarah broke free and flew downhill, blonde hair streaming behind her, compact body pitching forward, lunch box bobbing from her hand. Children's voices rose from the Old Mill School playground carried by the wind. Shouts, shrieks and the popping thunk of a kick ball filled the air. "Hurry up," Sarah yelled. "We'll be late."

The first buzzer sounded in the schoolyard. Students and teachers began to gather up balls and jackets. At the bottom of the hill, Sarah leapt to the edge of the curb, checked both ways and bolted across the street.

"Wait for me," Jess called, her feet flying over the ground.

The school, a classic, stucco, one-story building built in 1920 with wings that flared out from a central vestibule, occupied almost two acres directly across from Old Mill Park. Jess and Sarah skirted the playground along a cyclone fence and hurried along with other children who descended on the grounds like rabbits coming out of the field. They rode in on fat-tired, banana-seated, candy-apple red Schwins, silver, sleek Neshikis and battered skateboards as wide as shovels. They ran, skipped, and jostled on sidewalks. Jess and Sarah threaded their way through the throng.

At the front entrance to the school, Jess paused and laid her hand on Sarah's shoulder. "Mrs. Brush is your teacher and you're in room #3."

"I remember," Sarah said. Under her breath she whispered, "Please don't kiss me goodbye."

"I wouldn't think of it," Jess agreed. Sarah's confidence ultimately allowed her to navigate changes that other third-grade children might find rocky. She was curious about the world and content in it. Even as an infant she approached strangers with exuberance that Jess often had to monitor. This behavior wasn't something she learned; she was born that way.

"I'll see you after school," Jess said.

"Bye, Mom," Sarah said, darting into the crowd of children, a swift stream of red, green and navy sweaters and jackets.

* * *

As Sarah passed through the double doors of the school and into the arms of public education, Jess swung her bag over her shoulder and set off for the market. There was more than enough time to shop, meet Annie for a quick lunch, and return to the apartment to practice and continue to unpack and settle in. Humming to herself, her feet skimmed over the pavement. She considered the idea of popping into Village Music and checking out the latest vinyl, or maybe Mosher's Shoes just to peek at the latest arrival of knee-high leather boots. She wondered if Jake Zelinski was still operating the Royale Motors Garage up from the Fire Department. It had been a year since their paths had crossed. Jess had met Jake out in the valley when she and Mickey had stopped in at a bar for a drink, and he was shooting pool with Camilla.

A mental picture bloomed in her mind: Jake, an unshakeable optimist who favored the heft and lift of steel-toed black motorcycle boots to add height to his five foot six inch wiry frame, a man built for speed who loved nothing more than the challenge of restoring a mangled British racing car to its former glory. But it was the twinkle in his eye and his attraction to women that was both appealing and endearing, even though his style was the equivalent of a pit crew chief at the NASCAR races. No more had she finished the thought and turned at the corner when she heard the rumble of a motorcycle behind her.

A voice called, "Hey, babe! What's up?"

Jess swung her head toward the commotion without slowing her gait. A slow blush climbed from her throat into her cheeks.

Jake Zelinski himself was grinning at her like she was the opening act at the Sweetwater and he had all night to enjoy the show.

She sauntered between two parked cars over to his motorcycle gleaming in the sunshine. "Hi," she said, running her fingers through her hair and adjusting the strap of her bag that had fallen off her shoulder.

"Hi, yourself," Jake said. "It's been a long time. What are you doing in town?"

"I'm living here now." She shifted from foot to foot, pleased to see him, but suddenly self-conscious.

"No shit." He straddled the motorcycle and leaned back on the seat with his arms folded across his chest. "That blows me away."

"You haven't changed a bit," she said. "Still tearing up the streets in big flashy motorcycles."

He shrugged. "That's me, steady Eddie. Hey, I figured you had settled out in the valley for good."

"No, I joined a dance company in the city. The commute finally got to me. Some days I'd be driving back and forth twice because of Sarah."

"Wow. She must be grown up now. What is she, about twelve?"

"You're off by four years. You must be thinking of some other child."

"No," Jake said. "She seemed big or something. Give me a break. I don't know that many kids."

"Obviously," Jess said. Despite her annoyance she couldn't help but smile. His good humor was infectious.

A pack of cyclists pedaled by, thin tires humming in the street like bees. Jake was staring at her lips. She remembered the last time she had seen him. He had unexpectedly stopped by her place in Woodacre to see if she wanted to ride out to the beach with him. She was knee-deep in packing boxes to move in with Mickey, who had convinced her that if they lived together they could make a go of it. She was jittery as a fawn that Mickey might show up, find her with Jake and start a fight. Then, as if Jake was reading her mind, he had said goodbye, leaned into her face and kissed her lips. The tenderness of his kiss lingered in her mind longer than she would admit.

His voice surfaced over the roar of a passing bus. "I take it Mr. Wonderful is not in the picture?"

Jess shook her head no and studied the taxi drivers under the clock at the Depot. They leaned against their cabs, sipping from Styrofoam cups, waiting for the next fare.

"What was his name?"

"Mickey," she said, narrowing her eyes. She hated the scrutiny or arrogance of any man who seemed to have his life mapped out for him.

"Fireman, right?"

"What does that have to do with it?"

"The guy was an asshole. Significantly way out of control," he said.

"You can't blame me for trying," she flashed, her temper rising. "At least I gave it a shot."

"Take it easy. No offense. I'm on your side."

"What about you and Camilla?"

"We're the same. Nothing's changed. Business is booming."

Jess hitched the strap of the bag up onto her shoulder again. "Lucky you. I've got to get going."

"Now that you're in the neighborhood, drop by. Anytime. I'll show you my knife collection."

She burst out laughing. "You're really pushing it."

"What do you expect? I'm a rude guy."

"Sure. Whatever you say."

"Seriously, tell me you're not driving that heap of junk?"

"It suits me fine."

Jake grimaced. "The death trap. I can put you in something better. You should see the wrecks that get towed in. I make them so pretty." His dark eyes danced. "Don't put me off this time. Keep an open mind."

"I couldn't possibly afford one of your cars. Don't you know dancers are starving artists?"

"We'll work something out. Installment payments. Strictly on the up and up."

"That's all I need. *Me* in one of *your* big cars. Calling you from the road when it breaks down. And don't tell me you haven't seen those gas lines." She began backing away.

"That's no problem. I've got a connection."

"To Chevron?"

He tossed a triumphant smile at her. "Keep it in mind if you get hung up."

"I've really got to go," she explained.

"Where're you headed?"

"To the market." She glanced at her watch. "I'm pressed for time. My friend Annie is expecting me."

"Tell you what, I'll buy you coffee."

"Tell you what. I'll take a rain check."

"How about a lift?" he asked, cocking his wrist and opening up the throttle.

"Two blocks? You've got to be kidding?"

Jake flashed a grin.

"You're impossible," she said, transferring the bag to her other shoulder.

"Come on. I'll take you for a spin. For old time's sake." He held out his hand to hoist her aboard.

She balked like a cold engine that wouldn't turn over and then some impulse inside her fired. She took his outstretched hand, swinging one leg over the seat and settling close enough to feel his back against her body. He reached around and pulled her forward as if to resume a good thing they hadn't gotten into, like years hadn't passed, like he was her friend, like they could be lovers if she wanted. Then his body, lean and strong, sent out a current to her above the growl of the motorcycle and the voices in the street so that all traces of Camilla and a shadowy Mickey lifted past the sway of the redwood trees into the bluest sky, and suddenly, the coast was clear.

Chapter 2

ஒ

April 1

ANNIE MORRISON'S HEAD SPUN and oscillating points of white light burst across her vision. The sensation was similar to the time she dropped her first tab of sunshine acid and was convinced she'd seen the splendor of god radiating in fiery flames on the walls of her bedroom. Her body tingled like she'd been cavorting with angels. She hung up the phone and steadied herself against the kitchen counter.

An aide at Jerry Brown's campaign office had called from Sacramento. If elected Governor, Jerry was planning a different kind of inaugural ceremony, the aide explained. The gala ball would be cancelled, the Sufi Choir would sing at the swearing-in ceremony, and the walls of staterooms would be hung with paintings from California artists. Annie's name was at the top of the list. Would she be willing to send a painting?

She drifted from room to room of her Victorian home behind Dowd's Moving and Storage. Set by the creek in a grove of redwoods and abandoned by the locals because of its many frailties and oddities, including a reputation as a bordello, the house had stood vacant for years. Annie fell in love with it on first sight. She convinced the owner to accept her offer for less than the asking price—who would argue with cash? After selling off government bonds in her investment portfolio, she negotiated a quick close, moved in and started renovations. The cracked plaster, the chipped woodwork, and the layers of linoleum and plywood covering the wide-planked fir floors didn't faze Annie.

On the spot, she vowed to restore the house to a replica of its former splendor. She hired a contractor to shore up the foundation, an electrician to rewire the house, a plumber to install new fixtures, and a roofer to put down a new roof. She worked side-by-side with them plastering, painting and refinishing. True to her vision, in three months she had performed a miracle.

Annie sank onto the garnet brocade couch in the living room and admired the deep moss green she had painted the walls and the brilliant white of the twelve-foot ceilings. A sense of accomplishment and well-being washed over her. Then she rose, climbed the stairs to the second floor into a north-facing room and pushed open the door.

Three canvases, spanning a total of five feet high by fifteen feet long, hung on the wall. Across each canvas she had sketched elephants, rhinoceroses, monkeys, lions, and tigers. This morning she had begun to draw snakes that slithered and birds that soared. The eyes of creatures bulged; their hides rippled; their tongues flicked. Annie moved up to the canvases, backed off, turned and spun around to view them at various angles. She'd drench the jungle scenes in blues and greens and highlight the creatures with cadmium yellows and reds she craved. She'd call it "Biomorphic Blues Triptych."

In a near trance, she picked up a charcoal pencil and resumed drawing. Hours later, absorbed in rendering the leaves of a sword fern, she heard the front door open and close. A familiar voice called from below. Annie bit her lip. "Damn," she muttered. Reluctantly, she tore herself away from the canvas, laid down the pencil, and wiped her hands on her jeans.

She found Jess in the kitchen leaning against the sink, downing a glass of water.

"Sorry I'm late," Jess said, winding her tangled hair into a braid.

"Don't worry about it." Annie swallowed a complaint about being interrupted—after all she'd issued the invitation—and anyway it felt like old times to have Jess pop in.

"I'm starved," Jess said, opening the refrigerator door and peering in. "Let's have lunch."

Annie washed her hands at the sink. "Where have you been?"

Jess turned back and shrugged. "I bumped into Jake. We went for a ride on his motorcycle."

"I'm sure you did," Annie teased. "You probably ended up on a grassy hillside, flat on your back."

"Hardly," Jess protested. "It's not that way between us. But before I knew it, he was halfway up the mountain headed to Stinson Beach."

"Watch out. Whatever way it is between you now, he knows you're in town and free as a bird."

"He's devoted to Camilla."

"Since when does that keep a dog from sniffing around another tree?"

"I do have my standards."

"Would you stop? You're as obvious as an open-faced sandwich. Remember, I know about the hitch-hiker."

Jess set the glass down on the counter and folded her arms across her chest. "He was an exception," she said, straight-faced. "Besides, I thought he might run for president someday!"

"President, my ass," Annie laughed.

Jess pulled a stool from under the counter and slumped onto it. "Is it my imagination or is the field thinning out? I think one of my major talents is picking unsuitable men."

"That's ridiculous. What's wrong with a little experimentation? You know my motto: variety is the spice of life."

"There's something else." Jess fidgeted with the silver rings on her fingers. "It's probably nothing."

"Spit it out, Miss Goody Two Shoes." Annie perched on a stool on the opposite side of the counter and tried not to grumble. Often Jess would take a convoluted route to an obvious conclusion that made her cross. Annie chipped paint spatters off her fingernails and reminded herself that when she had freaked out during an acid flashback that paralyzed her at the post office, Jess responded with the speed of an emergency medical team. In the years they had known each other, no one but Jess could bring her down to the ground without a crash landing.

"Lately I've had the feeling I'm being watched."

"Watched?" Annie said, glancing up quickly. "What do you mean?"

Jess broke eye contact with Annie and peered over her head. "When I left the studio to walk to my car after rehearsal last week, I had a creepy feeling. All the hairs on the back of my neck stood straight up. Then the other day, I found one of those braided leather bracelets wedged under my windshield wiper."

"You mean the kind Mickey wore?" An alarm buzzed in Annie's brain.

"Yes, the same kind."

"I wouldn't put it past him to do something crazy. He could be stalking you."

Jess's eyes brimmed with tears and she rubbed them away with the back of her hand. "God, what is wrong with me? Just the idea of him trailing me is terrifying, but underneath is a sadness that I'll never find someone who will love me like he did. Is that sick or what?"

"Sometimes love and pain get mixed up together," Annie reassured her. "As beautiful as he was, and I'll give you that, he wanted to put you in chains. No one can live like that."

"You think Mickey was beautiful?"

"Christ, yes," Annie said. "Part of his act, if it was an act, was he didn't know it."

Jess looked astonished. "I thought you thought he was a walking nightmare."

"That, too."

"I can't go down that road again," Jess said.

Annie regarded Jess carefully. It was disturbing to recall the lethal escalation of intoxication mixed with danger that defined their relationship. Once in a blowup, he broke windows, smashed his fist through walls, and burned clothes he had given her. Their final break came after a period of arguing and fighting when a fire ignited inside his house while he was on duty in San Francisco. Jess and Sarah were trapped inside. The San Geronimo Valley firemen rescued them; the house burned to the foundation.

"Well, maybe finding that bracelet was a coincidence." Jess stood and stretched. "Anyway he's long gone."

"Don't be so sure of that. I don't trust him one bit."

"I heard he's back in the islands," Jess said. She waved her hand in front of her face as if to clear the air. "Living in Honolulu, or somewhere on Oahu."

"Good. He can stay there—permanently. I like the idea of three thousand miles of ocean between you and him." Annie softened her voice. "If anything else suspicious happens, you will let me know?"

"Of course," Jess said. "You don't have to worry about that."

"Good," Annie said and opened the cupboard. "All this talk makes me ravenous. You make sandwiches and I'll heat the soup. Is tomato okay?"

Together they prepared lunch while Annie told Jess about the unexpected phone call. "Pack your high heel sneakers. When Jerry is elected, we'll personally deliver my painting to Governor Moonbeam."

"You've been waiting for this kind of break," Jess exclaimed.

They sat at the counter, ate, laughed, and chatted about Annie's good fortune.

At the end of the meal, Jess pushed her plate away and leaned forward. "By the way, next week I have to stay late in the city. I hate to ask, but could Sarah come here and play with Noah after school? I should be back by dinnertime."

"You mean every day?" Annie raised her eyebrows.

"Just Wednesday and Friday. I wouldn't bother you, but I haven't met any other parents to ask." Jess blinked rapidly. "And, could you pick her up the first time?"

Annie scowled. "She's been here before. She knows the way." Jess's vigilance of Sarah's comings and goings annoyed Annie, provoking awkward disputes between them. Annie's philosophy was to encourage her sons to be independent, and they hadn't given her any cause to doubt her judgment. She'd chosen Mill Valley partially for their benefit: the schools were excellent, the town had a funky, live-and-let-live atmosphere, and the police kept the town safe. Matthew lived on his bike from morning to dark, hung out with his friends, and sometimes on weekends, when he spent the night at friends' houses, she wouldn't see him from Friday afternoon until Sunday dinner. Where Matthew was unbridled and whip smart, Noah was gentle and nurturing. He kept a menagerie of animals, and when Annie gave him her sewing machine he became absorbed in creating all manner of bivouac gear like tarps, tents and sleeping bags to camp and watch the animals in the woods. She concluded she couldn't have chosen a healthier community in which to raise her sons.

"Just for the first time," Jess said.

"It's only three blocks max."

"Four blocks," Jess corrected.

"All right, already, but really, you coddle her."

"New town, new school, new friends. I'm looking out for my daughter. Come on, Annie, don't be such a hard ass."

"You weren't so protective of Sarah before."

"Let's say I had a wake-up call. Anyway, she was one of thirty kids who knew each other by name and rode the school bus every day. Woodacre was a bump in the road compared to Mill Valley. If anyone sneezes in the valley, it's public knowledge by noon."

"You're exaggerating."

"Hardly. You've forgotten. Once you left you never came back. I was always the one who came over the hill to visit you."

As Jess hammered down on a sore point, Annie felt herself weaken.

"Pick her up just this once," Jess said. "Then she and Noah can play together."

"Okay, but don't expect me to jump in every time. Sarah's welcome, but she can fend for herself."

"She and Noah will make themselves invisible. Soon, I'll know a dozen parents, and I won't have to bother you."

Annie gave her a skeptical look. Jess hadn't been particularly social, nor was she a joiner. What other changes was she contemplating? She hoped her friend wasn't evolving into one of those annoying PTA mothers who volunteered for field trips and campouts. "Next thing you'll be petitioning me to co-chair an all-day bake sale."

Jess laughed. "Your brownies could convince the Sandinistas to lay down arms." She stood and reached for her bag.

"Before you dash out and sign on as homeroom mother, come upstairs and see my new painting. If I work day and night I can meet the deadline."

Daylight flooded into Annie's studio. She flicked on the overhead track lighting aimed at the walls. "I'm nearly ready to dive into the oils. What do you think?"

Jess stared at the canvases. "I feel like I'm in a jungle and can hear the munching of leaves and the screech of birds."

"Is it good enough?" Doubt perched on Annie's shoulder, driving its hard bargain.

"Good enough for what?" Jess asked. "Governor Moonbeam?"

"Hell, no. That's just a stepping-stone. I'm talking about work that will take me all the way—the SF MOMA, the LA County Museum, and right to the pinnacle, the MOMA in New York. Anything less is failure."

"That's putting a lot of pressure on yourself."

"Some days it feels like ambition is eating me alive."

"Can't you accept where you are right now?"

"If I could only find enough time," Annie snapped. "Some days I want to run away and hide." She inhaled deeply. "Lately when I have to shop for food and fix dinner for the boys, I resent it."

"You'd miss them if they weren't here."

"Try me. And don't look so horrified."

"Everything in balance," Jess said brightly.

Annie shook her head and turned back toward the canvases. "Right now, I'm at that hypnotic stage when the creatures are drawing themselves. The moral sensor is turned off. Everything flows. Most nights I turn out the light at 3 AM. But I can't completely block out the world. Speaking of which," she instructed, taking Jess by the arm, "turn around."

On the opposite wall, Annie had propped a painting she had entitled "Psychedelic Mambo." Five-feet high and ten-feet long, amoebae-like shapes of electric purple and red intertwined with ochre spheres and vibrated off the canvas. "This is a present for you. I think it'll look fantastic in your new apartment."

"I can't take this," Jess objected. "It's too valuable."

"If you don't accept, I'll be offended."

"When Parker and I divorced, I thought there goes all the fabulous art I could have had in my life."

"Nonsense. I hate it when you cry poor. Stop moaning about the past and your dead-ass ex."

"I'm a realist," Jess said, bristling. "I can't help it."

"Don't underestimate yourself." Impatience burned in Annie's throat. "You can do or be anything you want. Now let's get this painting out of here and up to your apartment."

"Right now?"

"Why not?" Annie pursed her lips. "We'll walk it up."

"Seven blocks?"

"We'll take breathers along the way."

"You're serious?"

"Yes, I am, you ninny."

"You don't do this for just anyone, do you?"

"Only the people I care about," Annie said.

Jess stepped forward and wrapped her slender arms around her friend's shoulders. "Thank you, Annie."

The sweep of Jess's hair that had fallen loose brushed past Annie's face. It smelled like citrus and orange blossoms. In that instant, she realized that Jess towered more than a foot above her. In her mind, she was the stronger one, wiser, more experienced. Jess's affection caught her off guard and touched a vulnerability that she hadn't expected to feel. She broke away first. "Come on," she said. "Let's go."

They grasped the cross bars of the frame at the back of the painting and maneuvered it down the stairs, out the front door, over the bridge that spanned the creek onto the avenue. Pedestrians turned their heads to glance at the two women advancing up the sidewalk, holding the painting like a banner. The red and purple shimmered against the ochre pigment, and Annie and Jess called to one another, giving encouragement along the way.

Chapter 3

April 9

AT NINE O'CLOCK SHARP, Mrs. Louise Terwilliger, affectionately known as Mrs. T. the Bird Lady, pulled her VW camper van in front of Old Mill School. Glee and anticipation seized students and teachers alike. Cheers echoed up and down the hallways. The decibel level in the building tripled.

In Stewart Merch's sixth-grade classroom, pandemonium swept through the air. At his desk, he tossed aside a bulletin from the school nurse about the scourge of head lice and joined the students who jostled at the windows for position. He was as pleased to see Mrs. T. as anyone else. Her legendary status as a goodwill ambassador of birds and their habitat was known throughout the county and her enthusiasm for all feathered, woodland and riparian creatures was contagious.

Mrs. T. emerged from the dusty van on legs as thin as a Snowy Egret and a bosom as generous as a Red Robin. Her appearance reinforced his good spirits and guaranteed a fine day. A billowing white shirt covered her stocky torso, khaki pants hung from her narrow hips and a wide brimmed straw hat was secured under her chin with a drawstring tie. Her eyes were a merry blue, her hands tan and freckled, and she waved to the children as she whisked by.

"Okay, kids, listen up," Stewart said. "Our class is scheduled to see Mrs. T. after morning recess. Right now, move your desks into three pods. Spread out and give yourselves plenty of room. Boys and girls together."

Stewart reached out and grabbed Matthew Morrison's arm as he streaked by. Matthew wore an orange T-shirt with a lion emblazoned on the front and his clear eyes showed a flicker of surprise. "I need your help," Stewart said.

"What's that, Mr. Merch?" Matthew asked.

"On the table under the window are three stacks of print-outs. Each one is color-coded. Bring them to me."

Matthew looked pained and mumbled something under his breath.

"What did you say?" Stewart asked. He kept his voice low, non-confrontational, and firm.

"Nothing," Matthew said, boldly meeting Stewart's gaze.

"All right then." Stewart motioned with his chin toward the table, and Matthew walked away.

There was a scraping of chairs as the children pulled their desks into circles. Stewart heard a tall boy named Luwellyn, his bleached blonde hair cut square at his shoulders like a knight in King Arthur's Court, snicker "Kiss ass," and stick out his foot in the aisle. Matthew gave Luwellyn the finger and shot something back.

Gradually the class assembled into two groups of eight and one group of seven. Stewart separated the boys who habitually sat together and reserved a place for Matthew in the first pod.

When the children turned their faces toward him, Stewart explained. "This morning we're going to read and discuss among your groups the early 1800's Westward Expansion that changed the shape of America. Each group will report on their subject. The following students will be team captains." He walked over to Matthew and placed his hand on his shoulder. "Matthew's group up front will take the Lewis and Clark expedition. Clarissa's group in the middle will take steamboat travel on the Hudson River, and Andy's group at the back will take the construction of the Erie Canal."

Protests and exclamations broke out among the children. "Let's keep our voices down so you can hear one another," Stewart announced, moving toward his desk. "You'll have an hour until morning recess to read and discuss the subjects. Later, each team captain will report."

Several hands shot up in unison.

"I'll take questions in a moment."

Stewart glanced at Matthew. A spark of recognition passed between them that Stewart chose to take as a shred of respect. The boy had a quick intelligence mixed with animal cunning that singled him out. Earlier, Mrs. Porter had stopped Stewart in the hall to report that the clerk at Lockwood's Pharmacy had called to say that the older Morrison boy had come into the store at noon yesterday. Right after he'd left, the counter where cigarette lighters and lighter fluid were displayed had been ransacked. Stewart was startled, but didn't want to corroborate this story with his own doubts about some materials that had gone missing in the classroom until he had a chance to talk with Matthew's mom. He told Mrs. Porter he'd look into it and report back.

"Mr. Merch, Mr. Merch," Mia called. "I have a question."

Stewart looked down at the chaos on his desk and back up at the girl. She had a voice like an axe splintering wood. Without a doubt she was destined for the stage. "Hold your horses, Mia," he said. "Everyone settle down. One question at a time."

He'd told himself that today he'd get a grip on the paperwork that went with the job, but he knew he was fooling himself. When the questions subsided, he'd make a stab at prioritizing the lot of it or dump it into the waste bin. Who would know the difference?

* * *

When the morning bell rang for recess, Stewart poured out of the classroom with the children onto the playground to take his turn as Yard Duty Teacher and saw that Mrs. T. was occupied with a class of younger children in the area used for kickball. He promptly guided the older students away from her demonstration. They scattered in all directions throughout the yard. He took notice of another teacher at the jungle gym and continued to watch Mrs. T.

She had parked the van under the spreading branches of the highest elm. A soft, clean spring breeze blew in the air dispersing the morning fog that had blown in off the beach from Tennessee Valley over the marshes and wetlands. She bustled in and out of the sliding door selecting birds and placing them in the center of the circle. The van was packed to the gills with stuffed birds, including a Great Horned Owl, a Red-shouldered Hawk, a Peregrine Falcon, a Western Gull, a Red-winged Blackbird, a Plain Titmouse, a Downy Woodpecker, and her pride and joy, a Great Blue Heron. Each bird was affixed to either a pole or piece of driftwood so they could stand upright when she mimicked the motion of birds in flight. Lizards and snakes were arranged on flat boards by means of glue or rubber bands. Some of the reptiles' scales had begun to flake, but this was of little concern. She'd repaired their papery scales with scotch tape as best she could and was done with it.

She shouted a cheery hello to the younger children as if they were visiting dignitaries and drew the tie of her hat tightly under her chin. "Today," she said, "we'll look at the Red-Shouldered Hawk and the Turkey Vulture." The children closest to her sucked in their breath and moved back.

"Remember, I have only one rule," Mrs. T. announced. "What is it?"

"Don't touch the birds!" the children chimed in.

"Excellent! Now, let's get started. Here is the beautiful hawk and next to it the mighty vulture. In the sky these birds look alike. But there is an easy way to know the difference between the two. When the hawk flies his wings are straight." With this, she spread her arms out from her shoulders and gracefully tilted her upper torso as though she was flying. The students next to her stepped back to give her more room. "When the vulture flies his wings are in the shape of a V." Now she held her arms in the shape of a V and sang, "V is for vulture."

The children raised their arms and joyfully shouted, "V is for vulture. V is for vulture." They swooped and darted and broke from the circle, screaming with delight.

Stewart pulled himself away from the hullabaloo and walked toward the middle of the playground where a group of boys he recognized from the fourth-grade were kicking a soccer ball back and forth. One of the boys was Matthew's younger brother, Noah. Stewart noticed him reaching down and picking up an object lying on the pebbly concrete. The boy hesitated, turning the object over in his hand. The intensity of his inquiry gave Stewart pause.

"Hey, Frodo," Stewart heard Noah call to another boy, "catch!"

The small object lofted in the air, a smooth trajectory sailing over the heads of students. The boys tossed it back and forth until Stewart watched Matthew run in, jump high, and snatch the object in mid-air. Noah and Frodo rushed at him.

"What the hell!" Matthew shouted, "Where'd you get this?"

"I found it," Noah said. "On the ground. Over there."

"Yeah," Frodo added. "What is it, anyway?"

Matthew ducked his head, and swiveled his hips, making graphic gestures with the object below the waist. The wind snatched his words away.

Hurriedly Stewart advanced on the boys. An expression of disbelief was etched Noah and Frodo's faces. He watched their childhood teeter in the air.

He heard Matthew laugh. "Women use it, you know…" He held the object in his fist and jerked it to and fro at his crotch.

Stewart walked faster.

"Give it here," Frodo threatened. "We found it first."

"Watch it," Noah said. "Here comes Merch."

A kickball whizzed on the ground past Stewart's feet and right behind him, a child ran and collided into his knees. She spilled onto the asphalt, hands out, breaking the fall. Nearly tripping, Stewart set her upright. "Are you okay?" he asked. The girl held back tears, her palms white, prickling with blood. Around them mayhem seemed to be breaking out. Boys rushed past them toward the fence. Stewart saw Luwellyn muscle in through the fracas and heard shouting and taunts.

Quickly Stewart found an older student to take the girl to the school nurse and pushed through the crowd to see Matthew throw the object so high it landed in the crotch of the elm tree right above the spot where Mrs. Terwilliger was demonstrating the behavior of the Western Sandpiper.

Stewart halted in front of Matthew. A slow burn filled his chest. "What did you throw in the tree?"

"Beats me, Mr. Merch." Matthew pushed up the sleeves of his orange shirt, jammed his hands into his pocket, and clenched his jaw.

The boys clustered around them. Stewart felt their gaze, boring into his back, waiting for his next move.

Stewart turned to Luwellyn who stood mutely next to Matthew. "What do you think it was?"

"Maybe some kind or tool or something." His blonde hair fell into his eyes and he swiped it away, his fingers smudged with dirt.

"Tell me this," Stewart said. "How smart was it to throw a tool over Mrs. T's head?"

Matthew raised his eyes, a smirk on his face. "I didn't mean anything by it."

Stewart's anger spiked. "Cut it out, Matthew. When Mrs. Terwilliger is here, give her your full respect. I saw what happened with your brother and his friend. Your behavior is out of bounds. Do we understand each other?"

Matthew hitched up his jeans. "Yes, Mr. Merch."

"Okay, let's break this up," Stewart said, waving away the circle of boys. A gust of wind picked up a plastic bag that flew over the cyclone fence. Seagulls dove at the edges of the playground, searching for spoils. He watched Matthew lope across the yard with his arm around Luwellyn's shoulder. Less than three months remained in the term before Matthew graduated to middle school. Had Stewart witnessed a cruel impulse in Matthew's behavior or was it the capriciousness of spring rising like sap? When he sang in class, his uplifted face showed no malice, his sure voice rising sweetly above the others. In the lunchroom he heard teachers assessing blame to "that Morrison boy" for every stolen bicycle, broken window and dead cat. Still, Stewart clung to a different take on Matthew: underneath that tough exterior were the markings of a born leader. He stored this impression alongside suspicions he could not square and joined the other teacher to survey the yard before he assembled his class for Mrs. T.

Chapter 4

ↂ

April 10

ANNIE SWISHED DOWN THE MAIN CORRIDOR of Old Mill Grammar School, her multi-colored skirt whipping against her legs, the mica stones on the fringe of her tan suede boots clicking against each other. She hurried on the polished linoleum floor trying to beat the clock. Most of the classroom doors were closed, afternoon light escaping through the transoms. Matthew's teacher had called yesterday and wanted to meet her after school. His voice had a serious note that she couldn't tease away when she tried to banter with him. She'd had her eye on Stewart since parents' night, but he wouldn't swallow the bait she had dangled in front of his nose. Maybe today she'd shake him loose.

The 3:00 bell jangled as she slid to a stop in front Noah's fourth-grade class. A stream of children shot through the doors. She nabbed Noah's collar from behind, bringing him up short.

"What are *you* doing here?" he asked incredulously.

"Hi, honey," she said. "Listen, do you know where Mrs. Brush's class is?"

"Yeah, up around the corner." He called to a boy who was disappearing down the hall in a trail of backpacks and bobbing heads, "Hey, Frodo, wait up!"

"I need you to go there, find Sarah, and take her home," Annie said.

"Me?" Noah whined.

"Am I speaking to anyone else?" When Noah stalled, feigning bafflement, she often wondered how she could possibly have two sons who were so completely opposite in every way.

"Why me?"

"Because you're friends and I promised her mom I'd meet her. But now I have an appointment with Matthew's teacher."

"Mom, I can't do that."

"Yes, you can."

"Ah, Mom. Come on. I want to go to Frodo's house today."

"Go tomorrow." She shoved a few dollars into his hand. "Take her downtown to Baskin-Robbins if you want. If you don't see her in the classroom, she'll be waiting outside on the corner." She pushed him away. "Now hurry up."

Annie turned on her heel and headed down the nearly deserted hall. Some of the classroom doors were open. A hush emanated from within the rooms. A frizzy-haired teacher in a smock slumped at her desk, glasses on the end of her nose, sorting through papers. The acrid odor of rodent cages gone too long without cleaning, soured milk cartons tossed in bins, and erasers choked with dust permeated the hallway. *Teaching,* Annie thought, *what a thankless profession. You couldn't pay me enough.*

"We might go up on the mountain," Noah called, his voice echoing down the corridor.

"Good idea," Annie called back. She hoped they'd stay out all afternoon. "See you later."

* * *

Anne stuck her head through the door at the threshold to Matthew's classroom. Stewart stood with his back toward the door in jeans and a khaki shirt. "Hi," she said. When he turned around, a smile on his face, she smiled back. Annie's earlier recollection of him as a fox was confirmed in an instant. He'd retained the charms of a boy in the healthy body of a man, a twinkle in his eye that signaled a quick mind, a strong jaw, straight teeth, tousled sandy hair. The third finger of his left hand was devoid of a wedding ring. He had the aura of a man up for grabs.

"Hello, Annie," he said. "Come in. Let me find you a chair."

As she approached his desk, she noticed him kicking aside a pair of athletic shoes, a tennis racket, and what looked like sweatpants. She swung her shoulders to and fro and stuck out her hand. "Good to see you again."

"Likewise," he said. His hand was warm in her grasp. He scooted a straight-backed chair up to the side of the desk. She sat, crossed one leg over the other, and arranged the folds of her skirt.

"Great spring weather we're having, isn't it?" he asked, clearing aside a vitamin bottle, a stopwatch, golf tees, a half-empty bottle of some kind of juice, a terrycloth headband, colored markers, a ring of keys, a bicycle tire pump, and the Sunday Examiner. He pulled a file from a stack and turned to Annie.

"I love spring," she said. "It's my favorite time of the year." If his desk was this messy, she could only imagine his house. Maybe he needed an incentive to get organized.

He dusted off his hands and leaned backwards balancing on the rear legs of the chair. "I'm glad we could meet today."

Annie decided to launch a full court press. "Lately, I've been thinking about getting into some kind of organized sport. Otherwise, before I know it, spring will be over and the fog will come rolling in."

"Is that right?" he said.

"I thought I'd take up tennis again." This part was true. She'd hit a mean backhand in college. If she could get him on the court, she wagered, it was a short distance to his bed.

"Heck of a game," he said.

"Do you play?" She swung her foot up and down, shaking the beads on her boots.

"I haven't got time." He waved his hand around the classroom as if to indicate that this was his entire world.

"Looks like you've got time for golf." She nodded at the tees on his desk. At this moment, she was on the verge of coming right out and saying teach me.

"I only play on weekends."

"Now there's a game that's intrigued me." She cocked her head and smiled as if she'd scored a point.

He tipped forwards and brought the chair to level. "I asked you to stop by so we could talk about Matthew."

His brusque manner brought her up short. "Of course." Her antennae recalibrated. She uncrossed her legs. "How's he doing?"

Stewart cleared his throat. "To tell you the truth, he's a talented kid and a natural athlete. He tests off the charts. What's difficult or challenging for other students comes easily to him. The other day he surprised me when the music teacher came to teach the class some Early American songs. We've been studying the westward expansion from New York State to the Appalachians. When she began "Fifteen Miles on the Erie Canal," Matthew joined in and belted out the lyrics."

"It's on a Pete Seeger record I used to play when he was a little boy." An initial stab of queasiness in her stomach turned to delight. "I had no idea he remembered it."

"The music teacher wants him to try out for the school pageant."

"He won't listen to me." Annie looked away from Stewart's inquisitive stare. Obviously he had no idea of what it took for a woman to raise two sons, and the tedious ineffectuality of making suggestions or setting down rules that would be scoffed at once they left her mouth. Couldn't the boys just magically grow up and become little men?

"Really?" He picked up a pencil and began to flip it back and forth between his fingers. "Well, talk to him about it. Give him some encouragement. He didn't seem interested, but we'll see." Stewart opened the file and glanced at his notes. "The other side of Matthew is that he can make or break a day in class by setting the tone. Whatever he says, other boys follow."

"Yes, he can be persuasive. To a fault." For months she had given up going toe-to-toe with Matthew when a conflict reared its head. He batted away her objections when she heard him on the roof—he was only playing war with his friends—and minimized her concern when he burned something foul in the yard. Noah's accusation that he had stolen his box turtle was bunk, he'd said. Rather than battle with him, she had struck a deal: he would bring home good grades and she would give him autonomy, unless an instance occurred that warranted action on her part. She wasn't sure at all how she could enforce discipline. His height and strength outweighed her by far, and when she challenged him his anger frightened her.

Stewart paused. "The principal got a call from Lockwood's Drug Store. Apparently Matthew came into the store at noon, which, as you know, is against school policy. And when he left the shelf where the lighters were displayed had been depleted."

She narrowed her eyes. "The lighters. You mean cigarette lighters?"

"That's right," he said.

The queasiness awakened and churned deeper in her stomach. "What else?" she asked.

"Lately some things have gone missing. My keys disappeared one morning but popped up in the afternoon. The milk money has legs. Some chemicals I use in science experiments walk away."

"Are you saying Matthew is stealing?" She was appalled, and then a sudden anger not unlike an animal's response to defend her young awakened in her. *Who was Stewart to accuse her son of stealing*? she thought. Just look around the room. It was a miracle the man could find anything in this clutter. The clerk at the drug store must have been mistaken. Matthew wouldn't be so stupid as to leave school at noon. It had to be another boy. Only she would be the judge of Matthew, not anyone else—not his teacher, and certainly not a clerk in a drug store.

Stewart picked up a rough stone from on top of a stack of papers. "I'm trying to sort this out. Is there anything going on with Matthew that I should know about?"

She fingered a turquoise necklace at her throat, a storm of contradictory feelings overwhelming her with force. Doubt, shame, and sadness rushed at her. She glanced at Stewart who was waiting, turning the stone in his hand. Without warning the memory of an afternoon with Matthew leapt into her mind.

"I don't mean to intrude," Stewart said.

"You're not intruding," she said, trying to figure out where to begin. She sighed, her throat dry. "I've been divorced for five years. The boys visit their father at Christmas and during summer vacation. He lives in Colorado."

"That's tough—especially on boys," Stewart said quietly.

"When we divorced I didn't realize how much the boys would need their father."

Stewart nodded his head, observant, still.

"I have the feeling Matthew blames me for the divorce," she continued.

"Why do you think that?"

She hesitated, peering out the window. When she looked back at Stewart his eyes had lost their smile. "The last fight Matthew and I had was a wake-up call. I can't even remember what it was about, probably to stop harassing his brother. Do you know, he punched me?" She raised her hand to the middle of her chest. "Right here. It knocked the wind out of me. I called his dad who luckily was home. He told Matthew if he ever hit me again, he'd beat the shit out of him. Can you imagine? What's his father going to do? Jump through the phone?" She touched the turquoise gems, cool to her touch. "Sometimes I feel I'm holding Matthew by a thread and if I let go, I'll lose him."

Silence hung between them. The afternoon light that filtered through the high green elms on the sidewalk fell through the windows into the classroom. The silence wrapped them in a moment of intimacy that she couldn't have predicted, and while she was unsure how to continue, the thing that was palpable, the thing that seemed to breathe between them was this moment of truth—hers to say and his to receive. When she lifted her eyes from her lap and met his gaze, it was as if she was seeing him clearly for the first time.

"Not many parents would tell me something so personal." He started to speak, stopped and started again. "This is a hard time for you and for Matthew. It's obvious he's acting out and needs limits—at home and in school. He may feel he's out of control. The principal will call him into her office. And I'll have a talk with him myself. Don't give up on encouraging him to audition for the school play."

Annie shook her head. "Do you really think that will make a difference?"

"You could try."

"You must be dreaming," she said.

Chapter 5

April 10

THE BUILDINGS SOUTH OF MARKET basked in late afternoon sunshine. At 16th and Mississippi a three-story brick warehouse that once clanged and shook in the manufacturing of electrical equipment now housed artists who had formed a collective and carved studios and illegal living spaces inside its cold, windy bowels and elevated floors. It was named Project Artaud after the French surrealist actor and poet, Antonin Artaud, the founder of the "Theatre of Cruelty." Inside disembodied voices echoed along its steel rafters and up and down its iron stairways.

In a dance studio tucked into the southwest corner of the building where maple floors gleamed and the floor-to-ceiling mirrors reflected the kinetic play of bodies in motion, Jess and her dance partners, Claire and Sebastian, changed into street clothes after a two-hour session of choreographing a performance piece.

"Sure you don't want to come with us?" Sebastian asked, buttoning skin-tight jeans and pulling an olive colored t-shirt over his shaved head. His body was honed to New York City Ballet Corps standards—long neck corded with muscle, thick shoulders, slim hips, attenuated rock-hard calves. Like a marble statue, he was lovely to admire, but icy to the touch. Although his skills intimidated her, he had something she wanted—star power.

"I'm beat," Jess replied, stepping into loose-fitting black pants. "I'd rather take a break." She rubbed a burning pain in her left hip flexor at the site of an old injury that wouldn't go away. Beyond the age when many dancers peak, she was just coming into her own and the constant throb of her hip annoyed her.

"We'll bring back some food," Claire said. She was the first to towel off and dress. The smallest of the trio, yet the most curvaceous, her every gesture was characterized by efficiency and speed. Her jumps and leaps inspired dumbstruck wonder.

"How about a sandwich?" Sebastian asked, wrapping a towel around his neck.

"I'm not hungry," Jess said. She slipped a black turtleneck over her head. "Bring me a coffee."

"How late can you stay tonight?" Sebastian asked. The tone of his voice was edgy and pitched higher than usual.

"As long as it takes," Jess replied. A familiar stab of duty gripped her chest. By early evening, Sarah would be waiting, and Annie would be watching the clock. The last thing Jess wanted was Annie harping about taking advantage of her goodwill.

"Can I make a phone call for you when we're out?" Claire asked.

Jess shook her head no and kept dressing. To explain in Sebastian's presence that she would put her daughter's needs before her devotion to the dance company was unthinkable. He wouldn't understand. Surely they would end rehearsal not later than 6 PM. She'd miss the rush hour traffic and be home in forty minutes.

"We need to tighten up the last section," Sebastian told them. "In the adagio I'm too far up stage. Jess, you have a tendency to get ahead of yourself. We all need to fill the movement with breath. Otherwise, the timing is off. We're at the point where we have to nail the work now. Time is going to fly."

"I agree," Claire said. She buttoned her shirt and grabbed her wallet.

"I brought the revised proposal for the grant committee. We need to check tour dates, workshop sites and finalize details. Let's wrap up these questions tonight," he urged. "Claire, can you type the final?"

"Sure. No problem."

"None of this feels real yet," Jess said. Her tendency to doubt success even when it was staring her in the face was an old pattern. Still, it leaked out. She wished she'd kept her mouth shut.

Sebastian mopped his face and grinned from underneath the towel. "We've made it this far. Tryouts in ten days. Grant notification in a month. When the contract comes in the mail, it will feel a hundred percent real!"

"I bet you're right," Jess said cheerfully.

Claire looped her arm through Jess's arm and together they walked outside into the sunshine. Jess watched as Claire and Sebastian strolled up 16th Street. Settling on the warm sidewalk, she squared her shoulders against the wall. Every muscle in her body hummed. She rested her back against the brick, knees bent and feet planted on the sidewalk.

Despite Sebastian's admonition to adjust her timing, the morning had been a triumph. The nagging worry that she was the weak link in the trio—the one with less professional training, less experience and less musical ability—stopped its chatter when she stepped onto the floor. She flung herself at the floor work in the same way Dylan sang "Tangled Up In Blue"—infusing the halting rhythms with urgency and going for broke on the crescendos. The music pulsed in her ears and she willed her muscles to execute the language of the choreography, sure that her legs and feet would support her as she moved in tandem with her partners or broke into a solo. She promised herself, from that moment forward, she'd banish any doubt that she didn't belong in the same league as Sebastian and Claire. They had chosen her; she wouldn't let them down.

The facades of the buildings dazzled a luminous pink and the sky swung bright blue overhead. The temperature was perfect—no wind, streets protected from chilly air off the bay, a Mediterranean light bathing sidewalks, back lots and pocket parks. She glanced at her watch—the black hands of the Timex read 3:00 PM. *Sarah's getting out of school,* Jess thought. She reassured herself—Annie agreed to meet Sarah and afterwards she and Noah would play together, their heads together, little chatterboxes, exploring outside and reading books in Noah's bedroom like they always did. There was no need for concern.

An engine backfired in the street and a plume of exhaust shot from the tailpipe. Jess squinted against the whiteout. A driver at the wheel of a VW bus idled in the street between two parked cars. She shaded her eyes with her hand, certain the driver was looking her way, his features obscured in shadow. Her body tensed, ready to stand, certain that Mickey's eyes would fasten into hers, a brittle smile would break across his face.

A black dog, with a red cotton handkerchief around his neck, shoved his nose from behind the man's shoulder and barked at Jess. The man spoke in a clear baritone, "Cut it out, Cody."

All the fight went out of Jess's body. She laughed at herself; Mickey detested VW buses—"hippie wheels" he called them. A surfboard was wedged in the back of the bus. A crystal dangled from the rearview mirror. The driver smiled at her. She smiled back, closed her eyes, and turned her shoulders a fraction as if to reclaim her solitude. She heard the motor cut off. The sounds of traffic subsided. Somewhere close a roof was being tarred, and dense fumes mingled with the scent of coconut oil baking on her skin. She lifted her face to the sun and closed her eyes.

It had been months since she had had a lover.

There had been the Australian wine merchant, a credit to his country, who read her like a book, took her to bed, and then surprised both of them by falling in love with her. She fell for him, but then so would most women—he was rugged, smart, funny, irreverent, and impossibly married. After another visit, phone calls in the early morning hours, and airmail letters, he promised to leave his wife and child to be with her. She panicked and called the whole thing off.

Then there was the real estate broker whose bold engaging patter was no cover for the shockingly small size of his sexual organ—she had been dumbfounded, even embarrassed. She recalled the joke passed between her girlfriends, "Are you in?" The real estate broker had labored over her body, worshipping at the altar of new sex. She thought the rumor of small penises mythical, a ruse, a fabrication of female gossip, but as the real estate broker's organ slipped inside her like a wet minnow, she had been silenced. A divide yawned across them. Hope capsized. The glaring inability of their bodies to fit only exacerbated her loneliness. She had wanted to disappear, to evaporate, and to pretend their coupling had never happened.

Finally, there was the civil service worker who had told her he was an engineer for the city. In fact, he worked for the sanitation district, drove a truck and monitored the flow of sewage at checkpoints in the financial district. It was his job to keep watch on the gauges in the concrete bunkers and climb down into the tanks if there was an obstruction—a solution called "butter worthing."

He had explained to Jess that his wife had, without explanation, left him with their two sons and moved out of state. The sanitation man moved into an apartment that resembled a set in a black and white TV drama in the 50s. Here is the living room—wall-to-wall carpeting, couch, chair, table, one-cut glass ashtray, and lamp. Here is the bedroom—shades drawn, each pleat equidistant from the other, blankets taut, sheet corners military straight. Here is the bathroom—tile shining, grout bleached, one towel crisply folded on each towel rack. She had rummaged through his immaculate drawers to find signs of life, stood in front of his stiffly hanging clothes to divine reason and wherefore, but there were no clues to what made him tick. He made love to her like a spy—expertly, bloodlessly, efficiently. He picked her like a lock, his cock a tool, head brimming with secrets, lips sealed.

Every encounter filled her with a wild and raunchy ache for Mickey. A year had passed since their affair had ended and she couldn't cauterize her emotions. He seemed to reside in the deepest pool of her psyche.

Jess heard the bus door unlatch. Her eyes watered momentarily adjusting to the glare. The dog bounded across the sidewalk and stood panting by her knee. She ran her fingers through his thick coat, the lanolin on his fur coating her fingers. He licked her cheek with his rough pink tongue. She instantly trusted the dog's sweet nature.

The stranger unfolded himself from the car seat. She guessed he was about six feet tall and not a day over twenty-one. "His name is Cody," he said, walking toward her. He wore cut-offs, zoris, and a faded blue windbreaker.

"Cody is a good name," she said. "Much better than Patches or Sparky."

"Way better." He stopped before the curb and planted one foot on its edge. His legs were tan and strong and the hair on his legs was bleached blonde.

"What kind of dog is he?" she asked.

"Part Australian Shepard for sure. The rest, who knows?" He nodded. "Looks like you've got a pal."

Cody nudged her arm with his black nose and climbed into her lap. She scratched him behind the ears, working her fingers up under the bandana and down into white markings that formed a V at his chest.

"He's a sucker for the female touch," he said. "Guess it's hard to have a dog in the city?"

"I wouldn't know. I don't live here." She nodded with her head toward the entry of the studio. "This is where I workout."

The man glanced at a sign over the door. "You're a dancer? That's cool. What kind of dance?"

"Modern," she answered.

"You mean Martha Graham or Merce Cunningham?"

"You know those dancers?" Her initial impression of him as another surfer on the loose did a somersault. She peered at him intently.

"I'm a newspaper junkie. I feel deprived if I don't get my daily fix," he said, folding his arms across his chest and switching feet on the curb. "Anyway, my sister used to drag me to the ballet when I was a kid."

"I bet she took you to the matinees with all the other screaming kids," she said, continuing to stroke the dog's chest. She hadn't had this much fun flirting in a long time. Obviously the difference in their ages didn't slow him down.

"Better than that." His lips parted, a smile teasing his mouth, fine granules of sand dusting his throat. "She'd go all out. She'd wrestle me into a sport coat and tie for an evening performance. We'd go out to dinner and she let me order whatever I wanted on the menu." He stepped up onto the curb closer to her and sat on his haunches. His sun-bleached hair fell forward into his green eyes flecked with hazel.

"Want to go for a ride?" he asked, brushing his hair away from his face. Cody leapt off her lap when he heard the word ride. Dashing to the bus, the dog's tail switched side-to-side propelling his rump back and forth.

"Me?" she asked, laughing. "I can't do that." She was taken aback by his confidence and intrigued that he would be so bold.

"Why not? You, me, and Cody. We could go out to Kelly's. Check out the surf. Or how about some food? I know the place in the Mission for burritos."

"Do you always park on the street, looking for someone to hang out with?" She was teasing him, but also cautious. She'd heard enough horror stories about women being picked up by handsome men and brutalized to put her on guard.

Amusement rumbled in his chest. "I suppose that is how it looks. Actually, I was waiting for a guy who wanted to sell me some stuff." He looked up at the windows. "I should have known better. Another no-show."

She believed him and felt a kind of giddy relief. She began to stand and he reached for her hands, pulling her to her feet. "Sorry to disappoint you, but I can't leave. We're in rehearsal."

His eyebrows lifted. "In rehearsal for what?"

"Tryouts for a grant to teach summer workshops in schools."

"How's your competition?" he asked, continuing to hold her hands.

"We stand a fair chance." Her hands felt small and protected in his.

"Good luck. Maybe I'll catch you another time."

Jess smiled, meeting his gaze, heat from his touch flowing into her arms. She wondered how his hands would feel on the rest of her body.

Footsteps approached from behind and as she turned she saw Claire and Sebastian stopping in front of the studio. "Hey, what's happening?" Sebastian asked.

"Just passing the time of day," Jess called. She dropped her hands.

"We're starting in a minute," Sebastian said.

"I'll be right there," Jess answered.

"Take your time," Claire said. "I've got your coffee." She shoved Sebastian in the small of the back and pushed him through the door.

"Well, I guess I'll hit the road." The man stepped off the curb and walked toward the bus. "Where do you live?" he called over his shoulder.

"Mill Valley." She stood at the edge of the curb, disappointed to see him go.

"Far out." He climbed behind the wheel and slammed the door shut. "My sister lives in Mill Valley."

"The sister who took you to the ballet?"

"Maybe you know her? She sings at the Sweetwater."

"What's her name?"

"Ceci."

"You mean Ceci Gessler?" She was amazed. The woman was a hometown phenomena, her name on the county's list of rising musical talents.

"That's her," he answered, switching on the motor.

"Where do you live?"

"Bolinas." He adjusted the rearview mirror and shifted into gear. "Your friends are waiting for you."

"I know." She lingered on the edge of the curb. "What's your name?"

"Daniel." He glanced her way. "And you?"

"Everyone calls me Jess."

"See you around then." He waved, punched the gas and drove down the street.

Jess stood motionless on the sidewalk. She watched Cody, head high, red bandana askew, through the dusty window until the bus careened around the corner.

She walked toward the studio and wondered how long she could go on like this—without a man to love and love her back—and she felt as adrift as an untethered kite floating in an empty sky.

Chapter 6

April 10

STEWART MERCH HAD EXPECTED THE LETTER, known full well it was coming, but spring in California wrapped its arms around his soul and sent him headlong into a frenzy of expectations. It drowned out obligations made in winter when spring seemed as unlikely as the probability of a bosomy woman, clad only in sensible black heels and a velvet hair ribbon, streaking past the steps of The Supreme Court on April Fools' Day.

Winding along the marshlands of Richardson Bay, Stewart pedaled his ten-speed bike from school toward the cottage he rented on a dappled lane on the outskirts of town in a neighborhood called Tam Valley. Today's meeting with Annie Morrison persisted in his thoughts. He had expected a typical parent meeting where he'd sit opposite a mother—usually—and discuss how to focus a rebellious son—usually—who was not reaching his potential. But there was nothing usual about Annie or Matthew. He'd never encountered a parent who made a pass at him, and he had never had a parent come clean about her son with such frankness. He'd considered consulting the school psychologist given what Annie had confided in him, but as soon as the idea entered his head, he knew he'd have to run it by her first—a chancy proposition. She had the air of a proud woman who'd refuse help unless she'd initiated the request.

In a burst of speed, Stewart skidded to the mailbox and yanked on the handle. The mailbox wobbled on the post. "Damn, I've got to fix this," he muttered, adding to a mental list of repairs he was known to make and promptly forget. Then his thumb touched a thin envelope and he knew the postmark was Houghton, Michigan. He anticipated the loops and flourishes of the handwriting flowed from the pen of his mother—a woman of continual high hopes inspired by vigorous living on the shores of Lake Superior.

Stewart tore open the envelope and read.

April 5, 1974

Dear Stewart,
Dad and I are so excited about our trip. He's going over the Winnebago with a fine-tooth comb. It took some doing to convince him that Herb can handle the yard and the business, but finally he's seeing things my way.

Aunt Shirl will watch after Bev. Bless Shirl's heart. Bev can't be left alone these days although her new job at the library has worked wonders. Anyway, we're not too sure how long it will take to drive because Dad wants to fish along the way. What else?

We're thinking we'll arrive in mid June so as not to conflict with your teaching schedule. I'm going to bring my recipe file so I can cook all your favorite dishes. Just think, I get to see you and the Pacific Ocean. I can't wait to meet your friends!
Love, Mom

P.S. Are you sure staying a week won't put you out?

Stewart struck his forehead with the heel of his hand. *What have I gotten myself into?* he thought. A whole week. It had been years since he had to play defense to his mother's offense. He was out of practice; his skills were rusty. He could easily occupy his father with fishing or hiking; their silent agreement was long-standing. But his mother would inquire about whom he was dating, the ways in which he was meeting women in the community, the frequency of potlucks with fellow teachers. She could never quite grasp why he had wanted to move west, much less to San Francisco. As far as she was concerned he had a perfectly fine future in Michigan.

His vision winnowed down to her vision. Rather than a cottage hideaway, he saw overgrown grass and flowerbeds choked with weeds, a shack with sub-standard plumbing and the daylight leaking through window jambs and doorframes. He saw her searching for telltale signs of female visitation, something frilly on the hook in the bathroom, bobby pins by his bedside, a dried bouquet of flowers tied in a ribbon, finding only a male lair. An accumulation of sports equipment and the brand new Olympic regulation trampoline set up in the front yard would send her into a paroxysm of doubt. What would she make of this? What would they think?

Dad would retreat to the rear; she would find it odd, out of step, and eager to know how much the trampoline cost. If he told her, she'd be dismayed. Didn't he have better things to do with his money? Saving for the future, investing in bonds, purchasing furniture, perhaps a washer-dryer. After all, someday he'd have a wife and a family.

No, Stewart thought, *it won't be that way.* He saw himself facing his mother, watching his father steeling himself for what was coming. "Mom," he'd say, "let's cut the pretense. I don't know how to say this any other way. Believe me I've wanted to tell you, there won't be a wife or children because…brace yourself, Mom, I'm queer."

A fist of nausea shot through Stewart's stomach and his parents' faces dissolved.

Inside the yard, Stewart dropped his backpack to the ground. Inside was a copy of *The Advocate,* student papers for correcting, lesson plans, and a bulletin from the Teachers' Union. *The Advocate*'s front-page news featured plans for the Gay Pride

Parade scheduled in June. His fingers curled around the metal frame of the trampoline, solid in his grasp, and he hoisted himself up onto the taut canvas. Air filled his lungs, and he sprang off the trampoline. But he jumped listlessly, his knees spongy, and giving into inertia he sank onto the center onto his back and stared up through the leaves of a maple to a sky dotted with clouds.

Stewart imagined his father fishing at Lake Lagunitas. From a distance they had the same compact body, although Stewart had inherited longer bones from his mother's side. His father was barrel-chested, with beefy shoulders, enough breadth for hockey, felling trees, building decks, and hauling rocks for the wall that ran the length of their lakefront summer property. This was the place where he and Stewart had spent the most companionable of times. There Stewart had grown from a sturdy child into awkward puberty, first recognizing without understanding that it wasn't the girls in his high school who attracted him, but the older boys in gym class—the boys whose bodies had taken on muscle shaped by physical work in the outdoors.

How confused he had been by his own desire, how weakened, and how he had turned it inward and fueled it with curiosity. How it had gnawed at him because he had no models for sex among men, much less teenage boys. Love between men was unthinkable. What future did he have? Surely, he was condemned.

Floundering, Stewart watched for clues. Within the context of his family—his father, solid, hard working, his mother laboring for the family, and his sister, Beverly, born mentally handicapped—his shame increased. Friends and extended family in the small, protected community of Houghton offered no assistance. There was no sex education beyond anatomy and reproduction in biology. There was no counter culture, literature, or movies into which he could escape. Meanwhile, the burden of desire compounded in his mind.

Then in the summer of his fifteenth year, a worker from Chicago moved into the bunkroom on the grounds of his father's oil distribution business. Bill Mitchell was a skilled mechanic, lean as a whip, and clever with his hands. He had been hired to temporarily replace Pete Duffy, who had suffered a back injury. Repairs on the equipment had fallen behind and Mitchell took command with cool determination.

Stewart had worked in the yard for several years and that summer was no different. He knew how to drive the trucks, operate the pumps, and be useful in the office. Stewart's father suggested that he team up beside Mitchell for a few hours each day and learn as much as he could about diesel rigs, pumps, and gasoline engines. Stewart had no objection—at least he could get out of the afternoon heat. He fell into a wordless rhythm beside the mechanic, passing him tools and watching him work. It wasn't long before Mitchell set aside jobs for Stewart and supervised him from across the shop.

Working beside men was nothing new for Stewart, but from the beginning there was something different about Mitchell. For starters, the scent of Mitchell's aftershave churned inside Stewart's stomach—it was sickeningly sweet, yet it triggered an attraction. When they were alone, he found himself staring at the ropy veins in Mitchell's forearms or the sharp edges of his shoulder blades underneath his white T-shirt. Mitchell would catch him staring and hold his gaze until Stewart looked away. No words were exchanged. As the weeks wore on, Stewart became more and more agitated. His wet dreams went on a rampage, disturbing his sleep.

Finally one humid July night at dusk when the office had closed and the men had clocked out, Mitchell broke the silence.

"You're working late these days." Mitchell's thin mouth curved in a rare smile. He leaned against a rusty rig and drew a cigarette out of a pack.

"I don't mind." The saliva dried in Stewart's mouth. "Not a lot going on anyway."

"Don't you have friends you hang out with?" Mitchell asked.

"Not really." Stewart's eyes locked into Mitchell's stare that pierced his soft shell. "This is more interesting."

"Yeah, I noticed you've got an aptitude for motors and that kind of shit."

"Thanks."

"You got a minute before you head home tonight?" Smoke curled around Mitchell's head.

Stewart nodded, unable to speak. His heart hammered in his chest.

"Let's wrap it up then. I got something I want to show you. In my bunk."

Mitchell led the way and locked the door when they were inside. Stewart stood in the middle of the floor, bug-eyed, arms slack and legs quaking. Mitchell dropped the cigarette into a beer can and moved towards Stewart, roughly taking his chin in his hand. "You know what we're going to do, don't you, boy?"

"I'm not sure." Real time slowed to dream time. Fear snaked around his ankles and slithered up his legs. The fear turned to heat and climbed higher.

"But you've thought about it. Right?"

"Yeah."

"You lie down and I'll show you." Mitchell backed Stewart onto the bed. He yanked Stewart's pants off his thin hips and stretched him out. Without remorse, he took his virginity as easily as butter sliding off a hot knife.

After it was over, Stewart lay mute beside Mitchell as the sky turned dark. He reached for a blanket and covered himself. Loneliness seeped into his soul, drop by drop. He stared into a tunnel of oblivion. The automatic lights in the yard switched on, shining against the blinds and filtering onto the floor. Mitchell lit a cigarette and blew smoke rings into the air above his head that spiraled above their naked bodies and turned the room hazy.

"Guess I better get going," Stewart said. He inched off the bed, picked his clothes off the floor, and dressed.

"Check out the window before you go. Make sure no one's in the yard."

Stewart crept across the floor and peered out the window. "All clear."

Mitchell eyes were hooded and flat and he offered no farewell.

Over the next few weeks, despite Stewart's guilt and remorse, Mitchell was a force he could not resist. Trips to the bunkhouse grew frequent. Stewart's mother insisted that he must stop missing dinner—he was beginning to look like a skeleton. Stewart felt like he was in free fall.

One night, blows on the door of the bunkhouse interrupted Mitchell and Stewart. Mitchell pushed Stewart away hard and bolted upright, standing naked when Stewart's father crashed through the door. The sound of splintering wood rented the airless room. He swung on Mitchell who ducked and jumped out of his reach. But Stewart's father lunged like a bear toward the mechanic and caught him from behind. Stewart was scrambling into his pants when he heard the sound of his father's fist cracking Mitchell's nose.

"Dad, stop, for god's sake, stop!" he shouted, trying to pry him off the bloodied Mitchell.

Stewart's father staggered to his feet, holding his son at arm's distance. "I want you out of here now," he panted to Mitchell. "Pack your clothes and get out!"

He shoved his son toward the door. Stewart stumbled across the yard, his father at his heels. Tears ran down his face and blinded his vision. Climbing into the company truck, he cowered against the door. The familiar bulk of the dash littered with scraps of paper, the round thick steering wheel and curved windshield seemed two-dimensional, flattened into bizarre patterns and distorted shapes.

His father hauled himself into the driver's seat. "That man is an animal," he growled, his face pinched with anger.

"Yes, sir," Stewart muttered, miserable beyond belief.

"But you are old enough to know the difference between right and wrong."

"Yes, sir."

"Let me make myself clear, I never want to catch you like this again. Your mother will not know. Is that understood?"

Stewart forced himself to look at his father whose sunken eyes burned with fury. "I understand," Stewart promised.

"I'm going to put the key in the ignition and start the engine. By the time we get home, forget this has happened. Go inside, clean yourself up, and go to bed. Mitchell will be gone by morning. I'll make sure of that."

* * *

In the years that followed, Stewart perfected the role of the good son. He assumed responsibility, interacted with his mother and sister, and demonstrated to his father that if he had fallen into disgrace he had the backbone to pull himself out of it. True to his word, he became a young man to count on. Redemption was a merciless cut, swift and binding.

In high school he made it his job to be everyone's loyal friend—the teachers, the town librarian, his mother's friends, the girls he dated, and a classmate he coveted. The coaches discovered he excelled in running track, jumping the hurdles, and working the balance beam. He learned to jump off the beam, flip in the air, and land on his feet; from there it was onto the trampoline where he jumped high, higher, the springs of the trampoline squealing as his body contacted the canvas, and he rebounded into the air, aloft, airborne.

The Mill Valley sky had turned a pale grey and the leaves fluttered high above Stewart's head as he lay on the trampoline. He was grateful for the breeze and the covering stillness of night coming on. The scene with his father seemed long ago. When Stewart left for Bowdoin College in Maine on an academic scholarship, his father let him go and never pressured him to return to join the business. Their agreement of silence had been honored; it was up to Stewart to change it.

Chapter 7

April 10

AS A COMMUTER BUS RUMBLED along the darkened avenue toward downtown Mill Valley at 7:30 PM, Jess bore down on the gas pedal of her car and drove around the rear of the bus, risking the wrath of Officer Ritter who zealously guarded the twenty-five mile an hour speed limit with the spiritual fervor of a Hare Krishna. The singsong admonition of "Lady bug, lady bug, fly away home, your house is on fire, your children will burn," played in her ear. Why hadn't she accepted Claire's offer in the afternoon to place a call to Annie? It would have been so easy then to warn her.

The thought of Parker flashed into Jess's head.

Damn it, why hadn't he called Sarah or returned her calls? Two weeks had gone by and not a word. Each time she contacted his Hartford office, either his secretary repeated he was out of town, or she was withholding information about his whereabouts—it could be London, Paris or Manhattan. If only she knew the hotels he booked she could track him down. Why was he stonewalling her? What was he up to?

His child support check of $250, due on April 1, was ten days late. Her bank balance was drained down to $75. She had $100 in cash from teaching dance classes. She calculated upcoming bills that would start to trickle in, the largest of which was $175 for rent due May 1. No matter which way she juggled her finances, there was never enough money, and the constant pressure worried at the edges of her mind.

Last month, she had slunk into the county's benefit office and applied for food stamps. If she had once worn poverty like a badge of honor, the allure was long gone. It was like sharing that you had psoriasis or your great aunt had been institutionalized—who would want to acknowledge such a demoralized state? Yet, there she was standing in line under the fluorescent lights in plain view. Her face burned as she stood at the counter in front of a little window, filled out the form, and passed it to a clerk who did not look directly into Jess's eyes. The woman's face was expressionless and indifferent. *I've reached a new low*, Jess thought. *College-educated and on the dole*. Miraculously, the county qualified her and Sarah for $200 a month in food stamps—a fortune compared to what she normally spent. The food stamps were in the mail; the idea of using them made her cringe.

Jess slammed into a parking place in front of the Odd Fellows Hall in front of Annie's house. Yellow pools of light from streetlights fell through the trees splashing grainy shadows onto the sidewalk. From the street, down the footpath, over the bridge, Jess saw Annie's porch light blazing, every window brightly lit. She hurried toward the house, stepping over a skateboard and baseball bats, and pushed open the door.

"Hello," she called. "I'm back!"

A draft laced with the acrid smell of pot met her nostrils. The high-pitched vibrato of Curtis Mayfield's voice spilled from speakers.

Annie, hair fanning out from her face, brow pinched, came rushing out of the kitchen toward her. "Are the kids with you?"

Matthew burst from the doorway. "They're in *big* trouble now!"

"With me?" Jess asked. "Why would they be with me?"

"Wait till I get my hands on them." Annie clenched her fists. "I'll kill the little bastards."

"Annie, it's pitch black outside. Where are they?"

"I don't know." Annie reached for her arm. "But it's not a problem."

"Let go of me," Jess snapped, yanking away from Annie's grasp. "What do you mean it's not a *problem*?"

Matthew did the funky chicken, executed an imaginary basket shot, and froze in a dead man's noose.

"Don't get your tail in a twist," Annie said. "I'm sure they're perfectly safe."

Jess drew back. "Damn it, tell me what's going on!" Annie's condescension lit her temper like a match to a smoldering fire.

"This afternoon when school let out, I forgot I had a meeting with Matthew's teacher."

"Mom's got the hots for Merch," Matthew chimed in. "How 'bout I whip up a few tasty TV dinners. What would you ladies prefer? Chicken or turkey?"

"For god's sake, Matthew, would you stop?" Jess said.

"I'm trying to tell you," Annie said, "I sent Noah to meet Sarah."

Jess shuddered with exasperation. "I asked you, Annie. Not Noah."

"Don't get all high and mighty with me. There was no harm done. When I came home, their lunch boxes were in the kitchen and I could see they raided the fridge. I knew they were playing in the neighborhood and would show up around dinnertime."

"So when that didn't happen, you hung out and smoked a joint?"

"Not me. A friend came over and he…"

"A *friend*? Oh, that's great. Just great. How could you let me down?" Jess exploded. "I was counting on you, and you don't know where she is! Or Noah! For god's sake, what is wrong with you?" Jess was as infuriated with herself as with Annie, but she couldn't stop.

"You're losing it, Jess."

"Losing it? I'm not even close," Jess shouted, shaking with frustration. Every part of her wanted to grab Annie by the shoulders and shake reason into her.

"Okay, ladies," Matthew said, stepping between them. "Let's take it easy. Noah is a retard. He probably doesn't know what time it is. What we need is a plan."

Jess faced Matthew and was startled to notice he was practically at eye-level with her. "Like what?" she asked.

"We need to fan out," Matthew said. "I'll get my posse."

"No," Annie intervened, her tone harsh and brittle. "Matthew, leave the room. I want to talk to Jess—alone."

"Really? I can..."

"I said 'leave the room' now! And stay off the roof."

"Bogus," Matthew said. "I'll go out on the street and set up watch."

"Stay put. I need you where I can find you."

When Matthew left the house an uneasy silence followed his departure. Jess was unable to look at Annie directly, certain she'd say something hateful. Everything in her body said, "Do something!"

Annie spoke first. "Leave Matthew out of this." She held her arms crossed at the waist, and regarded Jess dispassionately.

"But he could help."

"Not tonight. He's on restriction."

"What are you talking about?" To Jess's knowledge, Matthew didn't have limits or rules of any kind.

"I'll tell you later. Right now, you're over the top. Any minute the kids are going to show up or we can go out and start looking. This has happened with Noah before." The gleam in her eye was challenging. "Sometimes he comes home late. He roams around town with his friends. That's what kids do in Mill Valley. I've called the parents of his friends. One of the boys saw Noah and Sarah at the Depot earlier. I know what you're thinking, but drop it. Freaking out over everything that comes along with Sarah is getting old. By the way, where have you been? You said you'd be home by 6."

"Rehearsal went overtime. It couldn't be avoided."

"Well, there you are," Annie said, her voice laced with sarcasm. "A phone call would have been appreciated. If I had known you'd be late, I would have gone out and found them and we could have avoided all of this. That said, let's agree to what we're going to do now. Stay here and wait, or go out and look for them?"

Jess pressed her fingers to her temples. In the past there was a pattern between the women that when one faced a crisis, the other one would take charge. Not tonight. Jess held her ground. Even if she was over-reacting, she trusted her instincts. She checked her watch. "I can't wait. They may be in trouble. Let's go."

"You take the lead then." Annie grabbed a jacket off the coat tree and blew out of house. Up ahead, Jess saw Matthew standing on the sidewalk bouncing a basketball. She stopped next to him and searched and up and down the avenue. To all appearances it was a normal Wednesday night. Cars passed on the street, their engines muffled by the night air. People strolled along the sidewalk. The glow of light flickered from restaurant windows. The door of the Sweetwater swung open and the sound of loud voices blasted from within the club.

"No sign yet," Matthew said. "Man, they're seriously late."

"For starters, I think we should split up," Annie said to Jess. "We'd cover more ground."

"I wouldn't know where to look. Maybe this is a bad idea. Let's go to the police."

"That is totally unnecessary," Annie snapped. "I've got a good idea where they could be. Matthew, you stay here. If the kids come back, keep them in the house."

"Me and my friends can make a quick run through town," he said, continuing to bounce the ball, a steady cadence between the palm of his hand and the surface of the sidewalk, *slap, slap.*

"Not now. You keep watch right here."

"No sweat," he said. "10-4, buddy. I read you."

"Wait," Jess said. "Let's check my place first and make sure they're not there. You drive and I'll ride shot gun." She hopped into the van parked at the curb and slammed the door. Annie gunned the motor, raced up the hill, and screeched to a stop on the gravel drive in front of the apartment. Jess's budding hope dwindled—the second-story windows in her apartment were dark.

"That would have been too easy," Annie said, backing out of the driveway. "I know the route Noah uses when he goes up the mountain. We'll catch them if they're coming down." Annie drove down the hill and onto the road that cut through Old Mill Park.

Jess peered into the grounds that spilled out from the road. It was even darker inside the park, redwood trees towering above the earth, their branches bending low, and the weathered piers and beams of the ruins of the sawmill along the creek ghostly in the dim light from a light standard in the playground. The heavy wooden picnic tables abandoned and forlorn. She began to tremble. "I don't see anyone," she said. "How in the hell are we going to find them in here?"

"Keep looking," Annie replied, her eyes swiveling in her head like a game hunter.

"Where are you going?" Jess asked.

"We'll take Marion up to a trailhead that cuts through the woods. Noah has a camp there not more than a quarter of a mile in. I've hiked into it with him before. My hunch is that's where they are. Check the glove compartment. You'll find a flashlight."

Jess fished out the flashlight, chilled and hard in her hand.

Annie climbed higher, hugging the fern-lined road that skirted the woods in the night air that grew colder round every bend until a turnout appeared up ahead in the headlights. She parked, killed the lights, and turned off the motor.

Jess switched on the flashlight, and stepped out of the van. An owl hooted nearby. The air was damp, the smell of the woods herbaceous, tinged with the sharpness of mosses and lichens. The trees hovered nearby, their branches whispering overhead. She aimed the beam of the flashlight onto the ground, matted with layers of decayed earth and saw her shoes. Annie stood at the edge of the woods and called, "This way. Follow me."

Jess stepped forward when a boy answered, "Mom, is that you?" Jess's heart leapt in her throat. She swung the flashlight overhead onto the broad limb of an oak, its brown bark scrabbled with lichen. In the beam of light the pale face of Noah appeared, peering down toward her.

"Good god, Noah," Annie shouted. "What in the hell are you doing?"

"I'm cold," Noah said. He was belly down on the limb, shading his eyes with his hand. One pant leg was ripped and leaf-stained. The untied laces of his sneakers, caked with mud, dangled from his ankles.

"Uh-oh," Jess heard Sarah say. "Now we're in trouble."

For one insane moment, Jess felt like laughing. Panic drained away leaving her giddy and light. She turned the flashlight toward the voice of her daughter. Sarah's back was braced against the tree trunk, one leg swinging over the limb. Her face was smeared with dirt; bits of leaves stuck in her hair.

Instantly Annie was at Jess's side and wrested the flashlight out of her hand, focusing the beam back onto Noah. "Get down immediately, young man. Right now."

Jess grabbed the flashlight back and walked under the tree, shining its light up onto the limb, and watched Noah shimming along the trunk toward Sarah. When he reached the end of the limb, Jess heard them mumbling to each other, their arms embracing the tree trunk, their feet seeking purchase on limbs below until they let go, landing feet first on the earth at Jess's side. Noah crept away toward the van.

Jess bent down to Sarah and tried to hug her. "I'm so glad we found you," she said, brushing away strands of matted hair from her face.

"Sorry if we made you worry, Mom."

"What were you doing? Why didn't you come home?"

"It just got later and later. We were about to come down. Anyway, don't squeeze me so hard. You'll crush the bird."

The headlights of the van snapped on. Sarah reached in her jacket pocket and gently extracted a tiny grey sparrow, resting on its side, cupped in a nest of leaves and moss. "Look, his wing is broken. Do you think he'll will live?"

Annie shouted, "Get a move on it, you two. I can't wait all night."

The children huddled in the back, Annie stone silent at the wheel, the van bumping over the roads back to town. Repeatedly, Jess turned in the seat to study the children and then over at Annie who scowled at her. Sarah cooed at the bird, and Noah told her how to keep it warm in the oven. In minutes they were back, the woods behind them, the suburban street electric with human activity. After Annie pulled into a parking spot, they tumbled out of the van.

Matthew was waiting on the curb exactly where they had left him. "Man, where have you been? You're in deep shit!" Matthew shoved his brother. Noah shoved back.

"Lay off, dickhead," Noah declared.

"They were going to call the cops and put out a dragnet on you."

"So?" Noah said belligerently.

"So!" Matthew shoved his brother again.

"Okay, cut it out, you two," Annie said. "Into the house now. Noah clean up and go to bed. We'll discuss this when I come in."

"Bye, Noah," Sarah said. "Sure you don't want the bird?"

"You keep it," he said, shuffling off, the cuffs of his pants dragging on the ground. "See you tomorrow."

Annie leaned toward Sarah, touching her on the sleeve. "If anything happened to you, your mother wouldn't forgive me."

"It's mostly my fault. We were having an adventure."

Annie tousled her hair, "Get some sleep. I'll see you later." She regarded Jess with a sober stare and nodded. "I told you everything would turn out fine."

Jess twisted her mouth in a sour line, doubting the wisdom of any statement coming out of Annie's mouth.

Annie tossed up her arms. "Oh great, now you're going to sulk."

"Shut up. I've had enough."

Annie narrowed her eyes at Jess. "I'll expect you tomorrow afternoon. We'll finish this discussion."

"When are you going to give it a rest?" Jess shot back.

"Never," Annie said, walking away.

* * *

At home after a bath, Sarah found a shoebox for the bird, sat near the wall heater in her pajamas and fed a mixture of sugar and water into its yellow beak with a glass dropper. The cat mewed plaintively behind the closed door in the studio. Jess stood at the stove, stirring chicken noodle soup in a pot, watching Sarah from across the room.

"Sarah, I want you to understand you can't stay out past dark. It isn't safe."

"Even if I'm with Noah?" She rolled over onto her tummy, her blonde curls obscuring her face.

"Yes. The trails are slippery in the spring. Either of you could fall and hurt yourself. Or you could get lost."

Sarah lifted her head and looked directly at Jess. "We didn't get hurt today."

"You're not listening to me."

"I am, too. Noah knows all the trails. We didn't get lost once. He took me to a place in the creek where we fished for crawdads and at Four Wells we stood under a waterfall and drank the water. He even showed me his hidey hole where he camps."

"Playing in the woods with a friend is okay as long as you tell a grown up where you're going, but before dark you need to be either in their home or here." Jess turned down the burner under the soup and joined Sarah on the floor. She placed her hand on the small of her back and spoke candidly. "Sometimes there are people who want to hurt children."

"But we never saw anyone."

"I'm glad." Jess stroked Sarah's back. The bird lay quietly, wings drawn inward, short breaths filling its fragile lungs. "We don't have to dwell on this, but I want you to pay attention to what I'm saying. It's my job to protect you. Do you understand?"

Sarah bent her head to the bird again, her finger resting on its downy body. "I'm not a baby anymore," she said.

The pot sputtered on the stove, soup sizzling over the sides and spitting onto the burner. "Damn it," Jess said, jumping to her feet. She mopped up the mess and ladled what was left of the soup into bowls. "Let's eat, Sarah. It's getting late."

They sat beside each other at the kitchen table, sipping soup, and munching crackers. The bird was nestled inside the shoebox by the heater; the cat confined to the studio behind the closed door. Night gathered at their windows, settling around the apartment building.

"Can I still play with Noah on Friday after school?" Sarah asked, between spoonfuls of soup.

"I don't think so." Jess said. She was the verge of telling Sarah she would give her a key to let herself into the apartment after school and join the ranks of other latch-key children. If Jess stayed at rehearsal until just before 4, she could be home by 4:30.

"My friend, Amber, invited me to her house. And guess what? Her dad is a veterinarian. He can examine the bird."

"I haven't met her parents yet."

"That's okay. You can meet them tomorrow."

"You have an answer for everything, don't you?"

Sarah regarded her pensively. "How come you're mad at Annie?"

"It's complicated," Jess said.

Sarah spooned the last of the soup into her mouth. "Adults always say, 'it's complicated' when they think kids shouldn't hear stuff. I know more than you think." Sarah put her elbows on the table and rested her chin in her hands. "Will you still be best friends?"

Jess pushed the bowl away. When the fire broke out in Mickey's house, whom did she go to? Annie. Because she knew Annie would take them in, no questions asked, and listen to every detail, every nuance, every reason why she was leaving Mickey, and still understand that she was hopelessly entangled with him. Other people would judge. Not Annie. She'd empathize as if it was happening to her, stand back, survey the damage and suggest the right order, the order Jess could not see. Jess and Sarah had slept in Annie's living room under the swaying spider plants by the plate glass windows looking out to the valley until Jess found a rental on the flats. Annie knew her secrets; she was her staunchest ally, her confidante, and crusader. But something had shifted and Jess couldn't ignore the rift that had opened up between them. Suddenly she felt a chill and her eyes smarted like bits of sand were lodged under her eyelids. All she wanted to do was crawl into bed and sleep. "Come on, sweetie. We'll talk another time. I'll tuck you in."

Chapter 8

April 12

THE GESSLER SUMMERHOUSE had once been very grand. It was built on the Bolinas Mesa above the ocean with sea views to the knife-edge horizon. On sunny days, you could see clear to the Farallon Islands. Seals lazed at low tide on the mud flats in the Bolinas Lagoon like wet dogs basking in the sun and slid into the high tide in the hazy afternoon.

In times past, the house swarmed with family, friends, and political cronies of one Daniel Gessler, attorney and Superior Court Judge. Judge Gessler and his wife, Catherine, built the summerhouse as a retreat from San Francisco. Land in the beach town was bountiful, and the surrounding dairy farms shipped their milk and butter by boat to the city, which had risen shimmering by the sea.

Travel from San Francisco to Bolinas—by ferry, train, and lastly a 1921 Packard Touring Car—required hearty fortitude. Days of croquet, horse riding, and sailing were the reward. Family and guests picnicked on cold chicken, potato and macaroni salads, tomato aspic, and chocolate cake, atop white linen tablecloths on the clipped lawn. Afterwards the women strolled to the bluff and rested on wooden benches, men smoked cigars on the porch in wicker rocking chairs, and children rowed dinghies in the lagoon.

Gradually the decades rolled by. The property remained in the family trust, but some fifty years later it was like an aging country gentleman, clothes tattered and worn with age, but pedigree beyond question.

Occasionally a family reunion rekindled the comfort of the vast rooms, but in truth, no one cared about the property—save one member of the family, Daniel Gessler III. Judge Gessler and Catherine slept in the Bolinas Cemetery close by, and their grandson, Daniel, slept in the southwest wing of the old house at the far end of the driveway where the bluff plunged to the sea.

At a window to the sea, Daniel toyed with a wooden box of Mendocino weed, a roach clip, and a collection of matches from grocery stores up and down the coast. The haunting cry from a flock of common loon flying toward the shore drifted over the water. He lit a joint and aimed a telescope toward the dark horizon to search for lights on ships passing in the night.

On a round table near his bed, a collection of tide charts, geological maps, and books on birds, fish, and oceans of the world were stacked. Law texts that he hadn't cracked in weeks were shoved under his bed, their creased pages marked with scribbled notes, the oily residue of potato chips, and the occasional imprint from the bottom of a wet beer bottle. A portrait of his grandfather, Popee, and his grandmother, Catherine, hung on the wall; his sister's photograph, posing on the bay mare she rode throughout her school years, was propped beside the books. The inscription, penned in black ink, angular letters forming stiff peaks and downward strokes, read, "*To Daniel, Love Always, Ceci.*"

Daniel crept into bed and pushed his feet against Cody's warm flank. A memory of the woman he met in San Francisco surfaced in his mind. The warmth of her soft fingers in his hand lingered. He had wanted to reach out and touch the curve of her cheek. His body stirred in response. *This is a complication I don't need,* he reminded himself. Most of the women he knew were too quick to attach themselves to him. At first they made a show of independence, but their lives didn't seem to have any purpose. They drifted from one thing to another, living at home and either taking a few classes at the local college and hanging out with their friends or picking up part time jobs in bars and restaurants. They studied astrology or read Tarot cards as if the signs and symbols contained the mysteries of the Holy Grail. Annoyingly, they'd write him letters, wait on his doorstep, or show up stoned in the middle of the night. But Jess's clear-eyed gaze, like a brilliant opal in a matrix, had fixed in his imagination. He couldn't shake the picture of her, nor did he really want to. Some of his buddies accused him of turning into a loner. It was a reputation he didn't mind; he shrugged it off. He carried the image of the woman like a kernel in his pocket almost as if he planted her she'd take root in his future.

* * *

Dawn crested over the deep green Bolinas Ridge. Daniel awakened to the changing light and the sound of the ocean. He listened with his eyes closed. The air was calm; high tide filled the lagoon below, and swells from a storm at sea gathered off shore.

Cody snored at Daniel's feet and twitched in his sleep. "Wake up, old boy," Daniel said. "You're dreaming of rabbits."

Wearing faded swim trunks that had dried on his body, he slipped from under the red plaid flannel sleeping bag that smelled musty like childhood dreams and where, along its quilted seams, grains of sand had gathered like tiny ants. He moved with a loose-jointed grace and inhabited his body naturally. In the water, he was fearless.

"You coming with me or not?" Daniel asked. At the refrigerator, he chugged orange juice from the open neck of a plastic container. "This is the time, little dude. Tide is high. Swells coming in. No wind. Water like glass."

Cody jumped from the bed and shook his body so that all four paws lifted off the ground, his collar spinning in circles round his neck. Daniel slung a seven-foot surfboard under his arm and paused before a note he had tossed on the floor the day before. He glanced down at it: *Trust Meeting – Friday, 11AM, San Francisco, Popee's Office*.

Yesterday's phone call with Ceci came rushing back. Absorbed in *The History of Lewis and Clark*, he had avoided the jangling phone until the call came through a fourth time. Her voice, strident and bossy, ticked him off immediately.

"You know what tomorrow is?" she had asked.

"Give me a break. Estelle has called three times."

"You sound like a spoiled brat. Tomorrow is a big deal for me."

"You mean you'll come into even more money than you have now?"

"Don't be a smart ass. You may need me for backup, little brother. Charlie's on the war path."

"Don't worry. I've got that covered."

"Very wise," Ceci said.

"On second thought, I think I'll skip the meeting."

"Very unwise. You've got to show up."

"And be totally vibed by Uncle Charlie? And Dad with dumb-ass Melinda is pathetic. I'll be bummed out for a week. Why they can't they do this over the phone? Ceci, you handle it."

"Stop, Daniel. This is a legal procedure. It requires all beneficiaries to be present at the reading."

"Sometimes I'd just as soon kiss the money goodbye rather than deal with the bullshit."

"We've discussed this a hundred times before, and while I admire your purist soul, the truth is both of us would be up shit's creek without Popee's inheritance. Neither of us have a ton of ambition to save the world. I can hardly save myself."

"Are you drinking?"

"So what?"

"I don't want to talk to you when you're shit-faced."

Daniel threw the note back down on the floor and opened the door to the new morning.

The VW bus, patched with Bondo and held together with rope and duct tape, was parked on the grass. He strapped the surfboard to the rack on top and started the engine. The voice of Jerry Garcia poured from the 8-track. Daniel peeled around the gravel drive with Cody in the passenger seat.

Down at Stinson Beach, surfers stood silently on the ridge of a sand dune in the cool light, facing west. Zipped from neck to ankle in black wet suits, they were reading the waves, waiting for the swells to come in, looking for a channel. Single fin white surfboards lay at their feet. An aqua blue lifeguard station towered beside them.

Daniel walked toward the men, Big Daddy, Palo Dave, Titus, and Flea. Cody streaked ahead to the hard-packed grey sand. The surfers waited shoulder-to-shoulder, arms across their chests, hands tucked under their armpits.

Daniel took his place beside Big Daddy. "Hey, what's happening?"

"You ought to know, Weatherman," Big Daddy chuckled. At thirty-six, Big Daddy was considered the old man of the pack.

"It's going to go off any minute," Daniel said.

"Yeah, man, any minute," Flea echoed. He lit a joint, took a hit, and passed it on.

"I drove down to Four Mile yesterday," Titus said, taking the joint.

"That place goes off," Flea nodded.

"I caught a double overhead." Titus passed the joint to Palo Dave.

"This is good shit," Palo Dave said.

"I was totally in the green room."

"Awesome," Flea said.

"Completely," Titus said.

"Such a hairball drop."

"Off the lip."

"Totally righteous."

The joint made the rounds to each man and back to Flea. All that remained was a stubby, glowing orange tip. He took a final hit and dropped it on the sand. A set of perfect waves broke off to the south, and a channel opened up. Everyone saw it at once.

"Dudes, this is it," Daniel said.

"What are we waiting for?" Big Daddy asked.

Daniel hit the water first. The water sliced like razor blades cutting through bone. He dove under a wave and came up with his eyes wide open, searching for the channel. He turned to look back at the lifeguard station on the beach to get his bearings. Beyond the sand where the pavement began, he saw a figure in a wheelchair. Daniel knew it was Mole. It couldn't be anybody else, not at this hour, and in that spot. Mole had been the first to go to Nam and the first one back. On an airless afternoon near a village on the edge of rice paddies, he had been in the front line of his unit when the Viet Cong stepped out of the jungle and opened fire. His buddies saved his life by getting him into a chopper, but the doctors couldn't save his legs.

In that moment, for Daniel, every element churning around him knit into focus—the froth of the water, gulls swooping in the sky, the movement of the surging waves, men on boards stroking, and Mole pinned in the wheelchair—and he glimpsed into the long lens of time in which events can alter a life that was once solid and whole. He shuddered, the energy of the ocean coursing through him. The board shot through the channel. This one's for you, Mole, he promised.

He had to be the first one up, at the peak, where the waves set up. He had to be the one to catch the perfect wave.

* * *

Daniel paused in front of the high, wrought iron fence outside the offices of Gessler, Burrows, and Blake, Attorneys at Law. Thick vines twisted and clung to the rungs of the fence. The scent of jasmine, blossoming at the topmost spires, was cloying in the warmth of mid-day sun. Autumn claimed the best weather in the city, but spring ran a close second.

He glanced at the brass plaque on the fence. The shape of the embossed letters was as familiar to him as his own handwriting. With Popee gone, his Uncle Charles conducted the business of corporate law as was mandated by the original charter. He guided the firm toward greater profits, sat on civic boards, and endowed a chair at the University of California, Berkeley. He was also the executor of the family trusts. Daniel's father, nicknamed Duke, the youngest of the brothers, continued to play excellent tennis, sailed, and attended to Melinda, his fourth wife, who at thirty-six, was only two years older than Ceci.

Daniel unlatched the gate, crossed over the brick patio, and entered the offices.

"Good afternoon," Estelle said, walking toward him from the hallway. She wore a tailored, navy blue suit, pearls around her neck, and sensible low-heeled shoes. Daniel was surprised to see how much grey flecked her dark hair.

"Hey, Estelle. How's it going?" She was the one person he was unequivocally happy to see.

"Very well, dear," Estelle answered.

"Are the other freeloaders here?"

"Daniel, please. Show some respect. Your grandfather was very proud of the family."

"You're right, as usual." He swiped his fingers through his hair. "Do I pass inspection?"

"May I?" She straightened the collar of his shirt. The faint scent of violets accompanied her touch, and he noticed the slightest tremor of her hand.

"Are you working too hard, Estelle?" Every time he saw her, he noticed how the passage of time left its mark on her face.

"Of course not. Now hurry. There's a comb on the shelf in the powder room. They're waiting."

When Daniel emerged, Estelle nodded her approval. He had wrestled his hair into obedience, water dripping from the ends onto the shoulders of his rumpled jacket. Striding down the hall where gallery lights beamed onto a portrait of Popee and the ruddy faces of Burrows and Blake, Daniel burst into the meeting. His father, hail, hearty, in the pink of life, dressed in tennis whites, and winding out an imaginary serve, swung to greet him.

Daniel raised his hand in greeting, "I'm not late, am I?"

His father grasped Daniel's hand, pumping it up and down and clapping him on the back. "No, not at all. We're just getting started. Where have you been keeping yourself?"

"I've been busy, Dad." Daniel glanced quickly around the office noticing that little had changed since his grandfather's day—floor to ceiling built-in book cases lined with leather bound books, a blood red oriental carpet, and a game table in a window corner. The barely disguised hostility of his uncle, who presided at a baroque desk carved with lions' head and claw feet, permeated the room. His grandfather wouldn't have left a family member or guest standing without a firm handshake and welcome. Daniel stepped across the floor and shook Charles's hand, tepid as dishwater. "Hello, sir," Daniel said.

Charles, dressed in a pinstriped navy blue suit and a starched white shirt, released Daniel's hand and adjusted the gold wire-rim glasses perched on his nose.

Melinda rearranged herself on one of the wingback chairs arranged in a semi-circle toward the front of the desk. "Hey, Daniel, long time no see." Bare legs crossed at the knees, she tugged at the hem of a black mini skirt, one black leather boot swinging back and forth. A plume of "Charlie" broadcast into Daniel's nose.

"Hey, Melinda. What's going on?" Daniel flopped into a chair between Melinda and Ceci. He grinned to ease the tension. "Hi, Ceci. Right on time."

Ceci frowned at him. "Congratulations."

Estelle carried a silver tray and served coffee to a silent room. When she paused in front of Daniel, he put three heaping teaspoons of sugar into the cup, filled it to the brim with cream, and stirred. He winked at her. "This will hit the spot."

Charles waved Estelle aside. "Thank you. That will be all." He sipped from a glass of ice water. She set the tray on the sideboard and left.

"Shall we begin?" Charles asked. A fly, trapped behind slanted Venetian blinds, droned against the window. "As each of you know, we gather together at this time to consider the provisions of your individual trusts. Assets are reviewed and distributions are given, if deemed warranted and reasonable." He reclined against the back of the chair and peered over the top of his eyeglasses. "It is my responsibility to oversee the assets and ascertain that the recipients of the trusts conduct their lives within the guidelines of the trust and in the spirit of the family name."

Charles paused. The fly buzzed from between the slats. "I'll begin with you, Duke," he said. "There is no change in the provisions of your trust this year. You will continue to receive the interest on the assets on a quarterly basis."

In a chair next to Melinda, Duke leaned forward, placing his elbows on his bare knees and rubbed his hands.

"I have considered your request for an additional sum of cash, for a down payment on a condominium in …"

"Laguna," Melinda said. She jiggled her foot.

"Yes, I see, a condominium in Laguna," Charles said. He hesitated as if the words were distasteful in his mouth. "However, I see no reason why you can't make ends meet on the $80,000 you receive each quarter. Is this a hardship?"

Duke smacked his hands on his thighs. "No, it's not that." He gestured broadly toward Melinda, who glared back at him. "She's had her eye on a property, right on the beach. Hell of a view. You know how it is? On second thought, I don't suppose you do. Well, you're right, old man. What was I thinking?" He pulled himself to his feet. "Anyone want a gin? Sounds good to me."

Melinda sighed audibly.

Ceci looked at her lap and Daniel could hear her breath quicken.

Charles cleared his throat. "Then we'll continue." He turned to Ceci. "As you are aware, Catherine, this year the trust specifies that you receive a major distribution of cash. While I do not agree with some of the personal decisions you've made in your life, I can see you're serious about music. Duke tells me you're teaching music in the primary schools.

"Yes, that's true."

Daniel turned his head and stared at Ceci.

"Excellent. He also tells me you're thinking about opening a music school for disadvantaged children."

Daniel grimaced. "Since when?"

Ceci frowned. "I've begun talking to people who can help me with this project and we're developing a proposal. I know it's a big undertaking."

"Your grandparents would be proud." Charles jotted a note in a notebook. "They believed in service to the community."

"Yes, sir," Ceci said. "Thank you."

"You bet they would," Duke said, raising a glass of gin. "Damn proud. Here's to my girl! Hell of a musician."

"Catherine, since you seem to be making a worthwhile effort and applying yourself toward a worthy goal, I find that in accordance with the requirements of the trust, one third of the assets, a lump sum distribution of $500,000, will be deposited into your bank account on your thirty-fourth birthday."

Melinda gasped.

"Aw, cool it, Melinda. You're a pain in the ass." Duke said, pouring another shot.

"Thank you, Uncle Charles," Ceci said. She shifted in her seat and glanced nervously at Daniel. The weight of the inheritance seemed to settle on her skin like a pallor.

Daniel couldn't stand to look at her.

"The remainder of the trust will remain intact. I'd like to discuss ways to protect the distribution. Can you stay after the meeting?"

"Of course." Ceci's voice had dropped to a whisper.

"And now, young Daniel, we turn to you. Perhaps you can bring me up to the present."

"He's doing a hell of a job at Berkeley," Duke said. "Aren't you, son?"

"Yes, sir, I'm enrolled at Boalt Hall." Daniel's stomach rumbled, but his hands remained steady.

"Go Bears," Duke bellowed, his knees momentarily buckling.

"Dad, please sit down," Ceci said.

Duke hiccupped. "Not a bad idea. But I prefer standing. Right next to this lovely bar where I'll make myself one more teenie weenie drink."

"That is enough, Duke," Charles said. "Take a seat!"

"Ah, give me a break. Carry on, I say. You tell him, Daniel. One of these days you'll be joining the firm. Move over, Charlie. Here comes the kid."

Charles smoothed the lapels of his suit front. "As I was saying, first year law, is it?"

"Yes, sir." *Charlie's going for the kill,* Daniel thought. He could smell it.

Melinda stifled a laugh and tossed her hair over her shoulder.

"Then you'll pass exams this spring?" Charles asked.

Daniel turned to watch his father who raised his glass toward him in a toast. Then he looked at Ceci and shook his head from side to side. He gripped the arms of the chair. "I told you I'm enrolled."

"Do not trifle with me, young man," Charles said. "The Dean of Admissions at Boalt is a fraternity brother of mine. You haven't attended class in months."

Daniel's mouth curved in a smile.

"The guidelines of the trust specify that you are to actively and in good faith pursue an education. If your father allows you to live in the summer house that is his business, but as far as I'm concerned you are not meeting the requirements of the trust."

Daniel leapt to his feet. Ceci reached out and touched his sleeve.

"Sit down, young man!" Charles ordered.

"Don't mess with Charlie, son. He's the boss," Duke sputtered.

"Until you actively return to the University," Charles said, "I'm terminating any further distribution."

"Bullshit," Daniel said. "You know what you can do with the fucking money—!"

"The kid's got spunk. Just like his old man," Duke slurred. He slumped against the wall.

"You can take it and stuff it up your ass," Daniel shouted, staring into Charlie's mocking eyes that blazed through the lens of his glasses. He shook off Ceci's grasp and stormed out, deaf to the ringing phones and Estelle's voice calling to him.

On the sidewalk, the light of day temporarily blinded him. Taxis, cars, and bicycle messengers raced on the street. He dodged the honking horns, moving rapidly past glass-fronted antique stores, rare bookstores, and brick office buildings, filling his lungs with air. Gulls dove for spoils scattered under benches. People in hats and coats pushed into the wind. He found himself in alleyways he had traveled with his grandfather, toward the bay. The sound of Popee's silver-tipped cane tapping out a brisk rhythm returned to his ears. A vague memory of walking with his father and Uncle Charles flashed in his memory. Though his legs had to scurry, they urged him on. He could see their black pant legs flapping in the stiff breeze as he held their hands, calloused and broad.

Suddenly he was in the park at the edge of the Embarcadero where sunken ships lay buried under the sidewalk. So close were the sailing ships docked to each other during the Gold Rush, that the bay was a tangle of masts and more than one man had met his death overboard in foul play.

Daniel walked over the grass through the park and across six lanes of traffic onto the Embarcadero. On Pier 3, the choppy grey sea surging against the pilings, the scent of the kelp and sea salt in his lungs, he paused, turned and continued west, a free man at last.

Chapter 9

April 17

AFTER THE INCIDENT with their children, Annie's feelings towards Jess fluctuated like the barometer when a spring storm comes blowing in from Alaska. She wanted Jess to snap out of her ridiculous pout and apologize for her outburst. The sooner she accepted the messiness of parenting, the better off she'd be. Their friendship was surely built on firmer ground than a tiff about their kids.

Annie finally relented after realizing since neither of them would apologize, she would take the high road. In the spirit of solidarity and to coax Jess out of her silence, she decided to act on the article, "Go For it" that she'd read in *Ms.* magazine, with the stunning Gloria Steinem on the cover. The writer encouraged women to examine their cervixes and vaginas at group meetings as an educational practice and expression of their sexual identity. She dialed Jess's number and tried to breach the divide by suggesting a party.

"Are you out of your mind?" Jess protested.

"Come on. It's revolutionary," Annie insisted.

"The revolution may be happening at home, but not in a group viewing of my parts in your living room. Count me out."

"You're repressed."

"Hardly. Who's the one who gave you a copy of *Our Bodies, Ourselves*? You were the one who said you didn't want to investigate female plumbing and hook-ups."

"This is different—it will be fun. I'll serve wine and stuffed grape leaves, baba ghanoush and lavash—all your faves." Annie's voice dropped conspiratorially. "Haven't you wanted to see what's up there?"

"I already have."

"No," Annie shrieked. "Why didn't you tell me?"

"It was private."

"Well, I think privacy is highly overrated."

"That's your opinion," Jess said. "Not mine." And with that she hung up.

Annie determined it would take more than inspiration to draw Jess out of her corner, and because it was such a resplendent afternoon, she took a rare break from her work. Overnight, it seemed, the glory of April had struck. The air was clean, laced with the salty moisture of the sea that lay five miles to the west. Despite the second year of below-average rainfall, cherry, crabapple, and dogwood trees bloomed. Petals danced on soft breezes. Honeybees buzzed around the conical clusters hanging from lance-shaped leaves of California Walnuts, and redheaded Pileated Woodpeckers drilled holes into tree bark and feasted on grubs.

Annie wandered onto the porch and contemplated her work. She had finished the final brushstroke on the painting for Jerry Brown and hadn't entirely lost hope that she and Jess would someday make the trek to Sacramento. In the meantime, she had applied to the Fall Arts Festival, a juried art show and a three-day event that mixed talent, music, and food, in Old Mill Park. Marin County was home to artists of every stripe, and the festival was like a jubilee: artists at the peak of their skill who worked in sculpture, painting, pottery, woven textiles and exhibited their wares in open-air galleries fashioned amongst dappled groves while art lovers poured through the park. Magic spun in the warm amber air, the creek gurgling nearby, and the aroma of wine and sizzle of delectables rising from the food vendors' grills. Annie itched to be an exhibitor. It would add to her reputation as the cream of the crop in the art scene, and it didn't hurt that the returns were lucrative. Still, money wasn't the primary currency,

Annie mused. Greenbacks may have fueled the cogs of industry, but it dulled beside the quicksilver in the air that was free and plentiful.

The discussion with Stewart Merch about Matthew had quieted beside daily life. Matthew seemed to be in an exceptional frame of mind, cheerful and helpful around the house. So what if he did take a few items from Lockwood's? He was hardly a delinquent; he was smarter than that. She had to admit that he did have a propensity for setting things on fire. Earlier in the year he had been fooling around in his bedroom with a chemistry set she had given him for Christmas when he set a rug on fire and scorched a black hole into the polyester fibers, blistering the air with toxic fumes. Then there were odors of burning animal flesh she had smelled in the yard, but upon inspection she didn't find a thing. Possibly someone had been barbecuing. She settled for the adage, boys will be boys. For today at least, she put her concerns to rest and threw her energy into a new series of small collages.

She ambled across the bridge and down to the Book Depot, where she ordered a coffee and paused on the sidewalk, watching folks strolling around in the sunshine. Dogs frolicked on Lytton Square, sprinting between children who rode tricycles or ran around their mothers in circles. Business owners wandered out of their shops and chatted on the curb. As the crowd multiplied, she elbowed her way to the edge of the sidewalk on Miller Avenue and bumped into a man who sidestepped away.

"Whoops," she said, looking up into Jake Zelinski's face. "Sorry about that."

"Do we know each other?" he asked, his dark eyes roving over her face.

"I'm Annie. Jess's friend. We haven't met, but I've seen you around."

"How's she doing?"

"You know," she said, taking stock of his rough masculinity up close, an animal magnetism that projected street smarts. "Getting used to Mill Valley. The usual stuff."

"She's a righteous woman. Good to have her in town."

Annie shrugged off his remark and peered into the street. "Do you know what's going on?"

"I came down to the bank and thought I'd check out the action." He crossed his arms. "Something's going down."

The sidewalks on both sides of the street had thickened with people, and cars slowed in response and tooted their horns as if a parade was coming. Excitement buzzed in the square and rippled through the breeze.

As they stood chatting, Matthew sped up on his Schwinn along with two of his friends who rode identical bikes.

"Hi, boys," she said. "What's happening?"

"Hi, Mrs. Morrison," Kai said, popping a wheelie, and cutting a tight circle sideways.

Luwellyn was unusually silent, his eyes averted, appearing to scan the activity on the street.

"Hi, Mom," Matthew answered, glancing sideways at Jake and then at the spokes of his front wheel. He seemed to be looking for a malfunction that was wasn't there. The boys were acting uncharacteristically subdued like they'd bolt at any minute. She quickly introduced them to Jake.

"Hey, boys, what's happening?" Jake said.

"Suppose to be a happening," Matthew mumbled.

"No shit," Jake said.

"The cars you work on are cool," Matthew said, shooting a quick glance at Jake.

"I've seen you around." Jake narrowed his eyes. "You and your friends like to cruise by the shop."

Matthew gulped like he'd swallowed a fly, and his eyes opened wide and then became opaque. Annie had seen this look on his face before when he was around men with whom he felt unsure of himself. No doubt Matthew was awed by Jake and tongue-tied.

A roar sounded from further up the street, gathering volume, and before she could interject a comment, Matthew peeled off with the boys behind him. Typical behavior, she thought—always on the move, never a good-bye. Jostled by people pressing around her, Annie dismissed the encounter and was swept forward to see a pack of eight longhaired, virile young men streaking into the square on their bicycles—all naked, clad only in tennis shoes. One man wore an aardvark mask, another a ski mask. They waved as they triumphantly circled the square to the cheering crowd until they disappeared down a side street.

"Well, I'll be damned," Annie said. "A rite of spring in our own hometown." But when she turned to find Jake, he had disappeared into the crowd.

* * *

Back at home, Annie was seized with idea of spring-cleaning. It had been weeks since she'd set foot in either boy's bedroom. She had taught them how to do their own laundry so that she'd have little reason to enter the Dark Zone, as she called it. Noah kept a pet rat, and his antics on the whirling wheel inside the noxious cage made her gag. Usually Matthew's door was locked, or a "Do Not Enter" sign was posted on his door. Today the door was slightly ajar. She pushed on it and was hit with the heavy smell of cigarette smoke and boy sweat. Evil Kneviel, Led Zeppelin, and Planet of the Apes posters plastered the walls. A maze of colored buttons stuck to a cork board proclaimed "Bored Teenager," "Take a Hippy to Lunch," "Cleaver for President," "Am I Cool?" and "Cannibal Power."

She moved across the floor, over the burnt hole in the carpet, vinyl 33s, and a *Playboy* magazine, its pages flipped open to a buxom centerfold. As she turned to strip his bed, her toe slammed into a hard surface. She crouched on her hands and knees, lifted the edge of a sheet that had fallen over the bed and peered underneath. Dust balls, disturbed by the flow of air, scooted across the floor past mildewed yogurt cartons and crushed Frito Lay chips. A cardboard box was wedged under the bed. She yanked it out and flipped open the top. "What the hell," she said aloud. She reached in and pulled out the cold, smooth chrome of a Jaguar hood ornament, a perfect sculptural rendition of a leaping cat. Underneath the gleaming metal, she saw more jaguars and a cache of Mercedes hood emblems, three-pointed stars inside round circles. The rusty flat head of a hammer poked up through the jumble. She sat down hard. It was not a shock, but a reckoning, a sucker punch, delivered low and mean. She'd been had; she was a chump. Who could she blame if not herself? Was it pride or denial that prevented her from seeing the obvious? Her son was a thief. She could see Jake's eyes narrowing when the boys rode up on their bikes. They had been dying to get away, cornered like mice under his gaze.

Noah's voice cut through her thoughts, jerking her upright. "You don't know him, Mom," he had said.

Her throat was parched. She pushed the box under the bed and hauled herself off the floor. The sound of the front door banging shut rattled the house. She walked out of Matthew's bedroom and found Noah in the hall. He looked like a little man dressed in his red and white Little League outfit, hair sticking out from under a red ball cap pulled low on his forehead, grass stains on his knees.

"Who won?" she asked.

"Bombers rule," he said, he said lifting his hand for a high five. "I got a line drive down the first base line and brought in the winning run."

She smacked his hand, "Meet me in the kitchen and I'll fix you something to eat."

* * *

They sat on stools at the counter opposite one another. He wolfed down a peanut butter and jelly sandwich and drank two glasses of chocolate milk. Now he peeled an orange, belching loudly, eating the orange section by section. She sipped tea, hot and black.

"Is there anything going on with Matthew that I should know?"

His eyes did not leave her face. "Nope."

Annie considered how to phrase her next question. There had been a history between the boys of Noah complaining about Matthew abusing him when, in fact, Noah fabricated injury to get her attention. "I know he pushes you around and that kind of thing. But you hang out together. Has he ever beat you up or hurt you in any way?"

"Not really," he said. "But he likes to hide and jump out and scare me. Except most of the time, he ends up in my room. Sometimes when I wake up at night, he's asleep on the floor next to my bed."

Annie laughed. "Go figure," she said. She reached across the table and took his hand. "Matthew's in trouble."

"Matthew's not afraid of anything or anyone," he said, shaking off her grasp. His eyes were as clear as golden topaz. "I'm going to go watch 'Gilligan's Island.'"

The TV blared from the living room as she washed the dishes. Her mind wandered to Noah's room filled with Lego's that he had built into intricate constructions; a fish tank stocked with plants and fish purchased with his allowance; a prized collection of Matchbox cars and trucks arranged in rows on his bookcase; treasured books stacked in piles by his bedside.

It was so much easier when they were young, when their needs were uncomplicated. There was a simple rhythm to days of balancing her painting and their care: laughter and play, cooking and naps, friends coming and going, and long nights when the boys went to bed early and she could work at her easel in the kitchen without interruption. They were good kids, and she considered herself a good mother. She loved her boys. Now she recognized in herself an intense longing to live and work in different cities. She could imagine a life for herself in New York, London, and Rome. She had brought the boys this far. Wasn't it time for their father to step in?

Later that afternoon she found hubcaps hidden under the porch—Cadillac, Lincoln, Mustang, Porsche—all high end—arranged in stacks according to make. There was a secondhand hubcap dealer in San Rafael. She had seen the sign on the frontage road from the highway. "For Sale—Hubcaps, Any Brand, Any Year." Matthew hadn't asked her for money in months, but all along he had been buying pizzas, going to the movies, staying out all weekend at his friends' houses.

A line would have to be drawn, remedies taken for Matthew's future, and protection for Noah. She felt adrenaline shoot through her central nervous system. She could see the anger in Matthew's eyes, and hear him saying, "What are you going to do? Send me to live with Dad?" She could almost hear herself saying, "I'll help you pack."

* * *

Jess sailed down Blithedale Avenue on the way home from the city after wrapping a session early at Project Artaud. Earlier in the afternoon, Sebastian made the announcement that an anonymous benefactor had given the troupe one thousand dollars. With a euphoric grin on his face, he held out two three hundred dollar checks, pressing the first into Claire's hand, and then into hers. "This kind of support means we're in. After the tryouts, we'll be among the chosen. No doubt about it."

The act of receiving an infusion of cash gave her a sense of buoyancy. Now it seemed they were a hair's breath from receiving the grant and an actual living wage. In the meantime, if push came to shove, she could use the food stamps at the organic food store in town where the clerks wouldn't look at them like poison. Soon she wouldn't have to rely on Parker's child support. She'd put the money into a savings account for Sarah and let it accrue interest.

Passing by Boyle Park, she heard the thwack of tennis balls. Three courts facing the street were packed with players. She had an hour to spare since Sarah had joined an after-school playgroup. On impulse, she braked at the next corner and hung a U-turn.

Finding a bench, she watched old men dressed in Bermuda shorts, windbreakers zipped to the chin, and pork pie hats pulled snug over their heads, battle it out on the courts. Despite their stringy legs, rail thin chests, and eyes watering like turtles, they smacked the ball directly to one another's midsections with wicked forehands and stinging backhands. No wasted motion, they appeared to own the courts.

Jess kicked off her shoes and lifted her face to the warm sun. The creek on the outskirts of the park babbled, and birds chirped in willows overhanging the banks. As Sarah had predicted, Fred

Boynton had offered to take the sparrow to his office while it recovered. They dropped the bird off at the Boyntons' home on the afternoon after Sarah and Noah had been lost and were invited to stay for dinner. Fred, tall and gangly, was a little odd, though quite friendly; his wife, Renata, a striking, thin brunette, her bangs cut sharp above her eyebrows, remote. She was studying cello at the San Francisco Conservatory, and while Jess and Sarah were sharing a spaghetti dinner in their beautiful home, Renata announced she was off to a Breatherian meeting. This left Jess and Fred to chat while Amber and Sarah played together upstairs. It was all a little awkward. While they cleared the table, Jess spied a magnet on the refrigerator with the slogan, "The Revolution Begins at Home." She couldn't have agreed with it more, but she felt uneasy and longed for the easy, effortless banter that she and Annie shared.

As the old men shuffled off the court, Jess studied the tennis wives, sun-bleached blondes, bouncing down the steps and onto the courts. Did they wave their children off to school, giving instructions to housekeepers and then dropping off their husbands' dry cleaning? The wives wore short white tennis skirts, cropped socks that sported fuzzy bunny tails at the heels of blinding white Adidas, and cotton shirts the colors of Easter eggs. They lobbed the ball back and forth, and when an opponent's ball landed over the line, gestured politely, as if it was an error they ardently wished hadn't happened.

She had first noticed these women at the Mill Valley Market nearly two weeks ago on her first grocery trip. While she selected an onion, tomato, and garlic from one side of the produce bin, they were reaching over carrots and broccoli to select baby spring lettuces and asparagus. The produce man's hands paused on the navel oranges, eyes twirling in his head; the butcher peered over the meat case. The tennis wives leaned in deeper. The bag boys halted in mid-snap. Glimpses of buttock were revealed, cupped white cheeks against tan marks. Shoppers close to Jess turned their heads as if sensing an electrical disturbance, perhaps in the air-conditioning, and when the moment passed, resumed their selection.

On the court, the game the women played was insipid compared to the old duffers' fierce competition. The men hunkered down and met their opponents head on. They growled and shouted and took the court like champions. Down to a man, they stayed in the game until the final serve was smashed, the last ball sizzled over the net, and the score was called.

Jess recalled a game she and Annie had played. They had arrived at Boyle Park before dusk. Annie looked like she was dressed for the roller derby—high top red Keds, tight hibiscus-flowered shorts, and a lime green cropped top that exposed her ribcage; Jess wore ragged cut-offs over a leotard.

The first and middle courts were empty; they walked to the third court, closest to the cyclone fence bordering the creek.

"I feel like an imposter," Jess said. It wasn't the first occasion when Annie had convinced her to take up something she knew wouldn't last.

"Who's looking? There's nobody here." Annie said.

"Are you sure your shoes aren't too big for you?" Jess asked.

Annie stopped and tapped her toes. "Nope, they fit fine. Aren't they a dynamite red?"

"We're just going to rally first. A little friendly back and forth, right?"

"Sure thing." Annie executed a few jumping jacks, tucked her racket under her arm, and tightened her ponytail.

"Because neither of us has done this in a long time, right?"

"Come on Rosie Casals, hit me the ball." Annie pranced at the serve line like a filly at the gate.

Jess stood flat-footed mid-court. "You're so far away I can hardly see you."

Annie twitched her bottom impatiently. "So?"

"Can't you come a little closer?" Jess asked, trying to diffuse the intensity rising in stealth waves off Annie's shoulders.

"Are we going to play, or are you just going to talk about it?" Annie snapped.

"We agreed we'd rally first."

"All right, already." Annie scurried forward as if she was charging the net. The sudden movement was unusually predatory. Jess suppressed the urge to laugh. Annie crouched in an offensive position and raised her racket. "Is this close enough?"

Jess's wrists went loose as pudding. She felt like she was eight-years-old, at Girl Scout camp, challenged by the Scout mistress, ordinarily a kindly leader, to forge a raging creek over wet boulders, hack through poison oak, break camp, and start a fire with a flint.

"What are you waiting for?" Annie shouted.

Jess bounced a ball against the strings of the racket that veered off toward the sideline. She wrestled another ball out of her back pocket. When she glanced at Annie, she hadn't changed position. Jess whacked the ball and sliced it diagonally into the next court.

Annie looked like she wanted to beat the pants off her. Jess compressed her lips to keep from giggling. Annie didn't flinch. She held her ground, a pocket rocket of sheer concentration. Jess sputtered, laughter bursting from her mouth. Doubling over, she laughed until tears dribbled down her face. The racket fell to the ground.

Annie yelled at her, "Will you get a grip?"

Jess closed her eyes and drew herself up. Suddenly she heard swelling chords of symphonic music. Her arms lifted in a sweeping arch. She circled the court, once, twice, using the propelling one-two-three, one-two-three rhythm of triplets to gain momentum. At the serve line, she ran across the court and leapt over the net in a perfect grand *jete*. Soaring over the net, Jess saw Annie's mouth fall open as she landed and collapsed in a heap at Annie's feet.

"What is wrong with you? Get up," Annie said, grabbing a fistful of shirt.

"You look so funny," Jess wailed.

"I wouldn't talk," Annie said, starting to laugh.

"I'm going to wet my pants."

"Oh god, you are hopeless. We'll do this another time."

Jess nodded. "Whatever you say. You name the day. I'll be ready."

At that moment, a man appeared alone at the steps leading down to the courts, a tennis racket in hand. Annie combed her fingers through her hair and leaned in conspiratorially toward Jess. "Damn," she said, "There's Stewart Merch. Here's my chance. I'm going to snag him for a game right now. Would you mind?" Before Jess could respond, Annie sashayed across the courts straight toward an unsuspecting Stewart. A sharp undercurrent of disappointment swept away Jess's carefree mood. She shouldn't have felt let down. Annie had left her in the lurch before; her mercurial temperament often struck without any warning. Jess gathered her things together, hurried toward the bathroom, and waved as she passed them walking onto the first court.

But she and Annie hadn't made a return to the courts, and now, sitting on the bench, the warmth of the sun slipping behind a cloud, Jess wasn't sure if she would.

* * *

Cruising into town, Jess decided to stop at the organic food store and pick up strawberries for dessert. On the way, she passed by the Sweetwater, a club that brought the finest blues and rock acts onto its stage. Taped to the window was a poster featuring a photograph of a white woman and a black man, each holding a guitar.

Back by Popular Demand
April 26 & 27, Friday and Saturday Only, 9 & 11 PM
Ceci Gessler and Sam Johnstone
Play the Blues

Stepping closer, Jess read the poster and studied Ceci's face. There was no doubt about it—Ceci and Daniel resembled each other. It had less to do with their physical features and more to do with the expression in their eyes—as if they had nothing to prove, and you'd have everything to gain if you stepped into their universe.

Jess backed away from the poster. There was a vibrancy in the air. Down at the creek bank in the foliage, she could hear cicadas rubbing their wings together. She stopped and listened. Their ticking was a steady undercurrent that penetrated through the chatter of her mind and vibrated in her ears. She calculated that Daniel would make an appearance. How could he not? She could feel it in her bones.

Back at the apartment, Jess unlocked the door, and nudged Sarah toward the bathroom. "Go clean up for dinner. I'm going downstairs to check on the mail. I'll be right back." In the foyer, she slipped a key into the lock of the mailbox. A pale blue airmail envelope rested inside. It was addressed to her in unfamiliar handwriting. She peered at the Hartford postmark and tore at the envelope's navy blue and red edges. Parker's two hundred and fifty dollar child support check slipped from a single sheet of blank white paper into her fingers, exactly a month late. His signature jumped up at her, but the check was written in the same distinctly feminine handwriting as Jess's name and address on the envelope. The blank page fluttered to the floor. She ripped the envelope into tiny pieces, let it siphon through her fingers, and ground it into shreds with the heel of her shoe.

Chapter 10

April 27

THE SCENE AT THE SWEETWATER was jumping. Fans who had come to hear bluesman Sam Johnstone jam with local musician Ceci Gessler blocked the sidewalk and pressed toward the front. Two bouncers covered the door. Daniel waited across the street and watched them handle the crowd like carney men who work state fairs in the full blast of summer.

He had debated whether or not to show up. The morning after the meeting at the law office, the phone had rung in Bolinas at dawn and again late at night—the times Ceci usually tried to catch him. When the phone jangled repeatedly as he lay in bed reading by the glow of a lamp, he aimed a book at the phone and silenced its squawk. When they were growing up, Ceci had vowed they'd be different from the other misfits in their family, but in the end she buckled, concocted a lie, and swallowed the trust fund money whole. Her betrayal repelled him.

The next morning he packed the bus and headed down the coast to Santa Cruz. Camping in the dunes, he surfed, built campfires, and slept under the stars for a week until finally he gave in to what he knew was true: a recurring sense of obligation to his sister. She had been the one constant in his life—his loyalty to her would not release its hold. He was honor bound to be at the Sweetwater. He drove back up the coast, through the city and over the bridge into Mill Valley, all the while swallowing a bitter taste in his mouth.

In front of the club, he elbowed past bodies and approached the bouncers.

"House is full," said the lean one.

"Any way you can slip me in?"

"Don't see how."

"That's a bummer. What if I told you I'm related?"

"You don't look like no brother, dude," said the other bouncer, in a leather vest strained over his belly.

"He means to the white chick."

"Right. She's my sister."

The bouncers glanced at one another. "You believe him?"

Daniel dug inside his pocket. "Here's my driver's license."

They peered at his name. "Far out. On the house, dude."

He squeezed through the door into a thick screen of smoke and noise and threaded into the throng. Laughter punctuated the roar of voices. On one side of the club, a bar ran half the length of the dark, wood-paneled interior. Round tables and chairs spotted the floor, and along the other side, a bench was built against the wall. A low stage and small dance floor occupied the rear. There wasn't an empty seat. Two bartenders worked maniacally—slamming refrigerator doors, serving up bottles, flinging empties into buckets, splashing liquor over ice cubes into thick glasses, cursing the ringing phone. Waitresses waded through tables, delivering drinks and taking orders. He hung back and scanned the faces of the crowd. Just then the lights dimmed, and Ceci burst through a door at the rear. Fans clapped and the sound reverberated through the bar, setting Daniel back on his heels. The crowd's admiration was like a thunderbolt. Sam's reputation was renowned, but wasn't Ceci a newcomer?

Wearing a tight red jumpsuit, Ceci took the stairs to a stage like it was her sole pleasure to give everyone in the house the time of their lives. She had legs like an Olympian, and Daniel was reminded of the corkboard in her high school bedroom, choked with the ribbons she'd won in the high hurdle and the fifty-meter race. When she started playing music and hanging out in clubs, she turned in her cleats for a guitar and tossed out her ribbons.

"Good evening, ladies and gentlemen," she called. "Thank you for coming!"

Sam followed, filling the door with his bulk. He paused and moved gracefully forward with bones that seemed liquid under his dense muscle. Daniel smiled, watching him saunter up the stairs placing the sole of each snakeskin boot onto one step and then the next. For a humble dude Sam sure knew how to turn on the heat. As he stepped into the spotlight, a ripple of female appreciation rumbled through the audience. He lifted one hand in a salute, his pink lips widening to show white teeth, and strutting forward, he oozed a gentle message, as if to say, "Hey, baby, I got you covered. Cool your jets. Ain't no need to hurry 'cause we're going to set the house on fire." An expectant hush settled over the club. Sam dragged a chair in front of a microphone, settled onto it and lifted a black and white Fender onto his lap. Ceci strapped on an acoustic guitar and joked with the audience. A soundman darted around on the stage. When Sam plugged in the Fender, the techie circled the equipment. The air popped and crackled. "Hey, Sam," the techie called. "You plugged in all the way? We got rice crispies here."

Sam nodded and hooked up again. The soundman signaled thumbs up and hurried off the stage. Sam looked at Ceci who tapped her foot, one, two, three, four, and they broke into the opening bars of "Temptation Took Control of Me and I Fell." She swung toward the audience and belted out the lyrics as if her time had come.

The cords thundered and rocked, and Ceci's voice climbed higher. The music lifted the audience like a physical force; they clapped, stomped, and swayed. Daniel had heard Ceci and Sam play together at their place with friends and in venues when she'd joined Sam's band for a number or two, but tonight the frenzy of the audience astonished him. Envy lapped at his ankles. The emotion wasn't something he could articulate or explain; it lay buried beneath his mental awareness. Here she was in the limelight, at the zenith of her ambition, and when he was honest with himself he knew he was adrift.

Dumbfounded, he listened to her voice that lifted to startling crescendos and dipped to contraltos. She supplied the beat, the backbone of the rhythm, while Sam picked out a riff and repeated the musical line. They rolled through the numbers, bringing the audience higher and higher. While the crowd stomped their feet, Sam and Ceci slugged down beer from long necked bottles. In "Angel from Montgomery," Sam blew a mouth harp in the key of C while Ceci sang in a trance, eyelids fluttering. He read her the way a preacher in the Louisiana bayou reads his flock. In the instrumental sections of the songs, he played solo, plucking and picking the gleaming guitar strings. Her voice answered in response.

Daniel was riveted by their music. They invented new rules for "Mockingbird." By then everyone was up on their feet and straining toward the stage. Daniel was swept along in the pack of bodies. In front of the stage, he spotted a group of women who were dancing like rock 'n' roll sisters born to boogie. Abruptly he caught a glimpse of Jess as she twirled and spun in a tight circle, her face lit in joy, and he leaned forward to make sure it was she. Weeks had passed since he'd seen her on the street in San Francisco, and the memory of her had burned at the back of his mind.

From the stage, Sam's face glistened under a spotlight, and he picked up on the women dancing and shouted out, "All right, shake your thang!" The audience clapped and stomped for more. Waving his hand and talking sweetly, Sam quieted the crowd, nodding at Ceci who brought them down easy with "You Make Me Feel Like a Natural Woman."

The set finished; the applause died down. Daniel pulled up his collar and camouflaged himself behind two beefy men in front of him. He watched Sam pull Jess and each of the dancers onto the stage. A mob of people clustered around them. Daniel hesitated, his throat thick, torn between going forward or leaving. This was not his scene. He no longer recognized who Ceci had become. She had turned into a stranger. He pushed his way through the crowd and slipped out the door.

* * *

Jess stood on the stage packed in a crush of people. Glancing around at fans, she wanted to turn and discover Daniel. When she first saw the poster announcing Ceci's appearance, she decided then and there that she would be at the show. Still, coming tonight had been a gamble. Right up until the moment she closed the door to her apartment and walked to town, she wrestled with indecision. She didn't go into clubs alone, and she realized that her insecurity at traveling solo was born of old patterns. Usually none of this was an issue: she went with a date or a girlfriend, and most of the time she went with Annie. The very real prospect of crossing Annie's path at the Sweetwater left her feeling sick at heart.

She walked rapidly to town, and when she entered the club, she felt like a woman on the prowl. Jumpy and keyed up, she melted into the crowd, chose a seat against the bench along the wall and ordered a beer. Jake and his girlfriend Camilla sat at a table near the stage. She recognized a few other people she had seen in town, but neither Daniel or Annie was in sight. Once a group of women started boogying in the space that cleared in the front of the stage, the temptation to dance brought her to her feet. She elbowed through the crowd and jumped into the center of the dancing.

Now, she found herself jammed next to Camilla on the stage. Thin as a cipher, clad head to toe in black, she realized that Camilla had been dancing next to her the entire time. Jess stood on tiptoe to speak in her ear, "I didn't know you could dance."

"There's a lot you don't know about me, honey," Camilla said. She fanned her pale white face with her hand. "We should get to know each other better. Especially since you and my man are friends. Or so it seems."

Jess drew back, rebuked. "There's nothing between us, Camilla."

"Sure, sure. Whatever."

Jake popped up beside them, the pungent odor of weed wafting off his clothes. "Ladies, the planets are in alignment. The two best-looking women in the room strutting their stuff for the enjoyment of the house. Far out!" He planted a kiss on Camilla's cheek.

"Hey, baby," she said, "I've got to go to the john."

"Hurry back. We're going to party tonight."

"Later," she said, and slipped away.

"You are looking mighty fine," Jake said, squeezing Jess's shoulder. "Hanging out in the sun, I see. How about I introduce you to Sam?"

"He's a friend of yours?" she asked. She tried pull away from him, but his arm was planted around her shoulder. She blotted her perspiring face with the back of her hand.

"The cover photograph on his new album was taken at my garage."

Unexpectedly, the crowd parted and Sam loomed behind them. He clapped Jake on the back. "Little brother," he said, "I sure do love that car you sold Ceci. She knows how to spoil her man. Who would have thought old Sam would be driving such a fine automobile?"

"Anything I can do let me know. Have you met this lady?"

"Hey, it is indeed a pleasure. I like your style, all right."

Jess beamed at Sam. His skin, poreless and butter soft, was the texture of kid leather. "I'm a big fan," she said. The air was oppressive and hot, and she desperately wanted something cold to drink. Jostled by the crowd on stage, Jake dropped his arm from her shoulder and turned toward Sam. Camilla appeared and wedged herself between the men, forcing Jess out of the circle. Jess studied the faces of strangers who swirled around her and turning to get off the stage, she bumped against Ceci as she stood laughing, surrounded by a cluster of fans.

"Sorry," Jess said.

Ceci glanced at her over her shoulder.

Jess broke in, "I wanted to say hello."

"Really," Ceci replied. Her glittering eyes dimmed. "Do I know you?"

"No, but I know your brother, Daniel."

"Is that right?" Ceci arched one perfect eyebrow. "I've never seen him with you."

Jess tossed her hair over her shoulder. She'd encountered

arrogance before, but Ceci's hostility had a venomous sting. "I met him by chance in San Francisco," she said, squaring her shoulders.

"That explains it. He doesn't usually hang around with older women," Ceci said and turned away.

The flush of excitement drained from Jess's face, and she exited the stage onto the floor. At the bar, she downed a glass of water and caught a glimpse of Annie perched on a stool next to a man with a mustache.

Jess escaped into the brisk air, tinged with fog that bathed her hot face. People snaked clear down the street for the next set. Distractedly, she wandered down the sidewalk, her hopes for the night slipping through her fingers.

The last thing she wanted to do was go back into the club to look for Daniel. If he had been at the show, why hadn't he come forward to say hello? Maybe she had misread him. Jess recalled her initial impression that spoke of his self-assurance. But Ceci's air of superiority rankled her. *What a bitch*, she thought. Still, the evening was dissolving into another night alone. She didn't want to return home to an empty apartment without Sarah, who was at the Boynton's and wouldn't be back until late morning. Jess wandered farther up the street to the Edward Curtis Gallery and glanced through the plate-glass windows where beaded and feathered American Indian headdresses were on display. The old, familiar ache for Mickey surfaced. *How long will I have to battle this longing*? she wondered. How odd that days were filled with miracles of every kind—wonder, delight, comfort—but nights were often strewn with ghosts.

The crowd in front of the Sweetwater vanished. She reclined on the top stair of the gallery, her mood plummeting rapidly. The sidewalk filled with couples, heads close together, arms intertwined. Pinpoints of light from street lamps sparkled on the sidewalk, and the leaves in the trees spun and clicked, echoing her emptiness. Tonight Erica Jong's *Fear of Flying* waiting at her bedside would only exacerbate her desire for sex and passion. A figure appeared at the corner across the street and stepped off the curb, and as he drew closer, she recognized his casual gait.

"Hey," Daniel said, settling next to her.

"Where did you come from?" she asked, her heart rate accelerating in her chest. He was even more handsome than she remembered. A tangle of blonde hair spilled onto his shoulders, his physique lean and loose.

"I've been here all night. I didn't want to miss the show. Looks like my sister is a star." He stretched his legs out and crossed one foot over the other. Even though they weren't touching, his warmth radiated outwards, and she could feel it against her skin.

"Why aren't you inside? You're missing the party." She glimpsed at his profile, the smooth forehead, aquiline nose, chiseled cheekbones, and strong jaw. How unfair, she thought, that some men are physically flawless and other men, of all shapes, talents, and worthy attributes, even pure-hearted, will never know the allure that male beauty inspires.

"That's not my scene." He shrugged. "But she's entitled to whatever she wants. Sam makes her look good. I hope she can keep it together."

"Is there some reason why she wouldn't?" Jess fingered the splintered wood of the steps trying to appear nonchalant.

"She's running a fast race right now, that's all."

"I tried to say hello, but she cut me down about three pegs."

"She's riding high. That's a front." His eyes turned somber, concern filling his carefree voice. "Don't let her get to you."

"When I mentioned I had met you, she made a crack about the fact that her *younger* brother doesn't hang out with *older* women."

"Ouch. She's pushing that big sister thing way too far. I wish she'd lay off." He smiled. "The fact is Ceci pretty much raised me. We grew up with our dad here in town in an old shingled house up on Eldridge. Ceci and I have the same dad, but different moms. Each of them divorced our dad, and neither of them was ever in the picture. My dad hired housekeepers, but they were no match for us. We sent them packing."

Jess peered at him. "That must have been tough on both of you."

"Not really. We were a united front."

"Where is your mom?"

"I don't know." He shrugged. "When I was about four, she disappeared."

Jess was shocked. His tone of voice was so matter of fact. "And Ceci's mom?"

"She's in San Francisco. Ceci sees her every once in a while. You could say they're estranged."

Jess looked up to redwood trees on the hill and imagined the mountain where the darkness of night rested velvet in the ridges and granite outcroppings. Instantly she saw Daniel and Ceci in a different light. The reality of being abandoned and rejected by their mothers must have been a harsh blow. Jess and her mother weren't particularly close now—her parents lived in Hawaii—but she was raised in a traditional family, and her mom was at the center of it, ushering her through the stages of growth into adulthood. The thought of being separated from Sarah was inconceivable. How could Daniel and Ceci go through childhood and adolescence without their mothers?

"This is kind of heavy shit," he said. "Don't let it get to you."

"How much older is Ceci than you?" she asked.

"Eight years."

"And you are how old?"

"Twenty-six," he said.

Jess felt a karmic knock like she was being tested. "Don't you want to know how old I am?"

"Not really. Is it important?" He twisted toward her and squinted his eyes. "If you'd press me, I'd say you're in your late twenties."

"Daniel, I'm thirty-four, like Ceci."

He took her hand and laced his fingers between her fingers. "I don't have a problem with that. Do you?"

"When I was graduating from high school, you were ten. The eight years between you and me is a cultural divide."

"Not from where I sit. I grew up fast. I've been on my own for years. Anyway, I suspected you were older when I met you." He nudged her shoulder. "Why do you think I'm still here tonight? I'll wager a beer you're not here by accident either."

"You're pretty cocky."

"Speaking of cocky, I saw you up front."

The warmth of his body continued to flow into hers, and the confidence of his teasing tone made her smile. "Then you're witness to a secret ambition," she said.

"What's that?"

"If I tell you, you'll think I'm nuts." She tucked her feet up under her legs.

"Try me." He dropped her hand, reached over, caught a strand of hair that had fallen over her cheek and tucked it behind her ear. The gesture was surprisingly tender. She felt a shiver of delight.

"It's ridiculous."

"Come on. Out with it." His hand wandered gently under her hair to the nape of her neck and lingered there.

"To be a back-up dancer in a rock 'n roll band." She buried her head in her lap.

"Why not?" he laughed, his hand trailing down to her waist.

Did he know his touch was driving her crazy? "Among other things, I'm the wrong color."

"I agree the color thing isn't working for you. Plus, you're already a dancer. How did the tryouts go?"

"You remembered," she said, genuinely impressed.

"It sounded important."

"Life-changing," she confided. "About twelve groups all trying out for six positions. We think we stand a good chance. Now we wait. We'll know soon."

He stroked her back. "Waiting drives you crazy."

She laughed. He'd nailed her perfectly: she'd make split decisions and afterwards consider the consequences. "My initial impression of you is that you're patient to a fault and that you're perfectly content to hang back and watch what's happening to other people."

Again, he lifted her hand off her lap and smoothed her palm. "Mostly I watch the clouds, the sea, and the sky. Things that are worth studying." He turned her hand over and stroked each finger. "Your hands are cold," he said, tucking her hand under his shirt.

The pure animal pleasure of her hand on his warm belly made her moan. He turned her chin toward him and kissed her. The sweetness of his taste filled her mouth. He didn't hurry. He lavished care and attention to the shape of her lips and how his mouth fit hers. He kissed her eyes, cheeks, and neck.

"Are you hungry?" he murmured into her ear.

"No," she whispered. She wanted to say, don't stop touching me. Don't stop.

"Is there any reason you can't come home with me?" he asked.

"None that I can think of."

"It isn't much. My private world."

"I have to be back in the morning."

"That isn't a problem. I'm up with the dawn."

* * *

Daniel shifted into gear, drove through Old Mill Park and rumbled out of Cascade Canyon, where the dense air was as cold as creek stones. Jess clutched the door handle and braced her feet against the floor. The night breeze zipped through bullet-sized rust holes in the floorboards and chilled her legs. Cody stood on all fours against the seat behind them, wagging his tail. The dashboard was littered with shells, a plastic bag of trail mix, Zigzag papers, feathers, and pieces of pale driftwood shaped like dried lizards and snakes. As he careened around a turn, the pieces shifted like flotsam caught in a wave. A surfboard, lashed to a metal rack on the rooftop, rattled and shook. A flat can bounced across the floorboards over Jess's feet, and she bent over to retrieve it.

"Sex Wax," she said, squinting at the label. "What's that?"

"Tools of the trade."

"And what trade would that be?"

"I use it to wax my board. Honest." He cracked a smile. "Smell it."

Jess edged the lid off and dipped her finger into the center of the sticky wax. An aroma of vanilla tickled into her nose.

Daniel glanced at her. "Smells good, doesn't it?"

"Yes, it does." By the light of the dash, she discerned mischief in his eyes and wondered if she was crazy to be letting herself feel this way about a stranger.

The bus crawled up the steeply ascending road where redwoods pressed against the crumpling shoulder and buckled the pavement. The headlights dimly lit the white centerline. Dark shapes rushed by and a broken branch rasped at the windows. Jess experienced an intense keening for her daughter. She tried to calm herself and reasoned that other children spent the night with friends; other parents took time off from their children, and tomorrow would come soon enough.

But the further Daniel drove up the mountain, the more agitated she became. The winding road was as treacherous as any along the precipitous coast. One false move, even in daylight, could send you to an untimely death. Hairpin turns, relentless switchbacks, and harrowing descents had been carved from the mountain to gain delivery to the seashore. She would be breathless upon arrival.

"You know," she said, "I'm sitting here thinking maybe this isn't such a good idea."

"How can you say that?" he asked.

"For starters, I really don't know much about you."

"That's not true. Hey, boy," Daniel called over his shoulder, "you'll vouch for me, won't you?"

Head out the open window, nose up, Cody savored the aromatic smells of the woods.

Reaching over the gearshift, Daniel took her hand and placed it on his leg.

Jess sighed. Her mind veered away from its incessant examination and tallying, halted, and shifted instead to the warmth of Daniel's leg radiating into her palm.

"Why don't I fill in some of the blanks?" Daniel said.

"I'm listening," she said.

"I'm a Cancer, a vegetarian, and if I had been drafted I would have gone to Canada. Like a shot. You wouldn't even see my wake."

She let the husky overtones of his voice wash over her. A band of tension melted across the back of her shoulders. The throaty chug of the bus's motor soothed her fears. She imagined herself behind a camera, staring through the lens, taking in his voice, form, and essence.

Click. *She winds her fingers into his hair, surprisingly silky for its thickness. Her hands trail over his chest and downward to the furrowed muscle of his stomach.*

"I also think that Nixon is a lying, sorry crook. I'll wager the Senate will impeach him before the summer is over. Woodward, Bernstein, and the Washington Post should get the Pulitzer Prize."

Click. *The waistband of his Levi's is snug around his waist, the metal button cool. When she unfastens the button and pulls the zipper down, they crumple to the floor. She cups her hands on his hips and slowly kisses the small, vulnerable hollows at each hipbone.*

"Kennedy was shot by the Cubans who were the CIA's henchmen, and we've lost the stinking war in Vietnam, and corporations are in bed with the Government and are fouling the air and oceans."

Click. *She backs him onto a bed and buries her face in the musky smell of him. She cradles the soft heavy basket of his balls and tongues along the shaft of his cock that sails erect before her parted lips. Watching him watch her, she's poised above him, and then guides the full extent of him inside her, deep and up to the hilt.*

"This thing between you and me isn't complicated, but I don't blame you having second thoughts. If you want to, I'll turn around and take you home."

The bus crested the hill and broke into open space along the western ridge of Mt. Tamalpais. The Sleeping Lady was revealed in the jagged escarpment of the mountain looming outside the windshield. Moon shadows fell onto the road, and the starry sky stretched from the ocean to the ridge tops.

Daniel steered to the shoulder of the road and turned off the engine. He kissed her fingertips and released her hand. Leaning his head against the doorjamb, he waited. The scent of spring grasses salted by sea air streamed in through the open windows.

Behind them to the south, a glow from the streets of the city lit the horizon. The thrumming of their bodies filled the car.

Cody panted and raised his eyes to the slim moon hanging over the coast.

Daniel turned to her. "So what do you say?"

"How fast can you drive?" she asked in a reversal of heart.

He clicked on the ignition. "Hold on."

* * *

They drove in silence down the mountain along the lagoon's edge, up onto the mesa toward the sea until tall hedges of a property came into view.

Jess expected Daniel to bypass the stone pillars at the entry. In her mind, she situated him in a cottage closer to the village, perhaps rundown, certainly rustic. Daniel steered into the property, and the bus's headlights illuminated the brass plaque, engraved "Sea View." The tires crunched over gravel. A sprawling two-story house appeared in the moonlight. She counted three brick chimneys rising from the pitched rooftop. A low rock wall lined the circular drive. The outline of a gazebo appeared in the shadows of a garden. She expected him to veer off the drive toward one of the outbuildings barely visible under the trees. *He must be caretaking the property and living in the carriage house,* she mused. Perhaps he's exchanging rent for gardening or keeping away vandals. She glanced at him. He appeared unfazed.

"Home, sweet home," he announced, wheeling the bus past the wide porch that wrapped around the first floor toward a mound of grass at the far end of the estate.

"Oh my," she said. "How did you find this place?"

"You like it?"

"Anyone I know would kill for this."

"You're probably right," he replied.

"Do you live in the whole house?" She wanted to ask—*Is this yours?*

"Only one section," he said, breaking to a stop.

Jess let herself out of the bus, ambled to the center of the lawn, and turned back to gaze at the stately house. Loping across the grass, Daniel caught up with her and playfully grabbed her around the waist. Cody ran toward them, barking and yipping.

They headed toward the promontory where the cliff fell away to the ocean, their footprints leaving a trail in the dewy grass. Waves stacked offshore and shouldered onto the rocky beach below. The rollers pounding on the rocks sent a mist upwards that hung in the air like gauze. At the mouth of the lagoon, the incoming tide washed seawater into the estuary. Stinson Beach rolled southward, lights winking in the beach houses tucked along the pale sand spit.

"This is heaven," she said. "How can you be so lucky?"

"There's a price to pay," he answered, stroking her arms.

"Well, I assumed so. I mean you can't live here rent-free." She recalled her first impression of him that day he'd approached her on the street in front of the dance studio—the natural indifference he projected, aloof, almost wary, and most of all insulated. And then there's Ceci, Jess recalled. She stopped walking.

"Daniel, who owns this house?"

"What's this?" he asked, cocking his head. "An interview?"

"No fair answering a question with a question. Can't I just be curious?"

"Curious, yes, but prejudicial, no."

"You're implying something that isn't in my nature," she said. She'd have to coax the story out of him.

He shrugged. "You won't hold it against me?"

"Try me," she said.

"The property belongs to my family." She was close enough to see the consternation in his eyes.

"You mean the Gesslers of San Francisco?" she asked. She was floored.

"Yes, and I can see you're running through your head all that crap you've read about us in the newspapers."

"Can you blame me? Every week *The Examiner* is running a story about the firm's involvement in a controversial case or reporting a family scandal."

Daniel threw up his hands. "The part that's true is my family is certifiably nuts. Don't get me started on the firm. My grandfather is probably rolling in his grave. My grandparents were decent and honest to a fault."

Jess touched his arm. "I believe you. It's just that I'm stunned that I didn't put two and two together. I had you pegged as a rolling stone hiding out on the north coast."

"Well, you've got some of that right."

She ducked her head, acutely aware that she was withholding information about Sarah. She couldn't tell him yet. She needed to keep what was happening with this new man separate from her role as a mother. Telling him about her daughter would have felt like she was revealing the most intimate, precious fact of her existence.

"Let's go in. You're shivering. We'll talk about it another time," he said, guiding her toward a wing of the house. "I don't want to ruin a good night."

As she stepped through a doorway into a lofty expanse that seemed as grand as the living room of a hunting lodge, dampness seeped out of the dimness, interspersed with the clinging scent of Sex Wax and smoke from a fireplace.

Daniel crossed the floor and struck a match, lighting candles on a low table in front of the fireplace and a hurricane lamp over the mantle. A rocking chair was placed beside the table. Old paintings framed in glass caught the faint light and gleamed along the long walls; the spines of hardback books beckoned on bookshelves. It was like stepping back in time, and she was immediately taken with the old house's charm.

In the corner nearest the fireplace, a bed draped with rumpled covers was pushed up against the wall. Beside it, a row of windows faced west, panes of glass dark against the night sky. At the opposite end of the room, she made out a grouping of overstuffed chairs, a large roll-top desk and what appeared to be lumber stacked on saw horses. Directly across from the entry, cabinets were built under a row of windows. She noticed dishes stacked on the counter beside a sink and stove.

"This is an enormous space," she said. "In a way it's like my apartment, the spaciousness of it, I mean."

"Is that right?" he said. "I'd like to see it."

"Sure," she said. "We can arrange that." She was so tempted to say, *then you can meet my daughter*, but the words froze in her mouth.

"Come on in," Daniel said, removing clothes off the floor and tossing them aside. "Originally, this wing had been a game room that sometimes functioned as a ballroom. My grandparents liked to hold parties. It was easy to install a kitchen and there's a bathroom I added, too." He nodded toward the far end of the room. "Now I've got it just the way I like it. You sit here." He whisked a blanket off the floor, wrapped it around her shoulders, and backed her into the rocking chair. "I'll make a fire."

Jess hugged the blanket around her arms and watched Daniel whistle as he set the fire. Cody curled up by the hearth. Normally she considered herself a quick study, so it astounded her that she hadn't connected Daniel to the San Francisco Gesslers. On one knee, he built a tepee of kindling, branches, and logs, and lit the fire. Soon the logs began to crackle.

"I'll make tea," he said. "We'll get you warm in no time."

She heard him rustling in a cupboard. Water splashed in the sink. The click of a gas burner snapped. Watching the fire leap and dance, she rocked to and fro, transfixed by the leaping flames and the quiet that emanated from the timbers overhead.

Daniel returned holding a packet of Zigzag papers and a small wooden box, the top of which was intricately inlaid with darker woods. He sat cross-legged on the floor and extracted a paper from the packet. Flipping open the box, he sprinkled buds onto the paper, moistened the edge, rolled it, and pinched the ends. He lit one end, inhaled, and held it out to Jess who inhaled and passed it back to him. When the tea kettle whistled, he jumped to his feet.

The shadows of the room had lengthened, the red flames from the fire seemed to lick at the mantle, and the simple preparations of making tea seemed like a Kabuki ritual. When Daniel accidentally tapped the kettle with the spoon, it chimed like a gong; when he poured boiling water into the cups, the scent of mint curled into the air. His every movement seemed monumental, charged with meaning.

He passed her a cup, brimming with tea, and settled next to her on the floor. "I just got back from Santa Cruz today. I thought maybe I wouldn't come back. I seem to be running into walls and thought maybe a permanent change of scenery might be the answer. Do you know what I mean?"

She sipped the tea, the mint deliciously aromatic. "But that's never the answer, is it?" She looked at him over the rim of the cup. His face was illuminated by the firelight. "I'm glad you came back."

"Really?"

"Does that surprise you?"

"You could have any guy you want."

She shook her head. "It's not that easy. Believe me."

"I find that hard to believe."

"There are some things you don't want to talk about and there are some things I'd rather not talk about. Maybe another time, but like you said, not tonight."

"Fair enough," he said. "Are you warm?"

"Very warm," she smiled.

They sat quietly, passing the joint between them, drinking the tea and watching the burning wood in the fireplace shape-shift from human faces to animals to clouds.

"Would you like a tour?" he asked.

"Now?" she answered, her eyebrows rising. She glanced over her shoulder and down the length of the room that had felt cozy and safe. Now it appeared as dark as a cave. Talon-shaped shadows scraped along the length of the walls. "Is that a door down there?"

"Yes. It leads to the living room and my grandparents' library."

"Are there ghosts?" she asked.

He rolled his eyes in mock horror.

"You're frightening me," she whispered.

He tipped back his head and howled like a coyote. From the bed by the windows, Cody joined in chorus.

She toppled out of the rocker, falling into his lap, and he burst into laughter.

"Don't," she screamed, pummeling his chest. "This isn't funny."

"Yes, it is," he said, grabbing her in a bear hug. His merriment rumbled through her and she begged him to stop. Stumbling to his feet, he lifted her off the floor. She hugged her arms around his neck, pressed her face into his shoulder and inhaled his sun-drenched scent.

"Cody, get down," he said. "I've got company tonight."

Daniel walked across the floor and guided Jess onto the bed. Tenderly, he brushed her hair from her face. Unbuttoning her blouse, he planted a trail of kisses from her throat to her belly button. She felt luminous with desire, her body rising to meet his touch. When she attempted to remove his shirt, he gently held her hands away. Slipping his hands up her legs, he drew her panties down, and the fullness of her skirt slipped under her like a sail. With each caress of her skin, he erased all pictures in her mind, replacing them with the sliding, rocking dance of love. When she opened her eyes, moonlight bathed their bodies in a pale milky light as he paused above her, looking down into her face. She slid from beneath his body, climbed on top, and pressed her knees against his hipbones. The shadow of her loose hair fell across his face. Their longing was more real than the pictures in her mind when they drove over the mountain, and she trembled with desire given and returned in equal measure. She wove her fingers into his, stretched his arms above his head, her breasts poised above his chest, and kissed him in all the places she had wanted to taste. When his breath seemed to stop, he flipped her over, and entered her slowly. She wrapped her legs tight around his waist, driving him deeper. His lips upon her lips sealed off any final distance. She was lost in the movement of their bodies, flying on a high, cresting with him and riding into endless space, until they both came, and lay panting in each other's arms.

The fire cooled as Daniel spooned Jess, his arm heavy across her ribs. The pressure of his body along her back, rhythmic rise and fall of his breath, twitching of his legs, and softness of his cock gentled by sleep against her bottom was so unfamiliar she was sure she would lie awake until dawn.

The thought of Sarah floated into her mind, and she imagined her daughter sleeping on her stomach, burrowed under covers, one knee hugged up to her hip. After reassuring herself that Sarah was as safe in the Boynton household as she was under their own roof, Jess surrendered to the sweet sensation of Daniel's body against hers.

Cody rustled beside the bed, jumped up, and nestled against Jess's feet. The boards of the house creaked and snapped, the moon moved across the sky, and a light wind buffeted the windows. Jess closed her eyes and tried to match her breathing to Daniel's. The cadence of breaking waves finally pulled her into slumber.

* * *

The crunch of tires rolling over gravel teased her from her sleep. The noise increased in volume, drawing nearer. She tumbled from a dream, her eyes opening in the unfamiliar bed. The room was unlit; she could see through the windows that the sky was black, sprinkled with stars. A car door clicked sharply and slammed shut. A low growl rattled in Cody's throat.

She thought she heard a deep male voice call, "Baby, don't..." A door slammed again. A female voice shrill as knives replied, "Cool it, Sam," Footsteps, quick and sharp, approached.

Sliding away from Daniel's grasp, Jess whispered, "Daniel, wake up." She pressed her hand against his shoulder, dense as sand. "Someone's coming."

Outside, a woman's voice yelled, "Daniel, you asshole, I know you're in there."

A cry struck in Jess's heart where it lodged quivering and hot. She squeezed her eyes closed and ducked her head beneath the covers.

"Wake up, pisshead," the woman yelled again. "You missed the most important night of my life, and you better have a fucking good reason why."

Daniel bolted upright and sprang out of bed.

The front door flew open, and Jess heard a loud thud. "Oh my god! My head, I hit my head!"

"Ceci, what the fuck?" Daniel said.

"I'm Patty fucking Hearst, and this is a hold-up," she said, laughing hysterically.

Peeking out, Jess blinked as Daniel turned on the bedside lamp. He stood dressed in shorts and stepped away from the bed. Jess saw Ceci laying face down, legs splayed on the floor. She rolled onto her side, her arms caught in the sleeves of a black jacket, the top of the red pantsuit straining against her chest. "Whoa, the room is spinning," she mumbled. "Cody, stop licking me."

"God damn it," Daniel said. "What makes you think you can bust in here in the middle of the night?"

Jess crunched down farther. If an exit were possible, she would have made a run for it.

"I figured since you didn't make the party tonight, I'd bring the party to you." Ceci fished in a pocket, pulled out a flask, and tipped it to her lips. "Here's to me and my big night."

"You're drunk." He grabbed his shirt off the floor. "Where is Sam anyway?"

"No way. I want to tell you what happened tonight. You should have seen it. They loved me. Fucking loved me. Oh yeah, Sam was good, but he's always good. Tonight I was on."

"You had your night. It's over."

Jess continued to watch from the bed, transfixed by Ceci's drunken rage.

"You're no fun. I'm thirsty. Pour me a drink."

"You're drunk enough. Let's go."

"Wait one little minute." She lurched toward Daniel. "What's happened to you? Where were you tonight? You of all people. I'm the one who covers your ass and you…"

"I was there. I saw it. You're a big fucking deal. Now get off my back."

Ceci's face twisted in pain; she stepped back as if struck, weaving back and forth. "What do you mean?"

"You heard me. It's all coming your way now, but let's be clear about one thing. That story you invented about starting a music school is bullshit. You know it and I know it. Leave me out of your plans. I don't want any part of them."

"I don't understand."

"It doesn't matter. I'm taking you home." He scooped the keys off the low table and paused, "Jess, I'll be back. Like I was telling you, welcome to the zoo."

Jess pulled a blanket around her shoulders, fighting back embarrassment. "I heard a man's voice, Daniel," she said, reluctant to interject, but almost certain Sam was somewhere on the property.

Waving on her feet, Ceci staggered into the center of the room closer to the bed and gawked at Jess. Her eyes swam, pupils dilated, mouth slack.

"Hi," Jess said. "Remember me?"

"Fuck you." Ceci spun, lunged and swung at Daniel who caught her as she dropped into his arms.

Suddenly Sam appeared in the open doorway, sucking up the light. "Hey, what's the ruckus about?"

His presence broke the tension. Relief coursed through Jess. In his greeting was the suggestion that the paths of destruction Ceci cut were not out of the ordinary and entirely in his providence to rectify.

"She's all yours," Daniel said, still holding Ceci who had passed out. "Your timing is perfect."

"Could have been better, I suspect." He sauntered across the floor, a sense of calm in his carriage. "Caught a little sorely needed shut-eye behind the wheel. I am truly sorry for the intrusion, my man. But you know what Ceci wants, Ceci gets."

"You've got that right," Daniel said. He motioned toward the bed with his head. "Sam, did you meet Jess tonight?"

"Well, well. Look at this. It's the tiny dancer. Real nice to see you again."

Jess didn't hear one false note of disingenuousness in his words. "Hi, Sam. I didn't expect to see you so soon."

"I didn't expect to see *you* so soon. Yes, it's been a big night." Sam shook his head. "No need to worry. We'll leave you and head back over the mountain. In the morning we'll sort out whatever needs sorting out. Am I right? Sure as rain, I'm right. My, my, this lady of mine just doesn't know when to quit." He took Ceci from Daniel and lifted her in his arms. One of her arms fell free and her head lolled against his shoulder. "Ain't that a fact, baby doll?" he said and carried her out the door and into the night.

Chapter 11

April 28

AFTER CECI AND SAM LEFT, Daniel led Jess outside toward the bluff to dispel the acrimony left behind by his sister's drunken rage and his outburst. There was just enough light from stars to guide her over the grass where eucalyptus cones lay, spicing the cold, briny air with the scent of mentholatum. At the edge of the bluff, he looked out at the grey sea, the sound of churning waves floating up from below, soothing his nerves.

"Sorry for the dust-up," he said.

"It's nothing you could have controlled." She looped her arm through his and laughed softly. "I wanted to evaporate, but believe me, I've seen worse."

He looked at her sideways. The tone of her voice was light, without rancor. "You, too?"

"Different players, different circumstances, different times," she said. "Eventually it all works out."

He felt himself relax. "You sound confident. The fact is, she won't remember half of it."

"Does that worry you?"

"I've talked to her about binging, but she shuts down. I need to stay out of her business. Sam handles her better than anyone."

"I hope you resolve your differences. You've meant so much to each other."

"Don't worry about it," he said. He circled his arm around her waist and gazed out through the darkness to the misty horizon. He couldn't see what the future held. He needed time.

What seemed right was the woman beside him. At the edge of the bluff, the earth gave way to crumbling rock, roots, and shrubs. Soon it would be dawn. He suddenly felt tired. "Let's try to catch some shuteye," he said. Back inside the house, he felt his need for her rise. When he turned to her, she opened her arms, and afterwards they fell back asleep.

When they awoke, he brewed coffee, and they sauntered outside over the grass in the hazy sunshine, mugs in hand. She leaned against his shoulder, laughed at his jokes, and touched his face with her fingertips as if he was an unknown country. Several times, she acted like she was about to tell him something and then clammed up. As they drove through the gates and out onto the road bordering the Bolinas Lagoon, her mood seemed quixotic. She grew more remote the farther he drove. She kept glancing at her watch, and when he asked her if she was worried about the time, she looked at him and replied, "It's just that I've got a big day ahead."

Daniel continued to wind up and then down the mountain, delivering Jess over the same roads they had traveled the night before and emerging through the dark green cover of trees, pierced by diamond pinpoints of light spiraling down through dense branches, into the bustle of morning in Old Mill Park. Daniel watched runners, bicyclists and strollers parade along the paths on their Sunday morning constitutionals.

At the outside of the park, he stopped at the intersection and asked, "Which way?" Abruptly, she withdrew her hand from his and fidgeted with the contents of her bag until she fished out a ring of keys.

She straightened in the seat, distracted and distant. "One block up, left on Lovell, right on Summit," she said. "I'll show you when we get there."

As the road started to climb, she pointed to a building on the side of the hill. "This is it. You can stop here." She grasped a key.

"You live here? Cool. Wasn't this a church? I have a vague memory of services here."

"Really?" she replied, her hand on the door handle. "You're right. My place still has the air of the repentant." She opened the door. "Well, thanks for the ride home."

He reached out and grabbed her arm, unable to comprehend why she had turned so cold. "Wait a minute. You think I'm going to drop you off and say 'see you later'?"

Her face flushed, and she squirmed in the seat. "I'm awfully busy today."

"Come on," he insisted. "Just for awhile."

She stared at him for the longest minute, her eyes guileless. "Sure, come up."

In the entry hall, she took the stairs first, and he ambled behind. "Look at the paneling," he said, running his hand over the woodwork. "They don't build them like this any more."

At the top of a landing in front of a tall arched door, she slipped the key into the lock, and the door fell open.

"Wow, you lucked out," he said, strolling in. "What a far-out space. Look at that stained-glass window. Now that's a beauty." He gazed up into the rafters to admire the craftsmanship: the paneling, beamed ceiling, and the ogee-shaped windows bespoke of another era. "No doubt about it, the architect who designed this church was out to inspire redemption. What do you think? Are your dreams laced with visions of heaven?"

Jess stood at a table, sorting through a stack of mail. She cocked her head. "Yes, heaven and hell. But I only hear angels singing."

The morning light spilled across the burnished woodwork. Gradually he turned toward a painting hung on the wall next to the front door. Meticulously rendered red, purple and umber globes like bubbles floated on a large canvas held his gaze. "What a great painting," he said. "Who's the artist?"

"Her name is Annie Morrison." Jess said. Her brows knit together as she continued to rifle through the mail.

"She's talented," he said. "I like her work." He felt the subject was somehow off limits and decided not to press for more information. Oblivious to picture books randomly stacked in piles and pieces of a red, white, and blue Lego set scattered on the floor, he looked up into the rafters again. "This room is awesome."

"It functions as one big space. The kitchen is here," she said, pointing out the cabinets and countertop along one wall. "And I sleep in the alcove." She tossed her bag onto the bed. "There's a bedroom down the hall, a room where I practice and a bathroom."

A small powder blue sweatshirt lay on the floor, an arm casually flung in salute. He eyed the sweatshirt and the bed in the alcove. "Do you have a roommate?"

Her head was down, as she poured cat kibble into a dish on the floor, and as she stood she faced him. "Not exactly, Daniel. What I mean is ..." She halted, fumbling for words. "What I've been trying to tell you is, I don't have a roommate, but ..."

From the entry below, a heavy door slammed shut, and footsteps clattered on the hallway steps, drawing closer, loud and insistent.

She spoke louder, "I have a ..."

A young girl with wide oval eyes burst into the apartment, the tail of her shirt hanging out, shoelaces undone, a wad of gum bulging. "Mom, I missed you. Really I did. But guess what? Dr. Boynton has invited me to the *beach*! They're waiting for me. I only need my bathing suit. It's *really* warm today so I won't need a jacket. Can I go? Can I go? Please say yes!"

"Sarah," Jess said. "Say hello. This is Daniel. Daniel, this is my daughter, Sarah."

Daniel stood rooted to the floor, hands jammed in his jeans, blown away. The girl was a duplicate of Jess except for masses of blonde curls and a tan complexion. She was a beauty.

"Oh, sorry. Hi. Who are you?" Sarah hitched up her pants and emptied her pockets filled with gum wrappers and a brown banana peel onto the table. She spied the cat on the floor and flung herself beside it. "Triscuit, oh Triscuit. I didn't mean to ignore you. Really I didn't."

Daniel knew he had a shit-eating grin on his face that he couldn't wipe away. "I'm a friend," he stuttered. "I mean I'm your mom's friend." *I don't believe this*, he thought. *I don't fucking believe this.*

Ignoring him, Sarah jumped up and sidled over to Jess who smoothed her tangled hair perched like a swallow's nest at the back of her head. "Come on, Mom. Say yes. They're waiting for me. It's going to be so fun."

"I don't know, Sarah. Are you sure you're not too tired?"

"Amber and I went to bed *really, really* early."

"I thought we could ..."

"Pleeease," Sarah pleaded.

"Well, why not? It's a beautiful day."

"You're the best mom in the whole world. Can you help me find my bathing suit?"

"I'll be right back," Jess said to Daniel. Turning to Sarah, she said, "Spit out that gum and tie your shoelaces before you do another thing."

Ignoring her mother's instructions, Sarah dragged a chair to the countertop, stood on the seat, and strained to reach a box on the top shelf. "Can you help me?" She glanced at Daniel. "I'm starved."

Daniel started as if roused out of a trance. "What do you need?"

"That box of cornflakes," she said, jumping off the chair. "Get the bowls over there on the shelf. I'll get the milk." She jerked open the refrigerator door, bottles and jars on the door clanging against one another. "Quick, get the sugar before Mom comes back. She hates sugar. Here's a spoon for you." She dragged the chair back to the table, pushed Daniel into it, and poured cereal into the bowls. "You sit here. And I'll sit here. Go on. Eat. Isn't this yummy?"

Obediently, Daniel spooned a bite of cereal into his mouth. "What about the gum?"

"Oh, yeah," she said, spitting a pink wad into her hand. "We had a contest. I won. Five pieces of Bazooka."

"Does it still come in a comic strip wrapper?"

"Um hum," Sarah said, slurping the cereal, gaze pinned on Daniel. "I have a collection."

"Far out. I haven't had cornflakes since I was a kid."

"That's pretty silly."

"You know, you're right. I forgot how good they are." It occurred to him that an hour ago, he had no idea that Jess had a daughter and now here he was sitting next to her, munching on cornflakes drowned in cold milk like it was the most natural thing in the world.

"Mom makes me eat eggs sometimes in the morning. I hate eggs."

"You wouldn't hate the eggs I make. Cheese is my secret weapon."

"Sometime you can make them for me."

"Sure. Which beach are you going to?"

"Stinson. It's my favorite."

"That's cool. I live in Bolinas."

"Really? All the time?"

"Yep. I have a dog. Best dog in the county."

"You're lucky. Bolinas is my second favorite. Maybe we can come visit you sometime."

Daniel laughed. "Sure. Get your mom to bring you out someday. You better tie your shoelaces before she comes back."

She slurped the cereal into her mouth, her blue eyes examining his face. "I'm going to call you Danny," she said. "Cause that's way better than Daniel."

"That'll do," he said, an unfamiliar tenderness rising up in him that lodged in his throat.

Jess walked into the room carrying a canvas bag and a windbreaker. Sarah scooted off the chair and threw her arms around Jess. "I love you, Mom." She grabbed the bag and windbreaker, scooted toward the door, and stopped in mid-flight. "Uh-oh," she said, and circled in a wide arc, skidding to a stop at Daniel's chair. "Will you please tie my shoelaces for me?" she asked.

He bent over and quickly tied the laces. "There you go. All set."

She touched his shoulder, regarding him earnestly. "Will you be here when I get back?"

"When will that be?"

"Probably before dinner. Unless we barbecue at the beach."

"I don't think so. I'll be heading back home pretty soon."

"When will I see you again?" Sarah's eyes turned somber.

"Maybe in a few days."

"Wednesday is in a few days."

"I need to check this out with your mom," he said, glimpsing at Jess who leaned against the counter, arms crossed, cheeks flushed pink and eyes bright. She hitched her shoulders as if it was up to him.

"Wednesday it is then," Daniel said.

"Cross your heart."

"Cross my heart." She had him in her pocket, hook, line, and sinker.

Sarah stood on her tiptoes and planted a milky kiss on his cheek. Flying out the door, she cried, "Bye, Mom. Bye, Danny. Bye, Triscuit."

Silence settled over the room. Jess closed the front door and disappeared into the hallway. He heard water running behind a closed door, and after he had paced nervously from one end of the room to the other, she returned and wordlessly began to clear the dishes. He joined her at the kitchen counter while she worked briskly, which required him to step in one direction and then another to avoid getting in her way.

"Why didn't you tell me you had a daughter?" he asked.

"The topic never came up," she said, pivoting on her heel and sealing the top of the cereal box.

"Is that why you didn't want me to come up this morning?"

She shrugged, keeping her back to him.

"You could have told me." It was a balancing act to try and handle her defensiveness and contain his incredulity.

"Really?"

He rubbed his head. "It's a major surprise. I didn't have a clue."

She squirted a stream of liquid soap onto a sponge and started washing the bowls.

"Where's her dad?" he asked.

"Hartford." She rinsed the bowls and stacked them in a drainer.

Daniel whistled. "You're a fulltime parent."

"Obviously," she replied, wiping the counters.

He was losing patience fast. "Would you stop what you're doing and talk to me?"

Jess threw the sponge in the sink and dried her hands. "As I remember, you didn't want me to know about your family. I had to pry it out of you."

"You were righteously indignant," he said. "So, didn't it occur to you then that you were holding out on me?"

"It's not the same with Sarah."

"So there are two sets of rules—one for you and one for me."

"I didn't want to discuss Sarah last night because, to tell you the truth …"

"Because why?"

"It's not easy to explain."

"Let me guess." Color rose in his face. "I had to pass inspection like a USDA cut of meat?"

She grimaced. "God, no. Well, yes, but the way you're describing it sounds callous."

"Fill me in then."

"I didn't know if I'd ever see you again."

"Come on," he said. "Is that really why you didn't tell me?"

"No." she replied, her voice wooden and strained.

"So what is it?"

"I'd rather not go into it."

"Let's get this out of the way. It sounds important."

Jess looked up, a flash of defiance in her eyes. "If I told you last night that I had a daughter, I was afraid you'd ..." She bit down on the words.

"Spit it out."

"Run away," she confessed.

Daniel smiled. "Like a jackrabbit."

"Faster."

"I'll admit that used to be my style. But not right now. Sarah seems like a great kid. She doesn't change a thing." His reaction to Sarah was intuitive and genuine. He felt like he was waking up from a long lull where no one and nothing had much meaning in his life. He reached for Jess and took her into his arms, feeling her soften. "What about you?"

"Where would I run?" she mumbled into his chest.

"No fair answering a question with a question."

She drew back and squinted up at him. "You're a quick learner. But I can tell you're no bargain."

"Is that so?"

"As far as I can see you're a ne'er-do-well surfer with no particular sense of direction, but you're cute and decent and I suppose I can be persuaded to give you a try."

"That's big of you. Anyway, I made your daughter a promise." He tipped Jess's chin and kissed her mouth. "I'll see you both on Wednesday. Right now I need to get back to the beach to exercise my potential."

"The door is over there."

He kissed her again. "On second thought, why don't I fix you breakfast?"

* * *

Plundering the refrigerator, he found eggs, butter, and cheese. Jess ground inky black coffee beans, the blades whirring, releasing the aromatic vapors of French Roast. In the cupboard he unearthed a can of serrano chilies. She passed him the can opener as she held the kettle under the water faucet. Knife flying, he chopped an onion and garlic, wiping his burning eyes with the back of his sleeve. She poured hissing water into a paper cone filter while he melted butter in a fry pan browning it just short of smoking. The pungent aromas of the vegetables sizzling in the butter co-mingled with the sweet chocolate scent of the coffee and laced the air. They partnered the tasks in synchronicity, sensing each other's direction.

"So you're a local?" he asked, tossing whipped eggs into the sizzling fry pan.

"City girl, born and raised in San Francisco. Strictly public school," she said, setting the table. "I went east to school, B.U. I had some notion I'd get a better education back there."

"Were you right?"

She looked as him quickly, and her eyes brightened. "One semester I traveled through Europe. That was an eye-opener."

She turned back to the table. "That's where I met my ex-husband."

"How long were you married?" He added the eggs into the sautéed onion and garlic and stirred, watching the eggs set.

"Long enough for him to get the seven-year itch."

He detected an edge to her voice. "Was it mutual?"

"People can do terrible things to each other, but when you're the one in the dark, it's worse."

Her words hung in the air. Daniel didn't know how to respond. He kept the injustices he had experienced at a remove. He had cloaked himself in anonymity. It served him well.

She sliced sourdough bread and popped it into the toaster. "But that's water under the bridge. Marin has been home for years. I think the mountain is partially responsible."

"Don't tell me you believe in that Sleeping Lady crap?" He wrinkled his nose.

"You bet, Mr. Surfer Dude. All kidding aside, this is a town where I feel at home and where Sarah will thrive."

"You've got that right. My buddies and I owned the mountain when we were kids. We knew every trail, waterfall, and ravine." He tossed cheese on the scramble and turned off the burner. "Let's eat. Breakfast is served."

They ate ravenously, savoring the egg scramble, munching on buttered toast slathered with strawberry jam and sipping dark coffee laced with cream.

"Tell me about the rest of your family. Do you have any idea where your mother is?" Jess asked.

He shook his head. "No, I don't." He felt inadequate trying to explain something he had accepted long ago, something he knew sounded improbable. "I have a vague memory of her in Bolinas, but it's all mixed in with images of my grandparents. No one in the family talks about her. It's taboo."

"No pictures, or letters? She's never visited?"

"Nope. Weird, huh?"

"Something may have happened to her that you don't know about."

"It's possible. For as long as I can remember Ceci has been my protector. My grandparents felt like my real family, especially Popee. He was a great guy."

"You're lucky to live in their old house."

"Speaking of which, I should get back," he said, standing and stretching. "I'm sure you've got things to do. Let me help with the dishes."

"No, that's okay."

"At least I can clear the table."

She reached out and caught his hand. "Really, I'll do them later."

He lifted her to her feet, wrapped his arms around her shoulders and rested his chin on the top of her head. Crystal prisms of light flickered on the wall and set the stained glass window aflame. Her heartbeat drummed against his ribcage. "Wednesday is sounding like a long way off."

"Maybe too long," she sighed.

He ran his hands under her shirt up to the small of her back and traced her vertebrae with his fingertips. Her hair smelled faintly of peaches. He bent toward her, and she wove her arms around his neck. A low vibration gathered in his ears like the sound of the sea when he sensed the tide was gathering on shore. Under his hands, she arched her back, and balancing higher on tiptoe, teased the space between her body and his, swaying and touching his chest and legs, soft against hard, pliant against firm, the half wet shell of her mouth in his ear.

She half-hitched one leg around his leg and jumped into his arms, her legs wrapping around his waist, and he felt a jolt like the energy of the ocean, and he heard her voice calling to him the way the sea sang when he was paddling out through the salt spray toward the break gathering speed, through the wind, gulls crying caw, caw, caw, and diving through the sky, his heart pounding, plankton, jelly fish, sand swirling in phosphorous waves. He was moving her onto the bed, and her skin was sweeter than anything he had known, and he was over her. Now, now, now, she called to him, and he found her the way he took the waves, and there was no end to where he began, and she ended, and the world burst apart like water bending light, and she was calling now, now, now.

Chapter 12

May 17, 18, 19, and 20

ON FRIDAY NIGHT JESS WAS DAYDREAMING beside the kitchen table folding laundry when a sharp rap followed by four brisk knocks struck the front door. Before she could move, Sarah yelled, "I'll get it!" running from the bedroom toward the door, the sound of her shoes slapping the floor like a wet towel.

Daniel stood framed in the doorway wearing his standard uniform—T-shirt, cut-offs, and zori's. The olive green in his shirt brought out the green in his hazel eyes, the color of the light in the oak groves along the trails on Mt. Tamalpais. His hair was damp and wavy and tumbled toward his shoulders. He looked like a college drop-out, one of Hollywood's bronzed anointed who chucks a shot at Daddy's firm, hightails it to Oahu, stares into the all-powerful shimmering lapis surf with his buddies in a rusted beat-up convertible at the Pipeline on the North Shore, waiting to catch the biggest barrel, shit-kicking wave in the world. In short, he did not appear hopeful as a promising prospect for the long haul. She couldn't take her eyes off him.

He handed Sarah an oversized flat box and announced, "Pizza delivery at your service, Miss." The tone of his voice was teasing and light. He nodded at Jess and winked at the same time.

"Where have you been?" Sarah asked. She grabbed the box and hurried to the kitchen table. "I'm so hungry I could eat a bobcat."

Daniel struck his forehead with an open hand and pretended to lurch backwards.

"Where do you come up with this stuff? I bet you've never seen a bobcat."

"Did, too. Mrs. T. showed us one the other day. In the olden days, there were bobcats all over the mountain." She flapped her arms and whooped around the table.

"Okay, Miss Smarty-pants, you win."

Again, Jess's preconceptions about Daniel crumbled as she watched him deftly handle Sarah. In the three weeks since Daniel had driven Jess home from Bolinas and kept his promise to Sarah to return, not a day had passed without him calling or appearing at their doorstep. His consistency was so unfamiliar that each time the phone rang or she heard his gait hit the treads on the stairs, her pulse raced in anticipation. At first she was wary of his attentions, but his rock-steady presence faded her doubts. Their wishes became his to satisfy, their problems his to solve. Occasionally, the nagging question kept resurfacing, how long can this last? As the days passed, her objections faded. She let down her guard; she was learning to trust him. They developed a pattern: weekday nights, he would stay over at her place, and on weekends she and Sarah would join him in Bolinas.

He walked toward Jess and she met him halfway. "How's my girl? he asked, taking her in his arms and nestling her head against his T-shirt. "Don't you feed your daughter? If I hadn't shown up, she'd have wasted away."

"Food stamps make for lousy meals," she said, wrinkling her nose. "Impulse shopping, binge eating, and presto, before I know it, the cupboard is bare." She stuck out her bare arm. "I'm all skin and bones. Alms for the poor. Take pity, kind sir."

"No shit." He held her at a distance. "I better take you home with me. You can gather mushrooms and dandelions, I'll fish, the kid can hunt for berries. My idea of an awesome weekend."

"Stop it, you two," Sarah said, her voice high-pitched and scolding. "It's time to eat. I'm opening the box right now. You'll be sorry."

"Okay, Sarah, cool it," he said cheerfully. "Give your mom and me a minute." He peered down into Jess's eyes. "Let's eat.

Then we'll go to Bolinas. The weather forecast is clear and sunny. The kid and I will hit the beach while you practice."

"Come on, you guys. I'm opening the box right this minute," Sarah threatened. The scent of zesty pepperoni and yeasty crust wafted through the air. They crowded round the kitchen table, devouring the pizza and trading jokes. By dark they were in the bus, a few bags hastily packed, heading over the mountain.

* * *

On Saturday morning Jess lay on the floor in the living room of the Gessler house, a black leotard and tights clinging damply to her ribcage and legs. Through the open front door, she heard the boom of waves pounding the rocks. Rolling to one side, she scrubbed her perspiring face dry with a towel and draped it around her neck. She clicked off the tape deck, strolled out onto the porch, and gazed over the green lawn toward the navy blue line of the horizon.

Earlier in the morning, it had been Daniel's idea to transform the unused living room into her personal dance studio. "Use your imagination," he'd said, pulling her by the hand through the door of the closed-off west wing into a darkened room that filled with light once he opened the damask drapes. Plumes of dust cast off in every direction, and papery insect wings and tiny dead flies were scattered on the windowsill. He brushed them away with the palm of his hand. "It won't take us any time. Trust me."

He tossed aside sheets that had protected overstuffed horsehair furniture, dismantled a scarred leather-topped game table, and pushed back an oak table to a far wall where the swirling burnished patterns of the wood grain caught the glint of sunshine through the wavy glass windows. Together they heaved and strained to move a baby grand piano into a corner. He rolled up tattered oriental carpets, their colors faded and pile worn thin, hefted them onto his shoulder, and carried them up the stairs. He returned with rags, a broom, wet mop, and pail of water. "Okay, let's get going."

He popped a cassette into the tape recorder, whistling tunelessly to the reggae brew of Bob Marley's "Natty Dread." She smiled to herself thinking, just my luck, he's tone deaf. Every now and then she'd dance around him trying to entice him to join her. He'd feign two left feet, dodging out of her grasp. They rid the worn floors of grime, removed the cobwebs that clung to the corners and dangled from the ceiling, dusted the paintings and wall sconces, and shook a musty tapestry that hung over the fireplace.

"There," Daniel said. "Now it's all yours." He held his arms wide, eyebrows arched in anticipation, obviously pleased with himself. "What do you think?"

"I think it will do very nicely." She surveyed the room. "Thank you, Daniel."

He caught her in his arms and spun her around the room, humming in her ear. Abruptly he put her down. "Okay, your daughter and I are hitting the beach and you need to work out."

"Wait. Tell me. What would your grandparents think?" she asked.

"They'd get it. This was a home that buzzed with people; they wouldn't want it to be buried in ghosts."

"What about the rest of the family?"

"Believe me, none of them care. It won't even come up. Anyway, quit stalling. You're getting the final word on the grant this week, right?"

"If we don't hear soon, I think Sebastian will explode. We're all as jittery as claustrophobics in an elevator."

"Then work off some of that adrenaline. I'm out of here. It's all yours."

Hours later Jess walked across the porch and rested on the stoop in the sunshine. Daniel had told her the grounds occupied three acres; it seemed more like a park than a home. Around the perimeter of the house, juniper trees sculpted like giant bonsai had been shaped by perpetual coastal winds. At the road, climbing roses escaped from their beds, entangled in a row of twelve-foot privets. The great hedges were festooned with pink rosebuds. She stepped onto the lawn, turned, and looked back at the house. It had a serenely deserted air to it—the shingles were a faded grey and the white paint on the wood shutters was worn thin. Daniel had mentioned he'd paint the woodwork in the summer. A flat of white Impatiens lay on the porch. Tomorrow they would plant them in the window boxes.

Just then the bus came rolling into the driveway, Daniel grinning at the wheel and Sarah hanging out the passenger window. "I rode a wave, Mom," she shouted. "A real wave!"

Jess's heart lurched. *This is how it feels to be a family,* she thought. *This is how it could be.*

They spent the afternoon clamming on the narrow grey beach, shopping for bread at the bakery, and for beer, lemons, and butter at the old market with its creaky wide-planked floors and swinging screen door. Afterwards, Jess and Sarah baked chocolate chip cookies with walnuts, the butter and chocolate scent drifting out the windows, summoning Daniel in from tinkering on the bus.

After dinner, they built a fire in the fireplace and roasted marshmallows, and Sarah, sunburned and exhausted, fell asleep on the hearth in front of the fire. From the beginning, the sleeping arrangement for Sarah had been in question. They had proposed the idea to Sarah that she could bunk in the wing of old house with Cody, but she would have none of it, and in truth, Jess understood. The unused rooms, lofty and dank, seemed to whisper with voices from the past. To a child the prospect of staying alone in the deserted wing of the old house would feel lonely and frightening. Jess suggested that they could pitch a tent on the lawn where Sarah could sleep. Daniel vetoed that idea—if, for any reason, Sarah awoke and wandered too close to the cliffs, she would be in danger. Sarah begged to sleep in Daniel's VW bus, an idea both he and Jess turned down flat. He encouraged a bed by the fire. Jess concurred that this was the only option, not unlike the experience of camping when everyone slept in a tent, and so it was agreed: Sarah would "camp" at the hearth in her sleeping bag. What they relinquished in privacy was miniscule compared to the sense of contentment Jess felt that Daniel respected her daughter's needs.

Nearby Jess rested in the rocker, mesmerized by the fire's orange flames, smoke curling and twisting up the blackened bricks of the chimney. Daniel stretched out beside her on the floor, pushing the rung of the rocker. "This has been a lovely day," she whispered.

"I agree," he said, speaking low. "The surf was bitchin'. I even got in a few rides."

Jess looked down at him. "What did you say?"

"You know, the surf was better than I expected. Usually it's dead in the middle of the day."

She stiffened. "Where was Sarah?"

"On the beach. Cody was with her," he said in an off-handed way.

"Cody?" She stood abruptly. "Are you kidding?"

"Hey, don't get all exercised about this. You're going to wake the kid." He guided her away from the fire, out the door, and into the night. She paced on the lawn, her feet soaked with dew. When he attempted to catch her, she pulled away. "Will you stop and listen or do I have to pin you to the ground?"

She halted in front of him, her arms folded across her chest. "I'm listening."

"Before I went into the water, Sarah agreed to stay on the beach and play near the rocks. We had a system. If she needed me for any reason she would come to the edge of the surf and wave my red bandana. Under no condition would she leave the area or go into the water."

"You call that a system?" Jess nearly shouted. "What do you know? You're not a parent. She could have fallen on the rocks and hit her head. For god's sake, Daniel, you don't leave an eight-year-old on the beach, even in the company of the world's most amazing dog."

"Don't go ballistic on me, Jess, and don't accuse me of something that isn't true. I would never put Sarah in danger."

Standing her ground, Jess glared at Daniel, her pulse hammering in her head.

"Let me finish. After we made our agreement, we hung out for a while and Sarah made friends with a little boy. The mom was there. When I spoke to the woman she said she'd keep an eye on her. When I got back, Sarah and the boy were on a blanket eating brownies."

"Brownies?" she asked, a knot of distrust unspooling in her stomach.

"Homemade, in fact. No additives." he added, a smile teasing his lips. "I had a few myself."

"Do you know the woman?"

"I've seen her before. She's a weekender."

"How long were you gone?"

"Maybe thirty minutes."

She dropped her arms, anger draining completely out of her body. "At dinner, Sarah did mention playing with a little boy."

"They took to one another pretty fast."

"Now, I'm embarrassed."

"Don't be."

"Annie accuses me of being a neurotic who's always expecting disaster. What do you think?"

"Hey, what do I know? I'm not a parent." He laughed and reached for her. "Come here, psycho woman. Put your fears to rest."

* * *

Daniel and Jess lay in his bed facing one another. The briny ocean breeze lifted up from the beach, over the rocky cliffs onto the lawn, and through the open windows.

Daniel ran his fingers through her hair, speaking low. "Talk to me about dancing."

"I'm too tired," she said.

"Come on."

"Talking about dance is like talking about bowling." She fluttered her eyelids and spoke in sotto. "Boring."

"I've watched you work out. I can tell you're in the zone."

She stretched beside him like a cat waking up from a nap. "I'd rather you scratched my back."

She turned over, and he ran his hand from the small of her back up to her neck, his fingertips massaging her shoulder blades. His touch melted the soreness across her back.

"You're physically stronger than most women I know." He paused between long strokes. "Right?"

"Ummm," she said, her face pressed against a pillow. "I guess."

"When you dance you're moving over the floor in a kind of willful suspension. Maybe there's more risk in the water, but we're both working against gravity. You look like you'd fly if you could."

She smiled to herself. "You know, I could never resist dancing. Maybe it's the music. I was always the first one up—even as a child. It's never been a choice one way or the other. I studied ballet all through school, but as a teenager, modern dance fit my body. It spoke to me."

His hand lingered at the small of her back, pausing, smoothing her muscles, stroking her skin. "Keep talking," he said.

"Dance is making shapes with your body to tell a story. It's kinetic art, pure, absolute in the moment. Every detail is essential. Choreography is the challenge, technique the killer. Sometimes you're working with the music, sometimes against it. John Cage changed the landscape of sound. Sometimes his dancers move in silence. There isn't anything more perfect. You can't screw it up or wear it down or give it a disease. It doesn't go bad. I can't imagine doing anything else."

Daniel's hand rested on her hip and slowly grew heavier; his breathing deepened, smooth and even.

"Daniel," she whispered. "Are you awake?"

He sighed and pulled her closer. She turned to face him and hitched herself up onto one elbow to check on Sarah across the floor in front of the fire. The embers had extinguished. A feeling of contentment washed over her. She adjusted the pillow under her head, pulled her knees up, and spooned against his body. He murmured something low and unintelligible. She exhaled, closed her eyes, and thought about the grant. Tomorrow Daniel would take them home, and she would suggest to him that he return to Bolinas so that she and Sarah could get ready for the week ahead. Soon everything would change, she told herself. A new era would begin, and she would know how it feels to have a career that promises financial freedom.

* * *

After a glorious weekend of May's teasing promise of endless spring, the fog attacked the coast, rolled through the Gate, and descended on the city like a merciless captor.

Inside Project Artaud's dance studio, Jess straddled a metal folding chair in a corner under the clerestory windows latched tight against the cold. Beside her, Claire had lay on the floor, clutching her sweatshirt to her chest. Within the building, a cry echoed behind the double metal doors leading to the floors above.

Dressed in black jeans and a worn jacket, Sebastian darted across the floor, feinting and ducking, throwing punches like a street fighter. When he turned, the veins in his neck bulged, the skin at his throat purple and blotchy.

"We're screwed!" he shouted.

Questions lodged in Jess's throat. Months of studio work, selecting, and rejecting scores to fit the choreography, envisioning how the work would answer the mission to empower kids and change communities, countless revisions on the grant, the benefactor's stipend given as assurance that they would be among the selected—all of it evaporated.

Sebastian's fury drained the oxygen from the studio. Claire scooted closer to Jess, reached up, and took her hand. "I thought it was a done deal," she said.

Sebastian halted in front of them. "I thought, you thought—who the hell cares? The assholes selected companies they deemed had more inner city experience. I suppose if I was queer or a Chicano I might have qualified."

"Come on, man," Claire said. "You don't mean that. There must be some explanation. The benefactor said our acceptance was in the bag."

"Yeah, well, what did he know?" he said, pulling out a letter that he'd crumbled into a tight ball. Hand shaking, he thrust it at Claire. "It's here in black and white from *The Office of His Honor, Mayor Joseph Alioto*. We regret to inform you, blah blah blah. You read it. I'm out of here." He threw himself against the door to the street, the wind blasting into the studio.

Claire scooped up her bag off the floor. "Listen, Jess, I know this sounds like a train wreck. Don't give up yet."

"Where are you going?" Jess asked.

"After him. He shouldn't be alone. I'll call you later."

* * *

Jess slouched in her car, too stunned to turn on the ignition, too numb to think. Battered cars parked along the curb, figures huddled against the wind, pinched faces blank, hands jammed in their pockets.

It felt like a curtain was closing, and she couldn't see what was on the other side. She was tired of being broke, tired of scraping by each month. She needed legitimacy, recognition, a living wage. She turned on the motor and drove through the streets, barely noticing the traffic around her.

By the time she reached the bridge, she knew what she had to do. She stopped at the Book Depot in Mill Valley and bought a *Marin Independent Journal* and picked up a *Pacific Sun*. At home, she checked the mail slot. An airmail package was wedged in the box. In Parker's hand, addressed to Sarah, was a package post-marked London, May 13. "Now what?" she muttered. "Parker drops from sight for seven weeks, doesn't return my calls, and now he sends a souvenir?" She unlocked the door and furiously jammed the package into the top shelf in her studio closet. She would not allow Parker to buy Sarah's affections. She fed the cat, made a peanut butter and jelly sandwich, and poured the last of the cold morning coffee into a glass.

Nibbling on the sandwich, Jess spread open the *Pacific Sun* on the table and turned to the back of the paper to the classified ads. For years her one goal was to focus on dancing, juggle her time to be home for Sarah, and scrape together an existence as a dance teacher until she could support herself as a professional dancer. She had resisted working at any job that diluted her goal. Now she needed a paycheck. In Help Wanted, she traced the listings with her finger. Any job that began with secretary, office assistant, or receptionist she skipped. Then something caught her eye: *Mill Valley Unified School District needs summer school bus drivers.*

Experience not necessary. Will train. Part-time hours, benefits and good pay.

She circled it with a black felt pen and kept reading. *Local Pet Store needs part time worker for 20 hours a week. Minimum wage. Friendly staff.*

She hesitated, circled it, and then crossed it out. No way, she thought. One cat box was enough. At the bottom of the listings, she read: *Wanted: Cocktail Waitresses. Experience necessary. Mill Valley. Call 383-4747.*

She chewed on the end of her pen and looked up from the paper. How hard could it be? Annie had waitressed at the Kezar Bar and Grill a few years back when she hit a bad patch. Most nights she walked away with a wad of cash. "It's simple, honey," she told Jess. "The shorter the skirt, the bigger the tips."

"Mom, I'm home!" Sarah yelled, throwing open the door. Amber straggled in behind, jacket clutched in her hand as it dragged on the ground, leaves and twigs and bits of debris clinging to the frayed cuffs. Sarah slammed the door, sighed heavily, and tossed her backpack and Scooby Doo lunch box onto the table.

Jess closed the paper. "Hi Sarah. Hi, Amber. How are you?"

"Me and Amber are hungry," Sarah said. "What's to eat?"

"Fig Newton's are in the cabinet. Bananas on the countertop. Milk is in the fridge. Don't drink it all."

"Yuck, that's all you ever buy."

"Okay, Miss Fussy Budget, fix peanut butter and jelly sandwiches and don't be so ungrateful."

Sarah flopped on the floor next to Amber, who lazed in a patch of sun beside the cat who'd crawled out from under the bed. "What's to eat at your house?" Sarah asked.

"Umm," Amber said, stroking the fur on the cat's back, "maybe root beer, ice cream, bologna, chips, stuff like that."

Jess lifted her eyes from the Sun. Good nutrition versus sugar and salt? It was a losing battle.

"Hey, Mom, we're going down to Amber's." Sarah started for the door.

"Not so quickly, young lady."

Sarah looped back to her mother, put her arms around her neck, and leaned into shoulder.

"Guess the food down there is better. Just don't spoil dinner." Jess smoothed Sarah's hair from her face. "How was school today?"

"Fine. I got picked first in kick ball."

Jess continued to run her fingers through the tangles in Sarah's hair. "My star athlete," she said. "We'll have to shampoo your hair tonight. Don't be gone too long." She remembered the package from Parker hidden in her studio closet, and felt a stab of guilt. However feeble or infrequent, wasn't it her duty to foster their channels of communication? Both she and Annie had agreed they didn't want to be the kind of mothers who withheld visitation or complained bitterly to their children about their fathers. In restaurants, coffee houses, and on the street, they heard women gossiping loudly about their rotten ex-husbands. She told Sarah to wait one minute.

She retreated to her studio and emerged with the package in her hand.

Sarah read the address label. "It's from Dad. The stamps say Great Britain. What's he doing there?" she asked suspiciously.

Jess hunched her shoulders and shook her head. "I don't know. Probably business."

"How come he never calls anymore?"

Jess shrugged. "Go on. Open it."

Ripping at the string, Sarah tore open the brown paper to reveal a box wrapped in white issue paper, tied with red ribbon. A small card fell to the table. Sarah picked it up and read the inscription, "To Sarah. Love, Dad." She untied the ribbon, slipped off the tissue, and lifted the lid off the box. Inside, a brown bear was nestled in the folds of more tissue. He had long curved arms, matted fur, a black button nose and eyes, and was dressed in a faded red vest and a crumbling straw hat encircled by a black band.

"What's this?" she asked.

"He's Paddington Bear," Jess said. "A very famous English bear. Don't you remember reading about him?"

"Nope, not really." She fingered the edges of the vest and sniffed his fur. "He smells sour, and he's all worn out."

"He must be an antique, really quite special."

"Not to me," Sarah said. "I'm not a baby anymore."

"This is a more a collector's item. Something to hold onto for the future."

"Who cares," she said, dangling the bear by his arm, twirling him in jerky circles and flinging him across the room where he dropped onto the floor. "Come on, Amber. Let's go down to your house."

Amber scrambled to her feet and followed Sarah.

Jess watched in amazement. Never had Sarah rejected a gift from her father, nor criticized him in front of a friend. Usually a gift would be a source of pride to brag about, cherish, and add to a collection of other gifts arranged and displayed in her room for friends to see.

Sarah stopped at the door. "Hey, Mom, is Danny coming over tonight?"

Jess was staring at the card from Parker. The man she once knew intimately, his DNA stamped all over her daughter, was a stranger to her. Sarah's words brought her up short. "Yes. After dinner."

"That's good," she said. "I like it when he's here. I wish he lived with us."

Chapter 13

June 1

JACKET STRAINING ACROSS HIS BACK, doused with Aramis cologne, Stewart banked his car down Waldo Grade and cruised through the rainbow tunnel. Before him the twin International Orange towers of the Golden Gate Bridge pierced the night sky. Thin layers of fog twisted midway about the towers slicing them in half, so that the monolithic structures appeared to detach and float in the air. With the city in sight, a feeling akin to relief flooded through his chest.

As he sailed onto the deck of the bridge a chill ran down his back, though not from the brisk drop in temperature or the wind streaming through the open window. At the gateway to the City, an exhilarating sense of the unknown prickled his neck.

Passing under the arches of the north tower, he sniffed the air like a hound. The faces of his young students, fellow teachers, and parents faded as if they were apparitions. Ahead, the neon clock over the tollbooth read 9:22.

To his left, shrouded in fog, Alcatraz climbed out of the bay, fixed, immobile, its prison walls clinging to an island of granite soil and cliffs. Tonight it seemed close enough to touch, and for an instant, Stewart considered the men who had been incarcerated there. Abruptly, the memory of Bill Mitchell, the mechanic in his father's shop, crossed his mind. An underwater tow of emotions surfaced, part curiosity, part aversion, and underneath, the undeniable tug of lust, surprising Stewart with its intensity. It was as if Mitchell slouched beside him against the seat, cigarette burning in the cup of his callused hand, elbow balanced on the door. The sweet, gut-wrenching scent of Old Spice spun in Stewart's nostrils. Mitchell was the kind who'd land in jail, serve time in prison, or disappear into a city scraping by in seedy rent-by-the-week hotel and hanging out in porn shops. Or he could make it in the woods living like a lone wolf, getting by on fishing and odd jobs. Stewart speculated at his age, maybe fifty; in his memory Mitchell was ageless.

The roadway split, and Stewart veered onto Doyle Drive toward the Marina. The facades of the stucco Italianate homes along the bay were decorated with wrought-iron balconies and fluted columns. Here and there, a stark modern house interrupted the predictable and ordered architecture, fronted by formal gardens, all of which cheered Stewart. Through floor-to-ceiling plate glass windows he gazed into rooms lit by sparkling chandeliers and glimpsed people seated at dining tables. He placed himself at one of the long, polished tables and imagined his own guests, gay men mixing with straight friends, discussing politics, art, theater, and sports.

He breezed by the jaunty sailboats in the narrow berthing of St. Francis Yacht Club, bobbing masts strung with white lights, and hooked a turn onto Bay Street. The street ran steady for blocks, then crested over the lower hump of Russian Hill across the Hyde Street cable car tracks. A cable car carried tourists who white-knuckled the grip bars as it nose-dived off the hill, their gleeful cries sounding above the clang and shriek of steel wheels against steel tracks.

In North Beach, Stewart cruised the blocks at the brow of Telegraph Hill, found a parking spot near the top, hopped out of the car, and sauntered down the pitched street. On a side street off Grant Avenue, he entered through the swinging doors of the Silver Spur Bar and Restaurant.

Patrons at the front swiveled their heads to check out the newcomer. Men and women were smoking and drinking along the bar and jammed into tables. Heterosexual couples hobnobbed among gay couples, straight singles partied alongside gay singles. To the casual eye it looked like one big party. To Stewart, gay from straight was easily distinguishable. Here he could expect a certain full frontal male appraisal, a keening interest, unabashed and sexual. It stated loud and clear that any man was entitled to couple with another man, whenever and wherever he wished.

Stewart surveyed gay men who had wandered out of the financial district, ties loosened on their Oxford shirts, suited up from Brooks Brothers, wing-tip shoes polished to a high shine; men dressed to kill from the fashion salons of Wilkes Bashford, silk and cashmere draping their chiseled bodies; men from advertising in the Embarcadero who spun clever ideas and married words and jingles to subliminal desires; men from interior design in Jackson Square whose taste ran from Rococo to Bauhaus; men from the 'burbs dressed like urban cowboys in leather vests, jeans, and cowboy boots who switch-hit every chance they could; and men who were still boys from Ohio, Colorado, and Florida, whose uncles or cousins were showing them a night on the town. Light played on the planes of their faces and molecules collided in what little air was left around their bodies.

Savoring the moment to be in the company of gay men, Stewart pushed his way to the bar and ordered a Budweiser.

A pudgy, red-faced man whose button-down white collar was choking his neck shouted in Stewart's ear, "How's it going?" Perspiration trickled down his temples and onto his cheeks.

"Couldn't be better. How about you?"

"Hell of a night," the man said. "Love this town. A little bit of everything." His eyes twinkled behind large-framed glasses. He withdrew a pressed white linen handkerchief from the inside pocket of his suit jacket and mopped his brow. He offered a plump hand, "The name's Harry. Pleased to meet you."

His soft palm and feathery touch curled around Stewart's firm grip. They joined into easy banter while Stewart, hopped up on anticipation, continued to check out men of every imaginable shape and size, inclination and proclivity. Harry gazed up into Stewart's face, too adoringly, Stewart thought, and continued to dab his brow with the handkerchief.

A thin, razor-nosed man sporting a handlebar mustache and a black cowboy hat lounged at a table in the middle of the floor.

From a distance, he flirted brazenly with Stewart. Cowboys left him lukewarm, itchy for other bait. Another man with a receding hairline and watery blue eyes vied for Stewart's attention by smoothing the front of his raspberry pink Lacoste shirt and flaring his nostrils.

Stewart turned his shoulder, ordered a second beer, and listened to Harry with one ear while noticing a buff stranger who leaned against the wall at the far end of the restaurant. The hair on the back of Stewart's arms prickled with curiosity. The man stood with one foot crossed over the other, occasionally dipping his dark head toward a frizzy-haired blonde next to him. His hair was tied in a loose ponytail. The white T-shirt he wore gleamed against his olive-toned complexion; a tattoo wrapped around his bicep. He grasped the neck of a beer, black hair curling around his forearms. The thumb of his other hand was hooked into the pocket of his Levi's, fingers splayed against his hip. The stranger looked up at Stewart, his stare unflinching. They openly appraised one another; a perceptible stirring clicked between them. The stranger nodded at Stewart. Stewart nodded back.

"So, I'd judge you're not from these parts," Harry said.

"What did you say?" Stewart asked. Without a word exchanged, he felt as if the man had grasped him by the throat and held him captive.

"Am I right?"

"About what?" Harry's voice droned on in his ear.

"You're from somewhere else."

"Does it show?" Stewart asked. He watched the stranger set down his beer on a table where a group of men congregated. The stranger, without breaking eye contact with Stewart, leaned over the shoulder of one of the men and spoke in his ear.

"It's the way you talk. For instance you say about like it rhymes with shoot. Are you Canadian?"

Stewart laughed. "Hell, no. Guess I can't shake that Upper Michigan twang."

"I like it," Harry commented merrily.

The stranger straightened and began to thread a path between the chairs towards him. Stewart felt a surge of adrenaline.

Harry turned and followed Stewart's gaze.

"It's been nice talking to you, buddy," Stewart said. He clapped Harry on the shoulder.

"Indeed it has," Harry said, a note of genuine regret in his voice.

Stewart did not give Harry a backward glance. Hunger and desire had coalesced into one driving force that summoned him to the stranger's side. They met in the aisle, and the stranger parted his lips as if to speak, revealing a front tooth capped in gold. The stranger nodded, turned and walked rapidly toward a corridor where a woman stood in a phone booth, talking loudly. Stewart hesitated. He could hear blood pounding in his eardrums. The stranger walked down the corridor and disappeared around a corner. When Stewart reached the corner, he saw three closed doors at the far end. The first door was labeled "Ladies," the second "Gents." He tried the men's room, but it was locked. Confused, he paused, and wiped the sweat from his palms onto his jeans. The third door, past the bathrooms, was unmarked. Stewart placed his hand on the doorknob. It fell slowly open. Every fiber of his being was on alert. The interior was unlit and black. Something stringy and damp knocked against his ear. The sting of Lysol assaulted his nose. A primitive warning sounded in his brain but before he could move his feet, a hand reached out of the darkness and pulled him in. The man's face came in hard against his face, teeth smashing against Stewart's mouth. The salty taste of blood rippled on his tongue. Rough arms pushed him against a wall, a chokehold on his neck. A moan strangled in Stewart's throat; the throb of sexual desire flagged and vanished in one terrified instant.

The first blow hit him in the stomach. He buckled and fell to his knees, grunting for air. He tried to stand and fell against something hard and sharp. The sound of metal crashing to the floor split his ears. The second blow ripped across his shoulders, lancing like a blunt rod. He raised his hands to shield his head. Blows rained down on his back. The man trussed him like a hog and ripped his jeans down and raped him without a word. Stewart's body became a dark well of pain. Battered, he panted like a wounded animal. A crack of light shone from the door, and the room went black again. The man was gone. Stewart slumped to the floor and helplessly plummeted through ever narrowing bands of consciousness. When he came to, panic racked his half-naked body. Momentarily he didn't know where he was or what had happened until the sickening smell of Lysol jerked him back to the sensation of the cement floor that was gritty against his cheek, and he felt something wet under his fingers. He stumbled to his feet, tripping, freed his arms, and pulled up his jeans. Gasping for breath, he cracked open the door and crept into the hallway. The men's room was empty. He bolted the door.

Dizzy and sick with self-recrimination, he crouched over the sink, spitting out saliva flecked with blood. He ran his tongue over his teeth while washing his hands, letting cold water run over his arms and splashing it on his face and head. When he raised his eyes to the mirror, he recoiled from his image. His eyes were puffy. A red welt ran from his check to his neck and the collar of his jacket was ripped away at the seam. *You stupid son of a bitch,* he thought. *Mix with the rough trade and get your brains beaten out.* He applied wet paper towels to the pulpy tissue of his face and neck and attempted to clean himself, but unless he wore a mask there wasn't any way he could disguise his injuries. He patted his hair, zipped up his jacket, and tried to stop shivering.

Forcing himself out of the bathroom, he advanced down the corridor, using the walls to steady himself. The smell of red wine and garlic drifting down the hallway nauseated him. *All I have to do is get to the front door,* he thought. He braced himself and stepped into the bar. A wall of noise hit him. He stumbled forward in the aisle. People seemed to step aside as he navigated toward the exit. Above the din, he heard a female voice call his name. He flinched, turning up the collar of his jacket.

Jesus Christ, somebody's calling my name. Maybe a parent from school. Could this night go any worse? He shrunk inside his jacket and lurched away, walking as fast as he could, trying not to fall.

Abruptly, Harry appeared at Stewart's elbow, his touch gentle, voice high-pitched and urgent. "Hi there, buddy. Where you been? What happened?"

"I got tied up," Stewart said, trying to crack a smile, but wincing when a jolt of pain ripped across his back. "Get me out of here fast."

"Hang on," Harry said. "We're on our way."

"Thank you," Stewart mumbled, nearly crying with relief.

"Righto then," Harry said, and ushered him out the door.

The air was chilled, thick fog bathing Stewart's battered face. Cars and taxis zoomed by on the street. The beam of headlights jumped and flashed against the buildings and storefronts. A fire engine wailed across town.

Harry guided Stewart onto the sidewalk, continuing to hold his arm. "That dude worked you over hard."

"Hey, what do I know? I'm a fool hick from Michigan."

"It doesn't have to be like this."

"Please, spare the lectures," Stewart mumbled.

"I take it you drove?"

"Yes, I did."

"Can you make it home?" Harry asked, his eyes watery with worry.

"I think so."

"Where's your car?"

"Near the top of the hill."

"Let's walk. The air will do you good."

The men walked silently, pausing twice to stop and catch their breath. As they climbed higher, the harsh sounds from the neighborhood below became a distant babble meant for revelers whose luck was still running high. The wooden houses marched up the hill, side by side. A cat curled in a windowsill draped in lace curtains.

When they came abreast of Stewart's car, Harry waited as he unlocked the door. "Do you feel better?"

"I do," Stewart said, crawling inside, his legs stiff and shaking with fatigue. "Thank you."

"You sure?"

"All I want to do is get home." The insides of his mouth tasted like sour pulp and he kept wetting his lips.

Harry dug in his pocket and pulled out a leather cardholder. He withdrew a white business card and handed it to Stewart. By the lights in the dash, Stewart peered at the card, the print blurry:

Harry Dunbar
Sales Manager
Premier Printing

"Anytime you want to talk, give me a call."

"You've been a champ," Stewart offered.

"Yeah, that's me. A champ." Harry closed the door and backed away.

Stewart made a U-turn in the middle of the street. Eyes blind with tears, knuckles scraped, shoulders searing with pain, he gripped the steering wheel and braked down the hill.

Chapter 14

June 1

FROM A TABLE AT THE SILVER SPUR, Daniel peered through the smoky haze and observed Jess in the same way he studied the waves off the Bolinas coast—absorbed and alert—a master at detecting signs and waiting for optimum conditions. At the tables around him the crescendo of voices heightened the atmosphere of diners with unrestrained appetite and gusto enjoying a night on the town. Moments earlier, after finishing their meal, Jess had threaded her way through the tables toward the bathroom, but now she paused in the narrow aisle between the restaurant and bar, and appeared to be watching a man she seemed to recognize. From this distance, Daniel tried to capture the small motions of her head and expressions of her face. He kept asking himself how he could have fallen in love with her so quickly, and if by scrutinizing her from a distance, he could catch some detail or meaning he missed from close range and understand what had happened to him.

When she turned toward him, he noticed that her smile was false—it was separated from her eyes and pasted to her teeth. Then Daniel saw a man weaving on his feet, and he caught a raw, mask-like expression on the man's battered face. He felt something in his gut slide sideways, unforgiving and oily. The bitter taste of adrenaline filled his mouth. He was sure he noticed the same man earlier at the bar. *Goddamn,* he thought, *the dude looks like he just got the crap beaten out of him.* Instantly, he stood to help, but she held her hand up and waved him back. He hesitated and returned to the table. By then, an older gentleman had intervened, guiding the man toward the exit, and Jess had turned in the opposite direction, moving down the hall.

A childhood memory of a Christmas in San Francisco came to Daniel. Ceci had taken him to visit Santa Claus at Macy's Department Store; in preparation she'd polished him like an apple—hair wetted across his forehead, the tails of his plaid shirt tucked into dark pants, a clip-on tie fastened under his chin, and his arms stuffed into a green corduroy jacket that smelled like pennies. Buzzing with anticipation at seeing Santa, he'd held Ceci's hand as they strolled through Union Square between ladies pushing baby carriages, old people walking with canes, and men in business suits and hats.

The Christmas tree in Union Square, bigger than any he had ever seen, reached as tall as the stone statue holding a flame in the middle of the square. Festooned in red bows and tinsel, red lights twinkled in the tree's great branches. He strained to chase the pigeons, but Ceci grasped his hand firmly, guiding him at a steady pace. Alongside the walk where they passed, two men staggered from a patch of grass separated from the square by a low concrete wall. They stumbled toward one another bellowing insults. Only standing as tall as their belts, Daniel saw their dark forms lurch against one another. The heaviest man lunged with animal savagery. Daniel heard the impact of bone against cartilage. Bright blood spurted from the man's putty-colored nose and dribbled down the stubble of his chin. The fumes of stale beer and urine rushed from beneath their tattered coats. Terrified, Daniel sank to his knees, covering his eyes, until Ceci lifted him off the ground and sprinted with him across the square, where she held him until he could stand without his legs buckling.

Now the pulpy sound of the smashing fist and the trajectory of blood transposed itself across Daniel's vision. The same sense of revulsion that visited him as a child constricted his chest. His hands started to sweat, his breath quickened. Here in the restaurant there was no mistaking a sense of violation in this man's helpless face and Daniel felt an overwhelming tenderness toward Jess, who had wanted to come to his aid.

When she returned to their table, Daniel stood and pulled out her chair. "What was that about?" he asked.

She was visibly shaken, her face drained of color. "I know that guy."

Daniel pulled her chair closer. "Who is he?"

"His name is Stewart Merch. He's a sixth-grade teacher at Old Mill. Did you see his face?"

"I couldn't miss it," he said. "How well do you know him?"

"Not well. He's Annie's son's teacher, and she's been hustling him, but he doesn't seem interested . . ." her voice trailed off.

Daniel stared into her eyes. "Maybe there's a reason for that." He had heard the account of Jess's split with her friend and knew she was conflicted about their dispute. He understood her range of emotions—a righteous attitude that Annie had been in the wrong, anger that Annie wouldn't own up to it, and disappointment that the incident had torn them apart. Daniel empathized, but finding himself in that yawning middle ground that happens with families after a quarrel when no one makes a move to repair the damage, he wasn't in any position to give advice. Was it possible that neither Jess nor Annie picked up on what was here in plain sight?

"Like what?" Her eyes swept over the clientele as if she was in an arboretum trying to identify rare plant species.

"Take a look around." The crowd stood three deep. A backwash of voices and laughter bounced off the walls.

"What do you mean?"

"Half the men in here are gay."

"What?" Jess replied, stunned and unconsciously chewing on her lower lip.

"Check out the table over my shoulder. The guys drinking beer at the big round table. Do you see any women with them? And those dudes along the wall. Not a straight one in that line-up."

"What are you saying?"

"I'd bet money that Stewart Merch is gay."

"No way! Annie wouldn't be after him if he were gay." Jess's eyes continued to sweep over the faces of men and women in conversation, drinking and eating. "Why would she bother?"

"Maybe she doesn't know."

"Annie knows everything."

"Don't be so sure about that," he said. "Some guys keep it under wraps. Other guys flaunt it." He had known a few boys who appeared right from the get-go to be wired differently, and he had friends from Berkeley who were gay. "Come on, don't you read the papers? This is the City of Love. Where've you been? Under a rock?"

"You really think he's gay?" She seemed to be trying to break through a fog of incomprehension.

"It's possible he tangled with the wrong guy. Maybe dope or poppers got added into the mix and things got out of hand. It can get ugly fast. You saw the older guy who helped him out?"

"What about him?"

"Definitely gay."

Her eyes narrowed and fixed on a point across the room as if she was trying to bring into focus a picture that wouldn't jell.

"If I'm right, he's hurting right now." Daniel said. "He was pretty worked over."

"I should call Annie."

"There's someplace I've been meaning to show you. We'll find a phone booth along the way."

"Maybe tomorrow would be better."

"Whatever you want."

She reached for her jacket. "I could use some fresh air."

"Come on," he said, taking her by the arm. "We'll walk."

* * *

A street lamp illuminated the high wrought-iron fence at the front of the law firm of Gessler, Burrows, and Blake and the embossed letters of the sign on the gate. Old jasmine vines in full bloom twisted around the spires of the fence creating a screen and obscuring the interior courtyard. As Daniel approached the building, a strong sense of pride and ownership emerged from underneath the bitterness of his uncle's iron-fisted domination. A familiar yearning for his grandfather surfaced. Had he been alive, Daniel could have easily sought Popee's counsel concerning his ambivalence about studying law. He would have listened and given Daniel assurance about choosing a correct path, and, on any given day, no matter what his vigorous schedule, Daniel knew he would have welcomed Jess and shown her the same respect he extended to everyone regardless of age, social standing, or education.

At the gate, Jess stopped beside him. "Is this your family's law firm?"

"Yes." He unlatched it, and ushered Jess into the courtyard. "Now Charlie runs it like a cruise destroyer. I've been meaning to stop and pay a visit."

Two brass carriage lamps gleamed on either side of a carved oak door. Behind latticed windows, the heavy folds of drapes hung against the glass. Gritty shadows scattered across the brick entry.

"At this hour?" she asked.

He could see the wariness in her eyes. On the sidewalk he heard the voices of pedestrians as they drew closer. He waited until they passed. "Look, I'd rather have it out with Charlie face to face, but that's out of the question. Something he said to me in our last meeting keeps running through my mind."

"Like what?" she asked.

Headlights from a passing car flickered over the brick facade and crawled up the adjoining wall, cross-hatched in thick ivy. He backed Jess into the jasmine vines, the scent of their sweet milky fragrance unlocking a vault of memories when he was a child.

"A crack about knowing the Dean of Admissions. I don't buy it. Charlie is up to something. I can feel it in my blood." He realized he'd been brooding on this idea for weeks. Every part of him was fully awake. "Think of this as an undercover mission."

"Look, from everything you've told me, I can understand why you're angry at your uncle. But are you sure this is the way you want to go about it?"

"I am. But I don't want to force you into doing something you don't want to do."

"I've been known to act impulsively." She hesitated. "Especially in the name of justice."

"A freedom fighter," he said, grinning. "I should have known."

"Don't get carried away. Just tell me you've got a fail-safe plan for getting in. I'm not up for any more surprises tonight."

"I know every inch of this place." He wanted to assuage her fears and settle her jitters. "But I don't want to put you in jeopardy. City Lights is about six blocks away. You can walk there, and then I'll catch up with you later."

She glanced around the entry and toward the darkened windows of the buildings to either side of the law firm. "I don't know."

"It's up to you." With or without her he was going in.

"Is there an alarm?"

"There's a night patrol. Once we're inside we'll be safe."

She pulled her jacket tighter to her chest. "How long will it take you to get in?"

"Five minutes, max. I'll go in through the skylight on the roof." From up the street, a door slammed; shrill voices rang out.

"What about the patrol?"

"I saw the car cruise by when we were walking. They won't be back for at least an hour."

She nodded. "Make it quick. If anything goes wrong, I'm out of here."

"Trust me," he said, "I'll open the front door in five minutes. Stay right here." He stepped away and swiftly scaled a gnarled plum tree near the side of the building, hoisting himself from one branch to another and crawling onto the roof. Cat-walking to the skylight, he pried open the steel edge of the skylight with the flat screwdriver of a pocket knife. He lowered himself into the opening and dropped noiselessly onto the thick carpet of the center hallway. He inhaled deeply and surveyed the area. A hush emanated up and down the long hallway. Canister lights cast his shadow onto the floor. He moved down the hall, cracked open the front door and waved Jess inside. Exhilaration coursed through his body. She slipped in beside him. He closed the door and threw the deadbolts.

"Thank god," she said. "Waiting was driving me crazy."

"Sorry about that," he said, guiding her across the floor. The smell of leather-bound books and furniture wax wafted from the shadows.

He motioned to a group of upholstered chairs, couches, tables, and potted palms. "This is the reception area," he said, "and further down the hall is Estelle's office." Phone cords dropped from the desk and snaked across the floor. "Estelle is an institution here. She keeps an eagle eye on who comes and goes."

They moved down the hall past a succession of dour-faced males who peered out from oil portraits. Daniel paused in front of a door and opened it. It was like entering a portal to a lost world. "This is the conference room." From the coffered ceiling, low lights illuminated a massive oak table flanked by high-backed chairs. "When I was a kid, my grandfather let me play in here during annual meetings. Afterwards he'd take me out to lunch—just the two of us. Everywhere we went people loved him."

Farther down the hall, Daniel paused in front of the next door, turned the doorknob, and closed the door behind them. "This was my grandfather's office. Now it's Charlie's." His skin crawled recalling Charlie's attack on him during the meeting six weeks earlier. The semi-sweet leather aroma of cigar smoke laced the air. A mahogany desk dominated the room, claw feet grabbing at a Persian carpet and lions' heads silently roaring at his approach. Quickly Daniel crossed to the window and closed the drapes across the slanted Venetian blinds. A green glass lamp glowed on the desk. He sat down, leaned back, and laced his fingers behind his head. "Do I look like I belong here or what?" he said.

Jess shrugged her shoulders and walked across the carpet between the leather chairs towards the desk. "Hurry up, Sherlock. Get down to business. We're not here for fun and games."

"I know you're nervous, but don't sweat it. There's a secret chamber behind the bookcase." He pointed to a section of the floor-to-ceiling bookcases that stretched across the opposite wall. "It was grandfather's inner sanctum."

"I guess that makes you brilliant, but I'm barely holding it together." She rubbed her arms as if she had a chill.

"You can lend a hand," he said.

"That's okay," she said. "I'll just take a look around."

"Fine," he said. He put his head down and began searching through the desk drawers.

"Is this a family portrait?" she asked.

He glanced up. She was standing and looking up at a large oil painting hung over the bar. The portrait had been a passive presence for so long he had ceased to really see it.

"My grandfather is in the middle. Dad's on the left and Charlie's on the right."

Jess stepped closer to the painting. "You look more like your grandfather and your uncle than your father."

Her comment produced an uneasy reaction he couldn't dismiss. While he was proud to look like his grandfather, any physical link to Charlie was like poison in his gut. "That's what a lot of people have said."

"And your father and his brother hardly resemble each other."

"They never have. My grandfather commissioned the painting before he had given up on Dad. Charlie was hacking it out at Hastings while Dad was boozing at Bolt." He tried to tune her out.

"You sound exasperated," she said. "What are you looking for?"

He threw up his hands in frustration. "The keys to Charlie's files!" he snapped.

"Don't bark at me," she retorted. "His desk is too obvious." She paused, one finger on her lips. He watched begrudgingly as she walked to the bar, slid open the liquor compartment, and squatted in front of the bottles. As she rummaged through the cabinet, he kept pawing through the drawer.

"Well, well," she said. When he glanced up, she was holding a small brass monkey attached to a ring of keys from her fingers.

"Bingo!" Daniel exclaimed. "For a lightweight, you're not half-bad."

"It must be my devious mind," she said, walking back and dropping the keys into his hand. "What's next?"

"I'll know it when I find it," he said, crouching in front of a bank of low oak cabinets under the window, testing the keys until the first cabinet opened.

"While you hunt, I'm going to check out the titles on the bookshelves."

"Suit yourself." He bent his head to the task, rapidly searching the folders, returning the contents to their original place, and locking the cabinet before going to the next one. In the middle cabinet, near the back, he found a folder marked with his name. He pulled it out and moved closer to the light to examine its contents. A thick docket of statements from the brokerage firm of Sutro and Co. addressed to the trust of Daniel C. Gessler, III, were bound together. His pulse started to race. He read through the statements past the listing of equities, bonds, and T-bills that carried to a second and third page. The balance appeared at the bottom of the page. He peered at a series of numbers that blurred beyond the 1.8 million dollar figure. He whistled softly. In the next folder, he found a bill for $753.00 from Northrup Investigations, which listed its services as having conducted surveillance of Daniel Gessler, III, during the months of January, February, and March.

"Jesus," he said. "Take a look at this."

She replaced a book, returned to the desk, and took the page from him. As she read her eyebrows raised, and she shook her head. "Your hunch was right. Charles isn't above using whatever method he can to get what he wants." She balanced on the edge of the desk and handed the bill back to him.

"You can't change the stripes on a cat, hey?" he said, and jammed it back into the file. Memos penned with Charlie's handwriting fluttered in his fingers. At the rear of the file, sandwiched between trust papers, he noticed an envelope hand-addressed in blue ink to Charles Gessler. The penmanship, a graceful, feminine script, piqued his curiosity. He peered closer. It was postmarked Paris, January 3, 1970, but the return address was blank. Daniel held the envelope under the glow from the green light. He was about to pull the contents from the torn flap when he heard a metallic clink echo down the passageway that ran between the law office and the adjacent building. Daniel cocked his ear, adrenaline pumping into his system. In rapid motion he signaled Jess to hit the floor.

The beam of a utility flashlight, a brilliant white light, flooded the narrow passageway. Daniel rolled off the chair and flattened himself against the cabinets. The light swept over the windows, seeping in through the slats and against the drapes. Boots struck the concrete walkway.

When the light passed, he hopped up, slid the folder back into the desk, and locked the cabinet. Hoisting Jess to her knees, he whispered into her ear, "Stay next to me." As they crawled across the floor, she shoved the keys inside the liquor cabinet. Together they crab-walked to the bookshelf. He slipped his hand between *Paradise Lost* and *Shakespeare's Sonnets* and pressed a concealed button. The rumble of gears rent the air, and the bookshelf split down the middle.

From the back of the building he heard the sound of a door being slammed shut.

"Get in," Daniel said, pushing her into the cavity. A cellar-like dampness struck his clammy face, and, as he stepped forward reaching for the lever on the inside wall to close the bookshelf, something cold and hard bumped against his forehead.

"Oh," Jess shuddered, twisting herself around and moving in close against Daniel's back before burying her face between his shoulder blades.

Again, the gears rumbled and the partitions began to close. Daniel heard the click of a door latch, and a faint voice called out, "Mr. Gess…" just as the two halves of the bookshelf hinged shut.

Sweat dripped in Daniel's armpits. The chamber, sealed in darkness, reeked of whiskey. Something acidic burned his throat. Maneuvering Jess around to face him, he steadied her in his arms. The minutes dragged on. He heard her swallowing, a sibilant sound escaping from her lips. He covered her mouth with his hand. "Don't say a word." She shook her head violently, pushing his hand away. He repositioned himself against her body and held her tight as he listened for any noise above their shallow breathing. Time seemed to suspend. He couldn't be certain how long they waited before Jess began to strain again from his grasp.

"I'm going nuts." She rubbed her face against his shoulder. "I can't see a thing."

"Let's try to get through this. We have one chance to get out of here. If the guard hears us, we're screwed."

"It smells sick in here," she said. "I can't breathe."

He loosened his hold on her arms and rocked her gently. He concentrated on detecting any sound outside the chamber. Minutes passed.

"I thought you knew what you were doing," she whispered. "What tipped the guard off?"

"Maybe the closed blinds. I'm not sure. Jess, I found something in the folder."

"What?" She stopped fidgeting in his arms.

"A letter, postmarked from Paris."

"Did you put it back?"

"No, I've got it right here," he said, patting his chest.

"Is there a light?"

"Wait. You hold the letter." He felt her hand take the envelope. "I've got a lighter."

"Hurry up. This place gives me the creeps."

Daniel took a Zippo out of his pocket and in one motion flipped it open and drew his thumb across the striker. The flame flared in the darkness. He saw a flash of metal dangling from hooks, and in the same instant, Jess ducked, covering her head with her hands. Only inches above their heads, a metal chain, manacles, cuffs, and a leather whip swung from the ceiling. The mental picture of his uncle, a paragon of propriety, pontificating before a judge and jury, member of the Huntington Club, corporate board member, starched as stiff as his shirt collar, shattered as if an ice floe had cracked beneath his feet. "What the hell?" he said, his voice reverberating inside the airless chamber.

"I don't know," she cried. " Get me out of here now."

* * *

On the street, Jess gulped the night air. Daniel kept pace beside her, spewing vindictives about his uncle. She half-walked, half-ran, weaving through the back streets of Jackson Square as if pursued by ghouls. Anger seethed at the base of her skull aimed at Daniel. She allowed herself be swept away in a risky proposition.

She thought she was untouchable; she was deluding herself. The plate glass windows of antique showrooms and shuttered bookstores glittered under the streetlights. The noise of the City was brittle, the smell of sewage flowing down the storm drains and rising through the grates. The more distance they put between themselves and the law firm, the louder a voice of admonition rang in her head. *Why did I let myself be coerced into something so foolish?* The shriek of a siren, a police car speeding down Columbus Street caused her pulse to thud again, and she sprinted down an alley.

Daniel caught up with her and grasped her arm. "Slow down," he said.

"Damn it," she said, shaking free of his grasp. "I could have done without any of that bullshit."

"Oh, I don't know," Daniel said. "It turns out Charles, the sanctimonious prick, is a crook and a weird fuck."

Out of the shadows, a couple appeared on the sidewalk walking toward them. As soon as they'd passed, she swung toward Daniel. Was he suppressing a smile? Did he think this was a lark? "Are you kidding? I'm not talking about anything you may have found or the kinky factor in that hideous room. The real question is, what if we had have been caught and booked?"

"Wait a minute, Jess. I told you that wouldn't happen."

"I'm not sure about that," she said, watching his eyes turn smoky.

"I am sure," he insisted.

She turned away from him and stalked down the alley. She couldn't bear to look at his face. His priorities were different than hers. It was useless trying to make him understand. If they had been taken into custody, what did he have to lose? A crippling blow of shame shot through her mind. How could she have called the Boynton's and ask them to bail her out of jail? Who would she have gone to for backup?

They walked onto Broadway, the sidewalks thick with tourists. They passed Enrico's, where bohemians and longhairs sipped wine and espresso with prominent locals at café tables on the sidewalk and wandered by Finochio's, where drag queens staged the best musical revue in the City. They blended into the crowd outside jazz joints where horns blared through the doors, moved past clubs where go-go dancers dressed in platform shoes and G strings jerked the frug under glitter balls, and at the corner of Columbus, they elbowed through tourists under Carol Doda's red neon breasts beckoning outside The Condor Club.

Further up Grant Avenue, they climbed Telegraph Hill and slowed their pace. He took her arm again. Row houses shared common walls, lamps in their windows, iron gates shut at the bottom of brick stairs. She could hear him breathing, feel him matching his stride to hers, wordless and brooding.

Finally, she couldn't contain her frustration. "Tell me how would you have handled the guard tonight if we had been caught? By saying you're entitled to break into the firm because you're a relative? "

"You think some flat-footed guard is going to book us? Come on. Get real."

"You don't know what you're talking about."

"Don't tell me what I know and don't know. You're getting bent out of shape over nothing."

Every piece of her wanted to smash his face and wipe away his smirk of self-righteous entitlement. She dug her foot into the concrete ridges of uphill sidewalk ready to run. Instantly she felt his hands pull her back, pinning her body to his. She kicked wildly, trying to break free, but he lifted her off the ground. It was a move with which she was familiar, but only on the stage with men who were trained in the mechanics of dance.

The bells of Sts. Peter and Paul Church in Washington Square pealed over the rooftops. She fought to break free, but Daniel held her tightly. "Come on, Jess, don't do this," he said. "We're okay. Nothing happened."

Gradually she stopped struggling, spent and exhausted. As he set her on her feet, still holding her, a flutter insinuated itself, and, like pages of a book riffling in a draft, beckoned. Time focused backwards to a still point. A tiny pressure built and popped in her ears, and then muffled silence.

Gazing past Daniel's shoulder toward a row house across the street, Jess blinked, trying to focus her vision. Was that Mickey in the entryway, leaning against a brick wall, watching her? The thin divide between reality and a dream balanced precariously. More guts than sense, Mickey seemed to cock his head and smile, as if to mock her, as if to say, *Is this what you wanted?*

Jess ducked her face into Daniel's shoulder and whispered, "Leave me alone."

"What did you say?" Daniel asked.

She raised her head and looked into his face. She noticed laugh lines radiating out from the corners of his eyes and the dark arch of his brows knit together. She smelled the sun-dried scent of his shirt; his hands broadcast warmth through her clothes onto her skin. *This is what is real,* she thought—*this time, this place, this man.*

Again she heard the bells of Sts. Peter and Paul ring out. Across the street, the entryway was empty. The windows of parked cars against the curb were dark. The streets of the City spread below them, lights twinkling up and down the hills. "Daniel," she said. "I want to go home."

* * *

Inside her apartment, she collapsed onto her bed, so tired her bones ached. From across the room, she stared at Daniel who peered into the open refrigerator.

"Are you hungry?" he asked.

"All I want to do is sleep," she explained. She started to peel off her shirt when she noticed the envelope sticking out of the back pocket of Daniel's jeans. "Oh god, we forgot. What about the letter?"

He stood with his back toward her, an uncharacteristically defensive posture. A sixth sense told her that he was afraid of the contents of the envelope.

"I bet Charlie probably set up a bogus account in Paris and siphoned funds into it from Ceci's and my inheritance."

"Read the letter, Daniel."

"Here." He handed her the envelope. "You read it."

Flopping back on the pillows, Jess slipped the letter from the envelope and unfolded the page. The faint scent of lilies floated off the paper. The handwriting, small and old-fashioned, was penned in blue ink. She silently read from the single sheet of stationery.

12, rue de Richelieu
1st Arrondissement
Paris
July 4, 1970

Dear Charles,
I am writing to you from the Hotel Montpensier near the arcades of the Palais-Royal. Do you remember it? Madame Jumeau, now quite bent and deaf, continues to inquire about your health, hoping each year for more than I tell her. I believe she knows that my replies are fabrications, but she continues the game and I oblige her.

The hotel has not lost its charm although the floors are more crooked, the stairs creak dreadfully, and the window in my fifth floor room will not close. Even in the heat the courtyard is pleasant, and it is here that I sit now. Every summer I arrive on the occasion of Daniel's birthday. Although each year brings its own measure of sorrow and longing for him, the beauty of the City gives me courage. This year I can find no solace. Perhaps as my youth fades, it is the face of my son that I long to see. Today he is twenty one and my heart aches for him.

So, I come to you with a plea. Have I not kept my bargain? Have I not obeyed the terms of our agreement? What threat can I be now? I ask for the right to contact Daniel without fear of reprisal. In exchange for your permission, I promise not to reveal the circumstances that forced me to leave or the bargain we struck. I give you my word.

Please write without delay. I return home to Philadelphia by July 30.

Sincerely yours,
Margaret

Jess raised her eyes from the page to Daniel who stood at the sink, drinking from an open-necked bottle of orange juice. "This is important. You need to read this."

He glanced at her mid-gulp.

"Please," she said, holding out the letter.

He returned to the bed, sat down, and began to read.

When he lifted his face from the page, his voice was low and thick. "All these years I thought she had walked away and forgotten about me."

"Mothers don't walk away from their children and forget."

"They made it sound like she was crazy or institutionalized or had disappeared."

"Who said those things?"

"I don't remember anybody saying anything—my father or grandparents," he dropped the letter on the bed and began to pace. "It was a feeling I had. One day she was gone. No explanations, no comment, end of story."

"This is a mystery," Jess said, lifting the single page, holding it as if it was made of moth wings.

"I need time to think," he said, dragging his fingers through his hair, halting and pacing again.

"Daniel, get in touch with her." She wanted him to act immediately.

"How?" he demanded.

"Pick up the phone. Dial information in Philadelphia. Call her."

"I can't do that."

"Why not?" She couldn't comprehend his reluctance.

"It's not that simple. I need more information. Maybe Ceci knows something."

"And if she doesn't?"

"Then I'll go to Charlie."

"I don't think that's wise. Think about it. He had you trailed. He wants to cut you off. And it's obvious he has some kind of hold over your mother."

"Two can play as easily as one," he said.

Pausing, Jess reread the letter. She knew she had no right to rush or push him. There could be traps and dead ends, disappointments and delays. Her impatience would get in the way. She lingered at the top of the letter, staring at the date, before folding and slipping it inside the envelope. She ran her fingers over the handwriting, examined the postmark, and toyed with the edges of the Republique Francaise stamp. "There's one more thing. You told me you were twenty-six."

He threw his hands up. "Shit, I knew this would happen."

"You lied to me," she said, baffled that he would concoct an illusion from the beginning.

"A white lie."

"You're twenty-four," she said.

"Twenty-five on Independence Day," he said.

Without reply, she fell back onto the bed, hugged a pillow into her stomach, and closed her eyes. She was adrift in a sea of contradictions, deceptions, and half-truths.

She heard him walking across the floor, the click of the front door lock, water running in the sink. The lights snapped off; the apartment plunged into darkness. Beside her the mattress sagged under his weight.

Spooning against her back, he wrapped his arm around her shoulders, speaking into the nape of her neck. "Come on, Jess. We've been through this before. Why is my age so damn important? You know I've been on my own for years. What difference does it make anyway?"

It took monumental effort for her not to push him away. Her pride kept asserting itself, fighting for supremacy, sharp-edged, immovable. His breathing deepened, becoming more rhythmic, but he continued to hold her. It was as if she could hear the inner workings of his mind, and she knew he had to be thinking about his mother. Jess couldn't talk anymore; she longed for sleep; she prayed for grace. The lightest release like summer rain fell and cooled her resistance. Her thoughts quieted, her body settled, and she wove her fingers into his fingers and drifted into the embrace of Morpheus.

Chapter 15

June 2

AT DAWN A PALE PINK-TINGED GLOW spilled across the city. In Bernal Heights on Saturn Street, where the streets are named after planets, light glanced off the windows of a house clinging to rock. In the east-facing bedroom, Annie snapped out of sleep. *God,* she thought, *where am I?* Nothing in the room was familiar, much less the man who lay snoring beside her. Then she remembered: a happening in a loft south of Market, a wicked punch she kept pouring down her throat, the disco ball suspended from the rafters flashing pixilated rainbows onto the animated faces of strangers, the Bee Gees' incessant three-part harmonies, and the bearded sculptor who emerged out of the throng and came onto her like a steam roller, his rough hands roaming her back, his deep voice in her ear.

The next thought gripped her heart like an icy claw. "The kids," she whispered, and rolled out from under army-issue blankets. As her foot knocked over a half-empty bottle of tequila onto an ashtray containing a roach clip, she scrambled for her clothes, her toes squirming on the matted rug that upon contact seemed to release a sour vapor into the dank gloom. Shivering, she dressed, grabbed her purse off the floor, and crept down narrow wooden stairs and out onto the damp sidewalk where the moist breathe of a still morning cleansed her lungs. Not one soul was visible on the street. The world seemed to be sleeping.

"Shit, shit, shit," she said, looking at the vehicles parked along the curb. "Where in the hell is my van?" She dashed uphill and frantically searched both sides of the street. She held her head and willed herself to remember: I parked; he waited for me; we walked uphill. She turned around and flew down the sidewalk. At the bottom of the hill, she ran across the intersection and saw the van parked a half a block away. The skin on her forehead felt like it would explode and peel back to her hairline. When she unlocked the door and slid behind the wheel, the dashboard clock read 6:35 AM. "I'm a fucking fool," she ranted, driving through the city streets like an addict who pledges to enter a recovery program for the sake of her neglected children until the next score passes under her nose.

A vision of her house lying in smoky ruins jarred her senses. Hyperventilating, her eyesight blurred momentarily. When the approach to the Golden Gate Bridge came into view, she was on the verge of a full-blown anxiety attack. She white-knuckled the wheel, aiming the car through the tollbooth, and onto the suicide lane where only a painted line on the roadbed marked the division between her car that was traveling north and oncoming cars whizzing past. To choose otherwise, she'd risk the sensation of being sucked into the lane closest to the walkway, inevitably smashed against the guardrail, and flung into the choppy sea beneath the bridge. Sweat broke on her brow. The thump of the wheels against the swaying roadbed made her nauseous. She talked herself down until finally her car shot over the last lap of the bridge.

Racing against the clock toward home, a brilliant diversionary tactic struck like a pardon from the fates. "That's it!" she cried and veered off Highway 101 before the exit to Mill Valley. Ahead the golden arches of McDonald's glimmered in the distance.

Inside the booths were filled with sleepy parents and disheveled children, their hair smashed against the backs of their heads and fanned out in ragged combs. At the counter, she ordered from a perky teenager. "Give me three, no, make that four Egg McMuffins, four orange juices, and one large black coffee. Make it quick!" She paced nervously while the order was bagged.

The roads to town were serenely empty except for packs of cyclists, dressed in racing colors, hunched over the handlebars of their bikes. She sped toward home, parked, and raced to the edge of the footpath. Over the fern-edged creek that trickled over grey rocks, she saw her house, whole, intact, stately. The Tiffany lamp glowed in the downstairs window. "Oh god, thank you, thank you," she cried and hurried over the footbridge. She crept through the front door and tiptoed down the hall by the living room. The house seemed to have held its breath until her entry. Beanbag chairs lay crumpled in the center of the living room, shag rugs were kicked askew, and sticky glasses, half-drained of Hawaiian Punch were left on the living room tables.

Matthew's head appeared over the back of the couch, and he opened one sleep-sealed eye. "What time is it?" Behind him, the grainy screen of the television flickered noiselessly.

"Oh, it's pretty early." Her smile broadcast a radiant subterfuge.

"Where have you been?"

"I've been up for ages." She held up the McDonald's bags. "Want some breakfast?"

He scowled. "Bogus," he said, and dropped his head back down.

She laid the bags on the counter and crept upstairs. Inside Noah's humid bedroom, she found him asleep on top of his sleeping bag, fully dressed except for bare feet. His limbs appeared to have fought with one another and called a truce. The murky aquarium tank on his desk bubbled softly, supplying oxygen to goldfish that swam about undulating green ribbons of Waterweed, past a pink glazed underwater castle, and over turquoise shooters from the Toy Box. Nearby his malodorous rat nibbled on a limp stalk of pale green celery inside its cage.

With one hand pressed to her forehead, Annie tiptoed into her bedroom, closed the door, climbed onto her bed, and fell immediately asleep as if descending into a bottomless pit.

Two hours later when the phone jangled on her bedside table and jerked her awake, her hand automatically groped for the receiver. For the second time in one morning she was totally disoriented, but this time she had no idea what day it was.

Blinding sun spilled through her bedroom window and triggered an instant headache that stabbed her temples.

Jess's voice, modulated as if to inspire reason and calm, spilled into her ear. "Annie, it's me."

"Well, I'll be damned," Annie said, rearranging the pillow under her head and holding the receiver gingerly against one ear. Slowly the shadowy events of the previous night appeared in her vision like the shuffle of a deck of cards—the ace, king, queen, and jack revealing their suits. She grimaced, watching chagrin make its grand debut.

Jess cleared her throat and tripped over her words, as if she were attempting to form a thought that now seemed to escape articulation. Annie let her prattle on. She desperately needed water. But she couldn't imagine how she'd stand.

Eventually Jess seemed to reach the point of why she had called. In excruciating detail she explained that the previous night she and Daniel had seen Stewart Merch at a bar in San Francisco called the Silver Spur.

"Let me get this straight," Annie said. Her temper ignited like a match to a ragged string of firecrackers. "I haven't heard from you in a month, and without any apology, you're calling to tell me what?"

"This is important," Jess said doggedly. "You know the place."

"Of course," Annie barked. "I've been there before."

"A lot of gays hang out there."

"Spit it out."

"Stewart was with a gay man," Jess said.

"So?"

"I don't know how to tell you this," Jess continued, "but he looked like he had been attacked."

"Is this your idea of a joke?" Annie shot back.

"Daniel was with me, and he said 'it was possible that Stewart had tangled with the wrong guy.'"

"So you and your *boyfriend* are suddenly experts on human behavior. He's barely old enough to drive. What am I suppose to do about it, anyway?" she demanded.

"I thought you'd want to know." Jess cleared her throat again. "He looked like he could use a friend."

"We could all use a friend," Annie said.

A heartbeat passed by. "I can't be your friend right now," Jess said.

Annie slammed down the phone. She wanted to throttle Jess. How like her to play Mother Teresa! Without question, the woman had earned the distinction of being a major pain in the ass.

The angle of the sun cast brilliant reflections upon the ceiling above Annie's head. She rolled onto her back, shaded her eyes, and examined the hairline cracks that rippled under the white paint. The ceiling had the translucent texture of a sand painting, and the faint cracks were like a roadmap over the Kalahari. She could have been a nomadic traveler crossing a desert, unable to discern one swelling rise from the next. While it was true that she and Stewart had fallen into a habit of talking during the week, she could inevitably count on him declining any of her invitations. They'd meet in town and ramble over a variety of subjects: sports, art, politics, sometimes playfully, sometimes seriously, and it was in those moments that she felt a distinct, shared intimacy. Then they'd say good-bye, and his energy would shift from high to neutral, and she would feel the chill of rejection. Was he gay? Still, she couldn't see it. But then she couldn't see anything right now. An overpowering need to quench her thirst propelled her upright and onto her feet.

* * *

When Stewart Merch rolled over in bed close to noon, he moaned and brought both hands up to his face. His eyelids were crusted with sleep. He traced the swollen tissue around his eyes; a scratch extended from his temple to his jaw, and a welt bubbled on his neck. On his upper lip, a cold sore bloomed, and his tongue probed its glazed heat. His flaccid penis curled in the V of his crotch, and his anus stung and burned. Groaning, he stood and hobbled to the bathroom. There in the daylight he inspected the fleshy pulp of his face—the redness that would turn blue, and the blue that would fade to yellow-green. "You stupid son of a bitch," he said, gripping the rim of the bathroom sink. Cranking on the cold-water faucet, he gritted his teeth and splashed water on his face.

He shuffled to the kitchen, brewed coffee, and waited for it to cool. The hum of the clock on the wall registered each passing minute. He took up watch at the window, sipping from a mug, and saw squirrels scampering in the trees as they leapt from branch to branch. An idea formed in his brain, simple and reassuring: I need someone to care. I need someone with whom I can pretend. I need a partner who can mimic the straightforward details of give and take, tit for tat, you for me and all that crap. I need a woman.

He placed a call. On the first ring, he clutched the phone, his resolve wavering. On the fourth ring, just as he was ready to hang up, Annie's hello came over the line.

"Hi," he said. "How's your weekend?" There didn't seem to be much point in announcing his name; without fail, she'd recognize his voice. But today the phone line hummed as if the connection had failed.

"Annie," he said, "are you there?" Queasy panic rose up in his stomach as he recalled the female voice assailing him at the Silver Spur. Could it have been Annie? Impossible. He would have recognized her. He steadied himself, prepared for the worst, and made a feeble attempt to push away the humiliation that had brought him to this moment.

"I'm here," she finally said, an unfamiliar soberness in her voice compounding his alarm.

He pitched the question again. What else was there to do? "I asked, 'how are you?'"

"I'm not feeling too well right now," she answered.

"Under the weather?" He tried to imagine how anything could slow her down. He poured more coffee into his cup and slugged back a swallow.

"Kind of a rough night," she admitted.

"Sex, drugs, and rock and roll," he offered, and tried to laugh, but a dry cackle came out of his throat that sounded demented.

Help me here, he thought, *otherwise I'm sunk.* "I won't keep you. I called for a reason."

"Really?" Her voice, usually bubbly and animated, was flat and emotionless.

"I've haven't seen your studio," he ventured.

She didn't respond.

"How about I come over sometime next week?" he said, touching his face and wincing. "Does Wednesday work? Or maybe Thursday?"

"I can swing either way," she said.

Was she working him? He was as nervous as an outfielder roaming center field on his first day in the major leagues. "There is one other thing, while I'm thinking about it."

"You're full of surprises today," she said.

"What do you know about plants and flowers?"

"Whose plants and flowers?" she asked.

He noticed an uptick in her response, and he allowed himself to roll his neck that cracked with tension. "The non-existent ones in my yard."

"Sun or shade?"

"Both. And deer. I can't keep the buggers out of the yard. My parents are visiting. I've got to get this place in shape." A picture came to him: his parent's two-story brick house, sprawling lawn and tidy garden in Houghton, Michigan, dusted by a fine, powdery, spring snow; the Winnebago, shined and polished like it just rolled off the factory floor, rumbling in the driveway, packed for their trip; his dad, Clyde, his mom, Verna, stepping through the front door under the porch light in the grey of morning, wearing matching Hush Puppy shoes and rain slickers, ready to board the rig for the drive West.

"When does this happy event take place?" Annie's question, tinged with an ironic tone, brought him up short.

"In about two weeks." He could imagine his mother's face, her eyes sparkling behind her oval-shaped glasses, hair permed Midwestern style in curls around her face. Then, after introducing her to Annie, he could hear her whisper behind her hand to Clyde, "Good gracious is she what they call a 'hippie girl'?"

"In that case, we need to start right away," Annie said as. "I can come over this afternoon."

"That doesn't work for me."

"First we'll weed. Then we'll amend the soil. After that we'll plant. Rosemary, thyme, Mexican sage—all deer proof."

"Annie, are you listening? Don't come over today."

"There's always more work than you think and the plants need to establish themselves. First we need a plan. I'd like to walk around. Look at the beds. There are beds, aren't there?"

Stewart paused, imagining the transformation she would perform in the neglected garden beds. He steeled himself for other conquests she would be intending. He'd have to hold her at a distance, but not too far.

"We'll start at the beginning," he said. "What about next Saturday?"

"It's a deal," she said. "Be prepared. I'll work your butt off."

"That's what I'm afraid of," he said, with enormous relief and trepidation. "Thanks, Annie. When my parents are here, I'd like you to meet them."

Stewart hung up the phone, poured the last of the coffee into his cup, and pulled a baseball cap onto his head. Wandering into the yard, he rested his body on a plastic chair under a tree in the shade. An air of defeat hung over him, and he nursed a harsh reality: he didn't know how to make it as a gay man, and he wasn't ready to come out to anyone, especially his parents. It was necessary to build a line of defense, he reasoned. He needed Annie as a foil. It was a gamble he had to take. But of all the women he knew, if he had to choose, it would be Annie. He supposed that was worth something. Not enough, not even close enough, but it was something.

Chapter 16

June 2

KEYED UP BY THE EVENTS of the night before, Jess stepped out of a hot shower, toweled dry, and wrapped her shampooed hair turban style in a white towel. Her body ached like she had an emotional hangover. She and Daniel had awakened slowly that morning, lying in each other's arms without talking. Silently they had come to a mutual agreement to skirt the shoals of the conversation they'd had the night before. Then, while Daniel shopped at the market for breakfast, she'd forced herself to make the call to Annie. Her heartbeat accelerated as she dialed the number. When Annie answered, her words seemed to spill out all wrong until in the end Annie had slammed down the phone. She wished she could have done it differently.

Out the half-opened, steamy window in the bathroom, she heard the song of finches and sparrows that filtered down through the trees. Jess braced herself for a long day. Through the door, Sarah's easy banter with Daniel drifted down the hall from the kitchen. From the volume of her voice she had returned in high spirits from a sleepover at the Boynton's.

As she dressed, she cracked open the bathroom door and without a tinge of remorse eavesdropped on their conversation that was interspersed with the clink of dishes and the snap of drawers opening and closing.

"Are you hungry?" Daniel asked.

"Nope," Sarah said. "What does Mom do in the bathroom for so long?"

"Beats me," Daniel replied.

"You're more like me." The tone of her voice was conspiratorial, and Jess could picture the way Sarah sidled up to Daniel when she wanted something from him that he was inclined to give her.

"How's that?"

"You go to into the ocean to get clean. I go swimming. Even in the creek. And we don't have freckles like Mom. We get tan."

"Is that right?" Daniel commented.

"Can we go to the beach today?"

"We've got to clear it with the boss."

"You mean Mom? Don't worry about her. She'll say yes." Sarah laughed, and Jess suspected that Daniel was tussling her hair as part of a ritual they enacted—he trying to playfully tickle her, she escaping his attempts that, despite loud complaint, she adored.

The bond between Sarah and Daniel was growing stronger as each week passed. Their relationship seemed to have a momentum that was unstoppable, and the weight of Sarah's attachment to him filled Jess's soul with such gravity that there often wasn't room to sort out her own personal issues about a future that included him.

She lifted a green sundress off the hook on the back of the bathroom door and dressed quickly. As she walked into the kitchen, she was greeted by the scent of coffee and toast and the sight of Sarah sitting cross-legged on top of the kitchen counter next to Daniel who stood whipping eggs in a bowl.

"Hello, honey," she said, kissing Sarah's warm forehead. She ran her fingers through her tangled hair and hugged her. "What are you two plotting?"

"A day at the beach," Daniel said, smiling at Jess. "How about it?"

"Can we go, Mom?"

"We'll see," Jess said, stepping over Sarah's red tennies that had been tossed on the floor and touching Daniel lightly on the shoulder. She loosened the towel from her head and moved toward a patch of sun near the open window. "I'm not so sure about the beach today." She balanced on the windowsill and began to dry her hair.

Just as Sarah was about to send up a howl of protest, a knock sounded at the door.

"I'll get it," she said, jumping off the counter and skipping across the floor.

A beat of unmistakable silence hung in the room. Then Sarah stepped back from the open door and cried, "Daddy!" in a high-pitched voice. Shock rippled through Jess. Her breath stopped, and she froze in place, immobile, like a figure in a still life.

Parker blinked his eyes behind the lenses of his tortoise shell eyeglasses as if momentarily blinded by the sunshine. Jess hadn't seen him in over two years, and his unhealthy pallor jarred her senses. A sickly sheen of perspiration glazed his temples.

"Good morning," he said to no one in particular. "Hope I'm not interrupting anything." A white cuff pierced by a gold cufflink flashed out the sleeve of his wrinkled grey suit jacket that draped off his broad shoulders.

"Daddy!" Sarah squealed again, throwing herself into his arms.

"How's my girl?" Parker hoisted his daughter into his arms and walked into the apartment.

"Parker," Jess managed to say, the sound of her voice warped in her ear.

"Thought I'd drop by and say hello," he said.

"What are you doing here?"

"I'm on my way to Asia."

"Asia?" she repeated stupidly.

"My flight leaves later this afternoon." He shifted Sarah to his other arm and marched across the floor toward Daniel.

Meeting him halfway, Daniel offered his hand. "Hey, how's it going? I'm Daniel."

Jess watched in astonishment. Side by side, Parker looked pale and gaunt like he came from the dark side of the moon, Daniel a specimen of a superior race. Sympathy for Parker's ill health washed over her.

"Nice to meet you," Parker replied, pumping his hand. Sarah slid from his arms and landed on her feet, clinging to the tail of her father's suit jacket.

"Sounds like a great trip," Daniel said confidently. Jess was amazed at his composure. He appeared unperturbed, as if her ex showing up unannounced on a Sunday was a regular event. "Would you like a cup of coffee?" he asked. "Or how about some breakfast?"

"No, that's not necessary." Parker plunged his hands into his pockets. "I'd like to visit before I go."

"You can come to the beach with us," Sarah suggested. "Can't he, Mom?" Her gaze swept like antennae from one parent to the other and then quickly back to Daniel.

"Well, I don't…" Jess fumbled with the towel, rearranging it over her shoulders. Her heart was thumping wildly and her speech sounded strangled and unnatural.

"Tell you what," Daniel snatched his jacket and shoes off the floor, "I should cut out now. Give you folks a chance to---"

"Where are you going?" Sarah asked. Her downy cheeks crumpled and tears gathered in her eyes.

Jess's heart caught in her throat. "We'll go to the beach next time."

"But I want to go today," she pleaded, rushing to Daniel's side and tugging on his arm.

Daniel leaned over and lowered his voice. "Sarah, we'll go another time. I promise." He circled his arm around her waist, and she leaned into his shoulder. "You should be with your dad and mom today." He walked over to Parker with his hand outstretched.

He looked magnificent, his manners impeccable, his ease enviable. Jess almost said, "Don't go," but she held herself back. She suddenly wanted him to stay, but in equal measure she wished he hadn't been there to begin with. The awkwardness of the situation was excruciating.

"Have a good trip," Daniel said.

"I intend to," Parker said, clasping Daniel's hand.

Daniel led Sarah by the hand to Jess. The expression in his eyes signaled a mixture of concern and love. "I'll call you later," he said, lightly kissed her lips, and left, leaving the three of them in the sun-washed room.

* * *

"This is a terrific place you've got," Parker said, striding across the floor as if he was assessing the apartment for future occupancy. Jess roused herself from a stupor she knew she couldn't afford. This was her territory and she'd better defend it. Sarah ran toward the couch and threw herself onto the cushions, gazing out at Parker as if he was a ghost who would disappear at any moment.

Jess walked to the kitchen table and casually rearranged herself on a chair. Although six years had passed since their divorce, when he stepped through the door the specter of their former marriage entered beside him. Whatever direction he moved, the room seemed to tilt off kilter. Her mind cast about to reconcile his hail and hearty good humor that had formerly captivated her and measure it against his capacity for betrayal. She'd been sleepwalking through the last years of their marriage, unwilling or unable to recognize the danger signs. A familiar despondency clamped down on her chest.

He whipped his arms out of the suit jacket, draped it over the back of the kitchen chair opposite Jess, and appraised Annie's painting that hung on the wall. "I like the new canvas. Derivative of course. Frank Stella did it better. Still, it's gutsy."

Jess dug her nails into her palms, a coil of heat gathering in her chest.

Unexpectedly, Sarah ran from the couch, flung herself into Jess's lap, slung an arm around her shoulder, and twirled the ends of Jess's hair in her fingers.

"My school is right down the street," Sarah said, suddenly eager to report the neighborhood's credentials as if Mr. Rogers himself had come to call. Her body quivered like a colt. Barely two years old when Jess and Parker divorced, her knowledge of her father had been built on short visits, when Parker passed through San Francisco on business trips. And then the summer when she turned five, Jess boarded her onto an airplane with a nametag pinned to her jacket and into Parker's care for two weeks.

"No kidding. Do you like your teacher?" He turned back toward them, unclasped the gold cufflinks, and shoved them into his pants pocket. Dark rings of perspiration stained the armpits of his shirt.

"Her name is Mrs. Brush and we're number one in gymnastics and spelling." Sarah popped out of Jess's lap. "Watch me, Daddy!" she shouted and executed three cartwheels across the floor. Landing with a thud, she spun in a circle on her bottom then danced and leapt in circles around him. He shadowboxed with her, feigning punches and jabs, clipping her shoulders, and laughing. She skidded on the rug and sprawled at his feet, her cheeks rosy, and eyes aglow.

"That's swell, kitten." He dragged out the chair, loosened his tie, and addressed Jess. "How's the teaching staff at the school?"

"Excellent. The best in the county. I could arrange for you to visit Sarah's classroom," Jess said, certain he would not accept.

"Amber is my best friend." Sarah flopped back into Jess's lap. "She lives right down the street. We play after school and sometimes we go to the creek."

"This town looks like a page straight out of *The Whole Earth Catalogue*," he said, aiming the comment directly at Jess. The unmistakable disdain of East Coast superiority gleamed in his eyes. "I can see it fits your needs perfectly."

"Not up to your standards, I take it," she said, unwilling to suppress the contempt that laced her voice.

"That's not what I meant." He pushed his glasses up onto the bridge of his nose and squeezed his eyelids in rapid succession.

Jess recognized this reflex, and it transported her into a range of Parker's habits once as familiar to her as her own skin—the manner in which he pulled on his socks, hopping on one leg until he jabbed the toes of his free foot into the dangling sock; the way he stuffed the tails of a shirt into his pants round one way and back again; the habit of slicing an onion and endangering his fingers; the practice of licking an envelope by darting his tongue along the glue.

"You've lost weight," she said, casting about for conversation. "Have you been sick?"

"You know me. I put it on as fast as I take it off. The job was getting to me. That's all."

"What happened?" She braced herself. With Parker events didn't proceed logically; they labored under the weight of contradiction, exploded, and then whacked her from behind.

"You heard I worked as a consultant on the mayor's staff? I floated between different projects. The press got wind of allegations about mismanaged funds in Parks and Rec. The grand jury convened. Someone had to step down and I was burned out anyway. I figured it was a good time to travel, and I always wanted to fly around the world. First stop, Japan."

How like you, Parker, Jess thought; *trouble erupts, do something extravagant.*

"In fact, I declared bankruptcy." Parker's thin lips sealed shut in an expression beyond reproach.

Jess winced. "Bankruptcy?" She wrapped her arm protectively around her daughter's tummy.

"What's bankruptcy?" Sarah asked, straining against Jess's grasp.

"Well," Jess said, "it's when a person has spent more money than he can repay and the courts give him or her time to pay off his debts..."

"Don't you have any more money, Daddy?"

"Don't you worry, kitten. I've got an attorney handling the case. There'll be a job for me when I get back. Your dad always lands on his feet. In the meantime, off to Japan." He described a whirlwind of cities he'd sample across the globe, hotels and inns he'd booked, restaurants he was dying to try, friends of friends he'd visit in their chateaux and villas.

Sarah slumped against her mother's shoulder and played with the bits of toast and jam left on a plate. Oddly, Jess found herself reviewing the women Parker had slept with. Women, he had told her, who were educated, independently wealthy, sophisticated, and witty; women who were exceptionally talented, experts in their field, movers and shakers. Suddenly Sarah's weight became unbearably heavy, and Jess scooted her off her lap. "Why don't you show your father your room?"

Sarah sprang to action and ran toward her bedroom, calling out over her shoulder. "Come with me, Daddy."

Parker stood, shaking out the legs of his pants. "I'll be right there, buttercup." He planted his hands on the table and leaned forward. The chemical sweetness of Ban deodorant tinged with sweat wafted into her nose. "The boyfriend," he said into her ear. "What's his name?"

Jess drew back. "Daniel."

"Bad choice. He won't last."

"Get away from me," she hissed.

"Hey," he said, palms up in a flourish of surprise. "Don't take it so seriously."

"What gives you the right to barge in here and say anything about my life? You disregard my phone calls, neglect your daughter, and now you're making predictions about my future."

His shoulders slumped. "Things change. Nothing is set in stone. You know that."

"What I know is I have no idea why you're here or what you want."

"Mom," Sarah said, her voice barely above a whisper. She appeared in the doorway, clutching Paddington Bear. "What are you talking about?"

Jess pushed her chair back and began scraping and stacking the breakfast dishes. "Daddy and I were discussing business."

"It sounded like you were mad."

"Your mother's not mad at me," Parker said. "Are you, Jaybird?"

The nickname he had given her raked in her ears. "Your daughter wants to show you her room. Don't keep her waiting."

"Hurry up, Daddy."

"Sure, baby. I'm coming now. Isn't that the bear I sent you from England?" He ambled across the floor and followed Sarah into her room.

Jess walked to the sink, her insides rolling with fury. The air was burdened with recrimination and shame. She smoothed the front of her dress. At the outside corner of one eyelid she felt the recurring spasm of a tic and pressed her finger to still its beat. Sarah and Parker's voices drifted from the bedroom. When Sarah came back into the kitchen, she carried her jacket and Parker sauntered behind.

"Sarah and I have an idea," he said, unrolling his sleeves and reaching for his suit jacket. "Join us, and we'll go into the City."

From the floor near her father's feet, Sarah hunched over her shoes, tying the laces, and when she looked up into Jess's face, her eyes blinked rapidly like his. "Isn't that a fun idea?"

"No! I've got things to do."

"Come on, Jaybird. What's so important that you can't put it off until tomorrow?" Parker urged.

"Stop calling me that," she said sharply, and glanced at Sarah who held herself as still as water in a glass.

"We'll go to lunch." He jammed his glasses onto the bridge of his nose. "We'll show Sarah the places we lived."

"Please say yes," Sarah pleaded. "We'll have so much fun."

"We insist," Parker pressed. He stepped forward, hands outstretched.

"I'm not going! Leave me out of your plans."

The color drained from Sarah's face. "You don't have to, Mommy. You can stay here." She walked to Parker and took his hand. "Can't she, Daddy?"

"Why sure. That's fine with me."

"What will you do?" Sarah asked plaintively.

"Don't worry about me. I have plenty to do."

"Tell you what, Sarah," Parker said cheerfully. "We'll walk downtown and catch some lunch there. Didn't I see a pizza place down by the Depot? Then you can show me around town." He reached inside his jacket, pulled out an envelope and tossed it on the table. "This is for you, Jaybird. I'll get Sarah home by three o'clock, and have a taxi pick me up from here. I need to be at the airport by 5."

"I'll be here when you get back." Jess stooped to embrace her daughter and murmured into her ear. "Have fun. I'll see you soon."

"Well, off to town." Parker held his hand out to Sarah. "See you soon."

Every part of her wanted to snatch Sarah away from Parker,

but instead she watched them go, closed the door, and braced herself against it. "Damn, damn, damn," she swore. "Shit, shit, shit. This is not what I wanted. He is not the person I married. He is not the father I wanted for Sarah."

When Sarah and Parker's steps faded on the stairs, she surrendered to an anguish that bent her double and she sobbed, her fist jammed into her mouth. Grief scorched her as bare as bone left in desert sun. When she lifted her head, the light in the room had gone flat, changing the Kodachrome colors of day into black and white. Through the open windows, the wind carried the sound of birds, the bleat of a horn, and now and again the voice of a child shouting across the valley. She drank from the tap at the sink and fell back onto the bed, starring vacantly at the shifting shapes of daylight and shadow moving across the walls.

Gradually, her breath calmed and an urgency to speak to Annie became unbearable. Her finger poised above the phone. She started to dial her number, but stopped. She couldn't do it. She was in this alone, without Annie's keen appraisal or glib humor. By afternoon Parker would be gone, and she would be free of him. Suddenly she was fueled with adrenalin, and she swept through the apartment, trying to create order by making the beds, hanging bathroom towels, and folding clothes. She stuffed bread into its plastic wrapper and tossed scraps into the garbage. Armed in yellow rubber gloves up to her elbows and clutching a thick sponge, she washed plates, glasses, and cups. As she worked, she replayed the scene with Daniel and Sarah when Parker arrived, sometimes pausing and pushing strands of hair off her forehead with the back of the glove, and then plunging her hands back into the sink.

Jess leaned against the kitchen counter, the front of her sundress blotched with water stains. She had washed every dish, scrubbed the counters and the table. She squeezed the water out of the sponge and ripped off the gloves.

Inside the envelope that Parker had dropped on the table, she found a bank check payable to her in the amount of seven hundred and fifty dollars. On the memo line, Parker had scribbled, "June, July, August child support." She dropped the check into a drawer and looked around the apartment. Triscuit slept in a patch of sunshine on her bed. Grabbing a sweater and the house key, she fled.

Chapter 17

June 2

DANIEL HEADED OUT OF TOWN, down Miller Avenue, past the high school, and along the tide flats. As he drove, he tried to reconcile the impression he had of Parker married any length of time to Jess. He just couldn't see it. The guy looked like an overworked political hack that lived on airplanes and hustled deals. In his judgment there was no question that giving them space was the right move. He had confidence that once he left, Jess would handle the situation, and Sarah would recover from any letdown or disappointment.

The weight of the letter from his mother lay heavy on his mind.

At a curve in the road before the El Monte bus stop, he parked and hiked up a narrow footpath onto stone steps set into the hillside. Here gnarled pines bent their limbs to the constant chill of fog-tinged wind. Pine needles carpeted the sloping earth. A murder of crows screeched their disapproval at his ascent. Halfway up the hillside, a cabin, weathered by damp and decay, had been built into a clearing. Skirting the rear of the cabin, Daniel took the stairs that led to a wide porch. At the top of the landing, he saw Sam Johnstone in a protected corner of the porch, reclining in a rusted metal chair, nursing a cup of coffee.

Sam raised his hand in greeting. "Hey, man, look at what the cat dragged in." He wore a rumpled wool cardigan sweater the same toffee color as his skin.

A casualty of Daniel's dispute with Ceci had put a bump in

his friendship with Sam, and seeing him now produced the realization that giving up the man's company had hurt.

"I know," Daniel said. "Don't work me too hard."

"We haven't seen you in a month of Sundays."

"Come on." Sam's good humor disarmed him. He had a talent for shaking out the kinks and settling the meanest blues. Daniel had watched him break up brawls and flatten arguments by his sizeable presence and commanding voice. "It hasn't been that long."

"Suit yourself. Pull up a chair. What's shaking?"

"Not much." Nothing seemed to miss Sam's keen observation, but Daniel didn't want to confide in him right now. He knew if and when he needed him, Sam would be there like all the times he'd been there in the past. "And you?"

"We've been real busy. Phone keeps ringing. Club dates booked clear past New Year's. Can hardly find time to kick back. You know what I mean?"

"I do. Kicking back is my specialty. But you wouldn't like all that down time."

"I expect you're right about that." Sam would inevitably minimize his notoriety in favor of making Daniel comfortable—a trait he had seen Sam extend to friends and fans alike. "Hey, some days are better than others." A smile broke across the broad planes of his face. "You seeing that sweet girl, I take it?"

Daniel returned his smile.

"Ain't that fine. She's good to you, I can tell. Anyway, you didn't come here to pass the time of day. You've come to see your sister." Sam's eyes, soft in their deep sockets, fixed on Daniel's face.

"Is she here?" Daniel glanced nervously at the murky windows of the house, expecting to spot her.

"Oh, yes," Sam nodded thoughtfully, "she's here." He set the cup on the boards of the worn porch, reached inside his sweater pocket, and withdrew a pack Marlboros. "I've been meaning to tell you something and now that you're here you might as well hear me out." He lit a cigarette and stared at Daniel through smoke rings. "Something's been eating Ceci pretty bad these days. I'm not sure what it is, but some of it has to do with you."

From anyone else but Sam this statement would have sounded like an accusation that would have put Daniel on the defensive. Instead, he held Sam's gaze and waited. Lecturing wasn't in Sam's agenda. Daniel had learned that pearls of wisdom fell from his lips and seemed to clear a way.

"You see, she's been taking care of you for so long that she doesn't know how to stop. And now that you're opposed to this inheritance shit, it's driven a wedge between the two of you."

"She never wanted the money," Daniel said. "Why did she take it now?"

"I'm working on that question myself," Sam said. "But she's not talking. Give me time. I expect to get to the bottom of it."

"Not soon enough in my book," Daniel said. "But I've found something that may change her mind." He patted his pocket.

Sam looked at him quizzically. "Is that right? You going to share that with me?"

"I'd like to run this by Ceci first. It should get her thinking about putting her faith in Uncle Charlie. I'm sure she'll fill you in."

"That may be." Sam nodded. "There's one more thing and then I'm done talking. For some reason, she's taken an aversion to the lady in your life." Sam chuckled softly. "I suspect she might be a little jealous. You know what I mean?"

Daniel screwed up his mouth and shook his head. "I don't get that at all."

"Well, I've had a little more experience with women than you have, little dude."

"You've got that right," Daniel said. "I give you full respect."

"Hear me out then." Sam's voice dropped a register. "Ceci's been hitting the bottle pretty hard these days and mixing it up with some heavy shit." Sam held his hand up. "Not that I'm blaming you for that."

In spite of knowing about Ceci's habit, it was another thing to hear Sam say it. His stomach dropped. "What can I do?"

"I'm handling it. Not to worry. Your visit will help. So go on in. Take your medicine. I'll back you up."

Daniel's vision adjusted to the darkened room. The odor of

mold, rancid Chinese food, and cigarette smoke thickened the air. A black baby grand piano occupied one end of the living room. A couch, upholstered in a worn fabric, flanked the other end of the room, and in front of the couch, a glass coffee table was strewn with sheet music, greasy white cartons, chopsticks, and ashtrays crammed with cigarette butts.

Daniel called, "Ceci, it's me."

She appeared in the doorway. Her dark hair hung in flat strands against the sides of her face, and a chemical haze dulled her eyes. She tightened the sash of a frayed chenille robe at her waist and blinked at Daniel.

"Are you sick?" he asked, expressing genuine concern.

She held her hand up as if to say, don't, and made her way to the couch. She folded onto the cushions, a hand over her eyes. "Hell, no, you caught me at a bad time. It was dawn by the time I fell asleep." She yawned, pulled the robe tighter, and stretched her legs out along the length of the couch.

"Can I get you something?" he asked.

"Water," she answered.

The kitchen sink and counter were stacked with dirty dishes, glasses, and utensils. He turned on the faucet, and ran cold water in a glass. Grease swam over the rim of the dishes and coagulated in the sink.

She took the glass from his hand without looking at him. He settled onto a folding chair opposite the couch.

"Now, let's see," she began coldly. "The last time I saw you, you said something like you didn't want to see me again. What was it? Tell me."

"Ceci, I…" he faltered. "What I mean is…" he swallowed and rubbed his hands together. "You know I'm no good at this."

"Try. I like to watch you squirm."

"What's going on with you?" he asked, taken aback by her hostility. "You look like shit."

"The price of success, I guess," she laughed bitterly and coughed. Phlegm rattled in her throat. "Oh Christ, Daniel, don't be so serious. It doesn't become you. Light me a cigarette. They're over there on the piano."

He lit a cigarette and passed it to her. In slow motion, she brought the cigarette to her mouth and took a drag. A flake of tobacco clung to her lip. She peeled it off and flicked it onto the floor.

"To tell you the truth, whatever happened at your place is a blur. But Sam told me I made an ass of myself. He said to give you time to cool off. He was right, as usual." She took another drag and glanced at him, her eyes ringed with smeared black mascara. "You look disgustingly healthy. When are you going to leave the beach and join the human race? No, don't bother to answer." She stretched her legs again and sighed. "You still seeing that woman?"

It took every bit of his reserve to stay neutral. "Her name is Jess."

"That's nice, I guess. None of the others have lasted. Is she the one? No, don't answer that either." She propped herself up against a pillow and drank from the glass, her hand visibly shaking. "What's your status with Uncle Charlie these days? Has he still got the noose around your neck?"

"Not my neck," Daniel said firmly. He removed the envelope from his jacket and held it out to her.

"What's this?"

"Go ahead. Open it."

She examined the face of the envelope. "Where did you get this?"

"That's not important."

She shook her head from side to side, coaxed the letter from the envelope, and unfolded it. Her bloodshot eyes, puzzled and wide, flickered up to him, and then rapidly moved to the bottom of the page. "What the hell?" she mumbled, biting a thumbnail. Starting at the top again, she read slowly. When she finished her hands fell into her lap, the letter crinkling between her fingers. "This letter is written in," she glanced at the date, "July 4, 1970, on your twenty-first birthday. Your mother is in Paris. She's asking Charlie to release her from some kind of bargain they made so that she can contact you. This is bullshit. Pure unadulterated bullshit." Her gaze shifted vacantly to a point over his shoulder.

"What's this about?" Daniel asked impatiently.

"I don't know. The last time I saw your mother was twenty

years ago. I was fourteen, you were four. I was absorbed in horses and watching out for you. Their scene was a total turn-off. I made it my duty to stay clear of them."

"Don't you remember anything?" he asked, clinging to some hope that a recollection would jog her memory.

"Daniel, come on. They sequestered us. We were practically under house arrest."

"What about an incident? Something you saw. Something you overheard."

"They were traveling half the time, and when they were home, we weren't invited into the living room during cocktails or read bedtime stories or kissed goodnight. Miss Ida, Mrs. Friedlander, Mrs. Pain in the Ass raised us! I barely saw my own mother, and when I did it was by appointment."

"Damn it. There's got to be something."

"Don't count on any information from me." She rubbed her forehead and dropped the letter on the coffee table. "My brain cells are diminishing rapidly."

Daniel glared at her. He wanted to grab her by the shoulders and shake some life into her.

"You're a big boy. You figure it out. Frankly, right now I've got a headache that's making me want to puke. I need to sleep." She struggled to her feet and shuffled toward the bedroom. "I'd say bring your girlfriend over, but I'd be lying about wanting to see her." Ceci halted at the doorway. "She's not what I had in mind for you." Then she looked straight at Daniel. "Give me a break. Don't look so offended. Why is she hanging out with you? Shit! You haven't told her about your inheritance, have you?"

"Back off, Ceci! I'm not going to take the goddamn money."

"Oh, give me a fucking break," she shouted. "When push comes to shove, you'll fall. Just like I did."

"What is it with you?" Daniel shouted back. He jerked to his feet. "There's no filter between your brain and your mouth. And when have you ever had a corner on the truth?"

"There's one thing I've been, Daniel, and that is honest and up-front." She pointed her finger at him. "Don't expect me to change. Not now. Not even for you."

Daniel had heard enough. He stepped out the door, onto the porch, where Sam still reclined in the rusted metal chair, shaking his head, a mournful look in his eyes.

"She's all yours," Daniel said. "I don't know how you do it."

Chapter 18

June 3

BEYOND THE APARTMENT at a bend in the road, Jess stopped in a turnout and looked westward across the canyon toward the mountain that towered vertically into a brilliant sky. The craggy escarpment near the ridgeline, dotted with chaparral stands, appeared foreboding in the harsh sun. Suddenly she was at a loss as to what direction to go or how to fill the hours of the afternoon. The mountain offered no advice, nor gave any solace, and as her feet sought purchase on the crushed rock, she felt like she could slide away on the curvature of the earth and topple into space.

Around her a cluster of homes shouldered the knoll and hummed a mid-day drowsiness. She imagined their occupants, people who depended on one another, lounging over sections of the Sunday paper, calling out from the kitchen over coffee gone cold, "Honey, shall I make another pot?" She heard a radio tuned to gospel music and pictured a couple swaying to its good news and making sandwiches at a cutting board. A picture of Sarah and Parker flashed in her mind, and she forced herself to put aside her distrust of him. She asked only one thing from the silent mountain—let Parker take good care of Sarah. Then, after peering toward town as if she could see over the rooftops to where they might be walking side by side, she turned up the paved road.

In the fresh air, she swung her arms and quickened her pace. The road serpentined higher. The leaves of trees flipped in the sunshine, scattering verdant shapes over the pavement beneath her feet. Bicyclists in twos and threes pedaled by, their backs bent over handlebars, snippets of their conversations cast into the breeze. When she came upon railroad tie steps, scarred with tar and age, she followed their route as they switch-backed down a shaded canyon thick with sequoias, laurel and birch, flight after flight to a street she did not recognize. Here she took another unfamiliar route that wended back to town and deposited her in front of the Unknown Museum, next to Jake's garage that was locked and strangely quiet. She wondered what devilment he was up to on a Sunday. The avenue as well, usually a hubbub of activity and noise, was empty of cars and pedestrians, but the door to the museum was ajar, and in the window a bejeweled toilet perched on a dais under flashing colored lights. The tinkling of bells and faint music played from the second story.

Inside she saw a unicorn adorned with stars, bangles and beads, and beside it, an old drugstore display for trusses. A sign posted to the display read, "Museum Truss Fund. One: deposit money here. Two: rub my truss. Three: make a wish." She tiptoed into the museum. Art assemblage constructed from plumbing parts, prosthetic limbs, appliances large and small, and all manner of everyday things like steam irons, Disney lunch boxes, 45 rpm records, egg beaters, doll heads, and glass jewels filled the interior. She waited for someone to appear and when they did not, she wandered from creation to creation absorbed in the displays that pulsed and shined and radiated a world of uncommon joy made out of common things.

Finishing a tour of the museum, and still without an idea of what to do next, she suppressed a yearning to throw aside her vow to distance herself from Annie when the growl of a motorcycle approached from a distance. She stuck her head out the door to see the rider ripping up the street, and drawing closer, he bumped onto the driveway of the garage, swung one leg off the Triumph, and planted the kickstand.

She strolled out of the museum toward the garage watching Jake peel off his gloves, flip his goggles, and rub his hands over his face. When he looked in her direction a slow smile spread across his face, accentuating the dust and sweat smeared into the creases around his dark eyes.

"Hey, beautiful, what's happening?" he called.

"Nothing," she beamed back, suddenly happy to see an old friend. "I've been to the museum."

"That's a wacko place." He squinted at her. "You probably like it."

"I do," she said, walking toward him.

He slapped his forehead with his hand. "I knew it. Where's the kid?"

"My ex arrived and they're having a visit."

"And you're wandering around at loose ends."

"And you're covered with bugs." She reached out and plucked a small black winged creature out of his hair.

He caught her by the wrist. "Hey, don't mess with the goods."

"Where have you been?" she asked.

"To the coast."

"I should have known. You're one of the bikers who play god on the Sunday Morning Ride, screaming down Panoramic and striking fear into every unsuspecting motorist who doesn't know the road belongs to the mighty."

"I guess you could look at it that way," he grinned.

"Where's Camilla?"

"We have an agreement on Sundays. She does what she wants, and I do what I want. Why don't you come in? I still haven't shown you my collection of jackknifes."

"What is it with you and knives?" she laughed.

"Hey, it was part of my education."

In the office, the blinds were drawn casting thin strips of light over the metal desk and onto the floor. The smell of oil and gas fumes blanched the airless room. A large calendar hung on the wall. In dark block letters it advertised Sure Seal Piston Rings and under it an airbrushed blonde in a red polka-dot bikini held a piston ring in front of her large breasts. Jake unzipped his leather jacket and tossed it onto the desk.

"Have a seat." He turned back to the door. "I'm going to lock this, but don't get the wrong idea. Some wazoo will want to talk business and I can't be bothered." He slipped a Toots and Matoll cassette into the tape deck. No sooner had music flooded through the speakers than a shadow appeared on the opposite side of the door and the doorknob rattled.

"See, what did I tell you?" He peered through the blinds. "I've got to talk to this bozo. I'll be right back. Don't go anywhere."

"Take your time," she said, sinking into the chair and surveying his desk. Bills were skewered on a spindle. Manuals piled one on top of the other and were stacked the floor. Greasy handprints covered the desktop. The music lulled her mind and drowsiness settled over her shoulders like a warm cape.

She started when a door to the garage opened, and Jake walked in holding two beer cans. He had washed his face and his hair was damp. A white T-shirt accentuated the shadow of his beard, and his pale skin was as flawless as alabaster except for a scar than ran from under the sleeve of the T-shirt, over his triceps, and down to his elbow.

"You taking a nap?" he asked. He popped the tab of a can.

"No, I'm just unwinding." She sat up straighter and tucked the skirt of her dress around her knees.

"I haven't seen you in a while. Tell me what's going on." His dark gaze burrowed into a place soft and vulnerable and hidden.

To her surprise, tears filled her eyes and rolled down her cheeks.

"Hell," he said. "If there's one thing I hate to see it's a crying woman."

"I'm sorry." Waves of sadness rushed at her, filling her chest.

"You're not crying over your ex?"

"No, no, not him." Her emotions about Parker were as tangled as a Gordian knot. Try as she might to cut him loose, the knot only tightened. How could she explain this to Jake, a man who took mangled steel and made it smooth as glass?

"It must be some other son of a bitch. Tell me who he is and I'll cream him."

She laughed through her tears, shaking her head, and wiping her cheeks with the back of her hand. A vision of Daniel and his inherent goodness came to her, easing her sadness. There were so many ways in which he tried to please her.

"Here, take a swig." He passed her a beer. "What's eating you?"

"It's a little bit of everything." She took a pull from the icy beer. "My career is stalled. Finances are an issue. You know, the usual."

"It's none of my business, but I've wondered, how come a woman like you hasn't settled down?"

"If I knew that I wouldn't be here," she said. "Would I?"

"That would be a shame." His eyes swept over her face and then he nodded as if he'd lit on a novel idea. "You understand whatever I say isn't worth a hill of beans, but numero uno, I think you should lighten up. Don't take things so seriously." He rubbed his beard. "If you need a job, I could scare something up. Are you good with numbers?"

She practically gagged. "Now there's a disaster in the making."

"Just a suggestion," he said. He kicked his boots up on the desk and settled back in the chair. "As for men, you understand we're like dogs. One minute we're pissing on this bush, the next minute we're pissing on another." He rocked back and forth on the back rungs of the chair. "You're probably looking for the perfect guy, right? Let me tell you there's no such animal. But there is a guy for you." He chopped the air with his hand. "No question. It's all in the timing. Take me and Camilla. I'm no picnic, believe me, but we're cut from the same cloth. No matter what, I'm going to stick by her. And vice versa. It's that simple. So what if you picked a loser or two? Let it go. There's guys out there who'd give you their paycheck in a Chicago minute. In the meantime, like I said, stay loose. Don't get complicated."

Jess smiled weakly. "I wish it was that simple." Jake's outlook on life was as unfathomable to her as the theory of nuclear fusion.

"Okay, no more lecturing. Come with me. I want to show you my latest creation."

Inside the garage, it was dark and cool. Streaks of daylight peeked through openings around the roll-up doors. Three automobiles, huge and shadowed, rested in repose like warriors of the road under a spell.

"Watch your step," he said, taking her hand as she stepped over tools and steel fittings in the grease-slicked floor. He led her to a sedan in the middle bay, and opened the rear door. "Get in." The seats were tufted navy-blue leather, smooth as a kitten's ear, and penetrated the air with a scent like riding saddles polished to a luster. He closed the doors sealing her in the darkened, luxurious feel of British craftsmanship.

Jake climbed into the driver's seat and switched on the ignition. The electrical panel on the walnut dash lit up like the controls of a private airplane. He flipped the chrome toggles and ran his hands around the leather-stitched steering wheel. "What do you think?"

"It's lovely," she sighed. The opulence of the interior spun an air of foreign intrigue and illicit love affairs.

Leaning over the seat, he told her, "Pull down the section in the middle and lift up the top."

"Like this?" she asked. Her fingers searched between the leather folds to find the right opening.

He moved into the back, slipped down a leather sleeve and released a catch on a small walnut lid. She peered into a mirrored compartment illuminated by lights and stocked with a silver flask and crystal tumblers.

"Nice, huh?"

"First class," she answered.

"Wish I could offer you a shot, but it's empty."

"Then I'd know for sure you'd be trying to compromise me," she said. The comfort of the seat, cool and padded, cushioned her back.

"Not a bad idea," Jake said, and closed the lid to the compartment. He leaned next to her, his elbow touching hers. "Look, I've got a small Jag sedan coming in. It's been wrecked, but I can make it look like new."

She knew what was coming next. He'd been harping about the miserable condition of her car for months.

"I want you to have it," he said, his voice low, his breath

warm and moist beside her ear. "The car you drive is piece of shit. And don't talk to me about what it's going to cost. We'll figure out something."

"I can't accept that, Jake." She touched his cheek lightly. "Thank you for the offer." There was an intimacy to being alone with him as if the rest of the world was a dream.

"I knew you'd say that. I hate to see you hurting and, damn, you'd look so good in one of these." He lifted one of her hands from her lap and matched his fingers to hers. "I like to see my friends driving my cars."

His hands weren't much larger than hers, the calluses on his fingers deeply stained by grease. She felt a tensile energy coming off his body that was electrifying. She dropped her head onto his shoulder. As he stroked her forehead, brushing her hair from her face, she shivered. "What are we doing?" she asked, alarms sounding in her body. A scent was rising off his skin, musky, tinged with a faint sharpness of sweat. He didn't smell like Daniel. He didn't sound like Daniel. He didn't feel like Daniel.

"We're practicing?" He turned her hand over and stroked her open palm.

"What are we practicing?"

"Your new take on life."

"And what is that?"

"Staying loose." His fingertips slowly traced the outline of her cheekbone down to her chin. "You've got to admit, between you and me, it's been a long time coming."

She didn't say a word. He was like a foreign country, a dive off a cliff, a slide into oblivion.

He tilted her chin toward his face. "What do you think?"

"I think for someone who plays it tough that you are the sweetest man."

"Yeah." He brushed his lips against hers.

She pulled away, every part of her retracting. "But I can't do this."

"You sure?"

She nodded, "I'm sure," she said, kissing him lightly on the cheek.

"Ah, shit. Shot down again. I take it you don't subscribe to my theory of staying loose."

"I guess I'm just not wired like that. As you said before, it's all in the timing. Thanks for the tour." Her hand closed over the door handle. "And thanks for the beer and the offers, but I need to head for home."

* * *

Back in her apartment Jess brewed herself a strong cup of black tea and sifted through her emotions. Since she had known Jake, they each seemed to dodge around a sexual curiosity in the other that in the end never amounted to anything. Although her mind might vacillate, parry and divide about Daniel, her heart would not let her stray.

After she fed the cat, she decided to make macaroni and cheese for Sarah's dinner. She estimated she had at least an hour before Parker was due back. Between boiling the water for the macaroni and melting the butter to make a cheese sauce, she called Daniel in Bolinas, hoping to hear his voice and reconnect with him. When he didn't pick up, she assumed he was surfing, and she hurried to finish the meal.

As the clock bore down on 3:00, she steeled herself for Parker to deliver Sarah. When Sarah was younger, the transition had been painful; Sarah despondent, her forehead fevered and cheeks blotched, after saying good-bye to her father. "I miss my Daddy," she'd cry. "I miss my Daddy." The only remedy had been to hold Sarah and rock her to sleep, leaving Jess wide awake, the tick of the bedside clock echoing in the shadows cast from the hallway light. Now she speculated about Sarah's reaction. Since Sarah seemed spunkier and more independent, Jess was hopeful that she would be accepting of the fact that Parker was the distant parent and not so upset after he departed.

When 3:00 came and went, Jess assumed they had been delayed because Parker had either changed his mind about when he'd leave for the airport or had lost track of time. She made herself a sandwich, nibbled it at the sink, and dove into a Ms. Magazine with a stunning Gloria Steinem on the cover. The premise of an article, "Why Women Fear Success," by Vivian Gornick, sounded patently absurd to her—either you went for what you wanted or you didn't. The theory reeked of pure psychological babble that was offensive.

Eyeing the clock past 4:00, it occurred to her that maybe she hadn't heard Parker correctly. Given the state she had been in, she couldn't rely upon herself to remember what he had or hadn't told her. He must have said 5:00. Otherwise why wouldn't he have called to say he'd be late? She comforted herself with the assurance that Parker and Sarah were, at least, having a long visit. To stay busy, she scoured the bathroom floor, a chore she hated, and afterwards walked into the studio, clicked on the tape machine to a Joni Mitchell tape, lay on the floor, and stretched. She wished Daniel would call.

By 6:00, Jess watched from the window overlooking the drive. In the fading twilight, mosquitoes batted at the windowpanes. The headlights from cars flickered on the road and then passed; footsteps on the stairs brought a surge of relief until they passed her door. Hope faded to doubt, and doubt dueled with apprehension. She told herself that Parker and Sarah would appear any minute, and she was simply over-reacting. She called Daniel again, and when he didn't answer her frustration mounted. Why hadn't he called, she wondered. Where was he?

To kill time, she walked outside, stood on the stoop, and gazed out across the parking area. Twilight was gathering with each passing minute. The bushes bordering the parking area shape-shifted from figures hiding in the brush back to branches and foliage. She hugged her arms around her waist, stepped back inside the entry, and returned to the apartment.

Another hour ticked away. A suspicion that something had gone terribly wrong was replaced by mounting fear. Her mouth had turned to cotton; her heart raced with dread. Had they been in an accident? Did Parker call earlier in the afternoon while she was out? She began to question what he had told her about his flight. Maybe he wasn't flying at all. But why would he do that? And yet he hadn't mentioned when his flight departed or even what airlines he was flying.

She bargained with herself. If they didn't come back in ten, fifteen, twenty minutes at the latest, she'd take action. Anything was better than this escalating feeling of being out of control. Conversely, she reasoned that her fears were ill-founded. She'd feel ridiculous once they arrived. She could call San Francisco International and try to hunt down his flight. But if Parker tried to call, she'd tie up the line. She couldn't leave; she had promised she'd be home when they returned. Where were they?

By 8:00 she could no longer pretend. Darkness was closing in quickly. Pale white moths fluttered around the porch light. Hastily she left a note on the door, and drove to town while squinting into the windshield of each passing vehicle and hoping it were a taxi delivering Parker and Sarah. Jamming into a parking space, she watched people spilling from restaurants, flushed from dinner and lingering in groups. She hurried into the restaurants up and down the avenue and peered at the clientele who curiously met her stare. *What in the hell am I going to do?* she thought. She couldn't imagine going to the Boyntons. What would she say? I think my daughter is missing. Never.

In the center of town in front of the Depot, she stepped into the phone booth, and dialed Daniel's number. An automated, female voice said, "At the sound of the tone, please deposit seventy-five cents." She fished quarters out of her pocket, and dropped the coins into the slots. His phone rang unanswered, and her heart sank. There was only one option—the right option from the beginning if only she could have seen it. If she had to get down on her knees and beg, she would. She ran up the block, down the path, onto the bridge over the creek, and without knocking, burst through the door of the Annie's Victorian into the brightly lit hallway.

"Annie, where are you?" she called.

Annie appeared at the landing outside her studio, a paintbrush in her hand. "What the hell are you doing here?" The bottomless expression in her eyes was one that Jess had seen her turn on a fool more than once. It could shatter an offender or clear a room.

Jess held her ground, her insides churning. "I'm in trouble. You're the only person who can help me."

"This morning I'm not worthy of your friendship and now I'm sainted." Her mouth puckered like she had bitten down on bitter fruit.

Matthew and Noah popped their heads around the corner, their eyes bright with curiosity. Without turning her head, Annie ordered them back into Noah's room with instructions not to come out unless they were called.

"Where's the boyfriend?" Annie asked, crossing her arms under her ribcage.

"I really don't know." Jess leaned against the wall. She felt sick and frantic at the same time. "You've got to hear me out."

"This better be good," Annie said, her voice flat and emotionless.

"Parker's in town. I let him take Sarah. He said he'd be back by late afternoon to catch a plane. I shouldn't have let her go. I totally screwed up."

"Save the guilt," she said, walking quickly down the stairs. "The guy is a loaded gun."

"Can you help me find Sarah?" Jess asked.

"Of course I will!" She frowned as if there could any doubt. "Tell me everything that happened from the minute Parker arrived."

An enormous wave of relief washed over Jess. The walls of the house seemed to sigh in sympathy.

Annie sat on the bottom stair, her eyes riveted on Jess's face, her fingers working the bristles of the paintbrush while the Jess explained what had happened. Annie glanced at a watch on her wrist. "You mean you haven't heard from him since he left."

"Not a thing," Jess reported. Fear ran its cold fingers up her spine.

"Have you called the airlines?"

"What would I tell them? I don't know what time he's flying or what airline he's flying on. All I know is that he said he's flying to Japan."

"Give me a minute to think," Annie said. She tapped the paintbrush into the palm of her hand. "Was his behavior suspicious in any way?"

"What are you talking about?" Annie's estimation of Parker hadn't changed since the day they met, and the ferocity of her opinion never failed to surprise Jess.

"Come on, Jess, wake up. Was he straight up or his usual passive-aggressive, warped self?"

"How should I know? He's Parker. I can't read him."

"Goddamn it, that's part of the problem. But let's figure this out." She looked at her watch again. "It's 8:40, so he could be at the airport with Sarah. Does he have her birth certificate or passport?"

"I have her birth certificate. She doesn't have a passport."

"Could he be at the airport, and book a flight to somewhere else?"

"You've lost me, Annie. That's preposterous."

"Exactly. Look at it this way. Nothing is going his way. No job, no woman, no family. Now he's desperate."

Jess nerves lit up like a switchboard. "You're scaring me," she said, and as soon as the words were out of her mouth, the premonition she had been holding back crystallized: Parker's taken Sarah.

Annie grabbed her by her arm and shoved her towards the door. "Let's go."

"Where?"

"To pay a visit to Mill Valley's finest." Annie snatched a jacket off the coat tree in the hallway and shouted up the stairs. "Matthew, Noah. Listen up! I'm going out. If either of you lay a hand on each other, I'll kill you."

Jess stopped in her tracks. "Wait. Go up to my apartment. Wait there. If Parker shows, call me at the police station."

"Are you sure?"

"Annie, I'll make it up to you. I ..."

"Go on! You're wasting time."

* * *

Fluorescent light flooded the empty waiting room of the brick two-story Mill Valley Police Station. Radio static crackled from an adjoining room. A long wooden countertop and low gate blocked further entry. Leaning her elbows onto the countertop, Jess cleared her throat. "Hello," she called. Through a half open door, she heard a dispatcher's voice relaying a report about suspicious activity outside the 7-Eleven, and a reedy voice radioing back location details against scratchy interference. She stood on tiptoe, straining to see into the room. "Hello. Is there anyone here?"

Sharp heels echoed down a hallway. An officer appeared, clipboard in his hand. "Good evening, miss," he said. "What can I do for you?"

Jess looked into the lined, weathered face of a man whom she judged closer to retirement than active duty. His bald head gleamed above a fringe of salt and pepper hair.

"My daughter is missing," she said, the words catching in her throat. "My ex-husband, who is from out of town, didn't return with her this afternoon like he said he would and he's catching a plane to Tokyo and he hasn't called and you've got to call the airlines to stop him—"

The officer raised his hand, a worn gold band circling his third finger. His eyes were brown, deep set, and unblinking. "Take a breath," he said, and removed a pencil from behind his ear. Little tufts of grey hair sprouted from his earlobes. "Let's get some information down."

Jess clasped her hands together, damp with perspiration. A metal badge was pinned to the chest pocket of his blue shirt buttoned over his paunchy belly. Above the badge a thin bar read, "Brody."

A circular white-faced clock ticked loudly above the door on the wall.

Officer Brody laboriously wrote, June 2, 9:01 PM, onto a form attached to the clipboard. "You are?" he asked kindly. She reigned in her fear, and gave him her name, address and phone number, Sarah's name and the same for Parker, spelling the addresses when he inquired.

"State your daughter's age and describe what she wearing."

"She's eight." The smell of burnt coffee hanging in the air sickened her and she fumbled to remember exactly what outfit Sarah had chosen. "She was wearing red corduroy pants, a white cotton shirt imprinted with yellow and red flowers, and a navy blue jacket."

He repeated what Jess told him, paused, and asked, "Do I understand correctly that you are the custodial parent and your ex-husband arrived unexpectedly at your house today?" The radio crackled in the next room.

"Why is this taking so long?" she demanded, worrying her hands into her pockets.

"Please answer the question, Miss."

Jess glared at Officer Brody. "Yes," she sighed. "I'm the custodial parent and no, he did not tell me he was coming to visit."

"At what time did he arrive?"

"About eleven this morning."

"How did he arrive?"

"A taxi dropped him off."

"You saw the taxi?"

"I didn't see the taxi, but that's what he said." She hesitated, biting her lip. "At least I think that's what he said."

"What are his visitation rights?"

"He takes Sarah for a few weeks each summer or at times we mutually agree to," she explained. "But he rarely sees her. He lives three thousand miles away."

"Yes, I see. And how did he get into your house today?"

Jess flushed. "I let him in. Why wouldn't I?"

"Then you have an amicable relationship with your ex-husband?"

She faltered for an instant. What path was her leading her down? "You could say that."

Officer Brody's bushy eyebrows quivered. "No disagreements of any nature?"

Jess returned his inquiring gaze. "The child support checks are usually late."

Officer Brody paused. "Was he carrying any baggage?"

"Not with him. I suppose it's possible he could have stored baggage at the airport."

"You said he was catching a plane to Tokyo?"

"Yes, he told me he'd lost his job..." She caught herself in mid-sentence. "Wait. I'm not sure if he said Tokyo or Japan. No, he said Japan. Yes, that's it. Japan."

"What airline and when's the departure?"

"I don't know," she said. Did Officer Brody think she was hysterical by nature or stupid?

"Was he traveling alone?"

"To the best of my knowledge."

Officer Brody ran his hand over his baldhead and scratched his ear. "By your consent, he took your daughter out for the day, saying he'd return by three o'clock?"

"I've told you all that." A drop of perspiration formed in the center of her breastbone and began its lazy descent.

"Were you home all afternoon in the event he called to say he had a change of plans?"

Jess's eyes narrowed. "No, as a matter of fact, I went for a walk and visited a friend. I was home by two o'clock."

"Does your ex-husband have friends in the area?"

"No, I don't think so." She paused, remembering Parker boasting about an all-nighter he and a colleague pulled in San Francisco years ago. The next words out of Officer Brody's mouth threw her off track.

"Does your ex-husband have a history of violence?"

"No! Of course not."

"In the past has he threatened abduction?"

"God, no!" Her fist shot out and she pounded the countertop. "If he had, why would I let him take my daughter? Why are you asking me all these questions? He could be on an airplane right now with my daughter. Why can't you alert the airlines?"

Officer Brody pushed aside the clipboard and stuck the pencil back behind his ear. "Look, this is what I suggest. Go home. Wait. I've seen this kind of thing happen before."

Mustering what was left of her composure, Jess explained. "It's more complicated than that. This has never happened before."

"Give the situation a few more hours. If your ex-husband and daughter don't show up later tonight, we can issue a BOLO to our patrols and other agencies in the area."

She peered into his face, swiping away tears. "What's a BOLO?"

Officer Brody reached under the countertop and passed her a tissue. "It stands for 'be on the lookout.'" He blinked at her, his eyes red-rimmed, a pallor of fatigue passing over his face. "Like I said, go home. Keep us informed. Take my card. Call us at any time."

The radio in the adjoining room buzzed into action. Garbled voices broke through the static. The dispatcher's voice, clear and controlled, commanded, "High speed pursuit on 101. Driver is southbound at Strawberry exit. All cars on alert. All cars on alert."

Bewildered, Jess walked to the door, and stepped outside. The town seemed strangely shuttered, sidewalks lifeless. On either side of the walkway leading up to the station, sprinklers suddenly switched on, and she jerked back from the burst of cold water spraying across the grass and onto the walk.

A black dog with a white face trotted along the opposite side of the street, head high, tail up, sniffing the air. She watched him walk on the sidewalk in the direction of town until he vanished into the shadows.

* * *

From the parking lot, light streamed from the windows of Jess's apartment. As she walked into the entry, she heard the usual Sunday night sounds of music and voices from televisions and smelled the scents of cooked food that drifted in the hallways. A twinge of hope that Parker had called or even appeared with Sarah accompanied her up the stairs, but when she opened her front door, the look on Annie's face told her otherwise. Annie sat alone at her kitchen table, thumbing through a magazine.

"No word from Parker?" Jess asked.

"Not a damn thing," Annie. She slapped the magazine closed. "What happened with the police?"

"The Officer On Duty said a few more hours has to go by before they can issue something called a BOLO—be on the lookout."

"The assholes. I guess they have to go by the book, but it

doesn't help us. But what if we're on the wrong track altogether? Maybe Parker isn't at the airport. Maybe he's…"

"The officer asked me something that keeps rattling around in my brain."

"What?"

"He asked me if Parker has any friends in the area."

"And?"

"I told him no, but I vaguely recall Parker bragging about an all-nighter he pulled in the City. Most of the time his conversations are studded with names and exploitations that frankly, I just dismiss."

"Hmm," Annie said. "Maybe it will come to you, but in the meantime we can't just sit here like fools and do nothing," Annie said. "I've been thinking, if Sarah mentioned pizza in town that means one of two places," Annie said. "I know the owner of Lococo's. He's the type of guy who knows what's going on and how to make things happen. Let's start with him. If we can track down where Parker and Sarah were in town, maybe that will give us a lead."

* * *

Zahir's hooded eyes peered gravely at Jess, and then at Annie. His black eyebrows met in the middle between his eyes and dove onto hooked nose. "I see. Ladies, please take a seat at the bar. I'll be right back."

Jess watched Zahir pass through the restaurant to the elbow of a mustached waiter, lean in close, and speak into his ear. When he returned, his demeanor was a model of gentility tinged with caution. "This may take a little time, my friends. Are you sure I can't get you something to eat? Perhaps a dessert?" His eyebrows shot up inquisitively. "No? Then I'll make a few phone calls from my office and return as soon as possible."

Jess hoisted herself on a barstool and ordered a soft drink from the bartender.

Annie joined her and asked for a brandy. "You could use something stronger than bubble water," she said to Jess.

"All I want right now is this nightmare to go away."

"I'll tell you one thing, if you keep biting your nails you'll need medical attention."

Jess shoved her hands into her jacket. The bartender poured the drinks, a Hennessy neat, and a 7-Up over ice in a tall tumbler. Annie offered the brandy to Jess who tossed back a swallow, burning her tongue as it slid down her throat.

"We'll get through this one way or the other," Annie said. She touched her arm, squeezing gently. "And when we find Parker, I'll personally wring his neck."

"It won't be soon enough," Jess said, leaning against Annie's shoulder and taking consolation in her words.

"Let's see what the sultan digs up," Annie said.

"What's the story with him?" Jess asked.

"Small town rumors about his business that I don't pay attention to. He's obviously a mover and shaker. I thought he'd be worth a try."

From the mirror at wall, they watched a few patrons lingering over drinks at banquettes draped with white tablecloths. Waiters cleared dishes from empty tables, the ring of glassware and clink of china shattering the quiet of the restaurant.

"This is taking forever," Jess said. She watched the last patrons pay their bills and stroll out of the restaurant. One by one lights were dimmed. A waiter flipped the open sign on the front door to shut.

"My daughter is god knows where and I didn't see it coming."

"So you're normal like any other parent. Welcome to the club."

Something in her voice broke through Jess's misery, and she turned toward her. "What is it? Tell me what's going on."

"Later," she said. "Here comes Zahir."

Zahir approached moving quickly across the floor. They slid off the stools to meet him. Annie gripped Jess's arm. Zahir's eyes shone brightly in their deep sockets. "Aha, as I suspected. My day waiter remembers the party in question." He smiled slyly. "The gentleman was a big tipper. And your little girl made a charming impression. The gentleman had questions about transportation to the city. The waiter sent him across the street to the cabbies. I have spoken with the dispatcher there. The gentleman and your daughter were dropped off in Pacific Heights on the corner of Scott and Jackson at approximately 1:30 PM."

* * *

Jess tore out of the restaurant with Annie at her side. "Damn, Annie. You're a genius. It just hit me—Parker told me his colleague lived in Pacific Heights. That's where they've got to be."

"What are we waiting for?" Annie said. "I'll drive. You ride shotgun." She pointed across the street. "There's my van. I need to tell the boys we're going to the city."

Jess threw herself into the passenger seat and rolled down the window. She was seized by the unshakable belief that they were on the right course—any other possibility was madness.

Moments later, the door flew open and Annie jumped into the driver's seat, turned the key, and the engine rumbled awake. "Here we go," she said. "What's our plan?"

"Let's start at the corner where the cabbie said he dropped off Parker and Sarah. We'll fan out from there. Unless you've got another idea."

"Nope. Sit tight. We'll be there in thirty minutes max."

Once down Miller Avenue, Annie wound through the gears, getting the van up to speed, along the marshland, and out onto the highway. The cold wind streaming through the window tore tears from Jess's eyes.

"I'm feeling lucky about this, Annie. If I have to knock on every goddamn door in the neighborhood, I will."

"I'll bust down every door," Annie said, maneuvering through sparse traffic. The headlights from northbound traffic flashed past them as they rolled up the Waldo Grade and through the rainbow tunnel, the lights of the city blazing in the dark night. Soon they were over the bridge, tooling along Crissy Field, past the Palace of Fine Arts, and onto Lombard Street.

"We're almost there," Annie said. "Are you ready?"

"I'm so ready." Jess replied. The closer they drew to the corner where the cabbie had dropped off Parker and Sarah, the more attuned she became to each change or movement on the street. When Annie turned off Lombard onto Scott, the road began to climb. The neighborhood became more exclusive with each block—elegant period homes, chateaux, and mansions representing wealth passed down through generations. Manicured gardens fronted stately residences, spotlights aimed on sculpted trees, hedges, and iron gates. Every flicker and motion captured her attention.

At the top of the hill, Annie swung the van onto Jackson Street and pulled over in front of an imposing mansion across from Alta Plaza Park. "Which way?" she asked.

"Drive slowly. Let's circle the block and see what we find."

As Annie cruised, Jess watched. An air of privilege weighted the salty night air. Most of the homes were fronted with carved doors flanked by marble statuary and topiary. Chandeliers twinkled behind leaded windows. There was an aura of respectability and propriety behind each drawn drape. But when Annie turned the van onto Pacific Avenue, they both heard the thump of a deep base lifting out over the rooftops.

"Hot damn!" Annie said.

"I don't believe it." Jess squirmed on the seat, poised like a swimmer at the starting block. Annie drove faster, swinging around a corner and down two blocks toward the music that grew louder until up ahead in the middle of the street, she drew abreast of a mansion lit up like a palace. People milled around on the sidewalk. Limos were double-parked in the street. The bass thump of blues intermingled with brash voices.

"Why haven't the police shut this scene down?" Jess asked.

"You're looking at what money can buy," Annie said.

"No kidding! Park the van. I'll meet you inside," Jess said, leaping out the door. As she pushed her way through the gate, the path was crowded with men and women, holding cocktails, their eyes glittering. Guests stood on the balconies overlooking the street calling down to others below. Inside the black and white marble tiled entry, she took stock of the crowd and searched the faces of guests, trying to figure out what to do next. She noticed a young woman in a white blouse and black skirt, passing a platter of hors d'oeuvres.

Jess poised on the outside of a circle of guests and waited until the woman turned toward her. She lowered her voice. "Excuse me," she said. "Whose house is this?' The woman looked at her strangely.

"You see, I've lost my keys to my car and thought that maybe…" she paused.

"Why that would be Gardner and Posie…"

"Greene. Of course." Jess said. "Do you know where Gardner is right now?"

"I believe you'll find him in the pool house."

"Thank you," Jess said brightly. She stepped back, trying to gauge her next move when Annie tapped her on the shoulder.

"This is Gardner Greene's house," she reported. "That's the name I was trying to remember. I'm sure Parker is here. But where in the hell is Sarah in this zoo?"

"Let's split up," Annie said, gripping Jess's shoulder. "I'll take this floor. You take the second."

"No. Gardner is in the pool house. Let's start with him."

"These folks are high rollers." Annie appraised the walls in the foyer and along the staircase hung with paintings. "Already I've seen a de Kooning, Pollack, and Rausenberg." When a waiter moved by, she grabbed a flute of champagne off a tray, downing it in one swallow. She glanced at Jess. "Don't give me the stink eye. When have you known me to pass up Dom Perignon?"

They sauntered through the dining room, past the library, and into a kitchen that opened onto a garden patio. A turquoise pool sparkled. Foliage was thick with dense green palms. Industrial electric heaters warmed the cold air. Jess led Annie past unoccupied lounge chairs, a bar where Champagne corks popped, and a gleaming copper grill where chefs in white hats prepared food. Smoke rose from the grill carrying the scent of prawns, oysters and beef. At the far end of the patio, Jess saw the pool house, a striped awning overhanging its entry.

Jess marched up to wide doors folded open and into a wall of cigar smoke. She could feel Annie beside her keeping pace. The scent of whiskey pierced the dim. Middle-aged men slouched in low couches, many with silver at their temples, dressed in tuxedoes and suits, collars splayed at the neck. No one appeared to take notice as she advanced. She saw the back of Parker's head first, the gleam of a cufflink where his hand supported his neck. She walked toward him where he was slumped on a couch wedged between two older men. His eyes swam behind his glasses, trying to focus on her. She felt disgust and with it a swift rush of anger. His head flopped back as he tried to raise it. One foot was crossed over his knee. She kicked his foot hard. His head jerked up, his eyeglasses sliding sideways off his ears.

"Where's Sarah?" she demanded.

He opened his mouth, swallowing air; his eyes rolled in his head.

She wanted to scream, but Annie grabbed her arm and pulled her away. "What a sorry sack of shit," she said. "Don't waste your breath."

A man beside Parker struggled to his feet and tried to maintain his balance. "What's going on here?" he asked. He was distinguished looking, beautifully dressed and very drunk.

"Are you Gardner Greene?" Jess asked. He ducked his chin inside his neck and peer down at her quizzically. "Why, yes. Who are you?"

Annie planted herself directly in his path. A little more than half his height, she trembled with outrage. "Look, asshole," she said, poking her finger into a glittering stud on his shirtfront. "One simple question—where is Parker's daughter?"

His eyes blurred and he blinked, trying to focus. "All the children are in the gymnasium," he slurred, sputtering something else unintelligible, and flopped back on the couch.

* * *

The single entrance to the gymnasium was from the third floor. Jess and Annie found access up a twisting stairway. The din of children's voices grew louder as they climbed upwards. When they finally reached the top landing, they entered a small room stripped of furniture, and saw the descent of another staircase down to the gymnasium. They stepped up to a plate glass window built into a sidewall, cupped their hands to the window, and looked through the glass. Below, Jess saw a pack of boys and girls racing back and forth over the polished floor of a regulation-sized gymnasium. Floodlights shone as bright as day. Sarah, the smallest in the pack, fought for the ball, blonde hair flying and elbows jabbing.

"There she is!" Jess said, bounding down the stairs ahead of Annie and out onto the floor of the gymnasium. They halted on the sidelines, the smell of sweat and screech of tennis shoes swirling around their heads. A ball down court hit the rim and bounced off. A boy leapt and caught it in midair. The children turned in one unit and came racing up court toward Jess and Annie. Sarah was running behind, her legs, streaks of red corduroy, pumping hard.

Suddenly Sarah spotted them, and screamed, "Mommy!" She broke away and jogged over, looking up at her mother. Her chest was rising and falling as she panted for air, her cheeks flushed with excitement.

"Hi, honey." Jess said. "Looks like you found some friends?"

"Yeah!" A shadow of consternation passed over her face. She glanced at Annie, "Hi, Annie," and back at Jess. "How come you're here?" Her eyes grew wide. "Did Daddy call you? He said he called you."

"No, he didn't."

"Uh-oh." Comprehension wilted Sarah's pleasure, followed quickly by curiosity. "How did you know I was here?"

Jess pursed her lips. "It was kind of like following crumbs in the forest." She nodded at Annie. "I had a good scout."

"You're friends again?"

"We never really stopped," Annie said, elbowing Jess.

"That's right," Jess said.

"That's what I thought, too," Sarah said. Then she seemed to know what was coming next. Her eyes darted between Jess and Annie like she was trying to slow down an inevitable summons. "I'm having so much fun."

"Yes," Jess said. "I can see that."

"A real lot of fun," she said, drawing each word out for emphasis.

"Listen pumpkin," Jess said, "it's time to go home."

"You mean I can't stay and watch 'Creature Features'?" she asked.

"No, it's late."

Sarah stomped her foot on the floor. "Please, Mom," she whined. "Can't I stay?"

Jess leaned forward and reached for her. "It's been a big day."

Sarah pulled away, her arms stiff, hands clenched. "It's because of Daddy, isn't it?"

"Daddy is in no condition to bring you home," Jess said firmly.

Sarah's shoulders slumped in resignation. She scuffed her toe against the floor. Glancing over her shoulder at the children who continued to play, she sighed.

"Do you want to say goodbye to your friends?"

"No. I want to say goodbye to Daddy. I know where he is."

Annie stepped forward and spoke into Jess's ear. "Let her. She'll be okay."

* * *

Jess paused by the edge of the pool and watched Sarah walk straight-backed toward the men who still clustered on couches, their voices punctuated by occasional laughter. The bent notes of the blues wailed from the house, floating through the open windows and doors, over the turquoise water. The grill was closed, the cooks departed. Sarah had asked her mother not to come with her, and Jess had agreed.

Sarah waded in through the smoke and reek of whiskey. Jess's anger at Parker smoldered. But far larger, more consuming, was heartache for her daughter. There was no winning this crusade. There was only pressing on toward what seemed right.

Sarah stopped in front of the spot where Jess had confronted Parker. In that moment, each second held a universe of longing. Gradually Sarah leaned in toward Parker. Her face disappeared momentarily, and then Sarah's arms encircled his neck, her head buried in his shoulder.

* * *

As Annie drove down the hill toward the bridge, Jess cradled Sarah on her lap. Gradually, Sarah drifted into sleep. Her shoulders relaxed, her legs grew heavy, the fingers of her hands twitched and unfurled. Her tangy-sweet scent surrounded Jess. Ahead, the towers of the bridge, laced at the top with wisps of fog, ascended into the night sky like giant sentries.

Jess pulled her gaze away from Marin's broad headlands curving westward toward the ocean. "I'm finished with Parker."

"No shit."

"No, I mean I'm really finished."

"It's about time," Annie said, driving off the deck of the bridge, the tires clicking a final farewell, onto the highway, up the Waldo Grade, toward home. Behind, the city sparkled like a necklace of diamonds along the shore of the bay.

"You came through for me," Jess said.

"You would have done the same."

They shot through the tunnel, the van's headlights sweeping the road.

"Yes, I would," Jess said. Emerging from the narrow passage, Mt. Tamalpais loomed sovereign and majestic against the night sky. The power of the mountain infused her with strength. Homecoming promised peace. Morning would wash them clean.

Chapter 19

June 2, 3, and 4

NORMALLY A VETERAN at keeping trouble at a distance, the discovery of his mother's letter to Charles goaded Daniel to action. He drove to San Francisco, took a room at the San Remo Hotel, and after eating at a sidewalk joint in North Beach, he wandered the streets. He slept badly—noises of the city rattled the windows—sirens wailing, drunks shouting, and glass and metal crashing at 3 AM when sanitation trucks rumpled by.

At the Main Branch of the San Francisco Library in Civic Center, he walked through the door in the morning alongside students, the elderly, and men dressed in heavy coats and carrying briefcases who looked like they made the library their office annex. In the stacks, he searched through the Philadelphia phone books for Margaret's name and then spent the afternoon scrolling through two decades of '60s and '70s San Francisco newspaper articles on microfiche.

A recent article published in January 1974 about Judge Bertrand Hobart, who was retiring from San Francisco's Superior Court, jogged his memory. The article mentioned that before his appointment to the bench, Hobart had practiced at Gessler, Barrows, and Blake in the '50s. Daniel vaguely recalled meeting him at the firm when he was seven and witnessing the friendship between his grandfather and Bertrand. He mulled over the idea of contacting the judge on a hunch that he might air his distrust about Charles's leadership at the firm. He decided he didn't have a leg to stand on unless he had hard evidence, which meant another visit to the law office. It was worth a gamble.

He caught a bus back to North Beach and prowled down Columbus Avenue. Over the buildings, he saw the dark green shoulder of Mt. Tamalpais rise up against the horizon. He pushed aside a compunction to speak to Jess, anticipating that a conversation would dilute his efforts. He guarded his energy and focused on the hunt.

When night fell he broke into the law firm and had another look in Charles' files. He was familiar with properties held in the family trust—four office buildings in the financial district, an industrial warehouse in Mission Bay, and partial ownership of a new hotel, The Prescott, on Post Street in the theater district. He noticed an unusual number of billings for general repairs to all the properties except the Prescott. A roof job on the warehouse dated November 5, 1973 sparked his curiosity. The cost for the new roof was $48,500. The name of the contractor for all the repairs was Ching Kee Construction Company in Chinatown. He copied all the billings on the Xerox and returned the papers to the file.

That night he slept soundly.

As dawn broke over the city, he inspected the warehouse, a 40,000 square foot steel frame building. The sign over the rollup doors read, "Bay Cities Liquor Distribution." The doors were shut; no one was around, and the parking lot in front of the warehouse was empty. Daniel climbed up a ladder attached to the side of the building onto the flat roof. The tar and gravel roof was worn thin by sun, cold, and wind. He kicked at the sparse gravel with his shoe. His eyes swept over the roof surfaces, where blisters bubbled up through the asphalt. *Eureka!,* he thought. The billing from Ching Kee Construction was a blatant fraud. He pulled out an Instamatic camera and took photos.

He caught a bus back to Chinatown. The address for Ching Kee Construction led him down an alley off Grant Avenue. The alley reeked with the smell of fish, smoky incense, and trash. The sound of human voices and tinkling bells drifted from open shop doors. Telephone wires crossed overhead and clotheslines, strung with flapping shirts and trousers, draped the outside of buildings.

The address was the site of a fortune cookie factory on the ground floor and apartments on the second floor.

Now he had enough evidence to make a case against Charles.

He called the judge from a phone booth, introduced himself, and asked to see him. The judge expressed surprise and then seemed genuinely pleased. His afternoon was free, and he warmly extended an invitation to Daniel to visit.

After lunch, Daniel rode a cable car to Judge Hobart's home, a Nob Hill address on Sacramento Street bordering Grace Cathedral. As he jumped off and walked past the sweeping stairs to the Cathedral doors, he heard organ music pumping into the air. In Huntington Park across the street, pigeons flew in and out of a circular fountain that splashed water over bronze cherubs. His adrenaline ran high as he hiked up to the judge's house, climbed the brick stairs to a white door, and rang the bell.

The judge opened the door. "Good afternoon," he said, grasping Daniel's hand in a knuckle-gripping handshake. His keen blue eyes appraised Daniel. "Yes, you're a Gessler through and through. No doubt about it."

"How do you do, sir," Daniel said, immediately feeling welcomed. The demeanor of the man reminded Daniel of the ease of men like his grandfather who commanded respect by their presence. He had a shock of salt and pepper hair and displayed the vitality of someone as accustomed to navigating a sailboat on the bay as hearing a case in Superior Court.

"Come in," the judge said, preceding Daniel up two flights of stairs. They walked down a long hall into a study lined with books, a model yacht, and an enormous globe that occupied a pedestal table. The study afforded a view into grey ramparts of the nave rising against the jewel colors of the stain glass windows of the Cathedral. "Please, have a seat," the judge said. Bright afternoon light flooded through bay windows.

They sat in club chairs opposite one another. Daniel's anticipation mounted as he sat face to face with the judge. The hard moment for disclosure hovered at this back. Presenting his case wouldn't be as straightforward as he had contemplated. The judge's power of observation and knowledge of law was sharpened on cases far more egregious than this and far less personal. Daniel tried to cool his nerves. He was banking on the judge's loyalty to his grandfather.

The judge hooked his fingers into his suspenders and inquired politely about Daniel's family. After reminiscing about the law firm in the old days, he excused himself, and returned with two tumblers filled to the brim. He held one out to Daniel and settled back into his chair. "A little gin and tonic to wet the whistle," he said. "Here's to your grandfather," he said, raising his glass. He set down his glass, crossed one knee over the other and wove his fingers together. "Tell me, son. How can I help you today?"

Daniel sat forward, elbows on his knees, and began. He didn't spare the details of an acrimonious relationship between himself and Charles that had worsened over the years, or of his rocky tenure at Boalt Hall. The judge listened pensively. Daniel explained he had found evidence of a highly personal nature that he preferred to keep private, and how this evidence had, at first, aroused his suspicions about Charles's integrity. The judge's eyebrows shot up, but he didn't interrupt. Daniel continued that his reason for wanting to talk to the judge centered on properties held in a family trust. He slipped a list of properties, invoices, and photos of the liquor warehouse roof out of a manila envelope.

"Judge Hobart," he said, handing him the pages, "The construction on these properties wasn't performed, and I believe all the invoices are false."

The judge reached inside his shirt pocket, withdrew a pair of eyeglasses, and slipped them on his nose. As he examined the papers and photos, Daniel told him about his inspection and attempt to find the construction company in the alley in Chinatown.

The judge peered over the rim of his eyeglasses. "These are serious allegations."

"Yes, sir," Daniel answered. "I know."

"I presume you obtained this information unbeknownst to your uncle?"

Daniel swallowed. "I believe there may be other infractions."

"I see." The judge put a finger to his lips. "It would be helpful if you told me about the evidence you allude to that is a private matter."

"I'd rather not." Daniel said, nose to nose with the possibility of scandal. "Perhaps I could change my position on this, but not at this time."

The judge nodded thoughtfully. "Well, then, what are you proposing?"

"I intend to get to the bottom of this, sir. I believe Charles is siphoning money off the trust into his own pocket. It could be the tip of an iceberg."

"This is a grave matter indeed," the judge said. "It's enough if Charles is defrauding the family trust, but as senior member of the firm, I have a concern that's he may be defrauding clients as well.

"This isn't the legacy that my grandfather intended for our family or for the law firm," Daniel said.

"Hell, no." The judge pursed his lips.

"I've come to you for counsel, sir."

The judge stood, pacing between the chairs and the window. He regarded Daniel solemnly. "It's yours," he said, and launched into a discussion in which he outlined a course of legal actions that would, among other considerations, require an interim reorganization of the law firm. As he concluded his argument, he sat again, facing Daniel.

"Are you prepared to continue?"

"Yes, sir," Daniel said.

"You'll need to hire a professional who can investigate this matter. I recommend the principal investigator at Markewitz and Vetch. The firm deals with high profile cases of a sensitive and discreet nature. Roman Markewitz is a trusted ally."

The judge went to his desk and picked up the phone.

"Roman, it's Bertrand," he said. "Yes, I'm fine. And you?" He shifted in his seat, scratching his chin. "Say, is it possible for you to come over to the house?" He nodded. "Yes, this afternoon. Right away. It's urgent. I appreciate it. There's someone I want you to meet." He nodded at Daniel who knew he was at the starting line of a race, hearing a gun go off.

They didn't have long to wait. Shortly afterwards, Daniel heard a car door slam, and the bell ring at the front door.

An hour later, Daniel hired Roman Markewitz to undertake an investigation into the holdings in the Trust and dealings with the firm. Both the judge and investigator advised Daniel not to discuss the case with anyone. Markewitz said he'd report to Daniel within a week, shook Daniel's hand, the judge's hand, and said goodbye.

The judge stood at the top of the stairs as Daniel prepared to leave.

"Keep me appraised of the developments, son."

"Yes, I will." Daniel had gone from a standstill to warp speed within twelve hours.

"I suggest the three of us meet here, review Roman's findings, and talk about where we go. It's the least I can do for your grandfather."

"Thank you, sir," Daniel said gratefully.

"One more thing," the judge said sternly.

"Yes, sir?"

"Don't call me 'sir,'" he ordered, flashing a white-toothed smile and grasping Daniel's hand in another knuckle-gripping handshake.

* * *

At home later that evening, Daniel dragged a chair out onto the lawn at the edge of the cliff and gazed out to sea. Cody joined him in the grass, his head on his paws. Daniel's fingers stroked his head. He could feel in his gut that he had moved into a position he could only begin to assimilate. The seams were coming apart for Charles. There would be chaos. What would it mean for the firm? Daniel wanted a stake in the outcome, but he didn't know how or what. The hazy shape of an idea was forming in his mind. It was as distant as the horizon, but he sensed its solid presence.

He placed a call to Jess, and by the tone of her voice, he had the impression that she was holding him at arm's length. She barely responded when he explained that he had been San Francisco for a couple of days. He itched to tell her about Judge

Hobart and Roman Markewitz. When he suggested that she and Sarah join him in Bolinas the next weekend, she dodged the idea and the conversation idled.

"Maybe you want to hang out alone with Sarah," he said. "How is she?"

"What do you mean?"

"I mean, you know, how is she doing after Parker's visit?"

"She's rocky for a few days after he leaves and then she bounces back."

"I can come over."

"That's not necessary," she said. "Anyway, I want to concentrate on some things I've been putting off."

"Like what?"

"Some of us need to get a real job," she said acidly.

"You sound pissed off," he said. "What's going on?"

"Nothing. Apparently Sebastian has a new plan, but I've got to be realistic."

He hesitated. "Maybe being home when Sarah gets out of school rather than in rehearsal is a good call."

"If you have something to say, say it." She sounded like she wanted to bite his head off. "Anyway, I didn't say I'd *stop* dancing."

"Forget it. Why don't we talk later?"

"I may not be home."

He listened to the line go dead and stared out the window toward a rolling cloudbank gathering over the Pacific. Suddenly Jess was like a cold current coming down from the north meeting warm, moist air flowing up from the south—agitated and tempestuous. He couldn't read her temperature.

But another momentum was building, and her unpredictability added to his premonition that whatever road he was headed down, the shoulder would be strewn with bodies.

* * *

Bolstered by pillows, Jess was tucked in bed next to Sarah. A former tenant had painted green ivy intertwined with purple morning glories along the crown molding, and Jess's gaze wandered back and forth from the pages of the book she held in her lap to the leaves and flowers.

"Keep reading, Mom," Sarah said, spooning tapioca into her mouth. "You're getting to the good parts."

The book grew heavy in Jess's hands. Only a few days had passed since Parker's departure, and she had thrown herself into restoring normalcy to their daily pace of life. He had called before he boarded the airplane, offered a feeble apology, and said goodbye to Sarah who accepted his departure with a minimum of complaint. Jess sensed a new toughness in her that wasn't there before, and more and more, maturity uncommon for children her age who grow up in nuclear families. The bond between them seemed to grow stronger as they weathered new challenges. The warm bed, the familiar pressure of Sarah's knees shimmied against her hip, and the purring of the cat caused her eyelids to droop with sleep.

"Okay, we're ready now." Sarah repositioned the cat in her lap and the bowl on her chest.

Jess read:

> *Chapter V: Riddles in the Dark*
>
> *"When Bilbo opened his eyes, he wondered if he had; for it was just as dark as with them shut. No one was anywhere near him. Just imagine his fright! He could hear nothing, see nothing, and he could feel nothing except the stone of the floor.*
> *Very slowly he got up and groped about on all fours, till--"*

"I think someone's knocking," Sarah interrupted.

A six beat rap sounded from the front door.

A frown crossed Jess's brow. "You wait here," she said, and scooted from the bed. "I'll be right back."

Daniel slouched against the doorframe. "Hi. I didn't wake you, did I?"

Jess stepped slightly back and tightened the sash of the robe. "I was reading to Sarah," she said.

In a flash Sarah bounded across the floor, arms outstretched. "Danny," she cried. "I knew it was you."

"Hey, how's my girl?" He caught her flying body—a blur of blue fish pajamas, blond curls, and flushed cheeks.

"Ouff," he said, hoisting her higher into his arms. "You're getting heavy."

She clung to his neck. "Where have you been?"

The tenderness of their meeting silenced Jess.

"First I was in the city and then I was home fixing stuff."

"I missed you," she said, resting her head on his shoulder.

"Sarah," Jess said, "It's time for bed."

"But we didn't finish the chapter yet."

"We'll finish it tomorrow night."

"Can Danny put me to bed?"

Jess traded a quick look with Daniel who tipped his chin and smiled.

"Well, all right. But don't ask him to read to you."

In the kitchen, she rested her forehead on the windowpane and looked at stark outline of the dark trees standing against the night sky as her daughter launched into a discussion of Bilbo Baggins and Gandalf. Daniel confided that *The Hobbit* was one of his favorite books, and Sarah bombarded him with observations and inquiries, volleying question after question. The tiny muscles along Jess's jaw constricted, and her neck tightened. A tumult of emotions waged inside her head. Daniel's first phone call after the incident with Parker almost felt to her like a duty call. His absence when Sarah went missing chafed beneath her skin. She couldn't reveal to him what had happened with Parker. Sarah's feelings for Daniel were obvious; how could she ask her daughter to relinquish her attachment to him?

A hush emanated from the bedroom, and she went to investigate.

Daniel was straddling a stool beside the bed and holding Sarah's hand. Heads together, they each seemed absorbed in the flicking of the cat's tail.

Sarah swiveled her head toward her mother, her eyes widening and legs kicking. "Not yet," she moaned.

"Time's up." Jess insisted and straightened the bedcovers.

Sarah flopped back against the pillows, pouting at Daniel who leaned over and kissed her on the check. "Good night. Don't forget what I said." He held his fingers in a V, moved swiftly from the bedside and out of the room.

"Danny's going on a trip to see his mother," Sarah reported. "He said he wouldn't be gone long. He will come back, won't he?" A pucker of worry creased Sarah's forehead.

Jess folded the covers under her chin. "I'm sure he will."

"Where do you think Daddy is now?"

"Maybe he's in Kyoto," Jess said, stacking the books on the bedside table and perching on the edge of the bed.

"You're still not mad at him. I mean for getting drunk and stuff. Are you?"

"No, I'm not mad anymore…"

"Don't worry, Mom. I wasn't in real danger. Not like on TV or anything. Nothing bad happened. Anyway, you and Annie knew how to find me."

"Yes, we did." Jess kissed her cheek. "Now it's time for sleep.

Sarah yawned. "I love you, Mom. You can turn off the light, but don't shut the door."

Jess found Daniel leaning against the kitchen countertop, his energy contained and drawn about him.

"I guess Sarah let the cat out of the bag. I'm leaving for Philadelphia on the red-eye tonight."

"How did this happen?" She stood across the room from him, her arms folded tightly across her ribs.

"Ceci came through. She called Estelle who had maintained contact with my mother all along. Can you beat that?"

"It doesn't surprise me. Does your mother know you're coming?"

"No, I want to show up and see what happens."

"Sometimes that's all you can do." Jess stared at the floorboards. It was extraordinary to be in each other's presence and not be touching.

"What is it, Jess?" he asked. "Is something wrong? You didn't tell me about Parker's visit."

She turned and faced him. "You didn't ask!"

"I *did* ask. You brushed me off."

"Did I?" she said, unable to keep the sarcasm out of her voice.

"Come on," he said. "That's not fair."

"As a matter of a fact, Parker's visit was a disaster." She groped for words. "He disappeared with Sarah. I was terrified."

"Damn it!" he said, striding across the floor and taking her in his arms. "Why didn't you tell me?"

"Because by the time you called it was over. Annie helped me. I couldn't have done it without her. She was there when I needed her." She took a deep breath to clear her head and stepped away. "I've thought about this, believe me, what I need to do now is concentrate on Sarah, pay attention to what's important, and make a better home for her."

"What are you talking about?" he said. "You have made a home for her. Take a good look around. When has Sarah ever given you any reason to doubt that she isn't a perfectly normal, happy kid?"

"I have to do better."

"Not in my book. You're beating yourself up for something you couldn't have predicted. Come on, Jess. Give it up."

"Daniel, I can't be in a relationship right now."

"It's a little late for that," he said. "We're already in one."

She studied his face, the same clear, steady gaze, colors of the sea lighting his eyes, and her defense began to waiver.

"I wasn't by a phone when you needed me," he reasoned. "Be fair." He shook his head from side to side. "Christ, if anything had happened to Sarah I'd never forgive myself."

A weariness came over her that she hadn't allowed herself to feel.

Daniel's breath was warm against her cheek. "I'm here. I'll do everything I can to keep you and Sarah safe."

"I'm the one who has to make everything right for her."

"But that doesn't mean I can't be a part of it. No more talk about cutting out on me, okay?"

"Wasn't I convincing enough?" she asked.

He leaned back and looked at her. "You had me for a minute."

"Really?" she laughed softly.

"Well, not exactly." He held her gently and stroked her back.

"Daniel?"

"Yes?"

"Whatever happens in Philadelphia, your mother will feel blessed to find the boy she left behind has grown into a man."

Chapter 20

June 5

AT DUSK STEWART CRUISED DOWN the path to Annie's house and hiked up the collar of his shirt. The band-aid he'd placed over the scratch on his neck was a dead giveaway, but he couldn't do a damn thing about it. The bruises, he rationalized, weren't as noticeable. He felt like a chump at the poker table with a fool's hand—Jack 9, unsuited—betting against the house that would happily part a gambler from his money any time of the week.

He had checked the address twice; no doubt about it, this must be it. He hadn't noticed the house tucked behind Dowd's Moving and Storage, but then why would he? Walking over the footbridge that spanned the fern-banked creek was like walking into a different age. The paint job ranked right up there with the best of San Francisco's painted ladies.

Noah answered the door. "Hi, Mr. Merch," he said. The television blared from inside the house.

"Hey, Noah. Is your mom in?"

"She's upstairs," he said, tripping backwards. "She said you should go up."

Stewart paused in the hall, glancing at the high ceilings, wood moldings and burnished floors, and scrutinized a white marble-topped lowboy placed just inside the entry. Passing by the doorway to the living room, he stopped and found Matthew and Noah sprawled on the floor in front of the TV. Matthew rolled over, smacking a wad of pink gum in his mouth.

"Hello, Matthew. What's up?" Stewart asked. While he hadn't been able to break through Matthew's shell, the boy hadn't flamed out. There was some weak satisfaction to that. The school year wasn't quite over. Stewart was open to making a last ditch effort, and he watched for any opening.

Matthew eyed him coldly, working the gum between his teeth.

"Hey, that's Gilligan's Island," Stewart ventured. "Great show."

"Yeah, it's cool," Matthew said, rolling back to the TV.

Stewart spoke to his back, "I'm going up to see your mom," and walked up the stairs into the hallway toward an open door. "Annie," he called.

"I'm in here," she answered.

"You didn't tell me you lived in a showpiece," he said as he stepped into her studio.

"Welcome," she said, squeezing his arm.

Three canvases shimmered on the wall under the blast of track lighting. Interlocking creatures, part animal, part human, painted electric blue, undulated across the canvases.

Stewart gaped at the paintings. The visceral force of the images was like a blow to his chest. One thought resounded in his mind: I have underestimated this woman.

Leathery rings defined subterranean bodies. Bulging eyes leered from misshapen heads. A supplicating hand, palm up, grew out of a sinewy limb. Stumps of flesh dripped orange paint. Orifices gaped wetly.

"I'm almost finished with the last panel. What do you think?"

"It's like Henri Rousseau meets Dante's Inferno."

"Ah, I've never been compared to either of them, but I like it. I hope Governor Moonbeam will be as impressed as you are."

"This should knock everyone out. How do you come up with this stuff?"

"Sick, huh?" she beamed. "Dig deep, and you never know what you'll find." She picked up a bottle of wine from a worktable set with a plate of cheese and crackers, a bowl of olives, and two wine glasses. "How about some wine?"

"Sounds good." He ambled over to the portfolio by the window and flipped through the drawings.

The cork popped. "It's an unassuming, gay Sauvignon Blanc," she said. "Light and fruity on the palate."

He flinched, his hand flying to his collar, and swung around. She held out a wine glass, and as he took it, her fingertips brushed his hand. "Here's to you," she toasted. The glasses chimed a crystal clear bell note, and the creatures in the paintings seemed to freeze. Stewart gulped the cool grassy-scented wine.

"I heard you were out on the town in North Beach last weekend."

"News travels fast." He made a fast calculation. "A friend of yours at the Silver Spur?"

"Correct," Annie said, tipping her chin as if she was about to watch him stick his finger into a socket. "She said you looked like you'd run into some trouble."

"She saw me at my worst. That was the same day I wrecked my bicycle. Some nut ran into me in Golden Gate Park. I was trying to dull the pain."

"You can't be too careful these days," she said and refilled his glass.

He strolled back to the paintings and sipped the wine. "Tell me about your work."

She appeared at his shoulder. "Getting started is the tricky part," she explained. "It's like I'm trying to woo a cat. Try and catch her, and she'll dance away. But when I clear my mind, I begin to see organic shapes on the canvas. First I draw the shapes with a charcoal pencil, linking one to the other. Everything falls away. It's the most delicious process."

Her perfume wafted around his face, and the curve of her breast pressed against his arm. As he turned toward her, she kissed him full on the mouth.

The shock of her lips sent him backwards. "Take it easy," he said.

"What's the problem?" she objected.

"The boys are downstairs. I don't think we should fool around."

She laughed. "Are you kidding? They could care less."

"But I care," he said. "I wouldn't be comfortable. It would put me at a disadvantage I can't afford with Matthew."

Doubt passed over her face. "Give him an inch and he'll take a mile?"

"You got it. I'm on shaky ground with him as it is. You understand, right?"

"Of course. Still," she said, peering at him, "you're a hard one to button down. I never know where I stand with you."

"Then let's get to know one another better." He swept his hand toward the table. "You've got to understand that for me this is like dinner." He executed a quick shuffle like he was on the tennis court waiting for his opponent to smash the ball over the net. "Then I've got to get going. It's a school night, you know."

* * *

Night pressed against the weathered shingles of Stewart's cabin. Inside, he wandered aimlessly from room to room. From the kitchen, furnished with a Formica table and two metal folding chairs, an announcer's voice at the Giant's baseball game in Candlestick blared from a transistor radio perched on the refrigerator. He ambled into the bedroom and stepped over a pile of dirty sweatshirts and towels. At the bureau, an oak relic from college days, he shuffled through a stack of junk mail. Advertisements littered the pages: mega-vitamins, obscure book titles, wooden boats and the granddaddy of all outdoor equipment—the L.L. Bean catalogue. His favorite catalogue hawked bodybuilding machines. They guaranteed biceps like George Foreman, a neck like Hercules and the powers of Jack LaLanne. If used only minutes a day, the steel contraptions could transform a ninety-pound ectomorph and into a two hundred pound mesomorph the size of a Great Plains Buffalo. A sucker for the copy, he would pour over it for hours. He lifted another brochure, and a white business card fell onto the bureau. Harry Dunbar's name leapt into focus.

The scene at the bar materialized: he heard the ear-splitting roar of the crowd inside the bar; he saw the adoration in Harry's eyes, thin hair side-combed to conceal his balding head; he felt the stranger's hand on his shoulder, and the plunge into a well of blackness. Instantly lust had exploded into pain. How defenseless he was to ward off the blows.

Stewart walked into the kitchen and opened the refrigerator door. A carton of eggs, loaf of bread, six-pack of beer and tired apples had not changed position in a week. He sat at the table, head in his hands, and returning to the refrigerator, grabbed a beer and pulled the tab. The cool liquid hit the back of his throat and stung his eyes. At the phone, he lifted the receiver and dialed.

Harry's voice answered, clear and commanding. "May I ask who's calling?" he asked.

"I met you awhile back in North Beach."

"Of course. I thought I recognized your voice. It's Stewart, isn't it?"

"You remember me?"

"I do. How nice to hear from you."

"I meant to call earlier," Stewart said, thinking maybe placing the call wasn't such a good idea after all.

"I had rather hoped you would."

"I came across your card and I wanted to thank you for—"

"Don't mention it," Harry said. "What a dreadful night. Unfortunately not an isolated case. One must exercise caution. Are you well?"

"Yes, I'm fine."

"That is splendid," Harry plunged on about the beautiful spring weather and repeatedly mentioned how thoughtful it was that Stewart had called.

Stewart made several remarks about the kindness of strangers, and sensing the growing anticipation in Harry's voice, tried to wrap up the conversation.

"Say, let's have dinner this week," Harry suggested brightly.

"I'm pretty busy right now." *What a feeble excuse,* Stewart thought.

"Surely you could spare an evening?"

"I don't get to the city much."

"What a shame," Harry said. "Where do you live?"

"Mill Valley."

Harry gasped. "Why?"

"It beats the fog and I work here."

"Granted, but you're out of the loop, my man. Say, what line of work are you in?"

"I teach sixth grade." Stewart braced himself.

"Oh, I understand," Harry said. "Surrounded by god's little children, granola mothers, and drum-beating fathers champing at the bit for their neighbor's wives. But lovely indeed. All that fresh air."

A quick reply dried in Stewart's mouth.

"I can imagine," Harry's voice wavered dramatically. "Winsome sun-kissed women flocking to your door."

"You're way off base."

"Perhaps a young mother, red blood flowing in her veins and full of hormones? I take it you do look in the mirror now and again. Don't tell me you're not beating them off with a stick. Well, never mind. I hate to think of you stranded over there. Come meet my friends. This is where you belong."

"Back off, Harry." *Was the man a psychic?*

"It doesn't have to be like it was the other night."

"And how was that?" He steadied himself for the obvious.

"Do I have to remind you? Wandering around the City, dying to get laid, and nearly getting your head bashed to bits!"

"I had a lousy night. You were decent. I called to thank you for bailing me out."

"Damn," Harry said. "I didn't mean to scold."

"I've got to go."

"Blast!" Harry said. "Now I've gone and put you off."

"Whatever you say."

"Do keep in touch."

"Sure."

"I sincerely hope so."

Stewart slammed down the phone and tossed Harry's card into the trash.

Chapter 21

June 6

MARGARET RANZELL PAUSED in the walk-in closet of her bedroom and considered what to wear. This was the second time she would dress for the day, but it was no ordinary day. For a week she had cleared her calendar expecting a telephone call from her son whose voice she hadn't heard in twenty-one years. Her body, humming with nervous anticipation, bent to the task of waiting.

At dawn, as was her custom, she awakened. Her joints ached and her eyes burned from reading *Tinker, Tailor, Soldier, Spy* into the morning hours—none of which she could now recall. She stumbled into jodhpurs and pulled on a Hampton coat for a ride on the trails in Liberty Park. She reasoned that since California was three hours behind Philadelphia she could risk an outing to the stables and return in time to await a phone call. The bitter scent of coffee curling from the kitchen caused her to teeter momentarily on the stairs.

When Margaret tripped into the domain of her housekeeper and cook, Miss E. Temple exclaimed, "Gracious, you are in a state. Try at least to stomach some juice. But don't dilly-dally. The fresh air will do you good."

Now, her clothes lay in a pile on the bathroom floor. Bathed, she viewed her options. Distracted by the sight of her reddened toes peeking out from the hem of a silk dressing gown, she glanced down at her feet. Blue veins appeared like tributaries under her pale skin and ran up the bones of her once lovely ankles.

She curled her toes, the nails manicured and polished, into the white carpet and tipped her head, massaging the furrow between her eyebrows. She felt inept, unable to think clearly, by turns exhilarated and then swamped by a sorrow she had carried for so long that it threatened to drop her to her knees. The voice of Estelle, sensible and firm, returned in her head. "It's time Margaret. We knew this moment would come. Be strong, dear. He's a fine young man."

Her suits hung the length of one long rack. They were arranged by color, starting with cream and ending with black—Givenchy, Dior and Chanel—which she wore to the docent meetings she chaired at the museum and to charity luncheons. Her ball gowns and evening clothes were stored on another rack: satins and silks in brilliant jewel tones of amethyst, emerald, sapphire, flanked by a full-length mink coat and a short white fox stole. Her day clothes, mostly slacks, tweeds and wool flannel, some gabardine, hung next to blouses, jackets, and blazers. She quickly dressed in camel slacks, a cashmere cardigan to match, paisley scarf, and brown alligator slacks.

She had requested a salad and dry toast in the library from Miss E. Temple, and given her the afternoon off. After lunch Margaret swallowed two Darvon tablets, removed a notebook from the desk drawer, and forced herself to concentrate on notes for the caterer and florist in preparation of a gala celebration and fundraiser she was organizing at the Philadelphia Museum of Art.

Her efforts seemed hollow and meaningless; the pen she was holding slipped through her fingers, her hands collapsed in her lap. The pages of the notebook fluttered shut. Through the unlatched windows she heard a helicopter pass by, the sound of its blades blatting over the rooftops. The lace curtains stirred at the windows. She regarded the mute black telephone, an arm's length away, that shamed her. A migraine stabbed her temples creating an ocular aura the proportion of which she could not remember seeing since her horse had thrown her on a remote trail in the park, and she had lain in the brush until discovered by a hiker. She had been waiting for years, waiting to be reunited with her son. Now she was prisoner in her own home.

* * *

Daniel stood in the afternoon shadow of a tree on South Bank Street, opposite number 119, watching the front door. He had double-checked the address twice. His eyes smarted, and his mouth was dry from the red-eye that had been delayed in Chicago. The day was marked by a cloudless blue sky and a fresh breeze that delivered the smell of the sea and docks to the cobbled streets.

The Federal houses of old Philadelphia were remarkably similar—three story, red brick, and imposing. Along the narrow brim of sidewalks in front of the residences elm trees arched skyward. Their green leaves, twirling on branches, softened the imposing facades. What distinguished one house from another was the paint—glossy black, colonial green, and in some rare instances fire engine red—applied in thick layers to the front doors, broad shutters, and windowpane trim. The door at 119 South Bank Street was painted black, as were the shutters. The trim was bright white; lace curtains hung at the windows.

A black woman of considerable girth, dressed in a grey hat and coat, her handbag held tightly in the crook of her arm, exited the house and hurried along the sidewalk. Daniel turned his shoulder and walked in the opposite direction. Farther along, he stopped a teenage boy and bummed a cigarette. At the docks, he inhaled briny sea air and then retraced his steps back to South Bank Street.

When he pressed the doorbell, his hand was unsteady and he stuffed it into his jacket pocket. Tense and alert, he waited. A tall, small-boned woman, honey gold hair greying at the temples, opened the door. Her eyes, hazel flicked with the honey color of Baja sand, swept over his face.

The hello Daniel had prepared to deliver died in his mouth. They gazed mutely at one another. Finally he stepped forward. "Margaret?"

"Daniel?" she said and again, but quietly, the question lingering and then dissolving to certainty, "Daniel." She clasped her hands together and suddenly they flew apart like sparrows. "Forgive me. I wasn't expecting you. I mean I was expecting you."

"You knew I was coming?" he asked, completely thrown off-guard.

"Yes. Please come in," she said, gesturing to the entry where polished black and white marble floor tiles gleamed in the afternoon light.

He stepped over the threshold. "How did you know?"

"Estelle."

It took him a moment, but before he could ask another question, Margaret turned and led him down the hall and into the library.

"I think we'll be comfortable here. This is where I spend most of my time." She paused behind a low sofa upholstered in a red silk stripe. "Please, make yourself at home. Are you hungry? Thirsty? Of course you are. Let me get you something. I'll be right back."

In an odd reversal that he hadn't anticipated, he felt as if she had preempted his surprise. He roamed around the library studying somber oil portraitures he suspected were of Dutch origin, inspecting titles of leather bound books in the bookshelves, classics from Melville, Dickens, Thoreau, Bronte, Austin, Twain, and Tolstoy. *Had she read them all?* he wondered. The room smelled like furniture wax and dried roses. A sheaf of papers with the logo of the Philadelphia Museum of Art lay scattered on her desk. Sun streaming through the curtains cast shadowy snowflakes across the floor. On tables draped in white damask, he peered into photographs of a young Margaret posing with a distinguished couple who, in each photograph, aged as she grew into womanhood. Daniel lifted one of the photos and looked closer at the grandparents he had never known.

Gradually he noticed silver framed photographs of himself taken at various stages of his life on every table. He lifted each photo and set it down. Maybe she took these out when she heard he was coming. Wonder mixed with agitation flooded his chest. What kind of woman would arrange to have her son's photo taken yet never contact him? She had spied on him, fed off his innocence, robbed him of his privacy, and given nothing back in return.

She returned with a tray that she placed on a coffee table in front of the sofa.

"Where did you get these photographs?" he asked.

"Estelle kept me abreast of your every move."

"I had no idea," he bristled. "Your informant!"

"Please. Don't be angry with her. She meant well."

"Estelle was your shadow, and I didn't even know you existed."

She blanched and gestured toward the sofa. "Let's not start like this. It isn't the way you make it sound. Believe me. Won't you sit down? I only have tonic and lemon. And cashews. Do you like cashews?" She sat opposite him, on the edge of a wing-backed chair, smoothing the crease in her slacks.

He crossed his arms across his chest and sank into the seat. In the entry a grandfather clock ticked relentlessly. She inquired about his health and then veered into questions about his father's health and Ceci's activities. Daniel gave the briefest of answers, listening to her rattle on. She commented about the cosmopolitan nature of San Francisco, the extraordinary creation of Golden Gate Park, and the unparalleled beauty of Marin County. "We have so much to talk about," she said, her eyes searching his face, "I hardly know where to begin. I've dreamed of this moment. Now that you're here I'm afraid..." her voice drifted and she waved her hand in front of her face. "Estelle is a remarkable woman. There's so much I owe her. Do you remember getting my birthday and Christmas presents?"

He tucked in his chin, letting her carry the conversation as she damn well pleased. The drinks and nuts she had brought in lay untouched on the table.

"Oh, that doesn't matter. When you were young, she would try to route the gifts to you, but after awhile I wondered if they ever reached you so I stopped sending them. Estelle told me about your friends, school, and love of the ocean. I know how close you are to Ceci, and that you live in Popee and Grandma's house in Bolinas. Oh, yes, I also know there's a lady in your life."

Daniel shifted positions on the sofa. The fingers of his right hand toyed with a cut above his lip where he'd nicked himself shaving in the terminal restroom. He was unable to contain a hostility that escalated and subsided with her monologue. His eyes examined her face looking for himself in her, but he didn't recognize any features they shared in common except for one obvious similarity—her eyes. Across from him sat the woman who was his mother, and in spite of his anger, there was something that lodged in his throat about the cadence of her speech, the way she held her head and even laughed.

"Would you like to see the rest of the house?" A smile lit her face. "Yes, I think that's a splendid idea. It's been in the family for generations. You might as well learn something about its history."

Her comment roused him out of the chair. Following behind, he kept pace with her brisk walk. They toured every floor, examined every cubby and crevice, her explanations droning on. Daniel was transfixed by her ability to sustain an endless narrative about a collection of furnishings and art that had nothing to do with the confusion swirling inside of him. He watched her closely for a moment's respite until she brought the tour to a close in a guest room on the second floor with a view to the cobbled street. The late afternoon sun glanced off the paned windows.

"This will be your bedroom," Margaret said. "I hope you'll stay for a few days, longer if you wish. I see you didn't bring any luggage. Perhaps we can shop together?" She regarded him hopefully, and discerning a distant sound, held her fingertip to her lips. "I heard my housekeeper come in. I should let her know you'll be here for dinner. I'll leave you to rest." She moved toward the door, as if in retreat.

"Wait a second," Daniel said. He dug into the pocket of his jacket, his fingers closing around an envelope. "This is all very nice. The history I never knew, who my grandparents were, what it was like for you growing up and the cool shit you're into now. But there's a reason I came."

The high color in her face paled.

"I want to know why you left. I want to know what happened to you and Dad. You're acting like it was no big deal for me to grow up thinking you had disappeared, maybe even died, and now everything is going to be fine!" He withdrew the envelope and thrust it toward her. "What happened between you and Charlie?"

"Miss Ranzell?" A strong voice called from a distance. "Are you there?"

"Yes, Miss E. Temple, I'm here," Margaret replied. "Excuse me, Daniel."

Muffled conversation continued in the hall. A distinct, "Mercy!" reverberated, followed by hushed speaking and then quiet. Daniel paced in front of the windows until Margaret returned to the room. Eyes downward, she took the envelope from his hands and lowered into a chair by the fireplace. "Please, Daniel, sit down." The grandfather clock chimed four bells.

"I've imagined the time when we'd be reunited, but somehow I thought I wouldn't have to explain why I left. How absurd." A smile lifted the contours of her cheeks and then dissolved; she seemed to swallow with difficulty. "But really do we have to have this conversation now. I..."

"Damn it, yes. Or I'm leaving."

"No, don't. Please don't." She glanced at the envelope and smoothed it on her lap as she had smoothed the crease from her slacks earlier. "Your father and I were so young when we married. I think upon reflection that I married the family rather than the man. It was a glorious family. They were involved in politics, the arts, and mad about horses and sailing." She halted as if remembering faces and voices and events that she had erased from memory, their recollection momentarily dispelling doubt. She arranged one foot over the other. Her voice dropped. "Gradually it became clear to me that your father would not carry forward your grandfather's work. His drinking took priority over everything. He'd disappear for days and then reappear as if nothing was wrong."

Daniel gritted his teeth; he wasn't surprised, but hearing it from her tore at the defense he had built over the years about his father's alcoholism. "Charles, on the other hand, was everything your father was not: serious, hard-working, and ambitious. He was also attentive and charming." She fell back against the seat. "I'll make no apologies," she said. "We had an affair."

Daniel's jaw tightened. He recoiled remembering the fetid smell of Charles's chamber and cold brush of steel against his cheek. At once another memory surfaced—one he had entirely displaced—spring days when he was a boy and a younger Charles had taught him to ride at the beach. He recalled the pride he felt when one night Charles had announced to the family that Daniel had mastered the skills to ride on his own, and a cheer had gone up around the table.

Margaret's voice trailed to a whisper. "I tried to break it off, but Charles was very persuasive. And then, unexpectedly, your father and I went through a peaceful time. I was so hopeful. I thought that maybe our marriage had a chance. That's when I became pregnant with you." She smiled softly across the room at Daniel who was encased in a kind of gloom. She rushed on. "But as soon as you were born your father resumed his escapades. And Charles was waiting in the wings as if he knew your father would fail. He pursued me knowing when I was the most vulnerable until—" She twisted in the chair.

"Go on," Daniel said.

She buried her face in her hands, "I'm so ashamed," she said. "He found me—"

"Charles found you what?" Daniel said, sitting forward.

"With someone else." She pulled at the arms of the chair to stand. "I can't continue this."

"Sit down," Daniel said.

"This is torture."

"I need to know what happened."

Her body seemed to curve inward until she straightened her shoulders. "Charles was livid. He insisted I stopped seeing this man. He was an attorney, but he stood for everything Charles did not—organized labor, civil rights, farm workers' rights." She paused, catching her breath. "Charles threatened to reveal my affair to your father and the family. I called his bluff. Months went by. Just when I thought he had given up, he confronted me with photographs. He had us trailed." She gazed into a middle distance Daniel couldn't see. "He told me, 'If you don't agree to leave town, your affair will be on the front page of every newspaper. I'll expose you as an unfit mother and mentally unstable. We know the judges, and we know the courts. You won't have custody and you'll never have visitation rights. I'll ruin the reputation of that left-wing hotshot boyfriend of yours. If you stay, I'll make your life miserable. I'll destroy you. I don't care where you go, just get out of town."

"The son of a bitch," Daniel said.

"So I chose to leave," she said, as if she was weighing the measure of every year, birthday and holiday. "If I stayed I would have been locked out of your life. I couldn't have stood that. Maybe I should cry for what happened but I've cried too long." She adjusted the scarf around her neck and cleared her throat. "Now, if you'll excuse me, I'm going to rest."

Daniel felt like he'd been punched. As she turned to leave, she pivoted to face him. "I can't tell you what joy it gives me to have you here. If I had it to do again, I wouldn't have left you. I would have stayed and fought. Miss E. Temple said dinner will be served at 7:30. I'll see you downstairs."

* * *

Daniel shut the door and lay down on the bed. From below he heard a heavy object crash to the floor, and the clang of sharp surfaces banging together. He thought he heard singing. He half expected Margaret to knock at the door, to reappear, and he was relieved she did not. She'd been a ghost, a phantom in the ether of his memory, a swirling hologram tangled in the skeins of dream and recollection. In the waning afternoon light, memories surfaced when he knew Margaret's touch, the sound of her voice in his ear and her faint scent like roses. The same scent he recognized in the library, the same trace of sweetness in the air around her. Now she was whole, flesh and blood, sprung to life, imperfect—even damaged—but real. Now he would have to contend with the truth of who she was and what he found.

The roar in Daniel's head subsided and was replaced by humming in the base of his spine, a sensation he recognized when he was skimming the sea out beyond the break where the waves were setting up. The waves were gathering speed, and in a split second he knew that whatever had to be done, he could do it. He saw a green wave come barreling down on him, shimmering white foam on its lip, a monster wall, huge and taunting, and he knew he could take it.

* * *

At the stroke of 7:30, the grandfather clock chimed one bell. Daniel awoke with a jolt. He had slept hard, caught in a dream he couldn't recreate. When he sat up, a sense of equal parts dread and curiosity hit him. In the bathroom he stared at himself in the mirror. The skin on one cheek was creased from a fold in the pillow. He wet and combed his hair with his fingers, gave up, and muttered, "Hell, she'll have to take me as I am." Disoriented, he descended the circular staircase and walked down the wide hall toward the dining room. His fingers pressed against his wrinkled shirtfront. Ahead he saw the blaze of candlelight. He squinted into the spacious room, past a chandelier that cast light onto the dining table draped with white linen.

"Good evening," Margaret said, from the far end of the table. "Won't you come in?" Diamond earrings glittered in her earlobes. She wore a tailored black suit that accentuated the whiteness of her bare throat and face. "Please, sit down." She indicated the chair to her right. "I trust you're hungry?"

"I'm always hungry." His voice seemed unnaturally loud, and he coughed to clear his throat.

"Miss E. Temple has been in a flurry of preparation since I told her you arrived. And she's scolded me for not giving her proper notice, but…would you like some wine? Or would you rather have beer?" Her fingers fluttered against the stem of the wine glass.

"What makes you ask that?"

"Well, I don't know. Young men typically prefer beer."

"Some do. Some don't." His reply rang sour like he was an insolent jerk. He modulated his voice. "I drink my share of wine."

"Would you open it?" She nodded to a bottle submerged in a silver wine bucket near his elbow.

Daniel lifted the bottle out of the ice, placed it on a napkin, and holding the bottle firmly, he sunk the screw into the cork and withdrew it with a soft pop. He read the label, *Domaine de Chevalier, Graves, 1966*, nodded, and poured the pale gold wine into her glass and into his.

Margaret raised her glass, "*A votre sante,*" she said. Tears brimmed in her eyes.

"To your health, too," he toasted in return, staring at her like she one of the figures in the dark paintings on the walls of the room, remote and shrouded in mystery. "Nothing I've tasted compares with this," he said. "Popee used to lay in some fine wines, but I was too young to enjoy them."

"Yes," she said, "I tasted some of Popee's wine. He was quite proud of his cellar." She watched him over the brim of the wine glass. "I'm glad you like it."

He started to say that most of the wine he drank was from Napa and Sonoma, but the comment faltered on his tongue. His shirt grew damp. For the second time in the day he craved a cigarette although he had sworn off them.

Just then the swinging door flew open and Miss E. Temple emerged carrying a steaming platter. "No need for introductions now, Miss Ranzell," she announced. "I've been looking at this boy's picture for years, and I'd know him anywhere!"

Daniel stood. "How do you do?"

"How do you do yourself. Sit down, young man. Don't make a fuss. The important thing is to eat when it's hot, and I know you're starved." She paused at Margaret's elbow. "Your mother eats like a bird. From you I expect big things!"

"Yes, ma'am," he said, taking his seat.

She thrust a platter under his nose. "Try my crab cakes. Don't hold back. There's plenty more where this comes from. I'll leave this right here for you to help yourself. That's garlicky sauce there in the center. My own secret recipe." She beamed at him, "I'll be right back. Now you keep your mother's wine glass full," and swept back into the kitchen.

Color had risen in Margaret's cheeks. She lifted her fork and nodded, "Please, go ahead."

Daniel cut into the tender cake, dipped it into the sauce, and lifted it to his lips. A meld of succulent crab, onion, and spices flooded his mouth. "This is delicious!"

Before the door had stopped swinging, Miss E. Temple returned in its updraft. "I heard that!" she announced. "Why, honey, we're just getting started." She bustled back and forth with bowls and serving dishes heaped with catfish, collard greens, cornbread, and biscuits.

Daniel lowered his head and dug into the food.

"I don't mean to intrude, but— " Margaret said.

"What?" he said, reaching for another biscuit.

"May I ask you some questions?"

"As long as you don't ask me what I'm going to do with my life."

"No, nothing like that. I'm interested in the things you like to do."

Without warning his temper flared, and a reply flew out of his mouth before he could stop himself. "But not so interested all these years that you couldn't get in touch with me."

Her head snapped backwards like she had been struck.

"What the hell," he said, putting down his fork. "That came out of nowhere."

"No, you're right," she said and wiped her lips with the napkin. "Don't apologize. The funny thing is I did try, but I failed. I failed miserably."

He nodded, his eyes downcast.

"Believe me," she said, "above all else, I'm astonished at your presence."

He raised his eyes to her.

"This isn't easy for either of us," she said, "is it?"

"I guess I hadn't thought it through. If I had maybe I wouldn't have come."

She sipped from a water glass, the ice cubes clinking against the crystal. "However difficult and awkward any of the issues are that we face, I'm grateful for this moment." She laughed. "And I'm grateful for your appetite."

He laughed back.

"Miss E. Temple's food is wasted on me. I also give thanks that she can and will say what I cannot. Just you wait. She's a gift in my life. If you let her food get cold, she'll be insulted."

Daniel picked up his knife. "In that case, would you pass the honey?"

They ate in relieved silence as if they were strangers who had been trapped in an elevator between floors, and miraculously the power began to hum, the lights switch back on, and the gears in the elevator shaft crank.

"If I promise not to get too personal," she smiled, "will you tell me a bit about yourself?"

"Sure. That means no questions about my girlfriend, right?"

"Of course," Margaret said.

"Although I have to give her credit. She was the one who said I should find you."

"Really?" Margaret leaned forward on her elbows.

"She's all about going for what you want."

"I hope I can meet her someday."

Daniel helped himself to seconds, sidestepping her comment. "I've met a few radical guys at Berkeley. They think they're going to change the world. Not me. The longer I live in West Marin, the more I think about getting into some kind of environmental law before the coast is overrun by development and the lagoons and estuaries are spoiled."

"You're in first year law?"

"That's right," he said, and left it at that. He didn't want to get into an explanation of why he had stopped attending class.

"What do you like to read?"

"Natural history, world history, geography, that sort of thing."

"I read fiction," she said. "And mysteries."

"I noticed," he said. "To me, none of that is real."

"No, I guess it isn't," she laughed. "You're lucky. The Point Reyes Peninsula is a national treasure. I'd love to go back."

He looked at her quizzically thinking how her presence might begin to crack apart Charlie's lies and deceptions.

Miss E. Temple popped through the door. "Ready for dessert? Pecan pie or sweet potato pie? A la mode, of course."

"Miss E. Temple, where did you learn to cook?" Daniel asked.

"Learn to cook? Why I was born to cook. But that is a whole other story too long for the telling." She walked to his chair and placed her hand on his shoulder. "I've been with this family twice as long as you've been on this sweet earth, young man. This is my home. And these are glory days to have you here. Now what will it be?"

"Make it a slice of each," Daniel said.

"Good gracious! Music to my ears." She served pie and chicory coffee, all the while chatting and reflecting on the Forgiveness of the Lord and His Way to Perform Miracles. "Tomorrow morning I'm making Beignets with sausage and eggs, so I'll expect you down bright and early. We got a lot of catching up to do. We'll let your mother sleep in. Good night, now!"

When Daniel finished his coffee, Margaret smoothed back her hair. "There's an old telescope in the study. Shall we take a look?"

The telescope was propped at the back of the closet covered by a blanket. It was brass, heavy and equipped with wooden legs. The lens and filters were dusty, but preserved in their original box, fitted into green velvet slots. They hauled it up to the roof, and under the night sky in the City of Brotherly Love, peered through the lens until they found the rings of Saturn. The waxing moon hung on the southern horizon. Orion's Belt glittered next to Sirius' bright beam. Margaret kicked off her shoes and looked up into the heavens. "Since you're a student of the stars I'm sure you know why they twinkle."

"Debris and gases and atmospheric junk interrupt their steady light giving them the appearance of twinkling." He gazed up into the constellations. "I'm surprised that the sky is as clear as it is. You know, I just thought of something. The woman I'm seeing, her name is Jess, has a child, an eight-year old daughter."

"Jess is older than you?" Margaret asked.

"It doesn't matter to me, but she's always bringing it up like it's a deal breaker. Anyway, Jess is like one of those stars, a steady beam. And then last week, she threw me a curve. An event with her ex sent her into a downward spiral. Her head seemed filled with a language I couldn't translate."

"Did you ask her about this?"

"Sure. But it was touch and go."

"This will sound ironic coming from me," Margaret said.

"Fire away," Daniel said.

"She does have her child to consider."

Daniel glanced quickly at Margaret. "Believe me, I'm in the picture. Sarah is a great kid."

"I'm sure she is."

Daniel yawned. "All of a sudden, I'm shot. I think I'll get some shuteye. Let me take the telescope down."

"No, I'd like to stay a little longer. I'll cover it before I come down."

"You'll be okay?"

"Yes, I'll be fine. It's such a beautiful night." She tipped her head back and gazed up into the sky. "All these years, the stars have been a comfort to me. Sometimes I imagined you looking up at the same constellations as I was. Now here we are, looking at them together. I can't remember a lovelier evening." She took a small step toward him. "Thank you for coming, Daniel. Sleep well."

Tentatively, he advanced toward her, and as he moved closer she slowly embraced him, her arms reaching round his shoulders. He touched her lightly at the waist, the scent of roses encircling his head. With the city spread before them, they stood under the winking stars, Daniel holding her as if she might turn to smoke in his hands.

Chapter 22

June 8

ON SATURDAY THE WIND IN MILL VALLEY was cool, and the sun seemed to polish the air. Annie jumped into her van, a virtual greenhouse jammed into the rear of the cab. Between the plants, she had shoved gardening tools and gloves that she rounded up from her yard. On the passenger seat and floor, twenty-pound bags of chicken manure and compost were stacked one on top of the other. The combination of soil, fertilizer, and greenery emitted a fecund odor of steamy intoxication.

Annie had promised Stewart a garden, and what a garden it would be! It was in her nature to accept all challenges as a point of pride. His plight became her personal mission. He wanted to present a good face to his parents; she wanted to discover if he was gay or not. Yet it was more than just that. Since the day they'd met in Matthew's classroom, she believed they were on the same wavelength, and the possibility that there could be so much more to their relationship had tantalized her. When his request for help came, she threw herself full bore into the task at hand. And finally, there would be no more flirting, baiting, or stalling. Annie would take Stewart to bed and if not, she would know the reason why.

Stewart's neighborhood was a subdivision stitched together from flat residential tree-lined streets and simple one-story houses built on filled tidelands. Children's bikes were propped against fences and dogs trotted in the road. She pulled beside a tottering mailbox in front of a picket fence and turned off the motor. A row of privets inside the fence obscured the view into the yard.

She sprang from the van and wiped her hands on her overalls, cut off mid-thigh. Dashing through the gate, she nearly slammed into the cold metal frame of the trampoline. Instantly she felt a pent-up rush of frustration. "What in the hell!" she exclaimed.

"Hey," Stewart answered from the other side of the trampoline, swiping dew off the canvas. "How's it going?"

"I was doing great. Now I'm not so sure."

A look of puzzlement passed over his face. "What's wrong?"

"Are you kidding? How are we supposed to plant a garden with this contraption in the yard?"

"Does it matter?"

"Matter? I expected the yard to look neglected," she waved her hands at the expanse of dirt and weeds. "How do you expect me to work around this?"

He stared at her, his lips set in a hard line.

"Well, it will have to go," she ordered. "That's all there is to it."

"I have no place to put it."

"That's not my problem. Take the damn thing apart and store it somewhere. Anyway, we can't plant a garden in this…this disaster with a trampoline smack in the middle of it!" Hands on her hips, she held her ground. "Are we going to do this or not?"

He lifted his head and glared at her.

"Make up your mind." She turned on her heel and hurried away. "My van is loaded with plants. Help me take them out."

"Wait a minute!" he shouted and followed her out the gate. "I thought we were going to the nursery together!"

"I wanted to save time." She leaned against the van that was parked in the shade under the limbs of a maple. Two boys tossed a Frisbee in the street, its red disc whizzing low over the ground. "I drove by a nursery yesterday. They were having a sale and I decided why wait. From the look of things, we can use everything and more. Don't you think so?" She knew it was childish, but tears stung her eyes. Didn't he realize that she had relinquished precious time in her studio to please him? "Well, are you going to help or not?"

Stewart grimaced and began unloading the containers. She

blinked away tears, and began a breezy litany on the plants to dispel her outburst. "These are digitalis. Common name, foxglove. Hairy leaves sprout on a high stalk sending out a plume of pink bell-like flowers. Very pretty bedding plants. Look! They're already blooming."

He worked rapidly, lining up the plants along the fence. For every four containers he unloaded, she unloaded one. "These are rosemary plants," she continued. "I bought the bushy kind. They'll grow like weeds. Tiny blue flowers in the summer. Positively deer proof."

Head down, he grunted small declarations and kept unloading.

"I couldn't resist this daphne plant. We'll put it by your front door. Don't worry about the expense. They gave me an extra 10 percent off because I told them I was having a garden show. Now these are shade-loving plants," she added, "hellebores and ferns. The glossy leaf on the hellebores is lovely all year long and even though it's past its bloom, they'll be little workers for you. You know about ferns?"

"Yes," he mumbled opposite the foliage that concealed his face.

She chatted brightly through the fronds. "Good. Now, I probably overdid it on the oleander, but they are the warriors of the garden. I chose the white ones. You can never have enough white in a garden. They fill large empty spaces and bloom all summer. Some people call them highway plants, but the deer won't touch them."

He unloaded the last of the oleanders and as he stood to stretch his back, she touched him gently on his arm.

"Would you look at this gorgeous rhododendron! I couldn't resist. I bought some deer netting. Just in case the buggers want to nibble. So what do you think?"

"You know your stuff," he said, wiping the sweat off his brow.

"I want this to be really nice. Don't you?" An ache to connect with him welled up in her.

"Sure." He brushed her hand aside. "Let me finish, then I'll dismantle the trampoline."

She clung to the hope that by day's end their dance of push-pull would evaporate. "Can you get the manure and compost out of the van? I'll start clearing the garden beds and turning the soil. It looks as if the ground is still moist. Thank goodness."

He stopped, his hand on the rhododendron container. "Annie, I can only do one thing at a time."

"Whatever you say. One thing at a time."

* * *

The morning wore on, the sun blazed from the sky, and the air grew heavier, nearly tropical. Honeybees buzzed in the neighbor's wisteria that climbed the back fence. Two fat black crows cawed from the tall branches of a Monterey Pine and a calico cat wandered into the yard, curled up on the ground and fell asleep under the shade of the privets.

Annie had cleared the garden beds and dug along the back fence. Even though she wore gloves, small blisters were rising on the palms of her hands, and the skin on her shoulders was turning pink in the noonday sun. She was determined to work as hard as he was without complaint, but thirst was slowing her down. She felt by turns dizzy and then weak.

"Is there anything to drink?" she called to Stewart who was using the rake to jab at dry patches of crabgrass, thickening the air with dust.

"Water or beer." He had dismantled the trampoline, stacked it at the opposite side of the yard, pruned back the bushes, and badly mangled an ornamental plum. "Help yourself."

"Oh, my," Annie said to herself, as she stepped into his cabin. "Give me strength." A musty, dank smell scratched at her throat. In the worn kitchen, she found a glass in the paint-chipped cabinet, wiped the rim of the glass on her shirt, ran tap water into it, and drank. Passing through the living room, she entered his dim bedroom and saw the double mattress and box spring on the floor. The sheets were wadded in a tumble, a lumpy pillow was jammed up against a stained comforter, and dirty laundry was strewn about the floor around the bed. This will never do, she thought, and used the bathroom quickly, wondering why men were such slobs.

All afternoon, they labored side by side. Stewart dug holes, mixing in manure and compost while Annie shook plants from the containers, setting them into the holes. As they worked, he seemed to relax, but when she led the conversation toward his first girlfriend and how he lost his virginity, he stonewalled her. She turned to the news and discussed the kidnapping of Patty Hearst who had resurfaced as the gun-toting Tania, freedom fighter and urban terrorist. They bantered back and forth until the shadows lengthened in the yard, and they had planted all the containers with the exception of the ferns and hellebores.

"I don't know where these can go," Annie said, flopping down.

Stewart drove the shovel into the ground and leaned on the handle. He had taken off his shirt and changed into cut-offs. "I'm shot. I could have hired some day laborers and spent the day on the courts."

"Well, excuse me," she said. "I bust my butt and you're complaining. Your weed patch is now a garden. Thank you very much."

"Sorry, Annie. I sound like an asshole. I'll get the hose and start soaking the plants."

Annie watched him drag a hose from the side of the cabin. Didn't he know how she longed for his touch? As he passed by, she held out her hand. "Let me have a drink." She took the end of the hose and dipped her head toward the arcing cold stream.

Stewart had stepped back and was looking into the yard. The water dribbled down her chin and cooled her perspiring skin. On impulse, she lifted the hose and doused herself, splashing water in his direction.

Stewart jumped away. "Don't you dare," he warned.

"You're so hot," she taunted. "I know you're dying to cool off."

He back-stepped with his hands up. "You're asking for it."

She aimed the nozzle directly at his chest and blasted him. Ribbons of water shot in a wide arc that shimmered in the air over the grass.

He sputtered in disbelief. "You rat!"

She screamed with delight and pelted his legs with the spray. He rushed at her and grabbed at the hose that twisted and slipped in their hands. She hung on and they wrestled to the ground. He straddled her and wrenched the hose from her hands. She wrapped her arms around his neck and pulled his face toward her lips.

"Stop it," he shouted. "God damn it, would you stop!"

She fell back, squinting up into the blue sky. The earth was a slippery soup beneath her body. The skin on her legs and arms were caked with mud. The calico cat had crept from underneath the privets and sipped from a shallow puddle that had formed in the thin grass.

"God, you're a mess," he said, standing over her.

"Go fuck yourself," she said. She watched the cat dart across the yard and heard the crows scream from the top of the Monterey Pine.

He laughed bitterly. "That's not a bad idea."

"Tell me one thing. Is it me?"

"Oh, Annie. Come on, let's go in and dry off."

"Only if you tell me what's going on."

"That's asking a lot."

"You owe me."

* * *

They sat across from each other at the Formica table, nursing bottles of beer. Annie had showered and wore Stewart's terry cloth bathrobe. Her hair was wrapped in a towel.

"Talk to me," she said. The afternoon was fading, and a clock ticked on the wall over the refrigerator. She felt emotionally spent and physically exhausted.

"I don't know how."

"Start by opening your mouth and letting the words come out."

"I'm a private guy."

"I'm listening," she said. She toweled her damp hair.

"You asked me before how I lost my virginity." He picked at the metal edge of the table, twisting his mouth.

"Go on."

"The first time I had sex was with a man."

"I've had sexual experiences with women," she ventured. "Experimental forays into the unknown. You know how that kind of thing happens."

"I was seduced by an older man, and it was the biggest event of my adolescence. My dad found us. I thought my life was ruined."

"That must have been devastating."

"I dream about men, I want them and god knows even though I've tried, I can't change."

"You're queer," she said.

He swallowed and his Adam's apple bobbed. "That's right. I'm queer."

She watched him as moved towards the sink, his back turned away from her. In that moment, she sensed how her disappointment paled beside his anguish.

"Tell me, why this dance between us?"

He faced her. "I thought I'd give it one more try."

"Should I be flattered?" She worked up a smile.

"I know. I've been a prick, but Annie, think about it. If I come out, I'm afraid I'll lose my job."

"Well, Mill Valley isn't Kansas, but I understand why you wouldn't want to broadcast this around school. Sixth-grade boys are vicious. It isn't a problem for me or my friends, but if I were you, I wouldn't show up with a boyfriend at the Little League parade." She unloosed her hair, teasing the ends with her fingers. "The way I see it is you've got to live your life. What you choose to do in the bedroom is your business. Look at us—all this wasted energy. I'm not going to say I'm not let down, but the truth is, I'll be your friend no matter what."

He shook his head. "If I admit I'm gay to my parents, it will kill them."

"What do they think you're doing in San Francisco?"

"I don't discuss it with them."

"Your mom loves you, doesn't she?"

"She does," Stewart said.

"Then she knows."

"You don't understand."

"Yes, I do. It doesn't have to be this way. You don't have to hide."

He looked at her in disbelief.

"Tell you what. When your parents come to town, we'll have a dinner party." She examined the kitchen, the chipped cabinets, dented refrigerator and worn linoleum. "Ill have it at my house. I'll make my world-famous lasagna. You invite your gay friends. I'll invite my friends from both sides of the pew." She grinned. "We could even take them to Glide Church. That would blow their minds. We'll show your parents how we do it San Francisco style."

"I don't have any gay friends."

"You poor bastard. You better get some."

* * *

Annie dressed in Stewart's old clothes, and he walked her to the van. When they embraced good-bye, her knees buckled from fatigue. It was dusk, and up and down the block lamps snapped on in the windows of houses. Families clustered in living rooms. Tinny voices from portable televisions floated through screen doors and open windows. As Stewart walked back through the gate, Annie climbed into the van and closed the door. A chill ran across her sunburned shoulders and down her arms. She bowed her forehead, resting it on the steering wheel. Her hands lay limp in her lap and she resisted an impulse to cry. *You silly woman,* she thought. *When will you learn? You knew all along, but you wouldn't give up.* The illusive promise of the "whole package"—a full-blooded male to love—appeared out of nowhere and flashed across her vision. She lifted her head off the steering wheel, blew her nose, and laughed. She realized she was deceiving herself. She'd hate anyone, man or woman, who came between her and her art.

Chapter 23

June 10 and 11

AS COMMUTERS STREAMED down the highway toward San Francisco, Jess jockeyed for position, weaving in and out of traffic. Drivers sped past her, gunning their Mercedes Benzes, BMWs, Porsches, LTDs, and Lincolns—all glossy paint and grillwork. When she punched the gas pedal to the floorboard, the engine responded by knocking violently and shaking the chassis from front to back. Thirty-five minutes, maybe forty-five minutes max to the Mission, she calculated. On Saturday morning a phone call had come from Claire, who conveyed a summons from Sebastian, her voice bright and buoyant: "Be at the studio by nine on Monday. Something's up. Something big."

For the rest of the day, while Jess cooked and cared for Sarah, puttered and read, she intermittently thought about Daniel in Philadelphia and wondered about Sebastian's news. She wrestled with a decision that seemed inevitable: she could no longer exist as a dancer and make the other parts of her life work. For years she had confidently assumed she could dance full-time, work part-time, and be a full-time parent. Now something had to give. No matter what promising development Sebastian would announce about the next challenge, she was out. She was tired of living at the poverty line. It was time she faced it.

On Sunday she, Annie, and their children had hiked the mountain. It was like old times when the women had first met in Woodacre, reinventing their lives. They had attached an X in front of the word "husband" like marks on gravestones of unknown persons and crammed their wedding silver into their back closets. Their children were the first crop of post-modern children living without their fathers, and according to instructions, they had planted them in good soil and let them grow wild. They'd found a meadow with a view to the sea, spread a picnic on blankets, and spent the day confiding and laughing together while watching the children play Frisbee golf.

At the ascent to the Waldo Grade, Jess edged the car into the slow lane. Gusty wind blasted the car. Goose bumps freckled her arms. She gritted her teeth and mentally rehearsed the speech she had plotted to deliver to Claire and Sebastian. *It's been great dancing with you. A high water mark I'll never forget. I'm grateful, so please know how hard it is to come to this decision. After much deliberation, I'm bowing out. I need to concentrate on my future.*

She imagined the darkening scowl that crossed Sebastian's face whenever she or Claire strayed from his ethos of dedication. No doubt Claire would be upset about Jess quitting—that was a given. Still, she'd extend sympathy and understanding; Sebastian would wear her defection as a mortal wound. *So be it,* Jess thought. *I've got to make a living.*

The truth was she hadn't made progress toward solvency or applied for the jobs she'd found in the paper. The few tips she pursued had fizzled, and as vividly as she tried to imagine herself driving a bus or working in a bar, she couldn't make the leap. Nor had she broached the subject of more child support from Parker. Before he left for Japan, his refusal to admit he had been negligent with Sarah shocked her, and she allowed a perfect opportunity to demand more child support slip by. In the end, she'd be damned if she'd ask anything more from him. Let him wander the earth like a blind man, squandering his money. She wouldn't put herself in the position of being financially dependent on him, or on any man, especially Daniel, whose means of support was dubious, given his lack of ambition. Whatever was next, she told herself, she'd find gainful employment.

After exiting the Waldo Tunnel, she squinted into the sunlight and pumped the brakes for the downhill race. A five-axle truck, its black tires as high as the top of the VW, passed on the outside lane, sucking the car into its draft. Jess gripped the steering wheel and forced herself to ignore the tremor as if the hood might fly up into the windshield.

The city appeared in the distance against the sky like a crystal palace, the banks curving against the shores of the gunmetal-blue bay. She raced on, reshaping her speech and infusing the words with conviction so that no matter what Sebastian would know she was finished.

* * *

Bundled in sweats, Jess settled on the icy floor of the dance studio beside Claire, who paused to sip from a thermos filled to the brim with black coffee. They mirrored one another in a wide second position, both stretching the muscles of their hamstrings and calves, flexing and pointing their toes.

"Damn, it's freezing in here," Claire said, peeking from the hood of her sweatshirt, brown curls framing her oval face. "You'd think I'd get used to it."

"Where do you think Sebastian is?" Jess asked, blowing on her hands. "He's never late."

"Frankly, I could use a few minutes before he comes. He's wound tight as a tick. When we were passed over, he went into a total funk. I wasn't sure he'd come out of it."

"What's changed now?" Jess asked, glancing at the door to the street. She fidgeted and tugged at the wool socks that bagged down over her ankles.

"He wouldn't tell me." Claire tucked a stray curl around her ear. "He said he wanted to break the news to both of us. Say, how're you holding up?"

"I'm keeping busy. What's going on with you?"

"I'm teaching yoga. If you're interested I can get you a gig."

The door flung open, and Sebastian burst into the studio. The butterflies in Jess's stomach morphed into winged creatures batting their wings inside her ribs. His shaved head had sprouted pale, fuzzy curls close to his scalp; a turquoise earring studded one earlobe.

"Damn," he said, his bloodshot eyes blazing. "The frigging bus broke down on Mission and snarled up traffic." He flung his shoes across the floor and began to peel off his clothes down to narrow black dancer's briefs. He stepped into black sweats, pulled a black t-shirt over his head, and strode across the floor. "Ladies," he said, "I bring a startling development in the world of dance! Brace yourselves," he trumpeted. "We've been re-selected to join the Inter-City Summer Dance Festival." His smile accentuated his gaunt cheekbones. "We're back in the game!"

Jess felt like she'd walked under a ladder on a construction site and been beamed on the head by an object dropping from a scaffold. The logic of the speech she had memorized fizzled.

Claire remained strangely quiet. "Are you sure, Sebastian? Did you get it in writing."

"Hell, yes," he thundered. "What do you think this is?" He loped to his backpack and produced a letter, waving it above his head. "Here it is, direct from the office of the mayor. 'Due to a withdrawal, the committee has named your company as a replacement. Attached are the cities in July and August where you will conduct workshops and perform—Sacramento, Fresno, Los Angeles…'" He ticked off locations up and down California and swiped at a film of sweat on his forehead. "'Please advise immediately that your company is able to fulfill the position. Congratulations!'" In a single swoop he seized Jess and then Claire, and pulled them off the floor. "We're in!" he shouted. "We're in!"

"Stop," Jess said. "Please stop." She pulled away, circled the floor, and halted in front of them. "Look, this is great news. The best, really." The words tumbled out in a rush. "But I've had a heart-to-heart with myself. I've got to look to the future. I've thought about this long and hard." She rubbed her hands together. "I can't join you. For the festival or afterwards. I have to get a job. A real job."

Sebastian gripped her arm. "Wait a minute," he said. "We've hit the big time! We're a team. You're part of this company. You can't walk away. Hell, I won't let you!"

Claire pushed him aside and raised her hands. "Slow down! I've listened to you and your endless bullshit. Now you're going to listen to Jess." She slid down to the floor and patted a spot next to her. "Jess, sit here. Tell us what's going on."

Jess sunk to her knees, unable to look at Claire who lightly touched her arm. Her clean sweet scent filled Jess's nostrils, the scent she had grown to recognize on the dance floor for years, in dingy studios, backstreet warehouses, and worn school cafeterias.

Sebastian grunted, folding his legs beneath him, and hunched down.

Jess glanced warily at him and then at Claire. "The truth is I didn't think this whole summer festival thing through," she said. She felt exposed and vulnerable. "What would I do with Sarah? I'd be gone for days. Who would take care of her?"

"What about child care or summer school?" Claire asked.

"Yes, that would work, but how about at night?" Jess pursed her lips. Daniel entered her mind and she blinked away his image. "There's no one I can ask to take her for days at a time."

"Now you tell us?" Sebastian mumbled.

"Look, asshole. Could you give it a rest?' Claire's dark eyes regarded Jess softly. "No one?"

"There are friends, of course, schoolmates, that sort of thing, but there's isn't a family I would entrust her to. My best friend has boys, but her house is not an ideal place for Sarah."

"I see your point," Claire said. She stood and walked across the floor. On the street, a bus chugged by. Horns honked, and shouts were exchanged. She came back to Jess and pushed up her sleeves. "Well, I have an idea."

Sebastian stopped biting his fingernails and lifted his head.

"First of all, we need to apologize. Mr. Brilliant and I are clueless when it comes to kids—neither of us even owns a cat. We should have thought about from this from the get-go. It's a simple solution. This is a children's festival, right?" Claire held her hands out, palms up. "All kinds of kids, ages, and backgrounds. What if we petition for Sarah to join the workshops?"

Jess quickly looked at Sebastian who blanched.

"Hey, I like kids," he said. "In controlled environments."

Claire burst out laughing. "How about this? If she can't join the workshop, we could find someone or something to keep her occupied while we're working. Maybe we could even put her to work."

"Does she do laundry?" Sebastian asked.

"You're so lame," Claire exclaimed. "Anyway, Jess and I will be bunking together, and it's perfectly fine to have Sarah bunk with us. She's a good kid. What about that, Jess?"

Jess was dumbfounded. Claire's solution had been unthinkable.

"Okay, boss lady," Sebastian said to Claire. "I want to say something straight out." As he swiveled toward Jess, the intensity of his gaze held her rapt.

"I know I come across like a beast. Hey, it's part of my act. Whatever you want to arrange for your kid, and I'll bend on this one, it's up to you. Also, for your information, and I can say this with certainty, this gig will open doors. I'm already working on teaching positions in the fall, and you can bank on the fact that we'll be performing all year." He scrubbed his head as if he was releasing a torrent of energy. "But the thing is, you're an integral part of what we've created. I want you to stay. "

Jess was silenced. She couldn't remember ever seeing any sign of Sebastian's tenderness. Perhaps Claire knew this side of him. A fragile intimacy wove its spell around them. Above their heads, in the huge warehouse on the floors where artists lived and worked, steel doors slammed, sharp echoes ringing through the hallways.

Claire nodded toward Sebastian, who stood and tightened the drawstring on his sweats. They were looking directly at Jess. She quickly rose from the floor. "I don't know what to say."

"Say yes!" Claire said.

"Damn it, woman," Sebastian said. "We're waiting."

Jess grinned and spread her arms wide. "Yes!"

Immediately she was transported to another time when they had performed in a theater as part of a program with other companies. In the rear of the darkened theater, Jess had paused in an aisle between Claire and Sebastian, waiting for their cue. Listening to the murmurs of the seated audience, she regulated her breath and focused her mind. Further back on a dais, the whir of slide projectors grew louder. As Jess extended her hand toward

Claire, the skin on Claire's back cooled her fingertips, and Sebastian whispered, "Go."

They walked forward in a single file down the center aisle, the heads of the audience haloed by white light streaming from the slide projectors. Climbing the stairs to center stage, they faced one another in a circle, and in unison, tilted their faces upwards, arched their backs, and extended their arms. Gradually the light blurred as pigment heating on slides in the projector melted, splashed across the theater walls, and up onto the stage. They bent their front legs in a deep *plie* and thrust their back legs behind them. The theater was transformed into a universe of undulating rose and gold. Their skin glowed, stippled with watercolor tattoos. When the soundtrack opened with the symphonic woodwinds of cooing birds and rush of wind, tension rippled between them. Claire began the movement curving her spine inwards, then opening like a chrysalis, and spinning across the stage. Music filled the theater, lush and full, the violins and violas and cellos rising in volume and joining the woodwinds. Sebastian quivered like a horse starting at the gate, stretched to his full six-foot frame and leapt across the stage. The gold merged to green and to blue, and a tesserae of turquoise shimmered in the air, the violins calling to Jess who burst into the dance.

She came out of her reverie and saw Claire and Sebastian who were smiling at her. *Yes,* she thought, *this is what is right. I won't doubt it again. I'm all in.*

* * *

Sarah had fallen asleep in her bedroom, and Jess reclined in bed with a paperback of Ram Dass's *The Only Dance There Is* propped on her belly. At the section about "Consciousness as Freedom from Attachment," she read the same paragraph three times. Words like "polarity" and "*sangha*" and phrases like "cognitive centering device" and "karmic unfolding" merged in a murky stew on the page. She tossed the book aside, swung her feet to the floor and switched on the TV. After five minutes of staring at a reporter who described further allegations about the Nixon administration's deceit and deceptions at the Watergate hearings, she clicked it off.

Sore from rehearsals and tired from meetings, she was too keyed up to sleep. Her mind jumped from task to task that lay ahead. And while it would be days before an answer came from the Mayor's office about whether or not Sarah would be allowed to take part in the workshops, the waiting made her restless.

At her desk, she opened the drawer and removed a blue cotton bandana. She unfolded the bandana and lifted out Daniel's Puka shell necklace that she had discovered under the bathroom rug. She rolled the necklace between her palms and tried to imagine what had happened to Daniel in Philadelphia. Then she slipped the necklace back into the bandana, tucked it into the drawer, and flopped on her bed.

Far in the distance, from the direction of Old Mill Park, a lone dog barked. Soon other dogs reported, opening their throats, braying, barking, and yelping, their sharp voices converging and rising into the night. She resisted the urge to open the window and join into the howling. Instead, she closed her eyes and visualized the towns where they would travel, the workshops they would conduct, the dancers, educators, and parents they would meet, and the faces of the children they would come to know.

* * *

Daniel sat on the floor of the Philadelphia bedroom, a fire burning in the grate of the fireplace, and dialed Jess number. Pick up the phone, he willed, hearing her number ring two thousand miles away. I wonder what galaxy she's orbiting tonight. Earth to Venus, tune in.

"Hello." Her voice drifted into his ear like sweet California sunshine.

"I'm here in Philadelphia," he said. "I made it."

"Oh, I'm glad." She sounded genuinely happy. She sounded like she used to when her guard wasn't up.

"Did I wake you?"

"No, not really," she said. "And your mother? Are you with her?" she asked.

"You bet," he said, buoyed by her honeyed voice. "At first we were on shaky ground. I had to dig up some skeletons that won't be buried for a long time."

"Did you ask her about Charlie?"

"That's a nasty story. I won't kid you. It's been tough, but every day we get a little more used to each other. When I get home, I'll tell you the whole story." He paused to consider how his next words would sound, improbable as snow in July. "The thing is I'm even calling her 'Mom.' Don't laugh."

"I'm not," she said. "Really. This is such a turnaround."

"She wants to take me shopping. Right now I'm wearing one of my grandfather's cool old jackets." He watched the logs burn and smoke in the grate, the story spilling out in a rush, eager to bring her into the picture. "She lives with this amazing woman, Miss E. Temple. There're like a unit. Miss E. Temple is filling me in on ancient history. We spend hours talking; she cooks and talks, and I mostly eat." He sucked in his stomach, sure that he had gained weight. "Hey, enough about me. What's going on back home? How are you?"

"I've got something to tell you," she volunteered.

He held the phone tighter. "What?"

"We were asked by the Mayor's office to join the Summer Dance Festival." She laughed, and he could imagine the tawny sprinkle of freckles across her cheeks. She told him how quickly everything had fallen into place—the lucky break that moved their company into position, an orientation that was coming up, and cities where they would teach, and the real possibility that Sarah could go with them.

"This is great, no kidding. It's what you've wanted all along."

"Exactly. I'm still waiting for the go-ahead with Sarah, but if she can't come with us right away, Annie said she'd take her for a while. At least until after the first workshop."

"When do you go?" he asked. A buzzer went off in his brain—a buzzer that he had assumed had been disabled. He stood and walked as far as the phone cord would stretch. He was about to step into a hole.

"The rollout is right after the 4th of July."

He whistled. "That's good," he said, sidestepping his birthday. "By then, I can take Sarah."

"Really Daniel, you're not set up to care for Sarah."

"Give me some credit." An ember popped out from the logs and sizzled on the tile hearth. He stomped it out.

"We've discussed this before," she said. Her tone was resolute, immovable.

"You've got to trust me on this one," he said. "I know you and Annie are friends again, but I'm not sure you want Sarah staying at Annie's."

"What are you talking about?" she asked, her voice cold and flat.

The hole was directly in front of him. Unavoidable. His foot poised over the opening. "Shit, Jess. I gave Sarah my word. We had a confidence."

"A confidence? For god's sake, I'm her mother."

"Believe me, I get that." He switched the phone from one ear to the other. "I didn't see any reason to bring up an issue that I thought had blown over. Now my ass is on the line with Sarah. Do you understand my position?"

"I don't know what you're talking about," she insisted. "No deals until you tell me what's going on."

His tongue went deep in his cheek like he was probing a sore tooth. "The day Parker showed up, Sarah came home after spending the night at the Boyntons. Remember that?" The air in the room had turned hazy with smoke, and he wedged open a window.

"Of course," she snapped. "How could I forget it?"

"When you were in the shower, she told me that she and Amber went to Noah's to play. Annie wasn't home." He took a breath. "The action got kind of rough."

"Damn it." Jess said. "What 'action'?"

"They saw Matthew and his friends messing around on the roof of the gallery. Matthew found out they'd seen him and threatened them if they told anyone."

"For god's sake," Jess said.

"There isn't a boy in town that hasn't scaled rooftops or

pulled off some prank. Believe me. I'm living proof. It's normal."

"What about threatening younger kids," she said acidly. "Is that normal?"

"Some kids are bullies," he explained. "Sarah held her own. She wasn't intimidated."

"What about stealing?"

"What do you mean?" She was pushing him into a corner, and he didn't like it.

"Annie told me that Matthew's been stealing."

"That's different."

"So you'll admit there are holes in your argument?"

He crossed over to a chair near the fireplace. "I don't know Matthew. But I know Sarah. I've kept my eye on her. Nothing more came up. You obviously don't agree, but I gave it my best shot."

The line was as flat as dead air.

"Look," he said, "I know you're tired."

"I am," she said.

"Let's call it a night."

"I hope the rest of your visit goes well," she said and hung up.

He didn't have a chance to tell her the real reason he had called. The smell of the sea was close, and he mulled over their conversation. For the first time in his life it was becoming clear what he wanted to do and where he was headed. What would it take for her to trust him?

* * *

"Sarah, I want to talk to you," Jess said. She pulled a chair out at the kitchen table and patted the seat next to her.

"About what?" Sarah said, separating two round chocolate discs of an Oreo cookie and licking off the white sugary frosting. "I already did my homework."

"I know. I saw you working on it."

"I like division," Sarah said.

"Maybe you have a future as a mathematician."

"Nope. I'm going to be a veterinarian like Dr. Doolittle or a bird lady like Mrs. T." Sarah dug another cookie out of the cellophane wrapper, crunched it in half, and caught the crumbs with her tongue.

Jess drummed her fingers on the table. "I heard you and Amber were at Noah's house about a month ago."

Sarah wore a far-away stare. "That was a long time ago."

"What happened that night?"

"I think we played tag with Henry and then we watched 'Creature Features.'" Her eyebrows pinched together. "Yep, that's what we did."

"Is that all?"

"I'm going to go play in my room," Sarah said, rising from the chair.

"Sit down," Jess said firmly. "Did something happen with Matthew?"

Sarah held the cellophane cookie wrapper up to her eye and squinted through it, as if she was making it go blurry and measuring how far she could play dumb.

"I'm asking you a question."

"How come you're asking me?" Sarah asked defensively.

Jess reached across the table and took her hand. Sarah snatched it away. "Danny told you, didn't he? He promised me he wouldn't. He lied to me!"

"Danny called last night and…"

"You're spoiling everything," Sarah said, running across the room and flinging herself on the couch.

"Tell me what's going on," Jess said, joining her.

"I can't," Sarah said, pulling away and smothering her face into a couch cushion.

"Why not?"

"Because I promised," she mumbled.

"Whatever it is, we can solve it," Jess said, stroking her back.

"Something bad will happen," Sarah said, lifting her face.

Jess's heart jumped. "What will happen?"

"When is Danny coming home?"

"I'm not sure." Jess felt a twinge of bewilderment. She wanted to stand the tallest in Sarah's estimation. "Tell me what you know."

"You won't go to the police?" she asked.

"Is someone in danger?"

"Yes," Sarah said, her eyes wide with dismay. "Matthew is going to break into the gallery, and he's making Noah hold the ladder and be his guard when he goes through the broken window. And…"

"The gallery? Are you sure?"

"Un huh. The one in front of their house. The one with all the Indian stuff in it." Sarah's gulped. "Matthew was watching through the skylight when he saw some men in the storeroom."

"Go on," Jess said. She had a premonition where Sarah's confession was headed.

"He says there's marijuana in there, and he's going to steal it, and if Noah doesn't help, he's going to kill Henry. And…"

Jess's concern shot from borderline to high velocity.

"We've got to do something, Mom!" Sarah cried.

"Listen to me," Jess said, holding Sarah's arms. "I will do something. I'll tell Annie, and we'll get to the bottom of this."

"What about Noah? He'll get in big trouble."

"No, he won't," Jess said. "We'll solve this. Not you and not Noah. It's our job to protect you, all of you."

Sarah climbed up into her mother's lap and wrapped her arms around her neck.

"I want to help."

"I know you do." Jess felt Sarah's heartbeat skipping in her chest.

"Is Danny mad at me?"

"Of course not. Why would you think that?"

"Are you mad at him?"

"That's a complicated question."

"Don't be mad."

"Did he meet his mom?"

"Yes, he did."

"I'm glad of that."

"Me, too," Jess said, holding Sarah a while longer, knowing she would soon grow restless and slip off her lap. For one precious moment Sarah stilled in her embrace. Jess knew that Sarah and

Noah were rushing through their childhoods. Matthew had left behind his childhood long ago. He wore his defiance like a weapon. She desperately wanted to help Annie stop his fall.

Chapter 24

June 14

THE CRESCENT MOON GLIDED above the redwoods on the western ridge of Mt. Tamalpais, paused in the black sky, and caught by a wisp of fog, vanished over the treetops like a bride's smile dipping behind a veil. Annie patrolled the sidewalk outside of the Edward Curtis Gallery, the forlorn streets of town illuminated by streetlights, her shoulders hunched inside a jacket against the wind. It was past 2AM, the temperature cold, the air damp, seeping into every nook and cranny.

Less than three days ago, Jess had dropped a bomb in her lap: Matthew was planning a break-in at the gallery to steal the stash of marijuana. Sarah had broken down and delivered the news. Whether the gallery was a subterfuge for storing marijuana or not was secondary to Annie. How had Matthew come to this crossroads? The warning signs had been there all along—the school's suspicions about his behavior, her own discovery of stolen goods in the house, Noah's warning that Matthew wasn't afraid of anyone or anything, and finally Matthew's recent agreeability—a development she attributed to the school year ending.

Annie burned to stop Matthew dead in his tracks. After exploring every possible approach, none of which she deemed remotely effective unless she went to the police, Jess suggested they approach Jake. His solution was to allow Matthew to carry out the heist. Only, once inside the storeroom he would be apprehended not by the men he had seen through the skylight of the gallery, but by Jake and his "contacts." He and his "contacts" would clear the way to keep Matthew from falling into the wrong hands. This was a last-ditch effort. Annie's ability to exercise authority over Matthew was bankrupt. She felt as mean as a cornered rattlesnake.

From up the block beside a grove of redwoods, she heard footsteps, and turned to see Jess emerge from the tree limbs that overhung the shadowed ground, hurrying toward her on the sidewalk.

Jess looped her arm through Annie's arm. "When did you get here?"

"Just a minute ago," Annie said. "It's frigging cold. I'm twisted into knots."

"Try to get a grip on yourself. How's Noah holding up?"

"He was so brave," Annie said. "When he and Matthew crept out of the house, I pretended to be asleep in my bedroom. Then I watched from my studio. Noah held the ladder for Matthew until he climbed up and dropped through the window. When Noah got back into the house he fell apart. I put him to bed in my room. Last time I checked he was conked out."

"Good for him," Jess said, hugging her closer. "Jake called about thirty minutes ago to let me know everything is going as planned."

Annie swallowed hard. "That means he has Matthew?"

"Yes," Jess said. "Matthew thinks the drug dealers caught him!"

"Shit, I hope we're doing the right thing." Annie's anger withered. Her insides felt raw.

A gust of chilly wind blew up the block. "We didn't really have a choice, did we?" Jess asked.

"Not really," Annie said.

The door rattled and Jake appeared. Annie instantly began to shake. Jake checked up and down the avenue and stepped out onto the stoop. "Good evening, ladies. Let's get you inside."

Annie felt Jake's hand on her back as he guided them through the door and led them over old floorboards that creaked under their feet. A vapor of dust, smoke, and the smell of leather from saddles slung over sawhorses in the interior of the gallery closed around them. "Watch your step," he said as he pulled them into a huddle.

Annie peered at him. She could see the white of his eyes and the dark stubble of a beard. "How's my son, the second story man?"

Jake smiled, revealing the flash of teeth. "The guys worked him a little bit. Nothing brutal, you understand. Your son didn't give up easy. We let him stew, and then I had a little chat with him. He's ready to agree to some conditions. Give me a few more minutes. I'll be right back."

Jake's figure receded toward the back of the gallery. The rasp of a door opening and closing broke through the hush.

Jess pulled Annie toward her and whispered into her ear. "This is going like clockwork."

"Doesn't this strike you as ironic? I can't handle my son so I rely on the local grease monkey to rescue him."

"The local grease monkey saved Matthew's ass from getting busted by the dealers, and I don't even want to think about what they would have done to him."

"You're right. That was a stupid thing to say. It's just that I still feel duped by Matthew. I was a coward. I didn't confront him when I should have."

"Don't berate yourself," Jess said. "Think about it. In Matthew's eyes who's going to stop him from acting out? Not his dad. You must look like a pushover to him. We bought the psychobabble that said our children would thrive as long as both parents love them. Tell that to the kids who see their dads two weeks out of the year. Every divorced woman in this town is operating in the dark. I only hope Sarah won't hate me when she grows up."

"Sarah will never hate you," Annie said. "She adores you."

"I wouldn't dare predict the future."

The two women stood quietly sealed in their own thoughts. The feathers of a headdress that hung on the wall seemed to rustle as a draft swept through the gallery, and the images of the Native

American Indians in the black and white photographs that hung on the wall were mute.

A door creaked. Jake approached out of the shadowed rear of the gallery. "Okay, we're ready now. Jess, it's better if we take it from here."

"Sure," she said. "I need to get home anyway."

"Wait," Annie said. "You know…"

"I know," Jess said, hugging her. "Call me if you need anything. I'll have the phone by my bed."

Annie watched Jake walk Jess to the door, unlock the latch, and slip her out into the night. She reached for his sleeve as he led her across the floor toward the rear of the gallery. He stopped in front of a door. Slivers of light escaped from under the threshold. Her hands trembled, slick with perspiration.

"Let me handle this," he said.

Matthew slumped in a chair, bound by rope. She was shocked at how small and vulnerable he looked. The light over his head etched shadows around his eyes. "Mom," he said. He shuffled his feet against the floor, trying to sit up straighter.

"Matthew," she said. His name swam up from a place of love and protection that she hadn't felt since his first day in kindergarten. She looked helplessly at Jake who nodded at her.

"Matthew and I have come up with an agreement. First, he wants to tell you a few things." He turned to Matthew. "Isn't that right?"

Matthew blinked rapidly and opened his mouth as if to speak. A tear ran out of the corner of one eye.

A fist closed around Annie's heart.

"You understand you're in a lot of trouble, right?"

Matthew nodded. The blotchy skin on his face was smeared with sweat.

"Let me remind you," Jake said. "One night you saw some men in here. Right? You thought they were stashing marijuana in the storeroom. You thought you'd cash in on a deal?"

Matthew's eyes were riveted on Jake's face. Annie was transfixed by how defenseless he was.

"Answer me," Jake said.

"Yes," Matthew whimpered.

"Turns out what you thought you saw was wrong."

"I know it."

"That's good. Regardless, the big boys don't like some kid nosing around where they're not wanted." Jake paused. "They especially don't like stealing."

"I won't do it again."

Annie studied Matthew's shoes, the laces broken and untied, the tongues hanging out. She wanted to believe him, but there had been so many times when he made promises that he would break.

"What do you want to tell your mom?" Jake asked. He moved slowly behind Matthew and began to loosen the ropes around his shoulders.

Matthew's eyes fluttered toward Jake and then he looked at Annie. "I threatened Noah." He started to hiccup. "I told him if he didn't help me I'd...I'd hurt him."

The fist around her heart squeezed tighter. "Why?" she asked.

"I don't know," Matthew said. His lower lip quivered, and she could see he was struggling not to cry. "I really don't want anything bad to happen to him."

"And?" Jake asked. He put his hand on Matthew's shoulder.

"I'm going to work for Mr. Zelinski at his garage. He says he can teach me a few things. About cars and stuff." Matthew rubbed his arms.

"You're starting tomorrow, kid. Right?"

"Right. Can I get up now?"

Jake untied the rope, helping him to his feet. "See you, kid."

* * *

Annie rested in a chair beside Matthew's bed as he slept. She reached over, brushed away the hair from his brow, and lifted the corner of the blanket over his shoulder. His shifted slightly, inhaled, and drifted off to sleep again. She couldn't recall the last time he'd invited her into his room, and she glanced at the posters of motorcycle riders on the wall, board games stacked in piles on the floor, a skateboard upended amidst jackets, books, and food wrappers. She wondered what had happened to the box of stolen hood ornaments. Had he sold them, or were they still gathering dust?

His anger had been a wall she couldn't break through. Would Jake be able to knock some sense into him? She doubted it. If Matthew lived with his father he might change. It wouldn't be as if she was giving him up. Women in cities and towns across the country were making this decision. Matthew and his father were so close when he was little. It's a reasonable solution, she thought. They speak the same language. Denver isn't that far away. Maybe he and Noah could go together. They'd adjust. Their father would give them boundaries that he would enforce, and his wife seemed like a sensible woman. One loving home is the same as another loving home.

Annie thought about her dream of living in New York City. A studio right in The Village. The scene of the real art world. Gateway to London. The boys could visit her there. They'd think that traveling was an adventure.

A cool reality settled over her. The futility that had threatened to overwhelm her earlier had evaporated. She felt calm and resolved, and at a point when she could make sense out of what step to take next that would be best for her boys. She placed her hand on Matthew's shoulder and kissed his cheek. But she wasn't ready to leave him quite yet. Her hand lingered on his shoulder. The warmth of his body radiated into her hand. She felt his breath rising and falling. She stayed in the chair and watched him sleep.

Chapter 25

June 14

A FREAK STORM had deposited a fine powdery snow on the village square, neat lawns, and piney woods in Houghton, Michigan, and in its wake left patches of grey slush amongst spring's green carpet. The porch light at Clyde and Verna Merch's two-story brick house snapped on, flooding the tidy stoop as they stepped from their front door into the brisk morning. Verna, swathed in a vibrant yellow raincoat, wore a plastic rain bonnet to protect her salon-permed hair. Her heart was trilling like a robin's throat in full song. The day had arrived at last when they were beginning the journey to California to visit Stewart. It had been nearly two years since she laid eyes on him. She could barely contain her joy.

She clutched a cloth bag at her broad hip. Clyde, dressed in work khakis, a beige windbreaker, and lace-up cordovan boots, held her elbow and escorted her to the RV rumbling in the driveway. "What in the Be Jesus do you have in that bag?" he asked.

"Just a few things for the trip, dear. *My Ladies' Home Journal*, knitting, address book, recipes, and, would you believe, I almost forget the blueberry jam. You know it's Stewart's favorite."

"You better give that jam to me before it breaks," he warned. "I'll store it in the compartment behind your seat." He bundled Verna into the front seat where she arranged her belongings.

"Thank you, dear." He did make a fuss about her ways. Always rolling up her sleeve when she served soup or moving aside the furniture when what she wanted to do was quickly wash a window. But he had the best of intentions. He had seen awful accidents working around rigs and pumps that gave him nightmares. She knew she shouldn't be critical of his safety-conscious ways and vowed to curb her tongue. "You're right. My, isn't it nice and warm in here?"

Clyde unzipped his jacket, notched down the heat, and clicked on the headlights. Adjusting the rearview mirror and side mirrors, he pulled the rig out of the driveway and eased it onto the road.

"Good bye, good bye," Verna waved from the window, craning her neck until Clyde wheeled the Winnebago around a bend in the road and the silent house slipped from sight. "I do hope Beverly won't be too much trouble for Shirl." She untied the bow of the plastic rain cap underneath her chin, folded the accordion pleats into a single row, and tucked the cap into her bag. Her daughter, Beverly, three years younger than Stewart, was born mentally retarded. Verna had carried the burden of guilt thinking she was to blame until the doctor had helped her to see that sometimes there is no reason for misfortune. Wasn't Stewart as normal and healthy as a boy could be? So they loved Beverly just the same as any other child and raised her with care.

"If there's one woman who can take care of Bev, it's your sister."

"Yes, I know, but still. After a while it wears a body out. I'm used to it whereas Shirl hasn't been in charge for longer than a weekend."

"They'll get along fine. The family will be delivering casseroles and checking in every day." He raked the thin hair on his head with his fingers like he was furrowing rows of soil for planting. "Don't you worry. Right now we've got a lot of miles to cover. Your job is navigator. The atlas is right here," he said, nodding to a stack of maps between them. "I've marked the route in red pen."

She flipped open the pages to where Clyde had dog-eared a map of the United States and spread it across her lap. Her heart did another little giddy-up of pleasure. She traced the red line along the blue shore of Lake Superior from the upper Michigan peninsula shaded in green through the tip of pink Wisconsin and stopped at the orange Minnesota state line.

"Can we stop in Duluth at the Harbor Light for coffee?"

"Coffee? I thought we'd keep going until lunch, pull over, and heat up some of that Campbell's you've got stored in the kitchen."

'I'll be starved by then. Anyway, you know I need to stop at a restroom long before lunch. And you love watching the ore boats in the harbor."

"We've got to make Fargo by nightfall."

She continued to trace the red line passing through orange Minnesota to where Fargo was marked at the lavender North Dakota state line. "That usually takes us about six hours."

"Providing we don't run into bad weather or any damn road construction," Clyde said.

"Heck, we've got oodles of time. My cousin isn't expecting us until dinnertime. Let's stop, heh?"

"Sure, why not. But when we get to Fargo, keep your cousin away from me. She can talk the handle off a pisspot."

Verna laughed, leaning across the wide seat, and patted the back of Clyde's hand, the skin puckering on his broad knuckles, veins standing blue, a freckling of brown spots. "I'll make sure of that," she said. A sigh escaped her lips. Her hopes for the trip of a lifetime felt as high as whipped-cream clouds stacking over the lake before a cloudburst. "You know, this is a first for us, Clyde. We hardly ever get away alone except for a day trip. And it will be so nice to see the rest of the family. The twins are growing like weeds. And Harold bought a new boat."

"He's a big spender."

"Say, wasn't that a new rod and reel I saw you packing yesterday?" Clyde was a born fool for fishing, which was just fine with Verna. Once Verna helped Beverly dress, eat breakfast, and catch a bus to the handicap workshop center, she liked her mornings quiet.

"Watch out, I may buy me one of those new model Evenrudes."

"Don't be silly. Your boat is perfectly fine. Isn't this pleasant now?" She leaned her head onto the headrest, her grip loosening on the atlas, warmth and contentment easing her bones. "Say, how many days did you decide we'd take to drive?"

"I figure five to six days with a side trip to Yellowstone. If we can spare the time I've got a hankering to see the Grand Teton National Park." He puffed up his chest and exhaled. "Lake Tahoe is a beauty, I hear."

She didn't want to dampen his spirits with the admonition of foregoing a side trip to one of the parks. Still she couldn't help but ask the question to which she already knew the answer. "How long can we stay with Stewart?"

"Maybe a week."

"I wish it could be longer," she said wistfully.

"We'll have to get back."

"Yes, I suppose so. By the way, do you like my new glasses?"

"Kind of sparkly."

"Too sparkly?" She blinked her eyelids for maximum effect and plumped her perm.

"No, I guess not."

"Well, I thought since we're going to California where the folks are accustomed to Hollywood glamour, a few rhinestones would be pretty. For a change, I mean. I'm so excited to see Stewart I could sing."

"We need to go easy, Verna. He's been away for a long time now."

"Not even two years." She glanced at him wondering if there was some meaning to his words other than his usual practical outlook. "Surely we'll meet his friends and see where he teaches, and he'll want to show us San Francisco. I've always wanted to take a ride on one of those itty bitty cable cars and eat in a real Chinese restaurant."

"We shouldn't expect too much."

"My hunch is he has a girlfriend. Even if I am his mother, I've got eyes. A good-looking man like our Stewart won't be single for long. I hear those California girls are very forward and if they see a man they want they go after him. I read it in a Life Magazine. Oh, my, you don't think he's dating a hippie girl?"

"Verna, let's enjoy ourselves while we're there."

"Of course, dear." She reached into her bag and unfurled a knitted rectangle of heather blue wool.

"What are you making now?"

"A sweater vest," she said, smoothing it on her lap. "You've seen this before. I've almost finished the back." She tucked a ball of yarn between her knees and took up the knitting. Knit one. Purl one, she mouthed to herself. Knit one. Purl one.

"I can't keep all your projects straight. Who is this for?"

"Why Stewart, of course. Blue is his favorite color."

* * *

Stewart heard the Winnebago before he saw it. It sounded like a semi roaring at the front gate. He stood quickly and went to the window. The headlights filled the road from ditch to ditch, white running lights flashed along the side body, yellow parking lights blinked, red brake lights blazed. The Winnebago stopped. Then the gears shifted in reverse, tires crunching in the dirt, the engine coughing, spewing, and sputtering. The ignition clicked off.

Stewart went into high alert. The game plan he had prepared for his parents' visit was a hard-won truce between how and what he could imagine himself telling them, and Annie's advice to tell them the truth. He had sat with himself for a long time. He knew his cover of being straight was on borrowed time. Once his parents walked in his door, his sanctuary wasn't impenetrable from his mother's prying eyes. He assumed his father had kept the truth about Mitchell from his mother. Stewart's personal life was knee-deep in pretense. He was determined to shed the guilt he carried with the people who loved him the most.

Suddenly he saw his parents hurrying along the path, through the yard, his mother leading the way, calling his name, "Stewart! Stewart!" They were standing under the yellow porch light, moths fluttering around their heads. Stewart opened the door, his mother nearly collapsed into his arms. His father reached to steady her fall, and when his eyes met Stewart's gaze, they were unflinching and direct.

***

They had been on the go all weekend tramping up and down the hills of San Francisco and poking their noses into every damp Marin wood so that when Monday morning came, Verna couldn't help herself. While Stewart was clearing out the classroom, she and Clyde shopped at Safeway. Afterwards, she shooed Clyde off to the bait shop and filled a bucket of hot water with a dollop of Pine Sol. She was thankful she and Clyde were sleeping in the Winnebago. Although the yard was pretty enough, with its flowering plants and trees, housekeeping had no meaning to Stewart. She couldn't understand how he entertained anyone in such deplorable conditions.

With the vigor of a woman raised on a farm, she attacked the dust and cobwebs and scrubbed the kitchen from top to bottom—the windows, cabinets, countertop, and floor. She even lined the shelves with red and white checkered contact paper. All the while, a puzzle fueled her industry: not once had Stewart mentioned a someone special who would be joining them for coffee in the morning or dinner at the Italian restaurant in town where wine bottles hung through fishing net on the ceiling. When he announced they were invited to dinner at a friend's house—a friend named Annie—on the following Sunday, the last day of their stay, her heart gladdened. "Is Annie your girlfriend?" she asked.

Stewart cut her short. "She's just a friend," he said and changed the subject.

Now in his bedroom, she averted her eyes from his personal papers, but she couldn't help peeking about the bed and in his closet hoping to discover a female what-not or better yet a baby doll nightie hanging on the back of his bathroom door. When her search failed to produce results, she sighed, "What a shame," and resumed cleaning with renewed vigor, humming the catchy theme from "The Mary Tyler Moore Show."

The day before she had managed to secretly purchase a new shower curtain when they were in town at Varney's Hardware. After scouring the bathroom, she dismantled the mildewed curtain, hooked up the new one, stood back, and admired her selection. Goodness, didn't she just adore goldfish. She dumped the old one into the trashcan, declaring, "Good riddance." In the yard, she clipped baby roses from the back fence and arranged bouquets that she placed on the kitchen table, Stewart's nightstand, and the living room windowsill. She brewed herself a strong cup of Lipton tea that she sweetened with cream and honey and read over the recipes she had brought from home. She had decided on Swedish meatballs, mashed potatoes, fresh green beans, a molded orange carrot salad with raisins and walnuts, and for dessert, strawberry shortcake with whipped cream.

Stewart was picking up Clyde at the Bait Shop, and they were going fishing at Bon Tempe Lake. She had the afternoon to herself. She hoped to take a quick stroll around the neighborhood and afterwards apply a fresh coat of frosted raspberry polish to her nails that perfectly matched her new polyester pantsuit. She wanted to look especially nice for their first evening at home.

* * *

Icy spring fog churned off the Farallons, driving straight for the coast and extinguishing the sun beaming out of an agate blue sky. Visibility on the Bolinas Ridge dropped to less than two hundred feet. The fog rolled down the east side of the mountain blanketing the serpentine canyons and grassy hillsides. Soon the vaporous fog would drip from the forest's foliage and mingle with the clear song of the White-crowned Sparrow. A piercing wind swept over the watershed lakes. At Bon Tempe Lake, it whipped the deep emerald surface into stiff white peaks.

Stewart hiked up his collar around his neck and pulled the rods and reels from the back seat of his Mustang. "You going to be warm enough, Dad?" Stewart asked, tucking the tackle box under his arm.

"Hell, yes. Takes more than this to blow me over. This stuff just comes out of nowhere, heh?"

That's right," Stewart replied. "There's a spot round the lake where it's protected."

"Suits me. Looks like we've got the place to ourselves," Clyde said. "You fish here year round?"

"Yes, sun up to sun down. The lakes are stocked with trout in the spring. Lake Lagunitas is in that direction." Stewart pointed the tip of the rod toward a stand of redwood trees that marked the trail through a picnic area to a flume that carried overflow from the upper lake into Bon Tempe. "Today let's try our luck there." He started on the path toward a grassy meadow and matched his stride to his father's pace.

"If it ever warms up, this must be a piece of paradise," Clyde said.

Stewart laughed. "So, when are you going to quit the business and go to fishing full-time?" It seemed like they naturally turned to the same topics no matter what. The rhythm was comforting, and Stewart didn't mind it one bit.

"Me? I'll never quit. Plus your mother is not inclined to let me chase around in the Winnebago like tumbleweed. No, she likes me home by the fire every night."

"How many miles show on the odometer?"

"Pushing 60,000, but she's as good as new. I change the oil every 2,000 miles, keep her lubed; she's indoors all winter. Keeps the rust away." Clyde rubbed his nose vigorously. "That Mustang you have is a horse."

"I can do eighty, and it feels like I'm standing still."

"Detroit never made them better."

They crossed the grassy meadow and picked up the trail on the bank of the lake. The scene before them was rolling in slow motion, and Stewart glanced at his father, wondering at what point he could open the door to what was truly on his mind. Pacific pond turtles slid off a fallen log bleached to the color of ash and plopped into the shallows. Thickened roots from oak, madrone, and fir twisted up through the rocky soil. Above the trail, in an outcropping of boulders, a family of black-tailed deer raised their heads and watched them pass.

"Business is good?" Stewart asked, tossing the question over his shoulder.

"Can't complain. Steady demand, loyal customers. That damnable oil shortage was a bear, but Herb helped to shoulder the weight of that fiasco."

"He's doing a good job then?" A familiar feeling of guilt that he had abandoned his father and left a cousin to run the business made his voice thick. Stewart slowed his pace, stepping along the path.

"He's dependable all right, plus the boy's got a gift for gab. He can damn near talk to anyone and get results."

They tramped along the trail that rose and dipped. A pileated woodpecker hammered *rat-a-tat-tat* into the trunk of a towering fir and a flock of wild turkey grazed beneath the trees.

"Don't sell yourself short, Dad. You were the one who built the business."

"Yes, but nowadays, you've got to practice the skill of communication. I was never long on words. Herb's a natural."

"I'm glad to hear that," Stewart said and meant every word, but still he wished he could have fulfilled his father's ambition.

"Yes, he's a big help."

"I knew he had it in him."

"Seems like it was for the best…I mean, you coming out here and everything."

Stewart recognized the perfect opening. But he couldn't find a way to start.

They came to a narrow cove where the wind blew up little riffles. Clyde dug his handkerchief out of his pocket and blew his nose. "Is this your spot?"

For a moment, Stewart was confused. He turned and looked into his father's clear eyes. "Oh, you mean for fishing?"

"What did you think I meant?"

"I thought you meant is this where I'm going to settle permanently."

"Well, that too."

"I think so. I like it enough," he answered, prodding the wet earth with the toe of his boot and turning toward the lake.

"Can't say as I blame you. It's a sportsman's dream. You've got the ocean, the mountains, and the lakes. Maybe sometime we can take a fishing trip together."

"I'd like that, Dad."

"You going to stick with teaching?"

"For now. I can travel in the summer," he answered.

"You taking care of yourself?"

"Yes, sir," Stewart replied. Dryness parched the inside of his mouth. The gut-churning moment when his father found him with Mitchell flashed in his memory. He felt his father's eyes at the back of his head. The water slapped against the bank, and a gust of bracing wind drew tears from Stewart's eyes. He pushed against the feeling of shame. He couldn't find a way to confide in his father. He loved him. He didn't want to hurt him.

"What do you say we see if the fish are biting?" his father asked.

Stewart turned from the bank, set down the tackle box, and removed a plastic tub of live worms. He knelt, one knee tucked close against his chest, his foot slightly pigeon-toed, the other knee folded underneath him resting on the ground. The memory of being a kid came over him when he brought his bike to his father to fix.

Clyde stooped opposite him, and together they baited the hooks. Stewart waited while Clyde walked down the bank past the reed grasses, drew back, and cast the line over the rippling surface. The hook splashed into the lake. Stewart stepped to the water's edge, prepared to cast, but stopped in mid-swing. On cambered wings an osprey soared over the lake with a fish clutched in its talons. The osprey's sharp whistle called urgently and penetrated Stewart's full heart.

* * *

Dinner was heating in the oven, and the table was set when Verna saw Clyde and Stewart walking through the gate. She clapped her hands together, patted her hair and ran to greet them. "Hello!" she called, swinging open the door. "How was the fishing?"

"Strictly catch and release," Clyde answered, propping up the rod and reel by the door and kissing Verna on the cheek. "But what a spot. Something smells mighty good."

"You're just in time! Dinner is ready."

"I'm going to clean up." Stewart walked toward his bedroom.

Verna smiled to herself. Surely he'd notice the spic and span bathroom and the cheerful shower curtain. She bustled back into the kitchen, and Clyde followed her and began to wash up at the sink. She tied an apron around her waist and lifted the casseroles out of the oven racks. They chatted while she set the food onto trivets arranged on the table. She was dipping the Jell-O mold into a bath of warm water when Stewart appeared.

"What have you been doing all day?" he asked.

"Just a little cleaning, dear," she explained, ignoring the scowl on his face. She slipped the mold onto a plate and neatly tucked lettuce around its edges. "Now come and sit down. Everything is ready."

"It doesn't look like a *little* cleaning."

Verna cringed and looked to Clyde who shook his head.

"What's with the shower curtain?"

She ducked her head. "Don't you like it?"

"No, as a matter of fact, I don't like it at all."

"Oh, I'm sorry. I'll take it back and get something you like."

"That isn't the point."

"I didn't mean to disturb anything. Really I didn't. Can't we just sit down and enjoy our dinner." She glanced at the clock over the refrigerator. "Please, Clyde, take a seat."

"I wish you would have spent your time doing something else."

Verna scooted a chair out and sat down. "But I did, Stewart. I took a lovely walk around the neighborhood. In fact, I met one of your neighbors, and I've invited her for dessert."

"You what?"

"Why, yes, Leslie's the nicest girl. I know you'll get along." Verna began to slice the mold into sections.

"You've got no right!"

"Wait a minute, son." Clyde raised his hand. "Take it easy."

"For Christ's sake, Mom, put down the knife."

"Why, I hardly know what the fuss is." Why was Stewart getting so upset? she wondered. "Once you see her..."

"I have seen her."

"You have?" Verna paused, her hand poised over a salad plate, a scoop of Jell-O quivering in the spoon.

"Yes, she's at the end of the block. A tall blonde. She's an attractive woman, but.... please, listen to me. Both of you."

"Are you sick?" Verna asked, dropping the spoon to the plate, dread rushing toward her.

"No, I'm healthy as a horse. Look at me!"

"Thank goodness," she said. "You had me there for a minute."

Clyde moved to the table, pulled a chair up to his wife, and took her hand. "Let's listen to the boy, Verna."

She collected herself and gazed at Stewart who rested his head in his hands.

Gradually he lifted his head, looking first to Clyde, then to Verna. "I'm not attracted to women. I never have been."

"What are you talking about? Verna cried. "You had girlfriends in school. More than one as I recall. You went to all the proms!"

"That was an act."

"What do you mean?" Though she tried, she couldn't control her voice. "In college, you and Mary Beth were together for years. We thought you'd be married for sure."

Stewart shook his head. "She was a faithful friend who finally gave up on me."

Verna's eyes welled with tears, and she reached for Clyde who starred straight into Stewart's eyes.

"Mom, Dad," he said, "I'm gay."

Verna rocked backwards. Clyde closed his eyes and bowed his head. His hand gripped her fingers.

Finally Clyde raised his head and looked into Stewart's eyes. "Thank you, son, for telling us."

She searched the walls for someplace easy to rest her eyes, her lips trembling.

The coffee pot percolated on the stove; a cat scratched at the front door and down the block children called to one another from their skateboards.

"Mom, you do know what that means?"

"Heavens, do you think I'm stupid?" she scolded. "Of course, I know what that means."

"I don't want you to worry. I've got friends. There's a . . ."

Verna shook her head. "Give me a minute, Stewart. Just a minute."

She pulled herself up from the chair, swaying on her feet. Clyde reached out to her.

"I cannot breathe in this room," she announced, pulling away from Clyde. "If you'll excuse me." She rushed from the kitchen and hurried out the front door. In the yard, she dashed to a tree and steadied herself against its trunk. There in the shelter of its leafy canopy, despair rolled through her. She cried for everything: for the mother she may not have been, for her inability to detect the signs that Stewart must have given, and most of all, for her failure to protect him. Had she neglected him or had they represented married life in a way that was repugnant or unappealing? Worse yet, was there something in her that caused Stewart to find women undesirable? And she was sorry, sorry that she would never see Stewart's children, that they would not be grandparents, and frightened, frightened of what the family would surely think, what the neighbors would say, how people would talk behind their backs.

She bargained with herself that she and Clyde would keep this from everyone, and then she cried again, knowing her life was turning in a direction that she did not understand. How would she have the strength to carry on? She turned her face upwards and prayed to god for help until she stumbled through the gate and into the Winnebago. She felt her way to the narrow couch and fell upon it, surrendering to an anguish that threatened to engulf her. After a time, a knock sounded at the door, and Clyde entered. He came in quietly, sat on the edge of the couch, and placed his hand on her shoulder.

"Verna, are you all right?"

"I think I've cried myself out."

He stroked her shoulder. "Let me get you some water."

She propped herself on her elbow and drank from the glass. Cars passed on the street, and the wind rustled through the trees.

Clyde's hand found his wife's shoulder. When he spoke the words came softly. "Verna, you know me. All these years together, you pretty much get what you see." He paused. "There is something I've kept from you."

She tensed and peered at him.

"It happened when Stewart was about fourteen. I found Stewart with a part-time worker by the name of Mitchell, in the bunkhouse."

"Oh, my god." She gripped her forehead. "What do you mean 'found him'?"

Clyde's voice dropped to a whisper. "They were naked."

The years seemed to roll back and a vision of Mitchell chilled her to the bone. "You mean...you mean..." She couldn't bring herself to say the words. She had heard of these things, but it was unthinkable that this unnatural act could happen to her son.

"I didn't put two and two together until it was too late." He voice dropped to a growl. "I nearly killed the man."

Verna gasped. "How could you keep this from me?"

"What's done is done. The fact is, it doesn't change anything now."

"How can you say that?" she railed. "We could have done something!"

"Like what?"

"We could have gone to the pastor, or his school counselor, or to the librarian..."

"Listen to yourself. If we'd gone to the church, we'd have gotten an earful of Bible talk about sin and damnation, and I'm flat out against that. Anyway, what did they know then that we didn't know? And even if we did, Stewart would have been humiliated. I don't think we would have done any of that. I think we would have tried to handle it ourselves the same way I did. I thought it was a one-time thing. He never let on. It must have been hell for him."

"You are a damn fool for keeping this from me."

"I did what I thought was best."

She heard sadness in his voice. Wasn't he was protecting her like he always tried to do?

"What's clear now is that our son is hurting," Clyde said. "He's asking for something, and it's pretty clear he's asking for our understanding."

"Why, of course he is. Only I don't know how to act."

"Well, hell, neither do I."

"What do we do if he introduces us to a boyfriend?"

"Damn, Verna. You're moving way too fast here."

"He would have made such a fine father."

"Yes, that's true, but it's his life to live. Remember, he's still our son. That hasn't changed."

Verna shuddered. "Oh, enough of this wallowing. I can't stand myself any longer. You and I have a lot of talking to do. No more keeping things to yourself that you think I can't hear. It makes me steaming mad! I'm not made of sugar or salt, and I will not melt in the rain. We've met trouble before, and we'll stare it down again." She heaved herself up from the bed. "Get me a cold, wet washcloth. My eyes feel like burning coals. I didn't make dinner just for it to spoil!"

Clyde paused at the window. "Come here, Verna. You better look at this."

Verna squinted through swollen eyes and clutched her throat. "Mercy, why that's Leslie at the front door! When will this night end?"

Chapter 26

June 14

IN SAN FRANCISCO it was the kind of day that tourists dreamed about and residents, who shivered through spring's capriciousness, called their offices to say they were too ill to come to work. From daybreak to day's end, the city baked under a hot June sun. At dusk the air was balmy.

On the edge of Jackson Square, a half-block from the law offices of Gessler, Burrows, and Blake, Daniel struck a match and lit a cigarette that Sam held between his lips. He blew out the match and stepped farther back inside the cool alcove of a brick building. He was sweating and every screech of a horn jangled his nerves.

As Roman Markewitz's investigation proceeded, an idea hovered at the edges of Daniel's mind. The idea had taken hold in Philadelphia and grown in intensity—he would return to law school, pass the bar, and join the firm. He knew with certainty this was the path he was meant to take.

When he'd landed in San Francisco, Daniel consulted with Judge Hobart and Roman. In that meeting, Daniel confided about finding his mother and told them then what he couldn't tell them before—that his father had virtually abandoned her, that she and Charles had had an affair, and when she rejected him for another man, Charles blackmailed her. At the same time, he pled his case for joining the firm. He asked the judge to be his advisor, and without delay, the judge accepted.

In a subsequent meeting, Roman, speaking rapidly, exhibited copies of records that documented Charles's siphoning funds from three trusts that the firm represented into shell companies from which he cashed trustee checks as well as photographs of Charles gambling at casinos and club.

Judge Hobart said it was clear that Charles's intent was to defraud the family trust and clients' accounts. Unless Charles wanted a scandal, the evidence would force him to step down. The judge set up an emergency meeting with the other partners, Fritz Burrows and Herman Blake, and accepted their request to come onboard as part of the reorganization of the firm. Daniel announced that he wanted to break the news to Charles. The judge took a deep breath, and with the same respect he had shown Daniel from the instant they met, agreed.

* * *

Now Daniel stepped forward onto the sidewalk, surveyed the entrance to the law offices and ducked back into the shade.

Sam inhaled and blew the smoke toward a sky that was beginning to tinge flamenco pink. "New threads?" Sam asked.

"You like it?" Daniel dusted off the front of a navy blue blazer and rocked back on his heels. "A purchase in Philly."

"You look good. Just like a city boy."

"Yeah, well, you look like you could kick ass." Daniel observed the way Sam's neck disappeared into his shoulders and his biceps strained against the sleeves of a black leather jacket. Sam was the perfect backer—cool under pressure, street smart, and honest to the quick.

"Hey, not me," Sam chuckled, flecking a speck of tobacco off his tapered fingertip. "I am strictly a pacifist."

"I know you've seen some action in your time," Daniel said, remembering the stories Sam had let slip about touring in the South in the '50s and '60s when things got rough in towns where some people didn't like a black man and his band stirring up the audience, especially the women.

"Sure, but I don't go looking for it. I don't like to mess up my hands. Or my mouth. Speaking of which, I know you're hooked up with the judge on this takeover action, but you're going to be cool tonight." Sam's gaze bore into Daniel's eyes. "No personal vendettas you're intending to deliver. Correct?"

"I'm cool." Daniel rolled his shoulders and swiped the back of his hand over his perspiring lip.

"You heard the saying, 'Vengeance is a dish best served cold'?" Sam asked, dragging on his cigarette.

Daniel squinted at Sam. His litany of quotes was a rolling source of pleasure. "Yes, and I'm counting on you to help me keep it that way."

"Well, then we'll be fine," Sam said. "You got everything?"

"*I've* got the papers. *You've* got the photos. Right?"

"That's right," Sam said, tapping his inside breast pocket. "I was only making sure."

Daniel pushed up his cuff and checked his watch. The hour was pushing toward 6:30. By now, according to their timetable, Judge Hobart and the partners would be ensconced in the conference room. After Daniel's meeting with Charles, they would step in, outline their case, and offer him a termination package.

Sam dropped the cigarette and ground it with his shoe. "I'll hand it to you. You uncovered a shitload of bad business when you ran down that bogus roof job."

"Maybe, but the judge was brilliant and the private investigator did the heavy lifting." Daniel checked his watch again.

Sam clapped him on the back. "You're going to wear out that cuff."

Daniel nodded. "Let's go. It's time."

They crossed the street, walked down the block, and through the gates of the law firm. The door was unlocked.

Inside the hushed office, the receptionist's station was shut for the night, and doors along the corridor were closed. Daniel proceeded over the carpet at a brisk pace followed by Sam. They passed the entry to the conference room where a faint strip of light shone from under the door. They soundlessly slipped through the door marked "Miss Graves."

Estelle Graves secured the lock behind them, fumbling with

the latch. "You're here. Thank goodness." The usual crispness of her voice was diminished. "It's been a long day."

"Charles is in his office?" Daniel asked.

"Yes, he gave instructions not to be disturbed. Please tell me you'll be cautious," Estelle warned, a sober frown pinching her face. "Not headstrong."

"Nothing will go wrong," Daniel said. Against his better judgment, he wished that something would go wrong—very wrong. He'd like nothing better than to step in front of Charlie and plant a fist in his face.

"I expect not. I'm relying on you." She drew herself to her full height of five-feet-two inches and turned to Sam. "Mr. Johnstone," she said. "I'm pleased to see you again." She offered her hand, unembellished by rings, her clear polished nails neatly clipped.

"Miss Graves, the pleasure is mine," he said, gallantly bowing.

"I am grateful for your presence this afternoon."

"I suspect there won't be much reason for me to help."

"One can never tell." Estelle's grey-blue eyes sharpened behind silver-framed spectacles.

"That is the truth," Sam said. "You can't be too careful. In my experience it's situations like these when a wolf can read the wind."

"This is most unpleasant business. I'll be happy when it's over." Her fingers strayed to a gold pin in the shape of a swan fastened to the lapel of her suit jacket. "I hope we'll have another occasion less demanding when we can visit."

"I would be honored."

"There are only a handful of people in this world whom I cherish, and Ceci is one of them. I want her well, Mr. Johnstone."

"I'm doing my best."

"Estelle," Daniel interrupted. "It's time for you to leave." Informing Estelle about the extent of Charles's treachery had been difficult. When his mother had left San Francisco, she'd confided to Estelle only the barest reasons for her departure. She asked Estelle to honor her confidence, which she had faithfully done while continuing her work at the firm because of her allegiance to the memory of Daniel's grandfather and fondness for the family. When Estelle returned, he would need her by his side. Her forty-year devotion to the law practice was invaluable.

A slight tremor caused Estelle's head to shake on the thin stem of her neck and she responded in a near-whisper, "Of course."

"There's a car outside to take you to the airport. I don't want you to miss the flight." Daniel's first thought was to see that Estelle left the building safely. "There'll be a car waiting for you in Philadelphia. Mother is expecting you."

"Thank you, dear." She touched his sleeve. "I look forward to our reunion." She motioned toward her desk where files lay on top of a blotter, and an envelope was propped against a vase of white roses. "I've left everything in order. There's a letter for Charles. It seemed necessary even under the circumstances."

"I'll make sure he gets it," Daniel said.

She glanced around the office. "When I return we'll reorganize immediately." She lifted a small valise and pocketbook from a chair near the desk.

"May I escort you to the front door?" Sam asked.

"Why, no thank you." A smile deepened the lines around her eyes. "After all this time, I know the way." She brightened. "Soon we'll begin a new chapter."

Sam cracked open the door and peered into the empty corridor. He held her elbow and ushered her forward. Straight-backed and unswerving, she walked along the hallway, her sensible black pumps skimming over the carpet. In her departure, a faint trace of lavender lingering in the air.

They watched her go, and then Daniel nodded to Sam. Together they exited Estelle's office and stopped in front of Charles's door. Daniel looked at the brass plaque that read, "Charles W. Gessler, Esq." He rapped hard and twisted open the doorknob.

Charles was stationed behind the lion-footed desk, a glass tumbler held to his lips half-filled with amber-colored liquid. A legal-sized yellow tablet lay open before him. The whites of his eyes gleamed as white as his pinstriped shirt. "I beg your pardon," he protested. He slowly set the tumbler onto the desk, his head turning to Sam, who moved beside Daniel.

"Hello, Charles," Daniel said, striding into the room. He quickly assessed the details of the office: the placement of furniture—unchanged; blinds—drawn; the door to a private bathroom—closed. The smell of leather, books, and ink filled his nostrils, anchoring him to a past when civility was the order of the day.

"What is the meaning of this?" Charles demanded, his eyes darting back to Daniel.

"I'm here on business," Daniel said. He stopped at one of the leather chairs in front of the desk and ran his hand along the tufted seatback. "Or you could say, I'm here to settle a score."

Charles swallowed, adjusting the grey polka dot bow tie knotted squarely at his throat. He regarded his nephew as if he were evaluating the mettle of a prosecuting attorney. "State your business or get out of here."

Daniel searched his eyes for some sign of shock or irony. Instead he saw a chasm as deep as a pit. "The last time we met you were intent on shutting me out of the trust." He paused. "I thought about that, and the more I thought, it seemed to me that you knew a lot about how I was spending my time."Stale air circulated from the air-conditioner, churning the thickened atmosphere. "Northrup Investigations, was it?"

Charles gave no outward indication of surprise. A smirk of superiority soured his face. The smirk was a weapon Daniel had encountered before. The expression held its victim at bay. Today it was wasted on him.

"I resent this intrusion," Charles said. His forehead glistened with sweat.

Daniel smelled fear. He knew a bluff when he saw one. "The funny thing is, I have memories of you when I was young. Memories when you'd take me to some of your favorite haunts." He smiled. "You even taught me card tricks."

"Write me a letter," Charles said. His skin paled to grey ash. He half-swiveled toward Sam and gripped the armrests.

"Then I as grew older you changed." Daniel's pulse echoed in his ears. "I couldn't figure it out."

"I don't have time for this," Charles said, his lip quivering.

"Was it because of her?" Daniel asked. He reached inside his jacket pocket and withdrew a letter. Unfolding it slowly, he stepped up to the desk and dropped it on top of the yellow manila tablet.

"Where did you get this?" Charles demanded, his face twisting into a grimace.

"You sent my mother away like a criminal."

"You think I care?" Charles laughed contemptuously. "She deserved exactly what she got." He balled the letter in his fist and threw it at Daniel.

In a blinding move, Daniel jumped toward the desk, one leg hiked to vault, the taste of blood in his mouth. No sooner had his hands touched the desk than Sam clamped down on his arms and pulled him away.

Stumbling to his feet, Charles lurched backwards, his eyeglasses flying off his face.

Sam gripped Daniel's shoulder and led his away. He walked over to Charles, who was trying to get to his feet, hauled him off the floor, and handed him his eyeglasses. "Why don't you sit still and listen," Sam said. "It would be better for your health."

"I'll go to the police," Charles sputtered. "I'll sue the little bastard."

"You ain't the one who'll be doing any suing," Sam said.

"Get your henchman off my back," Charles spat at Daniel as he toppled back into the chair.

"Charles, meet Sam Johnstone. Sam is Ceci's boyfriend."

A deep red climbed from under Charles's collar and spread up to his forehead.

Daniel paced the floor, rubbing his knuckles as he turned back toward Charles. He produced a folded document from his pocket and tossed it onto the desk. "This is from the Registrar's Office at Berkeley. I'm enrolled in law school. In three years max, I'll pass the bar."

"You'll never amount to anything," Charles scoffed.

"Tell that to Judge Hobart and your partners. They're waiting for you in the conference room." He leveled a pitying stare into Charles's contorted face. "For years you've siphoned money off the family trust and at least three other clients of the firm. We know there's income missing from property accounts and expenses charged against shadow companies, and we know you've got a gambling problem." Daniel stepped back from the desk. "Show him the photos, Sam."

Sam flipped a brown manila envelope onto the desk.

Charles grimly opened the envelope. A blue vein bulged down the middle of his forehead. The eight by ten inch photographs were black and white and grainy in texture. The first revealed Charles entering a gambling club in Chinatown. In the second, he played cards with a group of men and women at a game table, foot-high poker chips stacked at his elbow. The third photograph caught him placing a bet at a roulette table in a Vegas casino.

Charles swallowed, his jaw rigid. He slumped, shoulders caved, eyes locked into Daniel's.

"There's one more thing," Daniel said. "You have no right to pass moral judgment on my mother."

Without breaking eye contact, Daniel stepped backwards until he reached the wall of bookshelves. He yanked a book from the shelf and slipped his hand into the opening.

Charles jerked upright, his mouth frozen in a rictus of dread.

Daniel pressed a button. The grinding sound of gears rumbled, and the bookshelf began to separate down the middle.

"You sonofabitch!" Charles shouted. "Shut it off! Shut the damn thing off!" Charles slumped in the chair, slack-mouthed and motionless.

"Right on, man." Sam strolled past the gap in the bookshelf and disappeared through the dark opening that gapped between the bookshelves. He whistled, and his voice rang out, "No shit." He stepped back into the office; a grin spread across his face and joined Daniel, who waited at the door.

"A pleasure meeting you," Sam called over his shoulder as he walked out.

"Starting now," Daniel said, "I'm taking my place here. Judge Hobart and the partners are waiting for my word. They're prepared to offer you a deal. Until I assume leadership, and believe me I will, this firm will operate the way my grandfather intended."

* * *

At Tosca's in North Beach, Daniel and Sam bellied up to the bar and each ordered a Moretti.

"Good work," Sam said, clapping him on the back.

"Couldn't have done it without you," Daniel replied, meaning every word of it.

The doors and windows were thrown open after the heat of the evening and the muffled sounds of traffic hummed by on Columbus Avenue. Between beers, Sam placed a call to Ceci, but got no answer. As he walked through the restaurant, the regulars gave him high fives. In a burst of good humor, Daniel grabbed a pool stick and challenged Sam to a game. They sank a few shots on the green velvet while they listened to the cognoscenti sing along with the arias being piped through the stereo speakers.

By the time they got back to Mill Valley, it was later than either of them had planned. Sam parked the Jag in the dirt turnout behind Daniel's bus, turned off the headlights, and looked up through the woods toward the rear of the cabin. Soft light flickered through the doors on the porch.

"You coming up?" Sam asked.

"I don't know. I've got one more stop to make."

"You going to see that sweet woman of yours?"

"I haven't seen her since I've been back."

"What?" Sam tilted his head back and moaned. "Are you crazy?"

Daniel shrugged. He knew his reasoning sounded downright foreign to Sam. "I had business to clean up. I didn't want any loose ends."

"I should say so. But Ceci will be pissed if I'm the one to tell her what went down."

"She's pissed all the time," Daniel said. He hoped, once he

explained, she'd be as supportive to his succession as the partners were. He wanted to assure her he'd be fair. Gradually his opposition to her acceptance of the trust fund distribution had shifted. She was entitled to whatever the trust stipulated.

"That's her crazy side acting up."

"You didn't let on about what we were up to tonight?"

Sam moved his head back and forth slowly in response. "Hell, no."

"I'm not sure I'm ready to break the news."

"She doesn't mean half of what she says." Sam's voice dropped. "Especially if she's been drinking."

"What's going on with her?"

"That woman is like a yo-yo. Some days she's up, some days she's down. If you stop in now it'll do her good."

Daniel looked askance at Sam. "You think she's home?"

"Most likely. She said something about stepping out with a girlfriend."

Daniel capitulated. He didn't intend to have any reason for disagreement from this moment on.

They walked single-file up the pathway through the warm earth-sweet evening. Their footfalls stilled the song of the crickets. Inside the air was stale with tobacco smoke and tinged with a slightly acrid scent of something gone awry.

"Baby girl, you home?" Sam called.

No one answered. The strains of Billie Holliday's voice played from the stereo in a corner of the room.

"She's not back," Daniel said, glancing around the living room.

"That's her purse on the couch," Sam said. "Let me check. Maybe she's sleeping."

Daniel watched Sam walk toward the hall and through the door of the bedroom. He was seized by a premonition that rippled down his spine.

He heard Sam bellow, "Ah, shit, Ceci! What have you done?"

Daniel moved quickly into the bedroom. The sour smell of sickness permeated the air. Ceci lay face down on the bed, her face into the pillow, hair tangled in vomit. A bottle of Jim Beam was caught in the covers beside an overturned prescription bottle.

Sam pulled her shoulders up and caught her in his arms. Her head lolled backwards and the whites of her eyes showed like milky slits. He howled in anguish. "Ceci, baby. Wake up! Ah, honey, wake up!"

Daniel crowded onto the bed, his hands pawing at Ceci's hair, his fingers palpating her neck. "Where's her pulse, Sam? "

Tears flooded Sam's eyes and ran down his cheeks, and he wailed, his voice keening like a wounded animal.

Daniel dragged Ceci off the bed onto the floor, pinched her nose, and pressed his mouth to her mouth, trying to force air into her lungs. He counted between breaths—one, two—and began again. He lifted his head and yelled at Sam who lay bawling on the floor, "Call the police! Get an ambulance!"

Death hovered in the room. Daniel cradled Ceci's body against his chest and rocked her like a child. "Come on. Damn it. Breathe. Breathe."

Chapter 27

June 17

MERCIFULLY THE FOG CREPT IN, the heat wave vanished, and, at the Bank of America, business was brisk. Jess waited in line for a teller; in her hand, she held a check for $2,500. The festival money from the mayor's office had arrived in full. Sebastian had split it three ways, and her bank account would increase five-fold.

The line crept ahead, and Jess people-watched: a collection of tennis wives, a few impatient shopkeepers, and a white-haired couple who chatted amiably with one another. She studied the legs of the tennis wife directly in front of her—legs flattered by smooth hamstrings and tanned *Ban de Soliel* brown. Jess guessed at the amount of money she might be depositing, certainly a staggering sum, and she could not fathom how every month all your material needs, and the needs of your children, would be taken care of.

In their last phone conversation, Daniel had exuded optimism. His reunion with his mother was a breakthrough. But Jess had cut him off when he revealed Sarah had confided in him about Matthew's plan to break in at the gallery. She wished she hadn't been so stubborn and unwilling to hear what he had been trying to explain. Gradually she decided that Daniel had acted on his own instincts, which were always to protect Sarah. His words were on her mind and in and out of her dreams. He said he'd be home from Philadelphia in a few days. A week had come and gone without hearing from him. He said they'd talk things out. Where was he?

A teller called, "Next, please."

A frizzy-haired shopkeeper with a large zippered bag hurried up to the window.

Jess stepped forward behind the tennis wife, and her gaze wandered across the floor over a low oak railing where she observed the obsequious demeanor of a bank manager, seated at a desk, facing a man in the adjoining chair. Her heart leapt in her throat. It was Daniel in profile, dressed in a white oxford shirt. Normally he wouldn't be caught dead in a shirt like that. What has he done to his hair? It was shorn up to his collar, and trimmed around his ears, causing him to appear older and shockingly conservative.

There was a flurry of papers over the desk. The manager was asking questions, listening closely to responses, and watching Daniel sign papers. The manager passed a document to Daniel, and as he raised one arm onto the desk, Jess noticed that his hand was wrapped in a white cast. An electrical current flashed in her wrists in sympathetic response.

Another teller called, "Next, please."

The tennis wife bounced forward on the toes of her Adidas leaving Jess in plain view. Somehow she wanted to hide as if seeing Daniel engaged in a financial transaction was like spying.

Daniel shook hands with the manager. He was opening the gate at the low railing when he angled her way. She looked down quickly, but he called her name. When she glanced up, he was coming toward her in long strides. Dark shadows ringed his eyes. He was holding his hand in the cast aloft. He pulled her toward him, kissing her mouth. The sensation of his lips on her lips, and the scent of his skin awakened all the ways in which he pleased and surprised her. She lingered in his embrace, the thrum of voices mixed with ringing phones, chattering typewriters, and adding machines in the background.

From behind a voice said, "Miss, you're next."

"Sorry," Daniel maneuvered Jess to one side. "It's good to see you," he said, dipping his mouth to her ear. "I can't tell you.

I was just on my way to your house."

"What's happened to your hand?" She tentatively reached out to soothe the injured fingers that protruded from the cast.

He winced and then frowned, and without his hair framing his face, she saw a furrow of faint lines crease his forehead. He looked more mature than before, and in a strange way that she couldn't have anticipated, she missed his long hair.

"I had an accident," he said. "It was a stupid thing."

The way he kept staring into her eyes disarmed her defenses. She remembered the first time she'd met him in San Francisco. She had thought he was an aimless surfer, belonging to no one and without a home or purpose. Now she knew differently. The strength and confidence that had attracted her in the beginning was even more intense now.

"Excuse me, dear," an older woman said, "there's a teller available for you."

"I'll wait." Daniel said. "Over by the door."

Jess stepped up to the teller and deposited her check. She kept glancing over her shoulder to make sure he was still there. As she walked toward him, he met her part way and looped his arm over her shoulder. "Can we go to your place?"

"I can't." She had a hundred questions to ask him. "I'm on my way to the city. We're pushing to get ready for the first workshop."

"Sorry, I've lost track of the days. Do you have time for a cup of coffee?"

Jess checked her watch. "I have to be on the road no later than ten."

"Let's go to the Depot."

* * *

Once they were in the bookstore, the clerks lounged at the counter, reading the morning paper, recovering from the early morning commuters, and fortifying themselves for an onslaught of mid-morning cyclists and joggers. Daniel found a table in the corner near a hanging fern. She brought two steaming mugs of French Roast and set them down. Daniel propped his elbow on the table, holding the cast upright. As soon as she settled, he reached for her hand with his good hand and caressed her fingers.

"Tell me what's happened," she said. "You hardly look like the same person who left for Philadelphia."

"I know," he said. "I've been making some changes."

"This sounds mysterious." She scanned his face trying to anticipate what he could possibly tell her that would have caused such a transformation.

"When I was in Philadelphia I made some decisions. One of them is to take control of my grandfather's law firm."

Was this a joke? she thought. The leap from law school dropout to attorney in the law firm was incomprehensible. "How in the world are you going to do that?"

"I know. It's a shocker. We need to talk. But right now I feel like hell."

The jittery cadence of his speech made her wary. "What's wrong?"

Daniel clenched his jaw. "It's Ceci. A few nights ago she overdosed."

A numbing void struck at Jess's soul. The leafy pattern of light falling onto their table, the voices around them, the bustle of book-buyers dimmed as if the earth, eclipsed by the sun, had fallen into shadow. "Is she alive?" she whispered.

"Yes. She's at Marin General." His face wore a mask of apprehension. "They had to pump her stomach. She isn't speaking, but she'll make it."

A wave of sadness rushed at her. The twin forces of loss and gain, triumph and failure, shuffled in again, side by side. "Daniel, I'm so sorry."

"I should have picked up on the signals, but she kept pushing me away."

"How could you have known?"

He shifted in the seat. "I was so damn involved in my own life, I let her down."

Jess winced. "What about Sam?" She knew he would be crippled if Ceci had passed from this planet.

"He's taking it bad. I'm going over to the hospital later on."

"What can I do?" Jess asked, feeling useless. She recognized in herself how darkness can swallow everything good and true in life. If it hadn't been for Sarah, there were frightening moments of despair when she would have wanted to sleep and never wake up.

"There's nothing to do," he said.

"And your hand?"

"When the ambulance took her to the hospital, I lost it. I punched the wall. Pretty stupid, huh?"

Jess leaned over and kissed his cheek. "You won't be able to surf."

He smiled grimly. "You know, this isn't the kind of reunion I had planned."

"I thought maybe you had changed your mind."

"No way. I meant everything I said on the phone." He drew his chair closer to her. "You'll be going on tour in less than two weeks. You haven't said where Sarah will be while you're out of town."

"She's going with me. Space has been made for her in the workshops."

"I've got another idea. My mother and Miss E. Temple are coming for the summer. Sarah can stay with us."

Jess looked at him in astonishment. He was like a force of nature whose internal compass was calibrated to true north.

"Come to Bolinas this weekend. Bring Sarah. We've got a lot of ground to cover. In fact, why doesn't Sarah spend the weekend with me? You can join us at night."

Love rose up inside her and the apparitions, pride and fear, dissolved under a tide of surprise. She smiled as if she could burst.

"I'll take that for a yes," he said, beaming at her.

They stood to leave, chairs scraping on the floor, coffee cups filled to the top left cold and untouched. The fern swayed slightly as they stood. At the counter, the clerks smoked another cigarette, skipped over the Sporting Green, and turning to the back section, chuckled over a scathing book review.

On the sidewalk in front of the Depot, Daniel tilted Jess's chin to his face. The sun drenched her shoulders. He kissed her mouth again. "I love you, Jess. Don't forget it."

In the deep-throated green canyons above the ridgelines the redwood trees stirred in the pearly light, their needles shimmering like emerald lace, and under the June sky, the Sleeping Lady showered down her blessings.

Chapter 28

June 23

VERNA WAS HAVING DIFFICULTY remembering everyone's name. As soon as she walked through the door into Annie's house with Stewart and Clyde by her side, introductions had happened so quickly that names flew by like dandelion wisps.

A more colorful group of people she hadn't seen since the "All State Country & Western Barn Dance" in Houghton two summers ago. They were different, of course, and more flamboyant than she was accustomed to, but still in keeping with the lively atmosphere. She wore her pink polyester pantsuit and matching white shell earrings, necklace and bracelet—very festive, if she did say so herself.

Everyone was so nice and friendly. The men greeted one another with a curious palm slap and thumb-twirling handshake, and the women kissed and hugged. They treated one another just like family. To a one they lingered a while to ask her and Clyde how they liked California, where had they been, and what the winters were like in Michigan.

She wistfully entertained the vision of Annie, resplendent in a purple blouse and skirt tied at the waist with a yellow scarf, as her daughter-in-law until she was invited to troop upstairs to the art studio. Land-a-Goshen, if she had a month of Sundays, she thought, she couldn't explain to her quilting bee how such a vibrant young woman could turn out such dreadful art. The primitive forms and hollow-eyed faces in the paintings unleashed a clammy disturbance in her chest.

Stewart interrupted her thoughts and handed her a glass of white wine, whispering, "Have a good time tonight, Mom. You deserve it." She nearly drained it dry on the spot. Even if her ankles swelled to the size of balloons, she wouldn't turn down another.

Thankfully they tromped back down the stairs into the living room. She found herself joined by a lovely creature named Jess who mentioned she was a dancer. *Didn't anyone have a regular job in these parts?* she thought. Together they took a seat on the couch, and Annie took the other seat next to Verna so that she was flanked on both sides by a female energy she hadn't encountered since she'd left her cousin's family in Fargo.

Annie mentioned to Verna how happy she was that she and Clyde had made the trip from Michigan to visit Stewart, and the two women took turns asking Verna questions, listening intently to her responses, and keeping the conversation going so that it was no problem at all to feel welcome.

Verna's eyes picked Stewart out of the crowd. It was his voice she strained to hear above the others. After the dreadful night of confessions, they had treated one another with infinite politeness, as if to regain their footing and weather the rest of the visit. She wondered if tonight she might meet one of his special friends. The possibility filled her with a flushed agitation. What does a body do when she meets her son's boyfriend? In her mind, she practiced the instant when she would look upon a man who might be, she shivered, her son's lover. She would be ready. She prepared her response—an interested, but not intrusive lift of her chin, a welcome, but not saccharin warmth in her eyes, a steady voice. She hoped words wouldn't fail her.

For the life of her, as Verna gazed around the room, she couldn't figure out who that special man might be. Across the room, Stewart talked with an exceptionally tall gangly man who had come in late from, she had overheard him mention, an all day cycle with his men's club. She thought his name was Fred. Yes, that was it, a doctor of some sorts though she didn't catch what. Verna frowned at the ill-fitting black wool pants he wore and wondered what would drive a grown man to dress like that. His daughter hung onto his leg, using it as a kind of May Pole from which she swung, flopping down to the floor and then crawling back up his leg. Verna turned to Jess and asked if Fred had a wife, and she said, yes, it was Renata, nodding across the room toward a woman of an exceptional porcelain complexion and dark clipped bangs. She hovered by a window discussing an obviously private subject with a very tall, emaciated woman. Verna vaguely recalled that woman's name was like a flower, but not quite. *Well, anyway,* she thought, *with the amount of make-up they're wearing they must be movie stars.*

Clyde had immediately taken up with a slim dark man who wore leather pants for the occasion. Verna suspected he was either a motorcycle gang member or a gangster. Then she remembered he owned a garage in town. Jaguars, is it? Well, if Clyde thinks he's going to buy one of those fancy British cars, he could think again.

There were other people roaming through the house: an elfin musician who wore a multi-colored knitted cap on his head; his exotic companion, a head taller, who revealed that she was a belly dancer and demonstrated, to Verna's astonishment, how swiveling one's hips was an excellent toner for female organs. A wild-haired owner of someplace called the Unknown Museum pondered one of Annie's disagreeable paintings on the living room wall beside a rather fat, swarthy man who looked like a sultan. Verna regarded the two of them suspiciously.

Verna was just about to ask Annie how all of these people fit together when a middle-aged, overweight gentleman dressed in a navy blue jacket, white shirt, red tie, and thick glasses threaded his way through the crowd. Earlier she had noticed him and Jess in the hall, their heads together, laughing and talking. He paused in front of Verna. "May I replenish your wine?"

"Aren't you thoughtful," she said, passing him her empty glass. "I'd be delighted."

"I'll be right back in a jiffy," he said.

"He is the most considerate man," Verna remarked to Jess. "Who is he?"

"That's Harry Dunbar. He lives in San Francisco."

She looked into Jess's eyes. "Have you been together long, dear?"

Jess's eyebrows snapped up her forehead like window shades. "Excuse me?"

Annie leaned forward. "What did you say, Verna?"

"I asked how long Harry and Jess have been together."

Annie smiled broadly, "Oh, no, Harry isn't Jess's boyfriend. Her boyfriend isn't here tonight."

"I just assumed from the way…well, forgive me."

"Don't think twice about it," Jess said, squeezing her arm.

Harry returned with Verna's glass and a cracker spread with Brie on a paper napkin.

"Why thank you. You're very kind. We don't have these fancy cheeses at home."

"You know, that's exactly what my aunt from Iowa says when she comes to visit."

"No! I have a cousin in Iowa."

"Isn't that a coincidence?" Harry said, cleaning his eyeglasses. "We'll have to compare notes."

Verna searched among the guests for Clyde. He hadn't moved from the huddle with the gangsterish man from the garage. "I'd like that. I swear you can't pry that husband of mine away once he starts talking about anything on wheels."

The most delectable garlicky and tomato scent wafted from the kitchen. Harry disappeared into the crowd to pour more wine, and the two ladies excused themselves to bring dinner into the dining room. Verna watched as several guests dashed back and forth delivering bowls while Annie placed a steaming casserole on the table. Annie's sweet young son, Noah, hot potatoed a loaf of bread wrapped in tin foil onto a cutting board.

Verna rose from the couch and nearly collided with the sultan as he slouched away, waving his hand good-bye, past an older wild-haired boy who dashed into the dining room.

"Don't come near this table, Matthew Morrison, until you clean up," Annie called.

"Far out, Mom! Lasagna! Way to go!"

Verna overheard Noah tell Jess who was lighting candles, "I told you my brother would show up."

Jess tousled his blonde hair. "What makes you so smart?"

"Years of experience," he said.

Harry walked toward her with a plate of food, which she gratefully accepted and edged toward a seat on the couch. As Clyde walked by, she lifted her wine glass. "Cheers, dear."

She watched guests circling round the table. Annie served steaming portions of lasagna and Stewart, positioned near a huge wooden salad bowl, scooped salad onto waiting plates.

Guests gathered in clusters in the living room, balancing plates on their laps and conversing freely. Noah and Matthew sat cross-legged on the floor, eating quickly and joking with each other. *How nicely they treat one another,* she thought. Real affection between brothers is a gift to behold.

Harry drew a chair up to Verna while Clyde sat across from them next to the garage man. While they ate, he chatted about his old widowed aunts, Aunt Frieda and Aunt Ann, from Galva, and his cousin, Andy Bill, who ran the family pig farm in Kingsley. When Verna spoke of her cousin, Lavon, Harry's gaze centered on her face, but soon a magnetic force seemed to pull Harry's eyes back to Stewart. When Stewart paused in front of them to refill their wine glasses, she saw a glimpse of longing flicker in Harry's eyes. She knew that look. She held her hand to her breast, an involuntary intake of breath rushing through her lips.

She continued to chat with Harry, waiting, and watching. When Stewart joined the boys on the floor to eat, a shadow of disappointment descended on Harry. Verna managed to get as far as describing Lavon, who married a man from Des Moines, and raised three boys all of whom became barbers like their dad, when her voice faded.

Harry sat up straighter. "You were saying."

"No," she said, "I've been talking too much."

"But I've enjoyed it."

"I know," she said softly. "So have I."

For the first time that evening a silence fell between them. Harry mumbled something about helping in the kitchen and excused himself. Verna turned and glanced out the windows. Through the wavy glass she recalled the sylvan scene of otherworldly beauty through which they had walked earlier: shaggy-needled giant redwood trees rising high toward the pale blue sky beside a creek laden with mossy ferns. Now the dusky light had faded to night. She observed it was common many afternoons for the wind, sharp and bone chilling, to come up out of nowhere and disperse a misty blanket of fog over the the land. Tonight was no different. A weary, out-of-sorts heaviness fell over her. However generous, these people were not her people. She ached for the familiar; she missed her Michigan family and the rhythms of home. The demands of caring for her daughter anchored her days and marked each one with a sense of accomplishment.

She watched Stewart and felt ready for their impending departure. Adoration was not too strong a word for how she held him in her heart, but now that emotion would dwell within more gently. Her love would be tempered by the reality of his choices that she couldn't readily understand. She longed for acceptance to inhabit her mind, and peace to enter her soul.

The voices of guests awakened her. The surprising Renata took her female friend by the arm and announced in a reedy voice, "Camilla and I are going upstairs to practice some restorative yoga poses. It's especially good for the digestion. If anybody wants to join us, that's cool."

Unexpectedly Stewart stopped at Verna's side and placed his hand on her arm. "I'm making coffee. Would you like a cup, Mom?"

"Yes, I would," she said.

Not a moment later, Harry, who seemed contrite, asked, "May I take your plate?"

"Of course. I enjoyed every bite," she answered.

Clyde caught Verna's eye, and she stood and walked gingerly to a chair beside him. Not only had her ankles swelled, but her feet as well.

He took her hand in his. "How are you doing?"

"Just fine."

"You sure?"

"I'm sure."

"Jake is going to take me to the garage and show me his beauties."

"Oh Clyde, really."

"You want to come?"

"Don't be ridiculous. I'm going to have a nice cup of coffee with my son, and then I'm going to go upstairs and see what those women are up to."

"I won't be long," he said.

"Go on with you." Normally she would have given him a push, but tonight she leaned over and rested her head on his shoulder.

* * *

Jess returned from the living room carrying a platter that had been laden with brownies. Every surface of the kitchen—countertops, table, stove—was piled high with dirty dishes, smudged glasses, utensils, bowls, pots, and pans. Harry stood valiantly at the sink, apron around his waist, briskly scraping and washing plates, attempting to reduce the damage.

"The brownies were a hit," Jess announced. "They took every single one." She set the platter down on the countertop next to Stewart, who was pouring boiling water into a Melitta cone coffee carafe. The rich scent of coffee steamed into the air.

"Not a problem," Annie said, reaching up into the cupboard beside Jess and taking down a glass platter heaped with more brownies. "I baked a triple batch."

Part of Jess wished that Daniel and Sarah had been able to come tonight, but it wouldn't have worked. He had picked up Sarah earlier in the morning and driven back to Bolinas while Jess was in rehearsal. They spent the day together getting the house ready for Daniel's mother and Miss E. Temple to arrive. The truth was he wasn't prepared yet for a celebration of any kind. Ceci's recovery had been slow, and he had taken charge of the details of her treatment.

Annie's voice brought her back to the moment. "Just in case you're wondering," she said, touching Stewart's arm, "I've set aside some very special brownies for my very special friends. I recommend only one—and I mean only one."

"You're an amazing woman," Stewart said, glancing down at Annie who stood barely to his shoulder.

"That's what I've been trying to tell you," she teased.

Jess was struck by how easy and close their friendship had become. Harry glanced at Daniel, yearning in his eyes. A part of her ached for Harry. Wasn't it the mystery of the human condition to feel alone until we find someone to love?

"I'm so proud of you tonight!" Annie said to Stewart. "Look at us. We pulled off a coup. Your mom and dad have been indoctrinated into straight and gay society, and they took it in good humor."

Harry had switched to drying the glasses. "I don't know." He hesitated, dishtowel in hand, and adjusted his tie to keep it from getting wet. "The psychiatric profession may have ruled that being gay is not a mental illness, but your mom looked at bit shell-shocked when she figured out who I am."

Stewart smiled warily. "Give her a chance. She's making strides."

"The ruling may have happened over a year ago," Jess said, reaching for the platter of brownies, "but it can't change how people think."

"Right on, sister," Annie said.

Harry tossed down the towel. "Isn't that the truth?"

Just then Matthew darted into the kitchen, scooted up to Jess, and snatched two brownies off the plate. "One for me and one for my brother."

Jess looked into Matthew's clear eyes and marveled. She knew Annie was holding her breath, but for now he was keeping his promise to work for Jake and make restitutions. Something in him had shifted. There was a sweetness to him she hadn't known.

"Hey, Mr. Merch," Matthew said. His face couldn't disguise an expression of devilment.

Stewart turned and looked. "Yes?"

"I think you're a great teacher."

Without missing a beat, Stewart grabbed Matthew around the neck and gave him a bear hug. Annie tucked her chin in surprise, a smile curving her mouth. Matthew laughed and ducked away, the brownies held aloft in one hand as he jogged out the kitchen.

"I hate to break up the party," Jess said, passing the platter to Harry, "but I've got to get going."

"Can't stay away from him, hey?" Annie said.

"Go on, work me over." Jess wrinkled her nose. "I knew this was coming."

"Where you going, honey?" Harry asked.

"Over the hill to Bolinas," Jess said.

"Jess is in love," Annie said. "In case you haven't noticed, she's a hopeless romantic."

"Nice work if you can get it," Harry said.

"And you can get it if you try." Annie hummed a few bars to the song and broke into voice, and Harry joined her in a lusty baritone while Stewart backed out of the kitchen carrying two cups of coffee.

* * *

The avenue was lively with people ambling past restaurants and strolling toward the Sweetwater. The air smelled fresh, and cars cruised by. Jess hadn't walked twenty steps before she noticed Clyde moving along at a fast clip on the other side of the street in the direction of Annie's house. She waved, and he waved back. Further along, Sam appeared, heading toward her.

"Hey, sweet thing," he called, grabbing her in a hug. "Where're you headed in such a hurry?"

"One guess," she said, staring up into his broad face.

He laughed heartily. "I'm surprised you're not out there right now. What's the problem?"

"No problem. My best friend had a party," she said. "And where are you going?"

"I'm stopping by for a little refreshment and no doubt some jammin'." He nodded in the direction of the Sweetwater. "Would you believe I've had a night off? House is pretty lonesome without my Ceci. But I'm not complaining. She's in good hands now."

"Daniel told me she's making progress," Jess said. "This has been hardest on you, Sam, hasn't it?"

"Ah, well, I expect she'll be coming home soon. That's when the real work will start. But I'm ready." His eyes softened. "Right now, I'm on the loose. Perfectly harmless though; strictly on the up and up." He patted Jess lightly on the shoulder. "Don't be standing here on the sidewalk talking to me when you got places to go. Say hello to the little dude."

"Bye, Sam. I'll see you soon!"

"Bye, sweet girl," he said, swinging his wide shoulders in a graceful turn. "Good luck on the road! Break a leg, you hear!"

* * *

Jess walked through downtown in the direction of The Royal Motors Garage. As she approached, she saw a light on in the office. The door was ajar. Drawing closer, she heard the pop of a dart hitting a cork target. She tapped lightly on the glass, and the door fell open.

"So, you came to your senses," Jake said, throwing the last dart.

"You could say that," she said.

"Like I told you, when you don't take things too seriously everything falls into place." His dark eyes teased her. He scooped a set of keys off the desk and took her by the arm.

The Jaguar sedan was parked in front of the last bay. Dove grey like Sam's car, the chrome grill glinted under the streetlight. Jake opened the door, and the courtesy lights clicked on, illuminating the leather interior. He handed Jess the keys. "There's a hell of a lot of power under the hood. More than you're used to, but she'll drive smooth. Take it easy on the curves."

"You received my first payment?" she said.

"Yeah, and the check cleared," he said.

She pushed him away, grinning at his perpetual bad jokes.

"Get in," he said.

Jess slid in. The leather was cool and smooth and cushioned the small of her back. She grasped the leather-wrapped steering wheel and fingered the stitching.

"Do you need to adjust the seat?" Jake crouched on his haunches at the open door.

"I don't think so." She touched her foot to the gas pedal and then the brake. "It feels right. Where are the headlights?"

"Here," he said and flipped up a chrome toggle on the wood dash.

"And the emergency brake?"

"Here." He pointed to a handle near her knee. "Okay, turn her on."

Jess slipped the key in the ignition and touched the gas pedal. The engine growled, and when she let off on the gas, it purred like a jungle cat. The luminous lights of the dash shone up into her eyes. The headlights beamed into the street.

"You look like a million bucks," he said.

"If I run into trouble, can I call you from the road?"

"Anytime. If you get in a pinch, there's a manual in the glove box. The boyfriend knows about cars, right?"

"Right," she said.

"And for luck, one of my finest switchblades."

"What is it with you and knives?" she laughed.

"Part of my culture, babe!"

"I'm heading to Bolinas."

"Piece of cake," he said.

She smiled, slipped the gear into drive, and released the emergency brake. Jake closed the door, rapped on the roof, and stepped away. She eased on the gas, rolled into the street, aiming the car down the avenue. She drove through town, the car's headlights cutting a wide path. The window was down, the cool wind blowing past her face. She knew the route by heart—into Cascade Canyon, up and over the same roads she had driven before, westward onto the shoulder of the mountain and toward the sea.

The car was like a cocoon, the lights of the dash shining green, the wheel handling as smooth as butter cream. The car took the roads like a champion. As she drove onto the mountain, the smell of sea streaming through the window, the realization came to her that we live our lives in layers that rest just under the skin. Events are woven into the layers—seams mismatched, folds and snags rippling the texture—that never quite disappear. Unseen by others, we feel each layer, our minds probing and roaming its contents. The memory ceaselessly explores what is given and what is taken away. What can we really know of another person's life? she wondered. Each life is like the miracle of dawn. How we hunger for light, for sight, for warmth. She heard Sarah's voice in her ear, laughing, telling her that tonight she and Daniel would look through his telescope to the stars, all the way to the edge of the earth. Jess was entrusting the care of her daughter to Daniel while she was away working. Months ago she wouldn't have bet on him. Now she was laying down another layer. They would be a family. The weight of it felt solid. She heard the song of her dreams in the wind, coaxing her on.

CPSIA information can be obtained at www.ICGtesting.com
Printed in the USA
BVOW042135141112

305616BV00002B/1/P